D0424308

Extraordinary praise for SENTINEL and
MATTHEW DUNN

"Not since Fleming charged Bond with the safety of the world has the international secret agent mystique been so anchored with an insider's reality. The pacing . . . is frenetic, and the plotting is meticulous as it continually doubles back on itself. Don't start it unless you have time to finish."

Noah Boyd, *New York Times* bestselling author of *Agent X*

"The cat-and-mouse game [is] a real surprise. An icy-edged psychological thriller."

Library Journal

"You can thrill to the high pressure intrigue as CIA and MI6 agents bumble into each other, unfortunately rubbing out the wrong principles in their haste to save their ideals. . . . *Sentinel*'s characters are thoroughly and irresistibly believable."

Examiner.com

"A spellbinding, realistic novel. . . . *Sentinel* is a fast-paced and riveting book with pure action and intrigue. The many twists and turns make for a very interesting and captivating book."

Blackfive.com

"An exciting novel that will keep you in suspense right up to the end. . . . espionage at its best."

Yahoo Voices

"A terrific thriller with a superb new hero. . . . Written with confidence by a man with the credentials to back him up . . . Bond and Bourne can take a back seat."

Matt Hilton, author of *Judgment and Wrath*

"Once in a while an espionage novelist comes along who has the smack of utter authenticity. Few are as daring as Matthew Dunn, fewer still as up-to-date. . . . Is there anyone writing today who knows more about the day-to-day operations of intelligence agencies in the field than Matthew Dunn?"

John Lawton, author of *A Lily of the Field*

By Matthew Dunn

SPYCATCHER
SENTINEL

MATTHEW DUNN

SENTINEL

A SPYCATCHER NOVEL

HARPER

An Imprint of HarperCollinsPublishers

This book is a work of fiction. References to real people, events, establishments, organizations, or locales are intended only to provide a sense of authenticity, and are used fictitiously. All other characters, and all incidents and dialogue, are drawn from the author's imagination and are not to be construed as real.

HARPER

An Imprint of HarperCollins*Publishers*
10 East 53rd Street
New York, New York 10022-5299

First Harper digest printing: April 2013
First Harper premium printing: April 2013
First William Morrow hardcover printing: August 2012

To my children and Margie, special operations personnel who operate within the four corners of Hell without a safety net, and to Russians and Americans

PART I

ONE

The Russian submarine captain ran through the woods, searching for signs of anyone who might kill him. It was night, and the forest was dense. Sleet struck his face. His body trembled with cold and fear.

Reaching a tiny area of open ground, he stopped, crouched, and listened. The sea was only a few hundred yards away, and he could hear the sounds of waves crashing over shingle. Turning slowly, he braced himself, half expecting to see men with flashlights, guns, and dogs rushing toward him.

He stayed like this for two minutes before glancing in the direction of his car. It was hidden from view, parked in the trees off the nearest road. It would take him one minute to get back to the vehicle and another twenty minutes to reach his submarine base. He was allowed off the base for only one hour. Time was running out.

Walking quickly, he moved out of the clearing and into more forest. He counted each step, stopped when he had gone eighty paces, changed direction, and walked a further fifty steps. The tree was before him. It looked like those around it—tall, thin, no foliage, and slightly bent from easterly winds—but he knew it was the right tree. He'd been here seven times before and despised the location because on each visit he'd always wondered if it was the place where he'd be trapped and killed.

He unwrapped a thin, waterproof poncho, draped it over his head and body, withdrew a small flashlight and penknife, and knelt at the base of the tree. The ground beneath him was sodden with an icy slush, and his pants quickly became saturated. After lifting the poncho's edge and positioning it against the tree, he switched on the flashlight and moved its beam over the trunk. He quickly found what he was looking for: a small circle with two horizontal lines within it carved into the bark. Around it were seven older carvings that had since been defaced. Flicking open the knife, he carefully cut a third horizontal line into the circle.

He bent down and let the poncho fall away from the tree so that it was completely covering his body and acting as a makeshift tent. Sleet banged against it. After putting the end of the light into his mouth, he used the knife and his other hand to dig in the ground directly beneath the symbol. Pain shot through his fingers as they removed cold, wet soil, but he kept digging, constantly aware that he had to do what was necessary as quickly as he could.

The knife struck something hard a few inches beneath the ground's surface. He tapped the blade against the thing to confirm that he'd not simply struck a root, but the object was clearly metallic. Discarding the knife, he eased both hands into the hole, wincing as more pain moved into his arms, and gripped tight when he felt the small box. After he pulled it out, he placed it next to his knife. Then he momentarily put his hands into his armpits to try to get them warm before shining the light directly on the container.

Brushing soil off its surface, he saw that it was the same gunmetal box he'd always used. But he had to be careful in case it was booby-trapped. He lifted it off the ground and thought that it felt the right weight, though he knew that told him nothing. Only a tiny piece of primed C4 would be needed to rip off his face. Grabbing the knife, he placed the tip under the container's latch, paused for a moment, and flicked it open. The rain drummed harder against his poncho.

He stared at the box for a while, his heart racing, sweat running down his back even though he was colder than he'd ever been in his life. Placing one hand on the base and the other on the lid, he began pulling it open. When he felt the hidden rubber seals resist, he closed his eyes and pulled harder until it was ajar. He opened his eyes. The only thing inside was a metal cigar tube. Lifting it carefully, he unscrewed the tube's cap, peered into the tube, and felt relief. Inside were a stubby pencil and a rolled sheet of plain paper. He flattened the paper and began to read.

The relief vanished.

His hand shook as he brought the pencil close to the paper.

The codes raced through his mind. He identified the numerical equivalent of each letter, added that to another set of memorized numbers that corresponded to the letters in order to determine the cipher text letters, and then began writing.

It took him six minutes to write the first sentence. He hated communicating this way but knew that the code was almost unbreakable unless the key code was discovered or he was tortured to reveal its detail. Communicating with anything more sophisticated was far too risky. All electronic communications signals into, out of, and near to the base were monitored. Sending an encrypted burst transmission from close to the base could easily pinpoint him as a spy.

He was about to begin the second sentence, but then he stopped, his hand hovering over the paper. A noise, distant but loud enough to be heard over the dreadful weather, was coming from the direction of the road. Then it grew louder. He thought it might be a car. Then he knew it was a truck. Only the military drove vehicles like that around here.

His hand unconsciously became a clenched fist. Tonight he was due to telephone his daughter to congratulate her on her promotion within Russian military intelligence. She would be pleased with his call because she respected her father's opinion and deeply admired his lifelong career of service to Russia. But he knew that if she could see him now she would be deeply ashamed of him.

The truck slowed. He wondered if the patrol had spotted his car and was worried about its owner or whether it had come here looking for a traitor. He tried to think clearly and wished the sleet and rain would stop.

An idea came to him: if his car had been spotted, he would confront the soldiers and tell them that he'd hit a deer and followed it into the woods, a likely enough occurrence on these forested roads. They'd probably even volunteer to help him kill the injured beast so that they could take it back to the base.

The truck braked; its engine idled.

The captain looked at the cipher. He had to write the next sentence, but time was short.

A door slammed. Then another.

He had no time.

He made a decision and muttered in Russian, "It's all I can give you."

Ramming the paper and pencil back into the cigar tube, he put it back into the box and buried the container in the same spot. Wind buffeted his poncho, the rain forcing it onto his face. He had to move, but he hesitated for a moment. Shivering, he silently recited the message he had just written.

"He has betrayed us and wants to go to war."

TWO

Will Cochrane stood alone on the deck of the rusty merchant cargo ship. It was night, and the boat rocked with the swell of the sea as a snowy wind blasted his face, but the MI6 officer ignored the vessel's movement and freezing weather. All that mattered to him was his destination. The desolate Russian coastline drew closer. He was being taken to a place where he knew he could die.

His objective was to get to shore, infiltrate the remote Rybachiy submarine base, and locate the captain. The Russian submariner, an MI6 agent code-named Svelte, had sent an encrypted message of such importance that it had been passed to the top secret joint MI6-CIA Spartan Section. It was clear that the message was incomplete, and a decision had been made to deploy the section's senior field operative to find out who had betrayed the West and wanted war.

The big officer brushed snow off his cropped dark hair, checked that his Heckler & Koch USP Compact Tactical pistol was secure in his jacket, and waited. He'd been on similar missions in the past during his nine years in MI6 and during the preceding five years as a French Foreign Legion Groupement des Commandos Parachutistes special forces soldier. But the thirty-five-year-old knew this was going to be particularly tough—even for a man who carried the code name Spartan, a title given to only the most effective and deadliest Western intelligence officer.

The boat slowed down.

It was time to go.

He was dressed head to toe in white arctic warfare clothes and boots; he pulled up the jacket hood. Walking carefully to a gap in the railings, he crouched down and ran a hand along the edge of the deck until he found what he was looking for. The rope ladder would take him thirty-five feet down the starboard side of the ship to the tiny rowboat.

The noise of the ocean and wind seemed even louder as he moved down. With every step he wrapped his forearms around the rope to stop him from being thrown away from the ladder as it slapped hard against the merchant ship's side. Reaching the rowboat, he found both ties and loosened them so that the vessel was free. The merchant ship moved on. Will was now on his own.

He waited until the barely lit ship was out of sight, then he gathered up the oars to his vessel and rowed toward his destination.

It took him four hours to reach the shore.

When he arrived, he got out carefully, grabbed the boat with both hands, and hauled it onto the slim beach of sand, loose rock, snow, and ice. Using his flashlight to check his compass, he mentally pictured the maps he had studied of this area. The base was ten miles away; the journey there would take him over forest-covered mountains before he reached the thin peninsula where the naval installation was located.

He pulled himself up a large snow-covered bank until he was off the beach and on higher ground. Snow was falling fast now, and the wind seemed even stronger. He started shaking and knew that he would have to move quickly to generate some warmth. He moved uphill through the forest. After two hours of running, walking, and clambering ever higher, he stopped.

He was on a mountain peak, and although little could be seen around him, in the distance and far below were numerous artificial lights. They came from an area of land that Will knew to be his destination: a peninsula three miles long and a quarter mile wide and accessible only via a bottleneck of land. The peninsula was surrounded by the icy waters of Avacha Bay, and the lights he could see ran from the bottleneck along the entire southern side of the peninsula. The lights belonged to the Rybachiy Nuclear Submarine Base.

Checking his watch, he saw that it was three A.M., and he began to run fast, knowing that he had a maximum of four hours to get into the base, find and speak to Svelte, and escape the military installation and its surrounding peninsula.

He covered two miles before throwing himself onto the ground. The bottleneck entrance to the peninsula was before him. It was three hundred yards below his position and contained medium-sized buildings and huts, a wide road, smaller adjacent tracks, and four stationary military jeeps. It also contained seven naval guards, two of whom had German shepherds on leashes. They were all dressed in navy blue overcoats and standing underneath streetlamps by a sign saying HALT in Russian. There were no barriers on the road, and the rest of the bottleneck was unprotected; its buildings would give him cover to enter the base easily.

Will smiled. Svelte had previously briefed MI6 that the land around the Rybachiy submarine base was so severe and remote that the base had small need for guards save for those who patrolled around the nuclear and diesel submarines. On top of that, those few guards were little more than poorly trained naval conscripts. Will had worried that Svelte's intelligence might be wrong, but he was relieved to see that it wasn't. He looked to his right and watched a four-ton truck drive slowly along a road toward the base. Glancing back at the guards, he saw that they were looking at the vehicle but had not raised their rifles. It clearly did not bother them.

Deciding that the vehicle's approach to the base would be a good distraction, Will got to his feet and ran fast to his right. After five hundred feet, he stopped and saw that the truck was now motionless by the entrance. The guards were standing by the driver's door and stamping their feet on the ground, their arms wrapped around their chests. To their right were the buildings and huts.

He moved diagonally so that he was heading toward the side of the bottleneck that was furthest away from the guards. Soon, trees and buildings obstructed his view of the truck. Slowing to a jog, he moved into open ground before reaching the wall of one of the huts. He placed himself flush against the building and listened for a moment. He could hear nothing save the sound of wind and the sea.

Moving along a gap between the hut and an adjacent larger building, he crouched down when he got to the end of the alley and slowly eased his head around the corner. The road entrance was visible on the other side of the bottleneck, but it was at least five hundred feet away. No one was looking his way. Glancing ahead, he saw more buildings beyond another area of open ground that was in darkness. He waited a few seconds, then sprinted toward them. After reaching the buildings, he spun around and looked toward the guards. They were still by the truck, doing nothing. He'd successfully entered the outer perimeter of Rybachiy submarine base.

He was about to move when he heard distant engine noises from the black sky. The noises grew louder until they were directly above him. They were clearly coming from aircraft, and their deep drone sounded very familiar. He briefly wondered if they were flying to the base, but Svelte had never mentioned that the base had an airstrip. He silently muttered "shit" as he realized why the sounds were so well known to him. Looking desperately at the black sky, he searched for what he knew was coming. There was nothing at first, but then he glimpsed the first one, followed by another, followed by several others. Paratroopers. They drifted silently through the sky before landing within one hundred feet of the guards behind him.

Will stayed very still. The soldiers were dressed in white combat clothes and had balaclavas, webbing, and tactical goggles. Assault rifles were strapped to their chests. He counted twenty-five of them as he watched the platoon gather up its parachutes, pack them away, and walk toward the guards.

Some of the airborne soldiers had unslung their weapons; some had not. The guards remained stationary and showed no signs of concern at the encroaching force, now clearly lit up by the lights of the base. The paratroopers moved right up to the guards, who seemed to be communicating with a handful of the men. The dogs were handed to two of the airborne soldiers. Then the guards turned and walked casually away from the entrance into the peninsula base.

The airborne soldiers split into groups. Four of them took two of the jeeps and drove into the base, six men and one dog took over protection of the entrance, the rest entered the base on foot. Now all of them had their weapons at the ready.

Will shook his head slowly; his heart beat fast. It seemed that the silent and clearly very professional Russian airborne troops had taken over security of the base. He had no idea why this had happened, but it meant everything had changed. His chances of completing his mission and escaping without being spotted were now nearly impossible.

He ran deeper into the base, using more buildings and the darkness as cover, but as he did so his mind raced with confusion. Only two men knew that he was attempting to infiltrate the Rybachiy submarine base—the CIA director and the MI6 controller who ran his covert unit—and he knew they would never betray him. A stark conclusion entered his mind: the Russian airborne troops were not searching for him; they were searching for another man.

He checked that his military knife was securely fastened at his waist, pulled out his pistol, looked left and right, and began to walk fast.

The area around him was a mixture of shadows, lights, long huts, warehouses, factory units, and roads. Snow carpeted everything. From his study of Svelte's map, Will knew that the submarine base was rectangular in shape and the size of a large town. He also knew from the map, and could see now, that the place was not densely built and that there were large gaps of open ground between buildings. Even though he still had the cover of night, he would have to be extremely careful moving through Rybachiy.

He stood in the blackness next to a building and watched everything around him for a while. Keeping low in the shadows, he moved carefully to the edge of the hut while staying flush against its wall. Another road was before him, and he looked left along its route. Buildings straddled the road; some were in darkness, and some had internal lights on. He knew that Svelte's quarters were approximately one mile farther along the route and adjacent to submarine pens. He saw two headlights in the distance and watched them draw closer. They seemed to be moving at a medium speed, and he could see they belonged to a civilian truck. He decided he would try to get onto the back of the vehicle and allow it to take him close to his destination.

The truck slowed and stopped about 250 feet from his position. Two men approached the vehicle. They were dressed in white and carrying guns. They spoke to the driver of the truck before waving him on. The truck drew nearer to Will, but the soldiers stayed motionless in the center of the road, watching the vehicle. He knew that if he stepped onto the road at this point he would be spotted and could easily be shot. The truck was now only a few feet from him. He kept staring at the soldiers. The truck drew alongside him, audibly changed gears, and started moving faster. One of the soldiers turned to face the other direction. The truck passed Will and in seconds would be out of range for what he needed to do. He stared at the other soldier, willing him to turn and join his colleague. The soldier placed the butt of his rifle into his shoulder, looked to his left and right, and turned. Will wasted no time. He jumped up, sprinted onto the road, and chased after the truck.

It was now fifty feet ahead of him and picking up speed. He wondered if he had the strength and pace to reach it and if the two soldiers would turn around and shoot him in the back. He lowered his head, ran faster, got closer to the truck, heard it change gears again, realized that it was about to accelerate away, pumped his legs and arms harder to bring him within five feet of its rear, and leapt forward.

He grabbed the vehicle's rear bumper and wrapped his arms tightly around it. Snow sprayed up either side of his body as he was dragged and tossed violently over the ground. He pulled with his arms and tried to move his body into a crouch position, but he slipped so that he was again horizontal and being dragged along the road. The soldiers were now 150 yards away, but the vehicle's rear lights would still allow them to see him if they turned to face in his direction. He ignored the paratroopers and looked quickly to his left and right in case the truck was passing one of the jeeps or other paratroopers on foot. Pulling again, he kicked at the rapidly moving ground, looked up, saw a rear door handle on the truck, took a deep breath, and lunged upward toward the handle. He grabbed it with one hand just as the truck made a slight turn on the road and lifted his whole body into the air. Yanking with the arm holding the handle and the arm holding the bumper, he slammed his body against the back of the truck and lifted his knees high before banging his feet down onto the bumper. Out of breath, he felt pain creep over his back and legs. But he was secure on the vehicle, out of sight of its driver, and now out of sight of the foot patrol.

The truck drove steadily for a minute before breaking hard, skidding over the icy ground, and stopping. Will kept his grip firm while desperately looking left and right. He heard a door on the vehicle open and close, men's voices and dogs barking, and he saw light on the ground. Standing fully on the bumper, he placed one foot on the door handle by his waist, thrust upward with his leg, and grabbed the top of the truck. Keeping his body flush against the vehicle, he pulled his body quickly onto the roof and lay there with his body pressed flat against its surface. The voices were all around the truck, and, judging by their noise, there was at least one dog to his right and one dog to his left. He was fifteen feet aboveground, hidden from view, and the snow-carrying wind would make his scent untraceable to the dogs. But he was surrounded, and if any of the men decided to check the truck's roof he would have no choice other than to fight his way out of the place that was clearly the main checkpoint entrance to the submarine pens and their surrounding quarters.

He heard the truck's rear door open and then footsteps

inside the vehicle, directly beneath him. At least one of the men was searching the interior. The door slammed shut, followed by the bark of a dog and more voices. Will resisted the temptation to look over the side to see how many soldiers were around him. He kept motionless and waited. A door from the truck's cabin opened and closed; then the vehicle shuddered as the driver engaged the gears and gunned the engine. A man said something loudly in Russian, and the truck moved slowly forward before picking up pace.

Will crawled quickly along the roof so that he was in the center of the truck, keeping low in case his increasing distance from the checkpoint gave the soldiers there visibility of him. As the truck moved onward he waited for thirty seconds before raising his head a few inches to look around. Everywhere was brightly illuminated. He saw buildings and submarines. The vessels were berthed alongside walkways, and as the truck continued on, Will counted sixteen craft. He saw four Delta IIIs, five Akula Is, one Akula II, and six Oscar IIs, one of which was captained by Svelte.

The truck slowed, and Will quickly crawled farther along its roof until he was close to the cabin. Three hundred feet ahead of him were six men standing on the road. Four of them looked like naval guards; the other two were airborne soldiers. Will crawled rapidly back along the roof and decided that he had to get off the vehicle before it reached the men. He looked around, lowered himself down the back of the truck, and waited while continuing to look left and right. When he saw nothing, he jumped to the ground.

He rolled over snow and lay flat for a moment, watching the taillights of the truck move away from his position. He waited until the truck was closer to the men and would hide his movements from their vision. After counting five seconds, he rose to one knee and looked around again before dashing off the road and into darkness. Pulling out his handgun, he attached the sound suppressor to the weapon and walked carefully alongside a building wall while tightly gripping the gun. Svelte's quarters were very close now.

He moved to the edge of the building and stood by a narrow road. There were buildings on either side of the route, and each one had an external lamp casting a dim light over the road. But none of the buildings had internal lights on, save one small hut. That building was Svelte's quarters and would be where the man slept, washed, dressed, and sometimes ate when not dining in the officers' mess or on board his submarine. It was about three hundred yards away from him on the left of the road. He looked up and down the route, checked his watch, and waited for a few seconds before deciding he had to move.

Moving out of the alley, he looked toward Svelte's residence and tightly gripped his handgun. He knew he needed to be within the man's quarters in seconds. He ran.

When he came to within a few feet of Svelte's hut, he slowed to a walk, crouched low, and pulled out his military knife. He moved carefully forward, looking around, with his gun in one hand and the knife in the other. The narrow street was still quiet as he looked up and down the route. His eyes narrowed. A streak of light began moving slowly down the road. It was daylight.

Moving up to the hut's door, he brought the knife up to force its lock. He frowned. The door was already ajar an inch. He pushed at it and immediately slammed his back against the adjacent wall so that he would not be visible to anyone inside. He waited, and when he heard nothing he swung himself low into the doorway with his handgun held forward. The room before him was small. It contained a tiny dining table and chair, a sofa, a television, an illuminated corner lamp, wall-mounted shelves filled with books, and a free-standing rack with a coat hanger holding an immaculately pressed naval captain's dress uniform. Beyond the room was a corridor, and Will moved silently into it. To his left was a room with a toilet, hand basin, and shower cubicle. To his right was a closed door. He crouched down and moved to one side of the door while placing his knife into its scabbard. Then he removed his jacket hood, lifted his handgun up high, and used his free hand to open the door.

A man was lying in the center of the room, moaning. Will ran to him and crouched down. Immediately, he recognized the man from a photograph he'd seen in MI6 headquarters. It was Svelte, and he was dressed in uniform. The MI6 Russian agent's face was screwed up in agony. His stomach had been torn open by a knife.

In Russian, Will said urgently, "I am a British intelligence officer." He cradled the back of Svelte's head and leaned down so that his face was inches away from the agent's. "Who did this to you?"

Svelte's eyes partially opened, his lips moved, but the only sound he made was a blood-filled guttural noise.

Will shook his head with disbelief. One of MI6's most prized Russian agents was dying, and there was nothing he could do to stop it from happening. Will had traveled halfway around the world to meet him, but now it seemed that his journey might have been a waste of time. He moved even closer to him. "You sent us a message. What did it mean?"

Svelte shook his head; tears streamed down the sides of his face.

"Who did this to you? Who wants to go to war?"

Svelte gripped Will's forearm tightly and opened his bloody mouth. But still no words came out.

Will felt anger, sorrow, and frustration that he'd not gotten to Svelte sooner. This was his fault. He'd failed the Russian officer. "Please . . . please try to speak." He made no attempt to hide the desperation he felt. "I'm so *very* sorry. I should have got to you sooner."

Svelte's back arched as his body went into a spasm, and he cried out in agony. His body slumped back to the floor; his breathing was fast and shallow. Unscrewing his eyes, he stared straight at Will. "Not . . . not your fault." He spoke with a barely audible voice. "Khmelnytsky . . . Colonel Taras Khmelnytsky. War between Russia and

America." He coughed blood and gritted his teeth. "Only Sentinel can stop him."

His grip on Will instantly relaxed and his hand fell away to the floor, but his eyes remained wide open. He was dead.

Will briefly closed his eyes and muttered, "Fuck." He lowered Svelte's head to the floor, placed his fingers gently onto the Russian's eyelids and closed them, and stared at the dead agent. Standing, he turned and kicked a bin across the room with a hushed "Damn it!"

Breathing deeply, he tried to control the anger he felt toward himself. He had to take control of the situation. Though Svelte's dying words had no meaning to him, his priority now was getting out of the base and taking the information back to people who almost certainly would know what Svelte had meant. But daylight and the presence of the paratroopers would make an attempted covert escape suicidal.

His eyes fixed onto a tumbler glass on a bedside table. Within it was an inch of clear liquid. Lifting it to his nose, he smelled vodka. He moved quickly around the room, opening the small number of cupboards and drawers. Only clothes and stationery. Entering the lounge, he spotted a small fridge unit in one corner. Pulling it open, he saw eight full bottles of vodka. He glanced at the sofa next to him. It was cheap and made of foam, ideal for what he needed. Opening the first bottle, he poured its contents over the sofa; then he did the same with a second bottle before splashing the contents of the remaining bottles over anything in Svelte's quarters that might be flammable. Grabbing a copy of an *Izvestia* newspaper from the dinner table, he tore it apart, wadded pieces of the paper into small balls, and scattered them over the sofa and elsewhere. He lit some of the balls, watched them start to burn, and then jogged back into the bedroom.

From the window, he saw that this side of the residence butted up against an alley and more buildings. Easing the window open, he clambered out of Svelte's quarters. The alley was empty; snow was falling thick and fast. Looking back into the quarters, he saw black smoke beginning to emerge from the lounge into the bedroom, and he walked quickly to the end of the alley before stopping. Ahead of him was open ground, and to his right was the main road. Smoke was now billowing out of Svelte's window. He ran north alongside a large warehouse and ducked into a narrow gap between buildings. His only hope lay in luring the paratroopers to Svelte's quarters so that he could escape on foot. It was a vain hope. He doubted they'd all break formation to come here.

Engine noises came from his right. Easing farther into the gap, he saw two jeeps emerge through the blizzard, driving off the road and stopping on the open ground ahead of him. Four troopers got out; one of them was shouting into a radio mic, the others had their rifles held ready to shoot. None of the men was wearing a balaclava. They sped toward the alley that led to the rear of Svelte's residence.

A minute later, a truck arrived and braked opposite

the jeeps. Six airborne soldiers and four navy conscripts jumped out of the truck and ran along the road toward the front entrance of the burning building. When they were out of sight, Will braced himself to sprint across the open ground to reach a cluster of more buildings and the cover they would provide. He hesitated as an idea came to him. Staying low, and with his pistol held with both hands, he moved to the jeeps. One of them had its engine idling, the keys still in the ignition.

Seeing that the soldiers were out of sight in Svelte's quarters, he got into the vehicle, jammed his handgun between the seat and door, and slowly drove away from the road across the open ground. Turning, he moved the jeep between two long huts before stopping and glancing over his shoulder. One white balaclava lay on a rear seat. He put it on and drove the vehicle out of the alley, across more snow-covered rough ground, and onto the main road.

Snow was hitting the windshield fast. He engaged the wipers on high, turned on the headlights, and lowered the driver's window. Depressing the accelerator, he increased speed until he was driving at fifty miles an hour. He saw a group of conscripts ahead of him, walking along the road. Flashing his lights and beeping the horn, he maintained his speed and pointed urgently out of the window in the direction of the fire behind him. As he passed the group, they broke into a run toward the fire.

He drove past the submarines until he was a mile and a half away from Svelte's residence. Checking the fuel gauge, he saw that the tank was half full. If he could escape the base, that would be more than enough. He only needed to drive fourteen miles south across roads and tracks to reach the coast. There, he'd be met by the Russian merchant navy captain who'd brought him to Russia. The captain, a CIA asset, would then take him to Alaska.

He saw the headlights of a four-ton truck. The vehicle stopped by the inner checkpoint to the submarine pens. As he neared it, five paratroopers emerged from the blizzard and got into the vehicle. The truck pulled away, coming right toward him, but it did not slow as it passed.

Will increased speed. Within five minutes he was nearing the outer perimeter of the base. He raced by more buildings, civilian workers, and two navy soldiers, who took no notice of him. His only hope was to put enough distance between him and the soldiers he'd lured to the fire. He needed that distance because in a few seconds the whole base would be alerted to his jeep and the paratroopers would be chasing after him. The alert would be raised by one of the six airborne soldiers now standing ahead of him at the bottleneck entrance to Rybachiy. They were five hundred feet away, and he could see that they were facing him but had not yet raised their weapons. He put his foot to the floor and got to within three hundred feet of them. The troopers remained still. When he was 150 feet away, he flashed his headlights. One of the soldiers raised a hand. Will returned the gesture. The soldiers moved away from the center of the road, no doubt expecting him to screech to a halt between them. He slowed down to half speed, got to within thirty feet of them, and gunned the engine again. The paratroopers leapt aside and fell to the ground as Will's vehicle sped by, spraying snow over the prone soldiers.

Swerving the jeep left and right, Will moved out of the base and onto the mountain road. Shots rang out. Two bullets smashed through the rear window and front windshield, narrowly missing Will's head. He swerved again just as more bullets slammed into the passenger door. One hundred feet ahead of him were the outskirts of the forest and a bend in the road that would take him out of the paratroopers' sight. His heart pounded. He was just as concerned about bullets striking the jeep's tires, fuel tank, or engine as he was about them hitting his body. A sustained burst of gunfire pounded the snow by his vehicle. More rounds rushed through the broken windows, one of them grazing his jacket. Yanking hard down on the steering wheel, he careered left and skidded, desperately trying to maintain control of the vehicle, then he yanked right, and momentarily took his foot off the accelerator. The jeep stayed on the road. Accelerating fast again, he approached the bend. Trees were now around him. He was just a few feet away from cover.

He heard a final volley of automatic gunfire.

THREE

"You were lucky to get out alive."

Will thought about Patrick's comment while looking around the large windowless room. He was sitting by a long oak table in the CIA's headquarters in Langley. Aside from the table and twelve chairs, the room was bare of any other furniture. Bright ceiling spotlights doused the room with an electric blue light.

Alongside Patrick sat Will's MI6 controller, Alistair. They were the coheads of the MI6-CIA Task Force. Both officers were immaculately dressed in suits. Though Patrick's hair was silver and Alistair's blond, in every other respect they looked physically similar—slender but strong, with faces that showed wisdom, humor, and sadness. Both men were in their fifties but appeared ten years younger.

"Yes, I suppose it was luck. What or who is Sentinel?"

Neither officer replied.

Will smoothed a hand over his smart suit. "Does it make sense?"

They remained silent.

"If it's classified, let me sign something to get clearance."

Patrick glanced at Alistair before speaking. "That won't be necessary." He returned his attention to Will. "We'll tell you everything we know, but"—he lifted a thick file that had the inscription SVELTE: ULTRA EYES ONLY, held it for a moment, and dropped it onto the table—"we'd know a lot more if Svelte was still alive."

Will was about to respond, but Alistair held up a hand and quietly said, "There was no way any of us could have predicted what happened in the base."

"True, but I should have got to him sooner."

"Get rid of that thought." Patrick picked up some papers. "Svelte died through no fault of yours. Thank God you escaped, because matters are escalating fast."

Alistair leaned forward and pointed at the papers in Patrick's hand while keeping his gaze fixed on Will. "We've got multiple reports from covert intelligence sources and overt diplomatic channels. Political and economic tensions between America and Russia are the highest they've been since the Cold War."

"I thought we were getting along quite nicely."

"So did the Russian and American premiers, until"—Patrick tossed the papers to one side—"we recently caught some Russian sleeper agents in America and interrogated them. Not to be outdone, the Russians rounded up a handful of our spies whom they'd had under surveillance and put the thumbscrews on them. As a result, some uncomfortable home truths, concerns, and agendas emerged."

Alistair checked the knot on his Royal Navy tie and leaned back, his eyes still locked on Will. "Collective lies were laid bare."

Patrick nodded. "Our spies confessed to the Russians that we're not as keen as we made ourselves out to be for Russia to have a dominant economic role in the WTO, that we'd no intention of removing our tactical nuclear weapons in Europe, that we'd never consider a joint missile defense system with the Russians, and that we're spying on them as much as we were in the fifties and sixties."

Alistair smiled, though his look was cold. "And the Russian men and women we spoke to in FBI cells told us that Russia is hell-bent on rebuilding itself into a superpower with a capitalist platform. It doesn't care whose toes it treads on to achieve that."

Patrick lifted a glass of water close to his mouth and held it there. "Given time, the diplomats and politicians might be able to smooth over the . . . *misunderstandings* to get relations back on track. But we've been reliably informed that right now nothing must happen to make the situation worse. The last thing we need is a flash point."

Glancing around the room, Will thought about Svelte's

dying words. Outside it was daytime, but in here it could have been any time at all. "Does the name Khmelnytsky mean anything to you?"

Patrick answered, "Yes."

Will looked at the two men. Though Alistair had always been his controller, Will had worked with both men for the first time during his last operation to capture an Iranian general, code name Megiddo. During that time he'd learned that Alistair and Patrick had a deep history of collaboration that had started when they were both young officers: when they had worked with Will's father, a CIA operative, and witnessed him being captured by Iranian revolutionaries. Their revenge-driven work against those revolutionaries had ensured that both had quickly risen in power to reach their now-unusual positions. The men before him had direct lines to the U.S. and British premiers, in practice did not answer to the heads of the CIA and MI6, and had personally killed many men. Though he rarely showed it, Will liked them, even though they had both made it clear that they viewed him as their most unpredictable and uncontrollable intelligence officer.

Will smiled. "Feel free to stop giving me monosyllabic answers to my questions."

"Watch your tone." Alistair glanced at Patrick, who nodded at him, then looked sharply at Will. "When I joined MI6, one of the recruits in the training program was different from the rest of us. He was quiet, kept away from the other students. We found out that he was a former SAS officer, but that's all we knew about him because two weeks into the course we were told that he was not deemed suitable material for the service and had been instructed to leave the program."

Alistair took a sip of his tea. Patrick watched Will.

Alistair continued, "Much later, I found out what had really happened. He hadn't failed the course at all. Instead, he'd been quickly identified by one of the instructors as highly unusual, as someone who could be deployed to help combat the Soviet Union. He was given secret MI6 training, and his identity was kept hidden from all within the service, save the chief and a tiny handful of other senior officers. After excelling in the training program, he was granted intelligence officer status while at the same time being told that officially he didn't exist." Alistair was very still. "The chief immediately sent him overseas in deep cover and his remit was to cause damage to the KGB: run agents against them, turn their officers into double agents, disrupt operations against us, and assassinate any Soviet officer who stood in his way. He operated in eastern Berlin, Poland, and the Soviet Union itself; always changing identity, always moving location, always aware that if he was caught he would be tortured and executed. He did this for years and was so successful that the KGB had an entire department dedicated to finding the man they suspected was causing untold damage to their intelligence activities.

"But he was always several steps ahead of them, always maintaining his security, his various covers, trusting no one and making no mistakes. However"—Alistair sighed—"a mistake was made by others. At the end of the Cold War there was a brief moment of euphoria from within the London-based ranks of MI6. That moment was extremely dangerous; it caused secrets to be shared between Great Britain and the reemerging Russia and its new neighboring states, caused many MI6 Soviet agents to wander back to their homeland, their work against the USSR done but their heads now stuffed with dangerous secrets. Of course, the Sluzhba Vneshney Razvedki was no different from the KGB and contained many of the same personnel who saw little difference between the Soviet Union and Russia. And many of those SVR men still wanted to capture our officer."

Will said, "They got to one of our recently retired Russian agents, made him tell them where they could find our man."

Alistair nodded. "We still don't know who betrayed him. But the location of one of our officer's many safe houses in Moscow was supplied and was put under observation by the SVR for weeks, until he finally showed up there and was captured after a gunfight. The FSB dragged him to the Lubyanka prison. They kept him in a tiny, dirty cell and tortured him for six years, but he told them nothing, not even his name. No doubt he'd have died there had Russia and the U.K. not decided that there would be an amnesty of sorts and certain key political prisoners would be exchanged. Our officer was one of those prisoners.

"When he got off the airplane at our military airport

in RAF Brize Norton, we expected him to be a broken man." Alistair smiled. "Instead, he stepped onto the tarmac, looked at the chief of MI6, told him that he wanted a hot meal, a glass of single-malt whiskey, a newspaper to catch up on world events, and a new suit, cash, and identity so that he could get on the next available flight back to Eastern Europe to continue his work. We had to force him to stay in the U.K. for a few days to undergo treatment for the torture inflicted on his body, but after that was done we gave him what he wanted. We sent him back to the Former Soviet Union." He tapped a finger on the table. "That was fifteen years ago. He's been in deep cover, acting as a businessman, in Central and Eastern Europe ever since, running numerous agents, and disrupting the SVR, GRU, and FSB. He's the West's most valuable intelligence resource for all intelligence matters Russia-related."

"He was Svelte's case officer?"

"Yes, Svelte was one of his agents, though the two rarely met. For security reasons, Svelte's DLB was always cleared by one of the case officer's Russian assets, who'd send the message direct to London. We'd decode it, recode it, and send it in a burst transmission to the officer. But after receiving Svelte's last message, we knew the officer was not contactable for two weeks while meeting one of his other agents. We couldn't afford to sit on it so sent you into the base." Alistair paused. "I've told you about this highly classified officer for two reasons. First, in the history of MI6 only two men have ever been kept so secret from others in our service. One of them is the man I've described; the other is you."

"He did the Program?"

Alistair gave a brief nod.

The Program to which Will referred was the Spartan Program, a twelve-month course of unrelenting extreme physical and mental tests. Only one MI6 applicant at a time was allowed to be enrolled in the course. Will had always thought that he was the first and last man to successfully go through the Spartan Program and carry its code name.

Will nodded slowly as understanding dawned on him. "He is Sentinel."

"Yes." Alistair took a sip of his tea. "Which leads me onto the second reason I'm telling you all this. Sentinel gets his intelligence from ten extremely valuable agents, individuals who have access to top secret Russian military and intelligence material, individuals who are being murdered one by one." Alistair frowned. "We had no idea who was doing this." His expression changed. "But you've given us the name."

"Khmelnytsky." Will pictured Svelte's dying body and felt a further wave of regret and failure rush over him. "Does Sentinel know him?"

"He does, though he doesn't yet know he's the murderer. Svelte was the fourth agent to have been assassinated so far." Alistair reached for his cup. "Taras Khmelnytsky is a colonel and the head of Spetsnaz Alpha."

Will knew that Spetsnaz Alpha was Russia's most

effective special forces unit, specializing in antiterrorist operations, intelligence gathering, close protection,
deployments behind enemy lines, and sabotage, surveillance, and direct action. It was part of the FSB, and its
elite members were shrouded in secrecy.

"Sentinel identified and recruited him three years ago
to become an MI6 agent. He gave him the code name
Razin and got him to spy on Russia."

"How in God's name did Sentinel do that?"

Patrick glanced at the papers in front of him. "He made
Razin an irresistible offer." The CIA officer slowly shook
his head, lowering his voice. "Or at least, that's what Sentinel thought."

Will silently swore as a realization struck him: Razin
had parachuted into Rybachiy with twenty-four of his
Alpha soldiers, having told the base that they were hunting an intruder, and murdered Svelte. "Why is Razin killing the agents?"

"We don't know. Perhaps he's doing it under FSB
orders."

"One man sent to kill ten agents? It would be easier
for the police just to arrest them and make them quietly
disappear." Will shook his head. "He's acting alone."

Nobody spoke for a moment.

"I need access to the files on Sentinel's agents."

"Of course." Patrick collected the papers and arranged
them into a pile. He was silent for a while, before saying,
"Tomorrow, you've got to go to Ukraine to meet Sentinel
and tell him that Razin is not only the killer but also

wants to create a flash point to bring Russia and America to war."

Will felt disbelief roll over him. "Whatever Razin does, Russia would be mad to go to war with the United States. It's completely outgunned."

"It is." Patrick's expression was somber. "Though it has one thing that we don't: a willingness to sacrifice millions of its countrymen."

Will was deep in thought. "He's going to use Alpha to create that flash point." He returned his attention to the coheads. "Though they'll be loyal to him, I doubt Razin's men know what he's planning. He'll use them in a way they won't suspect—maybe a covert training exercise. Razin's the key. If we can get rid of him, we'll stop his operation." He looked up. "Have you considered taking our information to the Russian premier?"

"We have, and my president has. But in order to do that we'd have to give him what little evidence we have. As a result, we'd risk compromising Sentinel, his agents, and maybe even our entire intelligence network in Russia. The consequences for us could be as devastating as Razin's actions."

Will knew that was true. He spoke fast. "I've got one chance to end this quickly: get Sentinel to set up a meeting with Razin, and I'll be there to kill him."

"Provided Razin attends the meeting."

"That's the problem." Will's mind raced. "Razin may attend if he believes that his treachery is still a secret. But I think I disturbed him at Svelte's quarters—he hadn't finished off Svelte. I think he heard me enter the building, might have thought I was a sailor, and got out quick before he was compromised. Later, Razin's men opened fire on me. Razin now knows that there was a genuine intruder and will be worried that I got to Svelte and spoke to him."

"Well, let's hope he makes the meeting."

Will shook his head. "There has to be a backup plan." He looked at Alistair. "As you know, I'll need some of my alias passports, but I'll also need an unused passport with a multiple-entry visa for Russia."

Alistair nodded. "We'll have the passport ready for you when you get back from Ukraine."

"When I get back?" Will shook his head. "I'll come back when I'm ready. Arrange for the passport to be available in Europe."

"What's your backup plan?"

Will relaxed his hand. "I have in mind a plan to discredit Razin, get him suspended, maybe even dismissed— regardless, to take him out of the equation." His words were measured, though privately he wondered if the plan would work. "Then, when he's isolated and powerless, I'll track him down and put a bullet in his head."

FOUR

That evening, Will sat at a corner table in the discreetly lit wine bar at Washington, D.C.'s, five-star Willard InterContinental hotel. The place was half full, and around him earnest-looking, sharp-suited men and women sat in couples, hunched over drinks, leaning close to each other, and talking in low voices.

A tall man walked across the bar, carrying drinks in one hand, and sat opposite him. He was wearing a suit but no tie, looked sinewy and very strong, was three years older than Will, had straw-colored hair, and a face that was handsome but etched with the weight of experiences that few men ever had. Placing two glasses of Maker's Mark whiskey on the table, the man looked at the people around him and smiled. "Lobbyists, senators, businessmen, political consultants. I know 'em all, but they don't know me." The man pushed one of the glasses across the table, looking at Will. "Have a drink."

Will glanced at his glass before looking at the CIA Special Operations Group paramilitary officer. He smiled. "Hello, Roger."

Roger Koenig lifted his glass and tapped it against Will's. "It's good to see you again."

The last time Will had seen Roger, the officer had had bullet wounds and had been lying on a hospital floor in the small village of Saranac Lake, New York. He was Will's only friend. "When did you get back on active duty?"

"Few months now." The former DEVGRU SEAL took a swig of his drink. "How long are you in town?"

Will drank some whiskey. "I'm leaving in a few hours."

"Shame. My wife wanted me to invite you over to our place for dinner."

"I—"

"Yeah, yeah. Your work comes first." He seemed to be studying Will. "Don't worry. I know, you'd have hated it." He grinned. "You can talk your way out of any situation, but you're terrified of a family dinner and idle chat. You really do need to lighten up a bit." His expression and tone of voice changed. "Patrick told me you just got back from Russia, that you were nearly killed."

"Did he send you here to check up on me?" The moment he said the words, Will regretted them.

Anger flashed across Roger's face. "You should know me better than that. I came here to have a drink with the man who saved my life."

"Stupid question. I'm sorry."

The anger on Roger's face receded, but his expression

remained stern. "Don't try to push me away, Cochrane. I'm not like the others."

Will nodded slowly. He wondered why Roger stuck by him. It was true that he'd saved the CIA officer's life, but he'd saved many people's lives and none of them had wanted to be in his presence for a second longer than they had to.

"Have you heard from your sister?"

Will shook his head. "She won't return my calls or reply to my letters."

"Give it time."

Will had given it time. He'd seen Sarah only once by chance during the last nine years. His existence reminded her of the day that criminals had come to kill her and their mother when Will and his sister had been teenagers. Will had killed the men but had been too late to stop his mother from dying. "I bought some gifts for your children." He handed Roger a duty-free carrier bag.

Roger looked inside. "Teddy bears? My twin sons are twelve and spend every free hour killing each other in Xbox games, and my daughter's just turned fourteen and is starting to think about cuddling other things." He smiled. "But thanks for the thought."

Will felt foolish. "How's Laith?"

Laith was a CIA SOG officer and ex–Delta Force operative who had worked with both men in their last mission. Like Roger, Will had last seen Laith in Saranac, though Laith's stomach had been slashed open with a knife.

"He was in the hospital for a while, but he's operational

again." Roger's cell phone bleeped. He checked the screen, his expression one of irritation.

Will smiled. "Work comes first."

"It thinks it does." He stood, a wry smile now on his face. "Find a nice woman and marry her. It'll be the solution to all your problems."

An hour later Will was in his hotel room. His bag was packed; he'd be checking out shortly. Turning on the television, he flicked through the channels until he found one devoted to classical music. An orchestra was playing Pyotr Ilyich Tchaikovsky's *Symphony No. 6*. He sat down, closed his eyes, and placed the tips of his fingers together.

As the third movement commenced, one of his rare good memories came to him. He was sixteen years old, and he was on his first proper date with a girl named Mary. He had known her for a couple of years—they played viola together in their school orchestra—but had only recently plucked up the courage to ask her out. They went to a National Symphony Orchestra performance in the John F. Kennedy Center for the Performing Arts. The musicians were delivering an excellent performance of *Symphony No. 6*. Will was nervous and his date looked nervous, but halfway during the third movement, he looked at Mary, smiled, and took her hand.

The television concert paused before commencing the fourth movement. The memory vanished and was replaced by another. He was twenty years old, and he was sitting in a café on the banks of the Barada River in

Syria's capital, Damascus. He was dressed in jeans and an open-neck shirt and was sipping a glass of arak. The early-evening sun felt good on his tanned skin, and he smiled as he listened to Tchaikovsky's fourth movement coming through the old speakers of the café. Several tables away from him sat a woman who looked to be around the same age as him. She was very pretty, had a glass of wine, and was reading a book. She glanced at him; Will smiled wider, and she responded. Three men walked in. Dressed in nice suits, they appeared middle-aged. Sitting down at a vacant table, they ordered drinks and began talking to each other with earnest expressions on their faces. Will looked at the woman again and wondered if she would be offended if he offered to buy her a drink. He looked at the three men and saw a waiter approaching them, carrying a tray with glasses. One of the men's cell phones rang. The man stood, listened to the call, closed his phone, and spoke to the other men while ushering the waiter away. The men clearly had urgent business elsewhere.

That was not supposed to happen just yet.

They were supposed to be there until closing time, when the café would be empty of innocents.

Will put cash onto his table to pay for his drink, stood, pulled out a handgun, and shot the three men in their heads.

Will opened his eyes as the memory faded, but he could still remember the expression on the woman's face turning from shock to disgust as she looked at him. He could still hear the screaming from the other people in the café; he could still remember standing in front of his GCP commanding officer and an anonymous French intelligence officer from the DGSE three days prior to that event. And he remembered his commander's words to him: *This is your first black operation. If you do well on this job, you'll be given plenty more just like it.*

FIVE

The business-class section of the Ukraine International Airlines Boeing 737 was at full capacity, with most passengers eating lunch. Will looked out of the window and saw that they were traveling over the snow-covered Transylvanian Alps of Romania. He'd not slept since departing Washington, D.C., fourteen hours before, taking flights to London, then Vienna, and now onward to Odessa. The plane would be landing in approximately one hour. Soon after that, he would be meeting Sentinel.

Not for the first time on the journey, Will wondered what Sentinel would be like. Alistair had forewarned him that Sentinel would be a complex and difficult man to deal with and rightly so. There were few men, if any, within the Western intelligence community who had proven, to such an extent, and over such a protracted period of time, that they were of such value.

He tried to sleep, but his mind was too active. More than anything, he felt an overwhelming sense of unease.

Will walked quickly through the lobby of the Hotel Otrada toward the entrance. He'd landed in Ukraine six hours ago, taken a room in the luxury hotel, and was now heading to his meeting with Sentinel. Outside, it was twilight and icy, and a heavy fog lay motionless over the city of Odessa. He entered a taxi and soon was being driven north along a coastal city road straddled with old-fashioned lamps that cast a dim golden glow over the route. The Black Sea was beside him but barely visible in the fading light. After two miles, he was nearing the city's old town and its adjacent port. The taxi slowed and the driver muttered in Russian, the common language of Ukraine, that they were close to his destination.

They moved northwest, with the port to their right. The place was better lit, but the fog seemed even heavier here, allowing only glimpses of the freight ships and ferries moored alongside large jetties. Pedestrians and cars milled around the area. The taxi stopped by an arterial road entrance to one of the jetties, and the driver held out a hand. Will thrust hryvnia notes at the expectant man and stepped out of the vehicle onto Prymors'ka street.

It was nearly night now and very cold, although the ground was free of snow. Will pulled up the collar of his overcoat and looked in the direction opposite to the port. Rising away from the road was the famous five-hundred-foot-long, broad stone Potemkin Stairs. On a normal day it would give tourists who climbed to its summit a view of the whole port. But tonight it was impossible to see much beyond a hundred feet.

Will frowned, looked left and right along the road, watched cars move cautiously through the fog, glanced at the port behind him, and looked back toward the Potemkin Stairs and the few tourists he could see on it. He'd been told that this was the meeting place, but now that he was here it felt wrong—too busy, too exposed, with too many routes into and out of the place.

An SUV passed him. He watched its taillights move away from his position and disappear into the thick fog. Glancing around again, he heard more engine noises; those sounded as though they belonged to other large vehicles, and they were moving fast. His heart missed a beat. Spinning to face the vehicles, Will saw two sets of headlights coming quickly toward him.

In an instant, he knew exactly what was happening.

He also knew that he had to allow it.

Two SUVs skidded to a halt by his position; eight men jumped out and ran to him. The SUV that had passed him seconds earlier reappeared, reversing fast to his position before stopping. The men grabbed and twisted him, ran him backward to the SUVs, threw him into one of the vehicles, and slammed boots and knees against his head. Everything happened in less than six seconds. Then the

SUVs lurched forward. Will was pinned to the floor of the vehicle by large and very strong men.

It was impossible to see where they were going. Will looked at the two men who held him firm. Their faces were in darkness; they said nothing. They seemed quite professional, though Will wouldn't know how good they were until he decided to do something.

The three-vehicle convoy drove for an hour before stopping. A cell phone rang. One of the five men in Will's vehicle pulled out his phone, listened to it, said nothing, then nodded at the two men holding Will. Doors were opened. Will was dragged out of the SUV and thrown onto the ground. Boots pressed his head against the frozen soil. The three SUVs were together, and the only light around them came from the vehicles. It showed that they were adjacent to a tree-lined road. Eleven men were on foot, all of them dressed in dark winter attire. One of them walked up to Will, nodded at the man pinning him down, took three paces away from them, and pointed a gun at Will's head.

Hands gripped Will's chin and forced his body into a kneeling position. All but the man with the gun moved to form a large circle around him. Will and the man holding the weapon were in the center of that circle.

Will raised his head and looked at the man holding the gun. "Fuck you."

The man smiled, took three paces forward, and kicked him in the chest, forcing him onto his back. Will's muscles instantly tensed. He thought about trying to escape, but he knew the thought was pointless.

The man punched the pistol into Will's mouth and smiled wider; then his face took on a cold look. He pulled out the weapon and nodded toward some of the men. One of them hit Will on the back of the head with sufficient force to send him to the ground. Immediately after his face hit the road, a boot stamped on his neck and held him still. Hands rummaged through his overcoat and suit pockets. He had nothing in them except his wallet and passport. Both were removed.

There was more rapid talking. The man with the gun moved in front of Will, crouched down, and tossed his passport and wallet onto the ground so that both were inches from his face.

Will looked at the man and spoke through gritted teeth. "Do I pass the test?"

The man said nothing for a while before nodding. "He had to be sure you were the right person and that you weren't being followed. You're in the outskirts of the village of Dalnik. Wait here."

The boot on Will's head was removed. All of the men entered two of the vehicles, then quickly sped away, leaving Will alone on the ground with the third empty SUV beside them, its engine and lights still on. Will hauled himself to his feet and picked up his ID and wallet. He looked at the area ahead of him that was illuminated by the vehicle's headlights. It was now very quiet, very still. The freezing fog was everywhere. He brushed ice from his clothes but kept his eyes on his surroundings, waiting, urgently trying to identify a new shape or movement. After taking two steps forward, he stood still for ten minutes, listening, watching. He moved forward again until he was standing fully in the headlights of the SUV and remained there for another fifteen minutes. The SUV behind him idled almost silently; fumes from its exhaust wafted through the air and mingled with the fog that now almost encapsulated him. He was exposed to anything around him, and he hated being this vulnerable. But he knew he had to remain calm. It was very cold now, cold enough to make every intake of air cause pain in his lungs.

The village of Dalnik sounded familiar, and he tried to remember why, something he'd learned about a long time before, maybe at school. It came to him. In 1941, Nazi-allied Romanian soldiers had rounded up twenty-five thousand Jews in Odessa and made them march along the twenty-mile road he'd been driven along to get here. Three thousand of them, mostly the elderly, children, and the physically and mentally handicapped, couldn't walk fast enough so were shot or hanged along the way. Those who made it here alive were herded into four warehouses, probably located very close to where Will was now standing. The Romanian troops made holes in the buildings big enough for machine guns, locked the doors, placed their guns into the holes, and opened fire. Later they set the buildings ablaze and tossed grenades into them to make sure no Jew survived.

He heard a sound and looked quickly in the direction from which it had come. There was nothing else at first, but then he heard what sounded like a footstep crunching over the icy ground, followed by another, then another. He waited. The noises stopped. The motionless fog blanketed everything. Nothing else could be seen. All was quiet again. Then there was another crunch over ground, followed by another.

Then he saw him. At first he was just a dark shape, but as he drew nearer, Will could see that it was a person who was taking careful, deliberate steps toward him. He was thirty feet away, his face was still hidden in the fog, and he was holding something. It was almost certainly a pistol, and it had probably been pointing at him since he arrived here. The man stopped far enough away for his features to still be hidden. He raised his weapon high so that Will could clearly see that it was aimed in his direction, held it with two hands, and suddenly walked quickly toward him. Within a split second, Will saw that the man was tall, athletic, middle-aged, and clean-shaven, had groomed short blond hair, and was dressed in a windbreaker jacket, jeans, and hiking boots.

Sentinel.

He came to within ten feet, stopped, and barked in a well-spoken English accent, "The service had better have a damn good reason for calling this meeting." He kept his gun pointed at Will's head. "You've got ten seconds to persuade me not to pull the trigger."

SIX

The first minutes of daylight showed woodland dotted with red berries, snow-covered ground, and snow-flakes falling serenely from the sky. Traces of the fog were still there and gave the place an eerie presence. Turning from the view, Will glanced around the large room. Six large windows surrounded what looked like a well-used spacious family kitchen. That was as it should be, for Sentinel's safe houses would all have been outfitted to look like genuine homes.

Sentinel was standing in the center of the room speaking rapid Slovene into his cell phone. He finished the call, poured black coffee into a mug, and sat down at the kitchen table.

Will joined him.

Sentinel withdrew three handgun magazines from his trouser pocket and carefully removed the bullets, resting each on its percussion cap on the table, until ten of them were lined up vertically. He took out another magazine, reached behind his back, withdrew a Sig Sauer P229 handgun, and slammed the fresh magazine into the weapon. Placing the muzzle of the gun against one of the bullets, he tapped the projectile over, then did the same with three more. He looked at Will with icy blue eyes. "I've now got two hundred and seventy-six assets. One hundred and eighty of them are Russians who operate inside their country, seventy are Ukrainian, Belarusian, Latvian, Estonian, and Finnish men, like those who grabbed you from the base of the Potemkin Stairs, and twenty of them are Western European support agents—mostly wealthy individuals, arms dealers, and forgers—who I use to finance and supply my operations when MI6 is unable to help me. But at the forefront of them all"—he looked back at the bullets—"are my Russian agents, my tier-one intelligence producers. There were ten of them, and now I have six. They all risk their lives for me so that the West can benefit from their intelligence about Russia. Do you know why they do that?"

Will said nothing.

Sentinel smoothed his fingers over the four prone cartridges and closed his eyes before opening them again. For the briefest moment his face was filled with sadness. His expression became cold. "They do it because they love Russia and hate the people that run it."

Will nodded.

Sentinel looked at the bullets. He pulled back the workings of the Sig Sauer, chambered a round, put the gun onto the table, and muttered to himself, "Bastard."

"You didn't suspect him?"

"I had no reason to. I've been investigating the deaths, but so far found nothing. I'd concluded the killers were SVR or FSB."

"How does Khmelnytsky know the identity of your agents?"

Sentinel stared at him.

"Did you make tradecraft mistakes? Perhaps you were followed by Razin to your agent meetings."

Sentinel remained motionless.

"You can trust me."

"Trust?" The room reverberated with the volume of Sentinel's voice. "I don't trust anyone, and I'm not about to start doing so with someone I've only known for a few hours." He spun the gun so that its nozzle was facing Will. "Do you work in the service's Russia team?"

"No."

"Security Department?"

"No."

"Then what's your fucking interest in my business?"

Will ignored the question. "You need to set up a meeting with Razin so that I can kill him."

Sentinel laughed. "Have you read his file?"

"Of course."

Sentinel's expression changed. "Then you'll know that it's more likely he'll kill us."

"I'm prepared to take that risk. Are you?"

Sentinel placed a hand over the gun. "How long have you been in the service?"

"Long enough not to have to prove my worth by answering questions like that."

"We'll see." Sentinel spoke fast. "I've no idea how Razin knows the identity of my other agents, nor do I know how Svelte found out he was a traitor." He raised his voice. "I made *no* tradecraft mistakes."

Will held his gaze. "Razin's command of Alpha gives him a very powerful weapon, but he's going to need more than that to try to spark a war. Any ideas what he might do?"

"Yes."

"I'm listening."

Silence.

Will put a finger against the tip of Sentinel's gun and yanked it sideways so that the gun was pointing away from him.

But Sentinel's hand remained over the weapon. "You shouldn't have come here. And you need to leave right now because there's nothing more I'm going to say to you."

Will pulled out his cell phone. "We thought you might say that." He punched some buttons, pressed SPEAKER-PHONE, and placed the phone on the table between them.

A man answered. "Hold while we route the call."

Thirty seconds later, the same man said, "Okay, you're through to the chief."

The chief of MI6.

Sentinel's expression remained hostile as he glanced at Will, then the cell. "Your messenger boy's asking too many questions. I've ordered him to leave."

The chief answered, his voice measured and deep. "He has my authority to stay."

Sentinel shook his head. "You have no authority over me."

"You can't speak to me like that."

"I can. Since I've been in the field, I've worked with six chiefs. They all come and go. But I've stayed."

"You'll do what you're told!"

Sentinel leaned closer to the phone. "I'll do what I damn well like. And if I *like*, I'll go above your head and speak directly to the prime minister. I'll tell him that you're interfering in my business and I don't like it. Our premiers have always done what I've told them to do." He leaned back. "You *know* that I have that power. Tell your messenger boy to leave, or things will get unpleasant for you."

The chief was silent for five seconds before saying, "I'm not interfering. I'm giving you help."

"Help that I didn't request. You don't make decisions like that without consulting with me first."

More silence. Then, "The man I sent is run by a controller who was on your intake when you joined MI6."

Sentinel's eyes narrowed. "Name?"

"Alistair McCulloch."

A thin smile emerged on Sentinel's face. "I'd heard he got promoted. I'd also heard that he'd been put in charge of a trivial administrative department."

"That's what you and everyone else were supposed to have heard."

The smile vanished. "The service doesn't withhold information from people like me."

"When did you last see Alistair?"

Sentinel answered through gritted teeth, "Nine years ago."

"It must have been an awkward meeting. After all, that's when you were stripped of your Spartan code name."

The mention of the code name clearly surprised Sentinel. "They were closing down the Spartan Section."

"Why?"

"Read the files."

"I wonder why my predecessor sent Alistair to break the news to you."

"Probably because the former chief was too scared to do it in person."

"I've read the files. You were stripped of your title because events had moved on since your imprisonment. Russia was no longer the only major threat. For the Spartan Section to have any relevance, its officer had to be globally deployable. They couldn't do that with you because you were too vital to the Russian operations."

Sentinel slid the gun close to his body, away from Will's reach.

"You'd become too . . . specialized."

"Their loss."

"Their gain. MI6 couldn't afford to underestimate your importance."

"You'd damn well better have a reason to be talking about this."

"Oh, I do. Alistair was sent to you for a very specific reason. It had to be him, because he'd just been given command of the revamped Spartan Section."

Sentinel stared at the phone, and his expression changed. He seemed to be deep in thought. Eventually, he brought his gaze up to Will and asked, "Is this him?"

"It is."

Sentinel nodded slowly, looked away, and muttered, "They kept it going."

"It wasn't easy. Eight recruits before him . . . failed. The future of the section was entirely reliant on someone passing the Program. I sent him to you out of respect for who you are." He paused. "I'd like you to work with him. But I concede that I can't order you to make that happen."

The room was silent. Will kept his eyes locked on Sentinel.

Sentinel picked the phone up. "Okay, I'll do it. But no more surprises. Understood?"

"I understand very well."

Sentinel ended the call and tossed the phone at Will. He spoke in a quiet, measured voice. "Razin and his men have been instructed by Russian high command to covertly train with twenty prototype weapons. These devices are about the size of small suitcases and are highly sophisticated. There's a view that the devices can be used in conventional battlefields and unconventional theaters of war and peace. Alpha's task is to prove this view correct and to also prove that the weapons can be smuggled into heavily defended areas. Over the last few months, Razin and his men have been secretly entering Russian air bases, navy installations, army depots, and government buildings to plant these devices. Every infiltration so far has been successful. The devices have since been removed by Razin's men and kept by them. The training exercise is due to be complete in the next few weeks, at which point the devices will be handed back to the army."

"This is how he'll spark a war?"

"It must be." Sentinel looked at the prone cartridges again and shook his head. "I'll send an urgent message to Razin that we need to meet in a safe house on the Russian border. We've used it before, so it shouldn't seem suspicious. The message will also say that people are being killed, I'm concerned for his safety, and I need to brief him on new security protocols."

Will's stomach muscles tightened. "The devices?"

Gun in hand, Sentinel rose and walked to the window. Outside, snow was falling faster and was being whipped up by a strong wind. Their surroundings no longer looked eerily serene; instead they appeared harsh and violent. Sentinel slowly turned to face Will. When he spoke, his voice was deep, and somber.

"The devices are nuclear bombs."

SEVEN

Will stood naked in his room in the Hotel Otrada, staring at his belongings laid out on the bed. He selected some clothes, carefully checked each item to ensure that none of them contained any compromising items such as receipts, and dressed. He examined himself in a mirror and decided that he looked as though he were about to embark on a winter hike. Stuffing cash into a jacket pocket, he repacked all of the remaining items, including his wallet and passport, into his case. The case he would leave with the concierge. He could see lunchtime traffic from the window, moving slowly below him through thick snow. There was no fog now. In the distance the Black Sea was easily visible.

He flicked on a kettle, tore open three tea bags, and

emptied their contents into a mug. He poured boiling water slowly over the loose tea, carefully stirring the brew. Grabbing the mug and looking at the sumptuous sofa and two armchairs in the room, he ignored them and sat instead on the floor with his back leaning against a wall. After waiting a few minutes for the tea leaves to settle to the base of the mug, he took a delicate sip of his drink and closed his eyes in appreciation. Though the drink was not up to the standard of his favorite Scottish breakfast tea blend, it was still good. He'd always known that even the coarsest of teas could be coaxed into tasting nice if one prepared its leaves properly and added nothing but hot water to them.

He thought about Sentinel, wondering if he would become the same as him by middle age unless something drastically changed the path of his life. There was so much about the man that Will not only understood but also saw in himself: mistrust of others, a life lived in extremes, a life lived with unrelenting focus, a life lived alone. But Sentinel had something that he did not yet have: an acceptance of that way of life, a realization that there would never be an alternative to his mode of existence.

Will recalled words spoken to him nine years before when an anonymous MI6 officer had asked if he was prepared to go into the Spartan Program.

Before you agree, understand this. There's no going back. If you survive the Program, everything will be different for you. Your body, your mind, your life. Everything.

He remembered being dragged to the edge of a forest in Scotland after two weeks of imprisonment, sleep deprivation, and torture by MI6 and special forces instructors, prior to which he had been chased by armed trackers and attack dogs over a hundred miles of frozen mountainous terrain. As he was dumped on the ground, an instructor walked quickly up to him, yanked his head up, pointed at the woods, and gave him his next task: "The forest is two miles long and one mile wide. Inside are four very skilled SBS soldiers. They're armed. You won't be. You've got to find them and render them immobile, but alive. If you exit the forest before doing so, you fail the program. And remember, this is not an artificial test. The men in there have authority to hurt you badly."

He took another sip of his tea and opened his eyes. Many years before Will had done so, Sentinel would have gone into that forest. He would have moved through the place exhausted, disoriented, desperate to find the men before they found him, but all the while doubting that he had the speed, strength, and skills to beat them. He would have wondered if that day was his last day on Earth, just as he had wondered every other day during the twelve-month Spartan Program.

Like Sentinel, Will had succeeded in that forest. But there was one thing he'd never been able to conquer: a fantasy about a different, normal life. Nine years before, he'd briefly had the opportunity to take that path. He was about to graduate from Cambridge University when one of his professors took him aside and offered him a full scholarship to do a Ph.D. and the chance to become an academic.

"I know how hard it's been for you, coming here after your experiences in the Legion. I know why you're quiet, while the other students like the sounds of their own mouths. But you've a razor-sharp intellect, and you have the chance now to put it to good use. Stay in Cambridge."

Will had answered, "I don't belong here."

The professor had countered, "So where do you belong? Do you really have a clear idea of where that place is? I suspect you don't. Be careful, because one day you'll stop, look around, and realize that you're totally alone."

Will knew that day had long since passed for Sentinel. But for a very brief moment, Will had seen real compassion and sadness on Sentinel's face as the officer recalled the memory of his four dead agents. Will understood. Sentinel's agents and assets were his kin, a disparate family.

But even though their work was dangerous and their lives isolated, Will was certain that none of them carried the burden that Sentinel did. Will had worked with many courageous and powerful men and women, but Sentinel was in a different league. To have survived so long in deep cover was in itself remarkable, but Sentinel had done so while at the same time building up an intelligence network that was second to none. Will had never met anyone so capable.

He finished his tea, checked his watch, and sighed. He needed to leave, to join forces with a man whom he was probably destined to become. Razin had responded to Sentinel's message, agreeing to the meeting. Nothing in Razin's response suggested he was suspicious.

But then again, Razin was a professional operator.

If the three of them did meet within the next twenty-four hours, in all probability at least one of them would end up dead.

EIGHT

The sedan drove east across the snow-covered Ukraine, covering four hundred miles, keeping the Black Sea and later the Sea of Azov to its right. Will sat in the back with Sentinel. A young Ukrainian man named Oleksandr was in the driver's seat. None of the men spoke during the journey.

It was night as the car reached the brightly illuminated industrial port city of Mariupol before traveling northeast for a further 180 miles. After fifteen hours of near-continuous driving since leaving Odessa, stopping only twice to refuel the vehicle, Oleksandr brought the car to a halt on a dimly lit deserted road, turned off its engine and lights, and pointed ahead into darkness. "Russia."

Sentinel opened a door, stretched, and got out. Will and Oleksandr followed suit, with the Ukrainian moving to the back of the vehicle to open the trunk. Snow fell fast around them. From within a rucksack, Oleksandr withdrew two HS 2000 handguns and spare magazines, then handed the items to the MI6 officers, who secreted the pistols and ammunition in their jackets.

The driver pulled up the collar of his thick coat and thrust his hands into his pockets. Light from an adjacent streetlamp showed that the man looked exhausted and cold. He glanced at Will. "Have you done this crossing before?"

"He hasn't." Sentinel looked in the direction of Russia.

Oleksandr nodded. "Normally it's easy. There're no barriers, just open fields covering the border, and the Ukrainian State Border Guard Service has been under-manned and underequipped to cover the thousands of miles of its borders. They've averaged one guard per twenty miles. On the other side, the Russians have faced the same problem." He looked at Sentinel. "Things have changed. The Russians and Ukrainians have recently strengthened their border, reinforced their guards, and equipped them with thermal and infrared surveillance and detection technology. They're worried about illegal immigrants coming over the border from Russia." Reaching back into the trunk of the car, he withdrew two IR/TG-7 thermal goggles with head straps. "These should help. But you'll still have to be very careful."

Sentinel looked at Oleksandr. "After five miles, pull

over somewhere quiet and get some sleep for a few hours. Wait for us there."

He nodded, rubbing his fatigued face. "Sure, boss."

Sentinel gave a sympathetic smile while gripping the young Ukrainian's shoulder. "Give my regards to your brother and uncle, and tell your mother that I will give her more cash for her husband's funeral when I'm back."

Oleksandr bristled. "My father would have wanted to be here with you now." He spat on the ground. "Fucking FSB. They should've arrested him when they trapped him in Moscow, not shot him like a dog."

Sentinel nodded slowly. "I was privileged to work with him."

"Bless you, boss." Oleksandr sighed, reached into a jacket pocket, and withdrew a small slim metal case. "Please give this to Polina. Twenty cigarettes, hand-rolled by my mother, containing her favorite sun-cured Ottoman tobacco." He gave the case to Sentinel. "We didn't have time to make more."

Sentinel secreted it within an inner jacket pocket. "She'll be very grateful."

Oleksandr wrapped his arms over his chest and glanced toward Russia. "Come home safely, boss."

"The border's five miles away; we've got to get there while it's still dark. Let's go."

Will strapped his thermal goggles onto his head and looked around. Even though there were no light sources, his TG-7 gave him perfect black-and-white vision of everything up to a range of three hundred yards. He and Sentinel were prone on the ground; the flat, open fields before them held no trees or other large features. It was still snowing. They were a mile from the border.

They stayed like that for ten minutes; then Sentinel slowly rose to a crouch, gripped his handgun, and moved quickly forward. After three hundred feet he stopped, dropped to the ground, and waited before beckoning to Will. Will moved fast but kept low, holding his gun ready to shoot. He reached Sentinel, lay flat on the ground next to him, looked around, saw nothing, and glanced at his colleague. Sentinel nodded, pointing ahead. Will got to his feet and sprinted forward for five hundred feet, the whole time glancing left and right and ahead. He reached the edge of the field, keeping his head below the low hedge. Another field was before him, but this one was much larger. Lifting his arm up, he waved Sentinel to join him.

When Sentinel reached him, he knelt on one knee, moving his head 180 degrees to examine everything before them. Then he jumped over the hedge and ran until he was approximately 250 yards in front of Will, before stopping. Will stayed still, focusing on only the white image of Sentinel. The MI6 man was flat on the ground, motionless. He stayed like that for nearly ten minutes. Will knew that something was wrong.

Sentinel raised a hand, gesturing for Will to come forward but stay low. Will moved, gripping his gun with both hands, running as fast as he could in his crouch stance, watching Sentinel the entire time. As he came to within 150 feet of the officer, Sentinel waved a hand downward. Will dived forward, thumping to the ground. He stayed still for several minutes, his eyes fixed on Sentinel and his surroundings. Sentinel moved his hand. Will leopard-crawled over the snow-covered ground between him and Sentinel.

Sentinel lay motionless, silent and staring ahead. Will followed his gaze. Five hundred feet ahead of them were two soldiers, both carrying assault rifles. One of the men was looking through binoculars.

Sentinel crawled right up to Will, cupped his hands around Will's ear, and whispered, "Ukrainian border guards. The man on the right has got thermal imagery, but he's not seen me, so the binoculars must have limited range. We'll take a route around them."

Will nodded as Sentinel moved away from him. The guard with the binoculars was rotating, then standing still for a few seconds before moving again. He was covering his entire surroundings but most likely was blind to anything beyond 150 yards from his position. The other soldier was still, gripping his rifle. Will rose carefully and moved back fifty feet. Sentinel did the same. Keeping his upper body low, Will ran to his left, examining the route ahead of him as he did so. Sentinel was directly behind him, and Will knew that he would not be looking ahead but instead would be watching the soldiers for signs that they had spotted the MI6 officers.

After a quarter mile, Will adjusted direction so that he

was running back toward the border but was far enough away from the two soldiers to remain out of their sight. To his right he could just make out the men; they were still stationary. He looked ahead and stopped abruptly, dropping to the ground. Two other soldiers were 150 yards away from him, sideways to his position. Both were on one knee; one was looking through a large rifle scope across the route directly in front of them, the other had his back to his colleague and was looking through his rifle scope in the other direction.

Sentinel crawled alongside Will. The man said nothing for a moment, but Will knew he would be thinking the same as him. The soldiers were also Ukrainian border guards. But these men looked as though they had very powerful night-vision equipment, and they were positioned in such a way to monitor at least a half mile of land on either side of them. The soldiers were motionless, not looking in their direction.

Sentinel again cupped his hands against Will's head. "It'll soon be daylight. Follow me, move fast."

A foot of snow already covered the ground, and more was quickly falling. They jumped to their feet and ran parallel to the guards. A further ten minutes and Sentinel stopped again, grabbing Will's arm and pulling him down. Both men were breathing hard. Sentinel glanced in the direction that they had come from before looking at Will. "I'm sure they can't see us now."

Sentinel swiveled to face Russia and walked fast, with Will close behind. It was clear that he knew exactly where he was going and was choosing his route with precision. Occasionally he would stop, motion to Will to do the same, look around, and move a few paces to his right or left before continuing. After two miles, he slowed, then stopped. The land around them was now undulating and forested.

"Welcome to Russia."

They moved toward an area of dense trees. Will was glad of their protection, though he continued to scrutinize his surroundings for hidden soldiers. A further twenty minutes and the trees thinned out. Will removed his night-vision equipment and looked around. The first signs of daylight were beginning to break into the forest, although it was still dark at ground level. He was about to move when he heard noises ahead of him. They were distant at first, but they quickly became recognizable.

"Dogs!" Sentinel looked around urgently.

The encroaching dogs meant that armed soldiers were close by. Will hoped that the dogs had not been unleashed, because they'd be spotted. But he knew that if he shot them, the border guards would be put on alert and their chances of getting back into the Ukraine much slimmer.

He saw them. There were two large German shepherds, and the first was fifty feet in front of the other. They were barking as they ran down a narrow route of open ground. They had clearly detected the MI6 officers. Will ran forward, crouched, and waited. The nearest dog was now 150 feet away.

Four seconds passed.

Suddenly the dog was just a few feet from him, jumping through the air with its mouth wide open.

Will dived at the airborne dog, wrapped an arm around its neck, squeezed tight while twisting his body against the dog's, and crashed to the ground. The dog was limp beneath him, its neck snapped. But he was totally vulnerable as the second dog launched its powerful body at him.

Sentinel stepped forward and punched the dog full force on the side of the head. Walking up to where it lay dazed, he stamped a boot onto its throat and held it there until the writhing creature had stopped breathing.

Both began covering the dogs with snow until the animals were hidden. They crept ahead along the track, which soon forked. They stopped, listened, and waited before taking the track on the left. The track forked again; this time they moved right. There was movement ahead. Crouching down, they sidestepped into foliage. Two soldiers were on the path two hundred feet ahead of them, coming slowly toward their position. They carried flashlights that they held alongside their assault rifles. They had not yet seen the MI6 officers. Moving farther into the foliage, Will and Sentinel lay carefully on the ground. The soldiers were silent, but Will caught glimpses of them between the snow-covered leaves around him. He placed his finger over the trigger of his handgun as the men came to within thirty feet of his position. They kept moving until they were right by his side. Will held his breath, remaining motionless. The men moved past him. They were almost certainly the dog handlers and were no doubt searching for the "immigrants" their dogs had detected.

When they were out of sight, Will and Sentinel continued deeper into the forest until they reached a small road. Will looked right and saw nothing. He looked left and saw a truck. It was two hundred feet away, and beside it were three soldiers and two more dogs on leashes. All of the soldiers were smoking. The heads of the dogs were twitching left and right.

They walked away from the patrol, keeping the road on their left, until trees obstructed their view of the soldiers. Crossing the road, they entered more forest.

Sentinel grabbed Will's arm. "They don't patrol this far away from the border. But stay alert."

They ran and walked for an hour, moving through forest and open fields, close to snow-covered vehicle tracks, over roads, through more woods and more open ground. Sentinel led the way, constantly changing direction, constantly looking around to check that they weren't being watched, always choosing routes that gave them cover when it was available.

When they stopped, it was full daylight. More open farmland was around them.

Sentinel's breathing was fast. "We're close."

Will followed his colleague, who now walked carefully ahead. They moved across more fields until they came to a six-bar gate. Beyond the gate was a vehicle track, and in the distance was a solitary farmhouse.

Sentinel moved to one side of the gate and knelt down. "That building's the safe house. We've made up time and are on schedule. The meeting's not due for another three hours."

They stayed like that for thirty minutes. Will heard the sound of a vehicle. Moving his head slowly out of his secreted position, he glanced down the track. A pickup was moving along the route, coming toward them. It passed the house, kept driving, and stopped 500 feet away from the building and 150 feet from their position. Will darted a look at Sentinel and saw that he was looking intently at the vehicle. Will glanced back at the truck. A small woman got out. She was dressed in thick dark clothes and wore a head scarf that hid her features, but judging by her posture and movements she was very old. The woman leaned back into the truck and flashed its headlights six times.

Sentinel instantly jumped over the fence. Will followed. They ran along the track and slowed as they approached the vehicle. Sentinel's gun was raised, but he was not pointing it at the woman; instead he was aiming it at the road beyond. The woman removed her scarf and walked toward Sentinel. She must have been at least seventy-five years old, maybe older.

She smiled and spoke in Russian. "My angel."

Sentinel lowered his weapon, walked up to the woman, hugged her, and responded in her language, "Polina. I shouldn't have asked you to come out in this weather."

Polina shrugged. "I have to unlock the house and get it ready for you." She rubbed her frail hands against

Sentinel's forearms. "I've bought some food for the freezer. Even though I don't live there anymore, I keep it stocked for your meetings. Would you like me to make you some nice shchi? The hot soup will do you good."

Sentinel smiled, shaking his head. "You need to be heading home in ten minutes." He extracted the slim metal case and handed it to the woman. "Oleksandr's mother made these for you. My Ukrainian friends send you their love."

Polina took the case, smiling. Then her smile faded. "Please tell them that I'm sorry for their loss. Juriy was a great soldier." She looked at Will. "Some of us here might live to old age, but in these parts few of us die from it."

Will saw that the sleeve on one of her arms had risen up to expose an inch of badly scarred skin on the underside of her forearm.

Polina caught his gaze and quickly pulled her sleeve down.

"I didn't mean to—"

"It's okay." She glanced at Sentinel before looking back at Will. "I was nine years old when Majdanek extermination camp was liberated by Soviet soldiers. Some other survivors told me to run away or hide because I had a Nazi tattoo that showed I was a Jew. Instead, I sat in a hut and peeled off the skin with my fingernails until the tattoo was gone. When I finished, I thought everything would be all right." She smiled, but the look was bitter. "I was a naive child. The Soviets knew that I'd tried to disguise my Jewish identity, and punished me by putting me in Kolyma gulag for fifteen years." She looked at Sentinel and reached out to him.

Sentinel kissed the old Russian woman's hand. "Next time I'll stay longer and make *you* some soup."

"I hope so." She entered the vehicle, turned it around, and drove toward the farmhouse.

Sentinel said, "We need to stay out of the house until he arrives. Then we'll shoot him and get back into Ukraine."

Polina stopped the vehicle by the building, paused by the front door as she released the locks, and stepped through the entrance.

As she did so, a massive explosion tore her body and most of the house apart.

NINE

It had taken them twenty hours to get back to the safe house in Odessa. Sentinel sat on the lounge floor, his head in his hands.

"We'll get him."

Sentinel looked up. "When we do, I'm going to be the one who kills him."

Will nodded and stretched his fatigued back muscles. He hadn't managed to sleep on the car journey back; all he'd thought about was Polina. He wondered what Sentinel thought of him. It had been Will's idea to set up the meeting with Razin. "I'm sorry."

Sentinel shook his head. "Razin's bomb was meant for us, not Polina." He bunched his hand into a fist. "We had to try getting him there."

"Let's hope he thinks we're dead."

"He knows we're alive."

Will thought for a moment. "Police records?"

Sentinel rubbed his unshaven face. "He'll use his FSB status to get access to them."

Minutes after the explosion, there had been a five-hundred-foot-high column of black smoke rising above the farmhouse. Though the property was remote, it wouldn't have taken long for emergency services to have been alerted. They'd have conducted a forensic analysis of the scene and ascertained that a conventional bomb had killed one old lady.

"Everything's different now that he knows we're after him." Will studied Sentinel. "What are you going to do?"

For ten seconds Sentinel said nothing. Then, "I've thought about every tier-one agent meeting I've had since I've known Razin—every antisurveillance route I've taken to the meetings, every covert communication I've made with them, *anything* that could have compromised their identities." He shook his head. "*Everything* was watertight."

"That can only mean one thing."

A breach of security by someone else who had access to their names.

Sentinel clasped his hands together. Now he looked focused. "It's a long shot, but one of my agents might be able to help. He's FSB. We need to meet him in Hungary."

"I can't join you."

"Why not?"

"I've got to be elsewhere."

Anger flashed across Sentinel's face. "What's more important than this?"

"Nothing." Will tried to keep his tone placatory. "But I need to set up my own operation to get Razin."

Sentinel's eyes narrowed. "Tell me."

"No. I'm going to work this from another angle, but I can't tell anyone what I'm doing. Not even Alistair's privy to the full details."

"You're in"—Sentinel's words were measured and clipped—"my territory. Tell me what you're planning."

Will shook his head. "It's because I'm in your territory that I can't tell you. For decades the Russians have wanted to get their hands on you. If they lifted you and tortured you, my operation would be dead in the water. We'd never be able to stop Razin."

"May I remind you that I resisted torture for six years."

"Techniques have become more . . . sophisticated."

Sentinel said nothing.

Will said, "Razin might lay low, not risk killing any more agents."

"Maybe"—Sentinel was hesitant—"though he's never been one to back off from danger."

"How did you recruit him?"

He expected Sentinel to stay silent. Instead, the MI6 officer muttered, "I turned his strength into a weakness."

"Ambition?"

Sentinel nodded. "You've clearly read his file thoroughly."

Will had.

The dossier had shown that Taras Khmelnytsky had been a brilliant student at Moscow State University and had been given the option of a fast-track career in the Russian diplomatic service or a prestigious commission into the military navy. He had refused both and instead joined the 98th Guards Airborne Division as a junior lieutenant. The people who knew him thought he was crazy to do so, but it turned out he was anything but that. He served with the Division's 217th Guards Airborne Regiment, based in Ivanovo, for three years before he was handpicked to undergo the grueling selection for Spetsnaz GRU. He had passed with distinction and served with the GRU for six years, stationed in Moscow, eventually attaining the rank of major while operating in deniable overseas operations. Unusually, he had then been asked to join Spetsnaz Vympel, which was under FSB rather than GRU control. The GRU had tried unsuccessfully to block the transfer, but it was clear that Razin had been noticed by Russian high command, which wanted to give him as wide-ranging special operations experience and action as possible. In Vympel he had been given further extensive training in marksmanship, unarmed combat, medicine, languages, and infiltration into and exfiltration out of hostile zones. He had seen covert action in a variety of theaters, including the northern Caucasus, and he was ultimately awarded Russia's highest honor, Hero of the Russian Federation, for single-handedly rescuing a four-man Spetsnaz GRU unit that had been compromised observing a nuclear plant in North Korea and was in danger of being captured and executed. Four years before, the FSB had promoted him to colonel and given him command of their jewel in the crown: Spetsnaz Alpha. At that time he had been thirty-five, the youngest colonel in the entire Russian army.

Sentinel said, "I knew that Razin was totally patriotic to the motherland and had no vices or any other chinks in his armor that could be used to coerce him to work for me." He smiled. "Anyone else in MI6 would have rightly concluded he was impossible to recruit." His face turned serious. "But his ambition intrigued me, and I wondered if that could be used against him."

Will stayed silent.

"My assets found out that Razin was on a brief visit to Africa as a military adviser. I went straight there and sat next to him as he flew from Nigeria to Moscow via Frankfurt in order to return to his duties in Alpha. Halfway during that flight, I placed a letter in his lap. The letter said that I worked for MI6, that I had an idea that could catapult his career to the very highest level, and that I had three very capable men around me on the flight who would slowly cut off his head with their onboard dinner knives if he tried to do anything silly.

"Razin and I got off the plane at Frankfurt, sat in the airport's Lufthansa business-class lounge, and spoke to each other for one hour." Sentinel's voice was very quiet. "I said that I wanted him to be my prime agent for all matters pertaining to Russian special operations activities.

He refused, saying that he'd never do anything to weaken the Spetsnaz units or the GRU and FSB. I responded with a lie, saying that, on the contrary, the West needed to see those units grow even stronger in order to justify U.S. and British expenditure on our own intelligence agencies and special forces; that the West needed a new, highly professional adversary now that the so-called war on terror was being won. I concluded that his intelligence would serve him and serve me." Sentinel paused. "He still gave me no commitment. So I gave him something irresistible that *was* true: I told him that I had intelligence about a twelve-strong terrorist unit from the northern Caucasus who were based in Moscow and planned to plant bombs in the city. I said that he should use his Alpha men to kill the terrorists and once again be hailed as Russia's hero; that if he did that for me, and if he gave me the intelligence I needed, I would continue to feed him missions that would inevitably gain him promotion to Russian high command and maybe even beyond." Sentinel folded his arms. "He agreed to my terms. I had him hook, line, and sinker."

Though Will didn't show it, he felt total admiration for the way Sentinel had approached Razin.

Sentinel sighed. "That was three years ago. It all seemed to be working out nicely." He stared at the wall and frowned. "Why does he want to kill my agents and start a war? How does he benefit from both events?"

Will's mind raced as he recalled the files he'd read in Langley. "Most of your tier-one agents are high-ranking military or intelligence officers. If they're all killed, how would that affect Russia's military capability?"

"It would be an inconvenience, but all of them are replaceable."

"I thought so."

Sentinel clearly could see where this was leading. "On the flip side, the agents' intelligence would give the United States a major advantage in a war with Russia."

Will agreed. "Advance knowledge of troop movements, the location of mobile strategic missile launch sites, naval deployments, among others. The war would be a one-sided bloodbath."

Sentinel placed the tips of his fingers together; his eyes were darting left and right. "And yet, America's military is far superior to Russia's. Even without my agents, it would still win the war."

Will remembered Patrick's words: "Russia has one thing that we don't: a willingness to sacrifice millions of its countrymen."

A thought came to his mind.

But before he could articulate it, Sentinel slapped his hands on his legs and expressed the same thought: "Stalemate."

"Precisely."

They discussed the fact that if Russia wanted to go to war with the United States, the United States would have no choice other than to react with overwhelming force. The intelligence from Sentinel's agents would make that reaction precise and swift. But if the agents were dead,

Russia would be able to draw out the war and throw millions of bodies at the U.S. military. And at some point during the ongoing massacre of Russians, the United States would have to ask itself if it could keep pushing ahead.

Will nodded. "That's what Razin's banking on."

"Russia can't be annihilated—"

"—because America won't have the stomach to do it."

"So halfway into the war a stalemate is reached."

"Peace is negotiated."

"And Russia will honor its heroes."

Both men stared at each other. Their thoughts were exactly the same, though it was Sentinel who gave voice to them. "The biggest hero of them all would be the man who stepped forward and said that he'd secretly killed my MI6 spies so that Russia wouldn't be crippled." He stood up quickly and banged a fist against the wall. "Razin's not going to lay low or stop; he's going to make himself that hero. And if he succeeds, he'll be handed the Russian presidency on a fucking plate."

TEN

The sun was setting over Istanbul as Will walked through the Turkish city's Grand Bazaar. The place was a vast warren of alleys, streets, and covered walkways—some pedestrian, others strewn with heavily laden cars and trucks carrying goods to and from the multitude of shops on either side of the routes. He was surrounded by the sounds of street vendors calling to crowds of shoppers, car horns, distorted transistor radios playing Ottoman folk music, and a nearby mosque giving the *aksam* call to prayer. Despite being winter, the air felt warm and was thick with the smells of kebabs, *gozleme* pancakes, roasted vegetables, *simit* bread, and spices. He passed shops selling clothes and fabrics, tea, dried fruits and nuts, kitchenware, backgammon sets, cinnamon, turmeric, and guns.

As he pushed his way through the crowds, the sound of the call to prayer grew nearer and soon he was by the front entrance of the small sixteenth-century Rüstem Pasha Mosque. Muslim men and women were lined up outside, queuing to enter the beautiful building. He watched them for a while before scanning the route he'd just covered. The place was a throng of bodies, jostling, moving into and out of shops, stopping, and walking. There were too many people for him to be sure that he wasn't being followed. But he looked anyway, just in case someone looked out of place.

Someone like a twenty- or thirty-something man or woman who could move fast if needed.

Someone whose posture suggested a heightened alertness to his surroundings.

Movement from one shop front to another that was too rapid and had no shopping pattern.

Anything about someone that just looked *wrong*.

He walked quickly away from the mosque toward the Bosphorus. Streetlamps, shop and residential lights, and car beams were being turned on as dusk fell. The sprawling city became bathed in an electric glow, below a clear sky with a sickle moon and stars.

Reaching the Eminönü docks, he stopped close to the traffic-laden Galata Bridge and waited. The Bosphorus was busy with brightly illuminated ferries, some berthing, others crossing the channel or heading up it to Asia. A gentle sea breeze ran over his face, and for a moment Will enjoyed the sensation. He checked his watch.

He saw the tram; his senses sharpened.

It was one of the modern Bombardier Flexity Swift fleet: two long carriages with concertina breaks half-way along that enabled them to bend with the curva-ture of the tracks. It was slowing down. Will hurried to a ticket kiosk and bought a token that would allow him to take the tram three stops to Yenikapı station. The tram stopped in front of him. Inside, it was at half capacity.

He walked along the aisle of the front carriage and took a vacant seat next to a middle-aged man. He hoped the journey would take no more than ten minutes. Any longer, and he would risk compromising the person he'd come to meet.

His name was Luka, an SVR officer stationed in Istan-bul whose presence in the city was fully declared to the Turkish intelligence service, Milli İstihbarat Teşkilatı. But even though his job required close collaboration with the MIT on issues of mutual Russian-Turkish concerns, that did not stop them from covertly following him every-where he went.

He'd known Luka for three years, during which time the Russian officer had often passed Will secrets. Luka wasn't a double agent; he was more complicated than that, and by his own admission he gave Will only infor-mation that he believed would foster better relations between West and East. Will knew that most of what Luka told him was lies, but occasionally he would pro-duce a gold-dust truth that served both him and MI6.

Not that Luka knew he was talking to MI6. As far as he was concerned, Will was called Émile Villon and was an officer of France's Direction Générale de la Sécurité Extérieure.

As the tram pulled away, Will turned to the man next to him.

Luka smiled, then spoke in fluent French. "My friends are in the carriage behind us."

The MIT surveillance detail.

Will returned his gaze to the front of the tram and responded in the same language. "Problem?"

"I don't think so. But you never know. They can be . . . nasty fellows when they want to be."

The tram followed the Turkish coastline. The evening was picturesque, though Will barely registered his surroundings, instead visualizing the rear carriage, knowing they were out of sight of the MIT team but also knowing they could be reached within seconds. "What's your view on current Russian-American relations?"

Luka answered with a trace of sarcasm in his voice, "You've come all this way to ask me that?"

"No, but I'll benefit from your opinion."

"Opinion?"

"Insight."

Luka was silent for a moment. "Relations are shit." He placed a hand on the back of the seat in front of him, exposing an expensive Cartier watch. "Read the papers."

"I have, but they don't tell me what you know."

"And you think I will?"

"I think you'd like to."

The tram stopped at Sirkeci station, alongside the

Marmara Sea. Both men were silent as people got onto and off the carriage. Two elderly ladies sat in the seats in front of them.

Luka stared at them before muttering, "Tomorrow morning the U.S. ambassador to Moscow will be summoned to the Kremlin to explain why the United States has pulled out of the economic talks with Russia. No doubt the ambassador will counter that Russia is taking a provocative stance by attempting to aggressively position its oil pricing while at the same trying to obtain a lead role in the WTO." As the tram pulled away, the noise within the carriage increased, but he kept his voice quiet. "The summons will have achieved nothing other than creating more paranoia, more anger, more distrust, more . . . shit."

Will chose his next words carefully, constantly aware that he had to be very careful with Luka. The slightest wrong word would be fed back to the SVR and could cause untold damage. "What would happen if there was an incident in Russia—an act of violence, maybe a bomb or several bombs detonating?"

Luka was silent for ten seconds before asking, "Is that going to happen?"

Will shook his head. "Not that I'm aware of. But America's petrified that a terrorist act could prompt Russia to jump to the wrong conclusions—maybe think it was a U.S. strike."

"America should be scared of that possibility. Russia's the twitchiest it's been in living memory."

The tram pulled into Cankurtaran. More people got off than on, leaving the carriage a third full. Will desperately wanted to look over his shoulder to see who was behind him. Time was running out; he had to get off at the next stop. "I have a favor to ask."

Luka laughed quietly. "Today's agenda seems a little one-sided."

Will ignored the comment. "I need a name—an arms dealer, preferably someone who specializes in military blueprints. Must be an SVR or FSB asset and currently active." He added, "Can you do a bit of digging to see if someone pops up with that profile?"

"I don't need to. I already have a name."

Will waited.

But Luka said, "Why should I give you that information? You've given me nothing today."

"What do you want?"

Luka placed a hand on Will's forearm. When he spoke, it was as if he was thinking aloud. "It would be interesting to know the French government's stance if tensions between my country and America were to increase."

Will's mind raced. He had absolutely no idea what the answer was. But Luka would expect Émile Villon of the DGSE to know. "You need this answer by—?"

"The same time you need the identity of the SVR asset."

Shit.

The tram was slowing. Yenikapı station was in view.

If Will gave him an answer, his information would almost certainly influence Russia's view of France. But he had to say something. "France is openly a staunch ally of America, though privately it's neutral."

"If a situation arose, France wouldn't stand in our way?"

Will hesitated. "No."

Luka nodded slowly. "And the rest of Europe?"

"That information's above my pay grade."

"I doubt that." Luka removed his hand.

The tram stopped.

People started to get off.

Will remained motionless. His heart raced. "Please. It's all I can give you."

Luka sighed. "Otto von Schiller. German. Lives in Berlin."

"How can I get to him?"

"That's all I can give *you*."

Will stood to leave but stopped as Luka raised a finger.

"Some of our generals would love those bombs to go off. It would give them the opportunity they've been waiting for."

ELEVEN

The following afternoon, Will was in an executive suite within Prague's Kempinski Hotel Hybernská, having arrived in the Czech Republic three hours before. Outside, snow was falling fast over heavy traffic and throngs of pedestrian shoppers, but inside the luxurious room it was warm and silent. Sitting at an ornate desk, he arranged some pens and papers before him and logged on to the room's computer. He felt exhausted, but his mind was completely alert and he smiled as he thought through every move of the chess game that he was about to commence.

After thirty minutes of browsing company websites, he found one that suited his purpose—a large, well-known, London-based accounting firm. Looking at the profiles

of the firm's partners, he decided on one of them, noted
the man's contact details, and called him. Introducing
himself as Thomas Eden, Will explained that he needed
the firm to act on his behalf to secure an off-the-shelf
limited company from Companies House, preferably one
that had at least ten years of audited accounts and a back-
ground in consultancy. That, he was advised, could be
obtained in under four hours. He told the partner that he
was to be listed as the sole director of the company, that
it needed to be renamed Thomas Eden Limited, and that
the company's function would be producing military
research and analysis to defense contractors and specialist military journals. The partner asked some questions.

Company bank account?

Already set up in London with HSBC in the name of
Thomas Eden, with a current balance of approximately
£90,000.

Address?

He gave him details of a private residence in Barnes,
London, omitting that it was an operational cover premise and run by a young woman who would collect his
mail and forward it on to a post office box run by MI6.

Contact details?

A BlackBerry cell number and e-mail address were
supplied. He added that he was traveling on business at
present in Europe and would not be back in London for
several weeks. Could all documentation requiring signatures be couriered to the Hotel Otrada in Ukraine?

Of course. They can be there tomorrow, and subject to our

receiving them a day later, the company's memorandum and articles of association and certificate of incorporation can be drawn up the same day.

The partner explained that he'd need a £1,000 down payment to be formally engaged and gave Will the firm's bank details. The man sounded delighted that he'd secured a new client and concluded that he was sure this was the start of a long business relationship.

Will ended the call and got back onto the Net to find another website. Thirty minutes later, he'd spoken to a manager at Servcorp, a company specializing in providing office space and other facilities, including telephone receptionists and individual phone lines with divert-to-cell capabilities. After agreeing on a monthly price for the deal and promising to send copies of the company documentation once it came through in the next few days, Will gave the woman his bank details. Thomas Eden Limited now had an address in Canary Wharf, London, and would seem legitimate to anyone who checked up on the company.

He made a final call to the Hotel Otrada, advised the receptionist that he'd be back at the hotel the next evening, and asked if there was anyone he could speak to about getting some business cards made. After being transferred to the concierge, he was told that it would come with a charge but was no problem. Will gave the man the company name, the Canary Wharf address, and all the contact details. Design? Will didn't care. Maybe plain white card with blue lettering and numbers.

Pouring himself a mug of black coffee, he turned off the computer and stretched his aching back muscles. He swiveled his chair to face the sumptuous bedroom. Five-star hotel rooms. He'd stayed in thousands of them but hated them all because they reminded him of his transitory existence and dislocation from a normal life.

He lay down on the double bed. In two hours, he needed to leave. Maybe that would give him enough time to get the rest he needed, though he didn't know if he could sleep. He moved his arm to the empty side of the bed, smoothed his hand over the quilt, and let it rest there.

Petrin Gardens was one of Prague's largest parks and usually very popular, but now it seemed almost empty of people. It was dusk, a thin layer of snow carpeted the park's ground and trees, and the temperature was well below zero. Will walked through the place, using his BlackBerry sat nav, until he found the lamppost. He checked his watch. Twenty-three minutes ahead of schedule. Looking ahead along the tree-lined footpath, he saw that it curved out of view approximately two hundred feet away. Checking his watch again, he waited for the second hand to reach 12 before beginning to walk at a normal pace. He turned the corner and saw a prominent tree. Reaching it, he stopped and looked at the second hand. It had taken him fifty-three seconds to walk the distance. Turning toward the hidden lamppost, he wrapped his arms over his chest, shivered a little from the cold, and waited.

Brush contacts rarely took place with people you

knew. Today, Will had no idea if his contact was male or female, young or old. For that reason, timing had to be precise down to the second. Alistair had been exact with his instructions: 1639hrs, Latitude 50°4'58.73"N, Longitude 14°23'58.19"E.

He looked around. The park was heavily wooded; no one else was on the path. He stayed like that for twenty minutes, only occasionally checking the time. But as the moment to move grew closer, he kept his eyes fixed on the illuminated surface of the watch.

Thirty seconds before moving.

Twenty.

Ten.

Now.

He moved, resisting the urge to walk faster. Nearing the bend in the path, he deeply hoped that the contact would be experienced in this drill and that he or she had remembered to synchronize their watch with the online atomic clock before coming here. Turning the corner, he saw that there were three people on the path, two quite close to each other, the other closer to him. He ignored them for now, focusing only on maintaining normal speed, knowing that keeping that pace was extremely hard to do when you're conscious of it.

He reached the nearest person but made no attempt to get close to him. Too bad if the man was the contact; he was beyond the lamppost and out of position. But the two people ahead of him were not. He tried to establish if they were together but couldn't be sure. The darkness hid their features.

He got closer and could now see that the two people were not side by side as he'd previously thought; one was slightly ahead of the other.

Thirty feet from the lamppost. The man in front was too close to it. But maybe he'd got his speed wrong by half a mile an hour. Soon he was beyond the lamppost and walking toward Will. They passed each other. Nothing happened. Will kept walking.

He was ten feet from the lamppost.

So was the old woman whose features were now vivid under the light's glow.

Older people walked at a more consistent speed than the young. They were a good choice for brush contacts.

He kept to the right-hand side of the track so that he'd be passing directly alongside the lamppost. By contrast, the woman was on a route that would take her a body width away from it.

Five feet. The woman's arms were by her sides.

Three feet.

The lamppost. They were directly alongside each other. The woman lifted her arm ever so slightly. A tiny package was in her hand.

Then it was in Will's hand.

Will kept walking as he secreted the alias passport containing the Russian multientry visa into a pocket.

One hour later, he entered Bunkr Parukářka bar. It had been difficult to find, hidden away in Prague, and as he walked down the winding metal staircase to the converted 1950s nuclear bunker, he wished he'd not worn a suit. The walls were covered with ghetto graffiti, industrial rock blared out of the windowless basement bar, and twenty-something clubbers eyed him with looks of suspicion, no doubt wondering if he was a secret policeman.

He ordered a beer and took a seat at a low table. The place was not full—it was too early in the evening—though it still felt claustrophobic and intense. After removing his tie and jacket and undoing a couple of his top shirt buttons, he stretched his legs out, took a big gulp of beer, ruffled his hair, and tried to do anything to make him look unlike an on-duty cop.

Looking around, he wondered why Kryštof had chosen this place to meet. The former Bezpečnostní Informační Služba intelligence officer, now private investigator, was in his midforties and would have as little in common with these kinds of bars as Will.

Kryštof was five minutes late. That wasn't unusual; sometimes he could be hours late. At the far end of the cavern, a band was setting up its instruments. Judging by the look of them, whatever they were going to play later that night would be loud and angst-ridden. Will took another swig of beer and looked at the groups of people scattered around the bar. Some were long-haired Goths, others bohemian slackers; all of them looked totally comfortable in their surroundings. He'd never experienced that kind of belonging or cultural rebellion, and for a moment he felt envious of the strangely pretty people around him. But then he wondered if he did have something in common with these men and women. Perhaps they were happy here because normal places made them deeply unhappy.

Kryštof emerged at the bottom of the staircase, dressed in a worn brown suit with his tie loosened and top button open. Cigarette dangling from one corner of his mouth, he stopped at the bar and leaned across it to say something to the barman before walking over to Will's table. Though the bunker's lighting was dim, Will could see that the Czech was unshaven and had dark bags under his eyes.

Will stood, held out his hand, and said in English, "We could have met somewhere else."

Kryštof shook his hand. "Where's the fun in that, David?"

David Becket. An MI6 officer whose profile deliberately approximated Kryštof's: passed over for promotion, in debt, weary, cynical, failed marriages, and adolescent children who no longer wanted to know him. The only difference between them was that David's fictitious older daughter was prospering in high school, whereas six months ago, Kryštof's real daughter had been brutally gang-raped and strangled to death.

They sat just as the barman came to them and thumped a bottle of Becherovka liquor and two glasses onto the table. Kryštof unscrewed the cap and poured the spirit into the glasses until they were nearly full. Stubbing out his cigarette and lifting his glass to his lips, he muttered, "Your health" and downed the drink.

"Your health." Will took a small sip and placed the glass down.

Kryštof refilled his glass to the top and gripped it while staring at Will. "You still in?"

Will shrugged. "I'm trying to last another ten years, until I can draw on my pension."

Becket was forty-five; youthful looks were the only thing he had going for him. Kryštof didn't even have that. Age, stress, and depression had been less kind to his once handsome face.

Kryštof drank some more and lit another cigarette. "I meant to thank you."

"What for?"

"The flowers and the card." He glanced away, his expression one of sadness and irritation. "Her mother wouldn't let me go to the funeral."

"I thought that might happen. That's why I sent them to your house."

Kryštof looked back at him. "She said that no doubt I was now happy that I had one less child to pay alimony for." He emptied the contents of his glass and topped it up.

Will sympathized with Kryštof's plight, though he worried that the man was losing his sanity. He twisted his glass on the table. "I have some work for you if you'd like it."

Kryštof blew out smoke. "They're still giving you tasks?"

"A few."

Kryštof nodded. "It's not a question of *like*, rather

need." He poured more drink down his throat. "What do you want?"

"Names."

"Price?"

Will sighed. "The service wanted me to get you on the cheap."

"Bastards."

"Bastards indeed." Will smiled. "It's okay. I held my ground and got them to agree to normal rates."

Kryštof would know what that meant: £5,000 up front, and a further £5,000 upon successful delivery.

Extinguishing his cigarette and lighting another, Kryštof asked, "Tell me."

"Otto von Schiller. Heard of him?"

The former Czech intelligence officer rubbed his facial stubble. "Sounds familiar." He narrowed his eyes. "Arms dealer?"

"Yes, lives in Berlin."

Kryštof drained the contents of his glass and poured more Becherovka into it. "I remember, few years ago"— his words were beginning to slur—"when I was still in BIS . . . we tried unsuccessfully to disrupt one of his Czech deals."

Will yawned in an attempt to make David look bored. "The service wants to find out about von Schiller's associates. Particularly if any of them are British or American."

Kryštof reached for the bottle, clearly forgetting that he'd already topped up his glass. "Sure. I'll make some inquiries."

Will handed the Czech a brown envelope containing the retainer and said, "Spend it on some food and new clothes"—he glanced at the bottle—"nothing else."

The Czech investigator looked around the bunker. "She used to come here." He smiled, but the look was bitter. "You'd have been shocked if you saw her. Pierced ears, nose . . . pierced everything. But I didn't mind; she was always my girl." Staring at the ceiling, he said through gritted teeth, "The men got her when she was walking home from here." He looked at Will, his eyes moist. "I couldn't come here on my own, but everyone I know stays away from me. When you asked to meet, I finally had the opportunity to come here to say my farewell to her." He pushed the bottle away. "Was that wrong?"

Will stared at him with no thoughts of being David anymore. Even though he couldn't tell Kryštof so, he knew exactly how he felt. And that was the curse of running agents like Kryštof. No matter how many layers of deceit there were, none of them could eradicate the real emotion in moments like this. Swallowing hard to control his voice, he placed his scarred hand over the Czech's and replied, "It was the right thing to do."

Kryštof looked at the table; a tear fell into his glass. "The name you need—is it going to make a difference to anything?"

Will leaned forward and said quietly, "Look after yourself, my friend. What you're doing for me is vital. The name is crucial to my plan. If you get it, you'll have helped stopped the potential slaughter of millions."

TWELVE

Sentinel weighed his cell phone in one hand and stared at it. His face looked fatigued. "Borzaya's got something for me. But this time I can't afford to take the risk of meeting him without you present."

Borzaya was the code name of the FSB officer Sentinel had met in Hungary three days before. He was one of the MI6 officer's tier-1 agents.

Will nodded. Now that he was back in Odessa, there was nothing he could do until Kryštof reported back. "Sure. I'm free for the next day or so."

"How very gracious of you."

Will frowned. "The chances of Razin being there are extremely remote. God knows what the odds are that he'll make an attempt on his life during your meeting with him."

Sentinel looked at Will and repeated, "I can't afford to take *any* risks."

"I understand."

"I'm delighted that you do!" Sentinel strode quickly across the room, pulled open the fridge, grabbed a fruit juice carton, and tore it open. After taking a swig of the drink, his expression softened. Speaking quietly he said, "I'm sorry. I'm not used to working with other MI6 officers. Ignore my tone."

The apology surprised Will. "For that matter, I normally work alone, too."

Sentinel asked, "How's it been for you—the nine years?"

Exhausting, dangerous, exhilarating, frustrating, and heartbreaking. But that wasn't the answer Sentinel was looking for.

Instead, Will said, "You *know* the worst of it."

The constant worry that one day he'd accept his isolated existence.

Sentinel understood. When he spoke, his voice held compassion. "That won't happen."

"It happened to you."

Sentinel frowned. "It . . . it may seem like that to you, but I can assure you that the reverse is true. When they finally pull me out of the field . . ." His voice trailed off. "Well, I guess I dream about having the same things that all normal people want." Sadness was now on his face. He nodded and seemed to speak to himself. "Yes, I want those things. Maybe more than most."

"You can leave."

Sentinel stared at him, shaking his head. "I volunteered to come back here after my imprisonment. I have to see this through."

Will felt a moment of anger. "The service knows that's how you think. It's exploiting your sense of duty."

"Of course." He smiled, then his expression turned serious. "There's a 1605 hours Malév flight to Budapest today, and we're going to be on it."

The Gresham Palace royal suite was one of the most luxurious in Budapest and overlooked the Danube, the Chain Bridge, the Royal Castle, and the Buda Hills. The suite's Art Deco lounge area contained two large sofas facing each other. Will and Sentinel were sitting on one, Borzaya was on the other. Between them was a glass coffee table, with mugs and a flask on it.

Will's presence in the hotel room clearly unsettled the FSB officer.

The chubby operative was sitting with his legs crossed. Immaculately groomed, he wore a charcoal gray suit, double-cuff shirt, and a silk tie bound in a Windsor knot. His hair was slicked back, and, judging by the scent emanating from him, he'd obviously applied a generous quantity of expensive eau de toilette to his smooth face.

He seemed reluctant to speak as he stared at Will. Then, "You know my language?"

Will answered in Russian, "Yes."

Borzaya glanced sharply at Sentinel. "One hundred percent sure that he's trustworthy?"

Sentinel leaned forward. "He wouldn't be here if I thought otherwise."

Borzaya's expression remained hostile. Looking back at Will, he asked, "Name?"

"Richard Bancroft."

"Real name?"

"No."

"The name you used to travel into Hungary?"

"No."

Borzaya nodded. "Good." He withdrew a slim silver cigarette case, flicked it open with one hand, withdrew a cigarette, and lit it with a gold lighter. "But you've still not explained why you're here."

Sentinel interjected. "Richard's from headquarters. Whatever you've found out, he can take back to London."

"London?" Borzaya clicked his tongue. "That would be a very bad mistake."

Will was about to speak, but Sentinel motioned for him to stay quiet.

Borzaya puffed on his cigarette for a while, his eyes flicking between the two MI6 officers. "I'm not cleared to know the whereabouts of Taras Khmelnytsky. I tried, but all I could find out was that he was on a top secret training exercise."

Sentinel slapped his hands on his legs. "Damn it!"

"The restriction on knowledge about his whereabouts is only temporary while the training exercise lasts. Once it's over, I'll be able to track him for you." Borzaya paused. "Unless . . . that's too late."

Sentinel shook his head. "Much too late."

The FSB officer carefully extinguished his cigarette and seemed deep in thought. Fixing his gaze directly on Sentinel, he said, "Not all is lost."

"You found something in the archives?"

Borzaya nodded. "Something very bad." He looked at Will. "If you intend to take what I say back to London, you need to leave this room right now."

Will shook his head. "I'm not going anywhere until Khmelnytsky's stopped."

"Stopped from doing what?" Borzaya glanced at Sentinel. "I know you want to find him, but you've not told me why."

Sentinel responded, "For your own safety."

Borzaya laughed, clearly not buying Sentinel's explanation as to why he was seeking Razin.

"What did you find in the archives?"

Borzaya darted a look at Will. "Leave or stay?"

Will held his gaze. "I'll stay."

"I hope it's the right decision." Borzaya lit another cigarette and gazed toward one of the hotel room windows. "There are tens of thousands of KGB files in the FSB and SVR archives. It would take years to read them all."

Sentinel snapped, "But you didn't need to read them all. I gave you a very specific task."

"You did." Borzaya looked mischievous. "'Find me evidence of an MI6 security breach.' Still, I was lucky."

"Why?"

The FSB officer shrugged. "The files you asked me to

read are still highly classified. I'd have needed to explain what my interest was in them to get permission to read them."

"Why were you lucky?" Sentinel repeated.

Borzaya smiled. "One of the files was missing. I thought that was curious, so I checked the registers to see who'd last read the file." He blew out smoke. "You remember that idiot Filip Chulkov?"

"I do."

Will glanced at Sentinel. "Chulkov? Was he one of ours?"

Sentinel shook his head. "No. He was an FSB officer. Murdered two years ago. Case unsolved." He looked back at Borzaya. "His name was in the register?"

Borzaya nodded. "The man was a moron, but he did have clearance to read the files." He chuckled. "Senior management probably gave that clearance to him because they thought he was too stupid to understand anything he read." His expression changed. "I spent the last two days checking lesser classified files to see if any of them cross-referenced to the missing file. Finally I found one. It contained a brief KGB report, dated 1987, saying that a young Moscow-based MI6 officer might be worth approaching. That report showed the MI6 officer's name in full."

Sentinel looked totally focused.

Borzaya eased back in his chair. "I looked into Chulkov's death. The reports included a list of the officer's cell phone records on the days preceding his death. All of the numbers dialed looked normal—calls made to FSB, SVR, and GRU colleagues, to senior military men, and certain politicians." He smiled. "I can see why none of them were considered suspects."

Will's mind raced. "One of the calls was to Taras Khmelnytsky."

"Correct, Mr. Bancroft."

"And who was the junior MI6 officer?"

Borzaya looked at Sentinel. When he spoke, his words were measured and tense. "Everything must be kept in this room."

"It will be."

Borzaya looked away again, deep in thought. After twenty seconds, he nodded slightly and said, "In the late eighties he was undercover as second secretary in the British Embassy in Moscow. The KGB found out that he was having an illicit affair with a Soviet diplomat, something that was completely forbidden in those days."

"Well, they obviously recruited him, or why would they have such a classified file on him?"

"Maybe."

"You have doubts?"

Borzaya shook his head. "I think the KGB got *something* out of him. But I found out the officer short-posted. Why would he run back to London midway through his posting if he was a KGB agent? They would have encouraged him to stay in Moscow for a full tour so that they could get everything out of him."

Sentinel said, "He ran away from them."

"I agree."

Sentinel lowered his head. "It's a shame we don't know what he told the KGB."

"We do know. It was clear in the file I read. The officer was deemed of interest because the KGB thought he could tell them the location of the various MI6 safe houses in Moscow."

"Safe houses?"

"Safe houses."

Safe houses, like the one where Sentinel was caught before he was put in the Lubyanka for six years.

Sentinel stood and walked to the window. With his back to Will and Borzaya, he said, "I'd always thought it was an agent who'd betrayed me to the Soviets, not a serving MI6 officer." He slowly turned and looked directly at Borzaya. "Who is he?"

Borzaya tapped his hand three times on his knee. "He's—"

Tap, tap.

"Nothing must go to London. You've given me your word."

Tap.

"I'm in enough danger without you using my name as part of an investigation."

He lifted his hand up again but held it in midair.

"The traitor is the current MI6 Head of Moscow Station."

THIRTEEN

Borzaya had left the hotel room fifteen minutes before. Will and Sentinel were sitting in a different part of the suite facing each other, mugs of black coffee on the floor between them.

"Let's think through the possibilities." Sentinel took a swig of the drink; his expression remained one of anger but also of focus. "The MI6 officer gets approached by the KGB and is told that they'll reveal his affair to British authorities unless he cooperates. He should have told them to go to hell, but he's young and scared."

"So he gives them the location of the houses and then flees to London before they get their hooks further into him."

"Normally"—Sentinel placed his mug down—"the KGB would've pursued him and tried to run him out of London, but—"

"The Soviet Union collapses, the Russian element of the KGB is transformed into the SVR, agendas change, and somewhere during that process the MI6 officer falls through the cracks."

Sentinel nodded. "Or a decision is made that he's of no further use to the revamped Russia—too junior, too out of reach."

"Either way, they went after you and got you at one of your safe houses." Will tried to picture that moment. Even for a veteran like Sentinel, it would have been a terrifying experience.

Sentinel looked away for a moment; his next words were quiet. "I heard them come into the building, looked out the windows, saw that I was completely surrounded, and knew that all was lost. So I put—" He sighed.

"You put your handgun to your head but couldn't pull the trigger."

Sentinel kept staring at nothing. "To this day, I still can't decide which of the two was the more cowardly."

Will leaned forward. "You can't think that way. It was an uncertain situation." He had no idea what he'd have done in similar circumstances.

"The *situation* was very certain. I had too many secrets and the knowledge of too many Russian MI6 agents who would have been executed if I'd buckled under torture."

"But you kept your mouth shut."

"I knew that if I told them what they wanted to know, I'd be walked out into a courtyard and executed by firing squad." Sentinel gripped his hands together. "The only reason I managed to keep my mouth shut was that

I steadfastly refused to let the Russians do to me what I couldn't do to myself." He looked at Will; his demeanor changed. "Back to work. Let's fast-forward to two years ago. Razin was now one of my agents and had decided that he must know the identity of my other agents."

"Though he knew he'd never get that information from you, so he wondered if it was possible to get it from another MI6 officer."

"A person who at some point in his career had betrayed secrets to the USSR or Russia."

"He discreetly tasked his contacts in Russian intelligence to try to find out if such a person existed."

Sentinel agreed. "One of those contacts was an FSB officer named Filip Chulkov. He had clearance to read the closed, top secret MI6 double-agent files."

"And in one of those files he read about the junior MI6 officer."

"Chulkov *was* a stupid man, but even he would have instantly recognized the name in the file."

"Though it seems his stupidity ultimately got the better of him. Instead of taking the file and the MI6 name to his FSB superiors so that they could reopen the case, he took it straight to Razin."

"Who thanked him and shot him in the head."

Will took a sip of his coffee. "Razin approaches the Head of Moscow Station and—"

"Blackmails him to get the names of my agents."

Though partly conjecture, their theory made sense to Will. But it didn't help them beyond explaining how

Razin had the names of the tier-1 agents. He felt overwhelming frustration. "We can't warn off your agents."

"I know that!" Sentinel sounded equally frustrated. "If we do, we take them out of the game. And if that happens, we'll get the same result we would if they're killed—a protracted war and all that will follow it." He muttered, "Shit, shit, shit," and looked at Will. "What's the likely success of the operation you're mounting?"

Will answered, "Provided I can get to the right people, I'm confident it will work, but I can't guarantee that more of your agents won't be killed."

"I thought so." Frustration was now replaced with a look of despair. "I can't let any more of them die."

"There's nothing you can do right now."

"There's one possibility."

Will waited.

Sentinel stared at the floor, clearly deep in thought. "Supposing we told Razin which agents I was going to next meet and when."

Will frowned. "That would only help if you were a target."

Sentinel smiled. "Maybe I am. He knows I'm after him and has already tried to kill me once. Plus, maybe my death would be the jewel in his crown. If he kills me, he's killed the man who runs the tier-1 agents, the man who has the capability to recruit more agents to replace those Razin's killed, the man the Russians stupidly released to carry on working against them."

Will's stomach muscles tensed. "We can't use you and your agents as bait."

"Why not? You'd be there to protect us."

"I might fail!"

"You will if you think like that."

"It's too damn risky."

For a moment, Sentinel seemed surprised by Will's reaction. "You care?"

"Of course." He pointed a finger at his colleague. "A huge number of people rely on you staying alive."

"Conversely . . ."

"Yes, *conversely*—but we don't need to play into that group's hands." Will shook his head. "How would you alert Razin to the meeting without him becoming suspicious?"

Sentinel looked up. "I'll liaise with Kiev Station and get them to send a telegram to London, telling them to instruct the Moscow Station that I'm reactivating the Minsk DLB. It's only ever cleared by Moscow Station— they have one officer who has official cover to travel in and out of Belarus. He gets my messages and takes them back into Russia in a diplomatic bag. Tomorrow, I'll deposit a coded message there saying that I'm meeting Shashka in three days' time." Code name Shashka was a tier-1 agent and a general in Russia's ground forces, based in the Western Operational Strategic Command in Saint Petersburg. "The message will be delivered to the head of station. Then I'm hoping he'll give the details to Razin."

"He might not do that."

Sentinel stood up and poured himself more coffee.

"Razin will be putting the squeeze on the head of station to find out anything he can about our plans. He'll have the man in his grip. The message will be passed, I'm certain."

Will said, "I'm strongly against using you as bait. I'm under orders to stop Razin, but I've also been instructed to protect you at all costs. Your idea feels wrong."

"Then give me an idea that feels *right* and doesn't allow more of my agents to be killed."

Will was silent.

Sentinel sat at a table, grabbed a piece of paper and a fountain pen, and began to write. When he finished, he stood, walked to Will, and thrust the paper toward him, saying, "I'll rewrite the message and encrypt it when I'm in Belarus."

MEETING SHASHKA AT 1800HRS ON 24TH THIS MONTH AT ST PETERSBURG SAFE HOUSE. VITAL THAT I'M ALERTED TO ANY SOURCE INTEL RELATING TO SHASHKA OR ST PETERSBURG PRIOR TO MEETING. MY RUSSIAN ASSETS CAN'T BE TRUSTED. BREACH OF SECURITY. NEED TWO HANDGUNS AND A TWO-PERSON COMMS SYSTEM. RESPOND ON 23RD WITH COLLECTION DETAILS.

SENTINEL.

Will tossed the paper to one side. "The other major risk is to Shashka himself. He's an extremely valuable agent."

"He has to be there. We can't use a stand-in."

"I know."

Shashka could have the ability to locate Razin. Meeting him to get that information would be vital. Moreover, it was possible that Razin would follow Shashka to the meeting. He'd easily spot a fake and would probably abort going to the meeting if he saw one.

But Will was still uncomfortable with the whole thing. "You're playing with fire."

"It's been ever thus."

Will looked at him. Over the last few days, Sentinel seemed to have aged. Will hesitated before quietly saying, "If we succeed in stopping Razin, you need to get out of the field. Make a home in England. You've done more than enough."

"I'd never request that."

"But by your own admission, you've thought about it." He leaned forward. "Maybe you'd not object if the decision was taken out of your hands."

Sentinel said nothing.

"Maybe . . . I could arrange for that to happen."

Sentinel was clearly digesting Will's idea. Then he beamed. "Get a wife, a nice house in the country, do some gardening, have an occasional pint at the local pub. And would I come to you to learn how to do all those things?"

Will laughed. "Fair point."

Sentinel smiled. "I think so." He sighed. "But still, it is a pleasant notion . . ." He folded his arms. "Tomorrow

I *will* be in Minsk. I don't need you for that, but I will need you for the Shashka meeting in Russia." His eyes became cold. "I'm going to kill Razin. And when I've finished with him, I'm going to visit the Head of Moscow Station."

PART II

FOURTEEN

The Russian intelligence officer drove his vehicle off the Moscow highway onto a minor road and headed north. Normally the journey to his home would take only thirty minutes, but it was dark and the snow was heavy. He hoped his wife wouldn't be angry with his delay. Tonight they were hosting a dinner party with friends and were allowing their young children to stay up and eat with them. Nikita and Ivan had been so excited at the prospect and had promised not to fall asleep before the meal.

Soon there were no streetlamps on the road; woods were either side of him. He increased the speed of the car's windshield wipers and squinted to try to focus through the snow. The car's heater was noisy and turned up high but barely seemed to be producing any heat. He recalled his wife nagging him to get a new car. She was right; this one was falling to pieces, and he doubted it would last through the winter.

A vehicle came toward him with its headlights on high. The officer swore as its glare nearly blinded him, and he slowed down until the car had passed. The road before him was now empty. He increased his speed, wondering if his wife would be preparing his favorite dish of kholodets. She had her own special recipe that eschewed veal in favor of pork legs and ears and beef tails.

He thought about the last few days. His work had been risky, and he was glad he'd completed his task successfully. Tonight he could relax, and he would uncork a few bottles of Pinot Noir. None of the guests knew what he did for a living, and even though his wife did know, she wasn't privy to the details. And she certainly didn't know his big secret. That didn't matter. He'd simply tell them all that tonight he was celebrating getting through a tough week of work.

With every mile he drove, his mood lightened. He pulled out a cigarette, lit it, and inhaled deeply. Picturing the dinner, he smiled. Maybe, when the evening was over and the children were asleep, his wife would make love to him.

Lowering his window a few inches, he moved the cigarette to the gap to tap ash outside of the car. A sudden gust of wind through the gap blew the cigarette out of his fingers and onto his chest. Cursing his stupidity, he looked down, searching for the glow of the cigarette's embers before it burned a hole in his clothes. He found it in his lap, grabbed it, and looked up.

As he did so a car rammed his vehicle from behind.

The officer lurched forward until the seat belt tightened and forced air out of his lungs. He moaned, heard tires screeching and metal grinding against metal, and felt the steering wheel shuddering in his grip. Lifting his head, he saw headlights in the rear mirror, urgently looked ahead, and realized that his car was being pushed diagonally across the road toward the dense forest. He yanked hard down on the steering wheel; his car went into a spin.

What was happening?

Drunk driver?

The car spun 360 degrees. The officer saw that it was still heading toward the forest, where upon impact it was sure to be squashed. There were no air bags in this heap of crap.

He was just a few feet from the trees.

Barely three seconds away.

No chance of regaining control of his car.

Releasing the seat belt, he pushed open the door and dived onto the road, a moment before he heard the vehicle smash against the large wooden trunks. His elbows and kneecaps screamed in pain. Breathing deeply, he looked to his right. The car that had rammed him was 150 feet away, stationary, its headlights pointing at him. A tall man was walking toward him, only his silhouette visible.

Coming to help?

No, not with a long knife in one hand.

He pushed himself off the ground, wincing as his legs nearly buckled.

Fear and adrenaline.

Limping away from the scene, he moved along the center of the road. His home was only a couple of miles away. That's all that mattered.

Two miles.

Home.

Lock the doors.

Get his gun.

He tried to run but could barely manage a jog; one of his legs was limping badly. Glancing urgently over his shoulder, he saw that the big man was still walking after him. He looked ahead. All was now in near darkness; snow was falling fast. The forest was on either side of him.

Go in there and hide?

And maybe freeze to death?

Or stay on the road in case help comes?

Just after the man easily caught up and murdered him?

He'd no idea what to do, so he kept moving along the road. His breathing was fast and shallow. Too many cigarettes. Too much rich food and wine. But he kept moving, even though every step sent shots of pain up his legs.

Get home.

Cuddle Nikita and Ivan.

Tell them he loved them.

Stay with them forever.

Don't die.

The blow to his back sent him flying forward. Lying on the ground, he tried to crawl forward, his fingers digging through the snow.

Something hard smacked onto the nape of his neck and held him still.

A boot.

No adrenaline now.

Only absolute terror.

The boot lifted. A hand grabbed his shoulder and spun him onto his back. Then two hands grabbed him by the throat and lifted him to his feet. The man's face was inches from his. There was just enough light to see that he looked calm.

That he was Taras Khmelnytsky.

The officer's legs kicked out, but it made no difference. Khmelnytsky held him firm, a smile now on his face.

Rapid movement.

Immense pain in his gut.

Of course.

The knife.

No chance now of cuddles with excited children, of consuming kholodets and Pinot Noir, of making love to his wife.

Khmelnytsky wrenched the knife up and dropped the officer.

He lay on the road, his whole body violently shaking. But his mind was still alive.

Khmelnytsky towered over him for a moment.

The officer thought about the secret that had made his week risky and tense. He wondered how his wife would've reacted if he'd told her about his work as an MI6 double agent.

He'd never know.

Khmelnytsky knelt down and thrust the knife into Borzaya's face.

FIFTEEN

Will was back in Ukraine, striding through the lobby of Kiev's Hyatt Regency, his cell phone against his ear. "I'm dining with him at seven tonight at the restaurant here. Will that give them enough time to assemble a team?"

Patrick's voice sounded hesitant. "It's going to be tight, but we'll mark the telegram as *urgent*."

Will sat on a corner sofa, away from other guests. "Tell them it's imperative that they get every word."

"Still can't guarantee you won't be lifted."

"I know."

Silence.

Will looked around the lobby. "When you get the transcript back, all I need to know is whether they've kept in the reference to the colonel."

"Understood. I'll send you an SMS."

"Not to my Eden phone."

"No shit."

The lobby was starting to fill up. Will decided he needed to move.

"If they do lift you, you're deniable—even if they throw you in prison for a few years."

Will smiled. "No shit."

It was early evening. Will was in his hotel room, finishing putting on his suit. Examining himself in a mirror, he was satisfied that he looked the part.

Thomas Eden. British national. Director of the London-based Thomas Eden Limited—a legitimate company but a suspected front for illegal arms procurement and one that had been under scrutiny by MI6 and the CIA.

This morning, the CIA had sent an urgent telegram to Ukraine's security service, the Sluzhba Bezpeky Ukray-iny, stating that Thomas Eden was meeting the defense attaché of the Iranian Embassy in Kiev at seven P.M. in the Hyatt Regency's restaurant. It requested that the SBU covertly record the conversation between the two men and send the transcript back to Langley; that Eden should not be touched, as to do so would compromise a bigger investigation into his arms deals; and that if the SBU did this the CIA would be very grateful and would supply some new intelligence on U.S.-Russian relations and the likely effect on Europe.

It was a straightforward request and the type that

intelligence services often made of each other. It also suggested that the CIA was behaving itself in Ukraine by not trying to do things in the country without the SBU knowing.

But the truth was not straightforward. The telegram was transmitted with the hope that the SBU would send the transcript not only to the CIA but also to the SBU's closest ally: the SVR.

Will gathered up his new business cards, which he'd collected from the Hotel Otrada the day before, after completing and couriering all Thomas Eden Limited documentation to his London accountant. It was time to go. He left his hotel room and took an elevator to the restaurant. As he descended, he began to get his mind into character.

Be gregarious, affable, money-driven, and occasionally crude, have an eye for anything in a skirt and no allegiances, and hate lawmakers. Be nothing like Will Cochrane.

The elevator doors opened; he walked into the restaurant. The 155-seat venue was three-quarters full. After giving his name to a waiter, he was shown to his table. The stocky, middle-aged Iranian DA was already there, dressed in a suit and sporting a mustache and lacquered black hair. He rose to shake Thomas Eden's hand.

Will grinned and said in a loud voice, "Mr. Mousavi, good to meet you."

The DA did not smile; instead, he looked cautious. "We could have met at the embassy."

Will smiled wider as he sat down at the table. "Embassies

are terribly dull places"—he grabbed a wine menu—"and they don't normally have a good wine cellar."

"Maybe I don't drink."

"If that's the case, maybe you're in the wrong job."

Mousavi's expression softened, though he still did not smile. Sitting down, he opened his white cloth napkin and placed it carefully over his lap. "Officially, I'm not supposed to meet strangers outside of the embassy."

Will leaned forward, a twinkle in his eye. "But unofficially"—he glanced around before looking back at the DA—"these types of places are where the real work is done." He whipped open his napkin and positioned it. "I'm so sorry, you need a business card."

He gave him one, certain that the two couples at the table next to him were the SBU surveillance team and could easily overhear his conversation.

Mousavi looked at the card for a while before stating, "Canary Wharf is a prestigious address."

Will shrugged. "I chose it because it gives me a good view of female bankers strutting to work in their tight office skirts."

Mousavi smiled. "Business must be good."

"Damn good." Will beckoned a waitress. "So good that demand is outweighing supply."

The waitress came over.

Will beamed at her. She was in her midtwenties and had short blond hair and no rings on her fingers.

In Russian, he asked, "What do you recommend to eat?"

She smiled, looked a little coy. "I've only just started working here and don't really know the menu. Let me get someone else to serve you."

Will wagged a finger. "That would ruin our evening. You're the prettiest woman in here."

She giggled. "Well, I've heard the steaks are good."

Will glanced at Mousavi, who nodded and said, "Make mine well done."

"And mine rare." Will hated rare steaks but thought that's how Thomas would like them. He opened the wine list, winked at the DA, and said while pointing at the list, "We'll have this bottle of Châteauneuf-du-Pape."

When the waitress left, Mousavi asked in English, "Where did you learn Russian?"

"Household Cavalry. They put me on a year's language course." He grinned. "One year of sitting opposite a Russian stunner. She taught me a lot of stuff. More than she was supposed to . . ."

"My Russian teacher was nothing like that—nothing like that at all." The DA looked serious. "Mr. Eden, your letter of introduction to me stated that you had an interesting business proposition to discuss."

Will pointed at the DA. "*Confidentially* discuss."

Mousavi seemed affronted. "I'm here in an official capacity."

"I know." Will leaned forward and lowered his voice a little. "But a man in my position has to be careful talking to someone from your country."

"And what is your . . . *position*?"

Will leaned back and rubbed his hands together. "I do a lot of the normal stuff—procurement and sales to clients all over the world. It pays the bills." He lost his smile. "But what I'm really good at, what I'm known for, is the classy high-end stuff."

The waitress brought their bottle to the table and poured two glasses of wine. Will looked at her, his smile back on. "Chanel No. 19 . . ." He shook his head. "No. Chanel No. 19 Poudré. Am I right?"

The waitress nodded. "My boyfriend bought it for me. I couldn't afford it on my salary."

Will laughed. "Boyfriend? Too bad—for me."

She smiled. "Not your lucky night."

As she left, Will stared at her bottom, sighed, then looked sharply at Mousavi. "Blueprints of prototypes. The classy stuff. That's what I deliver to discerning clients."

"And you think the Iranian government might be interested in what you have to offer?"

Will shrugged. "I'm here to find out." He lifted his glass and held it in midair over the table.

Mousavi stared at his own glass, then picked it up and chinked it against Will's. "And I'm listening."

Will took a sip of his wine and nodded approvingly. "This is a good drop."

The DA drank. "I agree, though it's a shame the restaurant doesn't stock any ninety-eight."

Will smiled. "I *knew* you'd know your wines."

Mousavi placed his glass down. "What do you have?"

Will hesitated. "A new weapons system is being tested.

It can easily be carried by one man and has a devastating effect." He lowered his voice. "An ideal weapon for Iranian special forces."

Mousavi seemed deep in thought. "Bombs?"

"Yes, but I can't go into detail yet until I know where this conversation's going."

The DA frowned. "You have a legitimate supplier of the blueprints for these weapons?"

This was the moment Will had been leading up to.

"Legitimate suppliers are rarely of use to me. I've got a contact in the Russian army, a colonel. He's involved with these weapons and has access to the blueprints. I've paid him a lot of money to copy the documents so that I can put them on the market. I'm giving you first refusal."

Mousavi stood quickly, anger on his face. "You have been deeply mistaken, Mr. Eden. I will have no involvement in illegal procurement."

"Mr. Mousavi—"

"No. This meeting is over!"

Mousavi stormed out of the restaurant just as the pretty waitress brought their steaks to the table. She looked concerned. "Is everything all right?"

Will tried to look disappointed, even though Mousavi had just said and done exactly what he'd hoped. "Tonight clearly is not my night."

She placed the plates down, glanced quickly around, and whispered, "I finish at eleven."

Will looked at her and wondered what it would feel like to meet her for a late drink. But he'd have to maintain

the arrogant and lecherous personality of Thomas Eden
in case the SBU detail was still on him. He couldn't do
that to the woman, nor could he do that to himself. His
smile masked an inner sadness. "That would have been
lovely, but I've got work to do."

The following day, Will walked through the arrivals section of Saint Petersburg's Pulkovo Airport. He'd entered
Russia using his multientry passport in the name of John
Lawrence. Sentinel had flown into the country earlier
that morning, and Will was going to meet him.

He turned on his cell phone. A message bleeped; he
recognized the number belonging to one of Patrick's
many cover phones.

They sent it over. No mention of the man or the items.

Will smiled. Langley had received the SBU transcript
with no reference to the "colonel" or the bombs. The
only reason they would have omitted those details was if
they thought they'd gain further favor with the SVR by
sending the information to the Russians so that the matter could be investigated by the FSB. His operation had
begun. By carefully drip feeding snippets of information
to the Russians, his hope was that Taras Khmelnytsky
would be discredited and sacked from the military.

As he continued walking toward the exit, his smile
faded. Two days ago, Sentinel had deposited his message in the Minsk DLB. Tonight they would be meeting
Shashka. And if everything went according to plan, they
would also be meeting Razin.

SIXTEEN

It was dusk as Will drove along a deserted, unlit road twenty miles outside Saint Petersburg. The road was straight as far as the eye could see and surrounded by woodland. Everywhere was icy, but the land was bare of snow.

Sentinel checked his watch before glancing at Will. "We're on time." He looked ahead. "Drive for another quarter mile, then get our vehicle off the road."

Will drove forward for ten seconds, brought the rental car to a halt, and reversed it over rough ground between trees. When he was satisfied that they were hidden from any cars that might drive by on the road, he stopped the vehicle and turned off its headlights.

Sentinel rubbed his hands together. "I'll wait here for her. I suggest you move up the road."

Will nodded and exited the vehicle. After having been in the heated car for nearly two hours, the sudden cold hit him hard. He jogged through the woods, keeping the road to his right, his breath steaming in the air. After five hundred feet, he moved closer to the road and crouched down beside a large tree, looking back down the road toward Sentinel's approximate location. He stayed like that for twenty minutes before he heard a vehicle. The road before him lit up; then a sedan drove by and stopped midway between Will's position and Sentinel's location. Nothing happened for a minute. Then a woman got out of the car.

Sentinel emerged on foot onto the road and called out, "7962."

The woman responded, "5389."

Sentinel walked quickly toward her and waved a hand to tell Will that the meeting was safe. Will approached the car with caution. Sentinel motioned to the woman. "This is Rebecca. She works out of Moscow."

Rebecca was petite, looked quite young, and was very nervous. Shaking Will's hand, the MI6 officer said, "This is the first time I've done this kind of thing outside of training."

Sentinel ignored her, and walked to the rear of her vehicle. Slapping a hand on the trunk, he asked, "In here?"

Rebecca nodded while looking around. She was clearly desperate to get away from this place. "It's open."

Sentinel withdrew a small cloth bag and walked back

to them. The bag contained the handguns and communications system he'd requested. He gave Will a Sig Sauer P226 and two spare clips and secreted his own weapon and magazines in his jacket. Looking sharply at Rebecca, he asked, "Anything suspicious?"

She shook her head. "Nothing. We've been talking to our sources. None of them has mentioned any deployment of FSB or SVR men to Saint Petersburg. Also, they've made no mention of Shashka."

"London or GCHQ traffic?"

"Again, nothing." She frowned. "I've been told by Guy to ask you about the security breach."

Guy—the MI6 Head of Moscow Station.

Sentinel was quiet for a moment. Then, "I don't have any evidence yet, but I suspect that one or more of my Russian assets may be working against me."

"Do you know their identities?"

Sentinel shook his head. "Tell your boss to be careful, because some of his own operations may be compromised."

"Thank you, I will." She looked at Will. "I've not met you before."

Sentinel glanced at his watch. "And it's unlikely you'll meet him again. You need to go."

She got into her car, and Will watched her taillights disappear from view. Then he turned to his colleague. "There's still time to cancel the meeting."

"I'm not going to."

"Razin could have rigged the safe house with explosives."

"We'll have to take that risk."

"Your course of action's wrong!"

"Meaning yours is right?" Sentinel shook his head. "Whatever you're doing, Razin's still loose." He turned to face Will. "Borzaya's been killed. I found out yesterday. Tomorrow I could find out that another agent has been killed because we did nothing. Stay here if you want, or come with me. Either way, tonight I'm going to try to kill Razin."

SEVENTEEN

I t was early evening as Will sat alone in his car, watching the stationary car ahead of him. Sentinel was in that vehicle. They were on Dvortsovaya Naberezhnaya, next to the wide Neva River, within the heart of Saint Petersburg. Close by was one of the city's main shopping areas of Nevskiy Prospekt, and pedestrian shoppers surrounded the MI6 men. Sentinel had wanted it that way. He needed his agent to have cover.

Sentinel was waiting for one of the many pedestrians to move to his car and sit alongside the MI6 officer. It was hoped that person would be Shashka. But the person could just as easily be Razin.

Will adjusted his earpiece, scrutinizing everything around him. It was nighttime, but bright street and building lights illuminated the entire area. Small motorized boats and larger cargo vessels moved slowly along the river. On land, families, couples, and solitary men and women walked by his car. Some carried shopping bags. Others had their hands thrust deep into their pockets. All of them wore overcoats and hats to protect them from the freezing cold.

Will spoke into his throat mic as he looked at the back of Sentinel's car. It was three hundred feet away. "Nothing yet."

Sentinel's voice was calm. "Okay. I bet he's watching me right now."

Will looked at the crowds of people. There were a number of men within their ranks who could be Shashka. That did not concern him. Shashka would reveal himself when he was ready to do so. What concerned Will was that he was certain that Razin was also close by, waiting to see Sentinel and his Russian agent sitting together in the car so that he could gun them down before they had the chance to escape.

He moved a hand over the pistol by his side, mentally picturing what could happen and how he would respond. If Razin walked up to the car and raised a gun toward it, Will knew he could swing his handgun up, shoot through the windshield, and put a bullet into the man's head within half a second. But if Razin had a higher-powered gun, he could shoot Sentinel and Shashka from a distance while hidden in the crowds. The people would panic; Razin would disappear before Will could even get out of his car. He looked around, silently cursing. His eyes locked on one man. He was 150 feet away from Sentinel's vehicle and appeared to be looking at it. The man was tall and dressed in a long overcoat and fur hat. His arms were folded.

"Possible sighting." Will spoke quietly. "He's on your four o'clock, out of your line of sight."

Sentinel replied, "Understood."

The man continued to stare at the vehicle. Will looked at him but also darted glances at others near Sentinel's vehicle in case the man was not Shashka. The crowds around him were getting thicker. Will imagined that shops were now closing, evicting their occupants onto the streets. A car drove by him, and Will looked at the people inside it: a man, a woman, and a child. The car continued onward, passing the man who might be Shashka and then passing Sentinel's vehicle. The man remained where he was but now started looking left and right. Then he started walking.

"He's on the move. Heading toward you."

"All right." Sentinel's voice remained calm.

"He's crossing the road." Will gripped his gun. "He's moving behind your vehicle. He's stopped. Now he's moving again." Will waited a few seconds. "You should see him in your wing mirrors."

Sentinel said nothing for a moment. Then, "It's him. Radio silence from here on out, as I don't want to spook the guy."

Shashka hadn't been told that Will would be attending the meeting.

Will looked back toward the crowds on the other side

of the road. They were starting to thin; many people had clearly decided it was time to get off the freezing streets and head home. Will moved his eyes from one person to the next, searching for a killer. He looked back at Sentinel's car and saw Shashka open the door and lower himself into the vehicle. Will moved his gun up to the vehicle dashboard. If anything bad was going to happen, it would happen now. Shashka shut the door. Will turned on his vehicle's ignition, looking back at the few remaining people who were near Sentinel's car. None of them looked as though they were armed and ready to shoot a senior MI6 officer and a general of Russia's Western Operational Strategic Command.

Sentinel's car moved quickly forward. Will depressed his vehicle's accelerator, causing his tires to skid over the ice before they gained traction and forced the car to lunge forward. Soon he was a hundred feet behind Sentinel, traveling northeast on Dvortsovaya Naberezhnaya. They passed more pedestrians, but Will made no effort to look at them. Now that he and Sentinel were mobile, any threat against them would almost certainly come from another vehicle. They turned south onto Liteyniy Prospekt, and then southwest onto Zagorodniy Prospekt. All around them were shops, residential buildings, and offices. Traffic was heavy. They were moving through the center of the city.

Will kept very close to Sentinel's car so that no other vehicle could move into the space between them. Snow began to fall, and he put the windshield wipers on. He scrutinized every vehicle close to him as well as the side roads to his left and right in case any vehicles were waiting there to speed out and ram Sentinel's vehicle. They turned west onto the Naberezhnaya Obvodnogo Kanala and drove along the road, with the canal by their side. After ten minutes, they turned south again. Soon buildings became sparse. They were heading out of the city. Will's observation of all around him intensified. He knew that a mobile assault on Sentinel's car would be easier now that they were more exposed.

Sentinel drove faster, and Will kept up with him. They continued driving south for six miles before going west on the A121, with the Baltic Sea by their side. Fewer cars were on this road. They had left Saint Petersburg. Will kept looking in his mirror to check for signs that they were being followed but he saw nothing unusual.

They followed the A121 for 110 miles before Sentinel's car began to slow down. Will adjusted his speed and watched his colleague's vehicle drive off the road onto a small track. Turning off his headlights, he slowed until he was traveling at only ten miles per hour. Then he watched Sentinel's vehicle's taillights disappear up the track and followed them. The track was a mile long. Sentinel drove all the way along it before stopping by a house beside the Baltic Sea. It was another of his safe houses. All around them was darkness. There were no streetlights or other forms of illumination. Will stopped his car three hundred yards away from the house, briefly saw the interior lights of Sentinel's car come on as its occupants exited the vehicle, and soon after saw lights within the residence. Sentinel and Shashka were in the building.

Disabling his interior light so that it would not come on when he opened the car door, he got out, raised his handgun, and pointed it back down the route he had driven. He waited for the sounds of a vehicle, a sight of its headlights, or the noise of a man moving rapidly on foot toward him. But he heard and saw nothing.

He got back into his car and drove slowly to minimize noise. Parking it to one side of the house, he got out again and looked around. Aside from the building next to him, everything remained in darkness. The sounds of the sea were right beside him, and he could smell the salty air coming from it. Tucking his handgun into his belt, he entered the house.

He locked the door behind him and walked along the hallway. He could hear Sentinel and Shashka talking in Russian. He saw them sitting in the lounge facing each other. But as soon as Will entered the room, Shashka jumped up, his face angry and shocked. Sentinel also stood, speaking rapidly and placing a hand on Shashka's arm.

Shashka broke away from Sentinel's grip, stepping toward Will. The Russian was in his fifties, was as tall as Will, had neatly cropped gray hair, was clean-shaven, and had removed his overcoat to reveal an immaculate three-piece suit. The anger in his green eyes was vivid. When he spoke, his voice was a deep growl. "I'm told that I must trust you. But I hate being taken for a fool."

Sentinel moved up to him. "Sir, nobody has done that. My colleague's here to make sure that you are safe."

Shashka looked sharply at Sentinel. "We've never met with others present before. What's so different about this meeting?"

Sentinel shrugged. "These are difficult times. I'm merely being cautious."

Shashka shook his head, remaining angry.

Will held out his hand. "I'm sorry that I startled you."

Shashka looked at Will's outstretched hand. His anger remained, but his expression changed a little. He sighed and gripped Will's hand with strength. "No more surprises. I'm too old for them." He released his grip and moved to a corner liquor cabinet, extracted a bottle of vodka and three tumblers, and poured the spirit into the glasses. Handing them a drink each, he lifted his own glass. "To peace."

"To peace," the MI6 officers responded in unison.

Will took a tiny sip of the liquor, then placed his glass down on a side table. Sentinel and Shashka sat back down in their armchairs while Will moved around the room, pulling curtains over its windows. He shut the lounge door, grabbed a dining chair, and sat so that he was partially facing the entrance. Glancing at Shashka, he could see that the man was not looking in his direction. Discreetly, Will removed his handgun from his belt and gripped it by his side, hiding it from view.

Shashka took a big gulp of vodka and wiped his mouth with the back of his hand. "Why was this meeting so urgent?"

Sentinel answered, "Taras Khmelnytsky. Head of Spetsnaz Alpha. Is there any way of locating him?"

Shashka frowned. "Why do you need to find him?"

"I can't tell you anything, other than it's vital I know where he is."

"That's not much incentive to help you." The Russian general swirled the vodka in his glass. "He's on a classified training exercise with elements of Alpha. For most of the time, even high command doesn't know where he is because the exercise requires Colonel Khmelnytsky and his men to retain an element of surprise."

Like placing a nuclear bomb in an army barracks without anyone knowing.

"Someone must know where he is."

The general took out an elegant cigarette holder and cigarette. Attaching them to each other, he lit the cigarette with a gunmetal lighter, snapped the lighter shut, and blew a thin stream of smoke. "In case of emergency, he can be tracked. My colleagues choose not to know where he is because it benefits them not to know. But they're not stupid. Khmelnytsky's working with some very . . . valuable equipment. If anything happens to the colonel or his men, it's vital the equipment be recovered and returned to a safe location."

"There are beacons on the equipment?"

Shashka nodded. "Yes, and they're visible. But the colonel and his men are unaware that their civilian vehicles have been secretly equipped with tracking devices."

"Are they activated?"

"No. As long as the colonel provides his daily reports on time, the beacons are kept off to make the exercise as realistic as possible."

Sweat began to trickle down Will's back. He desperately wanted the meeting to end, because he knew that Razin could strike at any moment. But what Shashka was saying was adding a whole new range of possibilities to capturing the man.

Sentinel asked, "Can they be turned on?"

Shashka smiled. "Even I don't have that authority. The only men who could authorize that are my boss Luchinski, Barkov, Nikitin, Fursenko, or the big man himself—Platonov."

Lieutenant General Vladimirsky Luchinski, Lieutenant General Ilya Barkov, Lieutenant General Daniil Nikitin, and Lieutenant General Viktor Fursenko. Respectively, heads of the Western, Central, Southern, and Eastern Commands. Colonel General Platonov was their superior and answered only to the Russian president and prime minister.

"You could try to persuade Luchinski to activate the beacons. Maybe say they need to be tested."

Shashka shook his head quickly. "I'm quite happy to feed you information. But if I make a request like that, it'll be viewed as highly suspicious. The only reason I know about Alpha's training exercise is because it falls under Western Command and sometimes I have to countersign some of Luchinski's orders. But I'm not special forces. For me to attempt to interfere would seem odd, to say the least."

Will stood, knowing that Sentinel would be feeling overwhelming disappointment and also knowing that the three of them were sitting ducks. He moved around the room carefully, so as not to let Shashka see his gun.

Shashka looked at him. "Why are you pacing? Is there something out there that I should be aware of?"

Will smiled. "Ignore me. I'm just here to make sure you're safe."

A bullet tore a hole in the lounge wall, traveled across the room, and removed a large part of Shashka's head from his body.

Sentinel dived to the ground, shouting, "Fifty caliber with thermal!"

Razin.

With a precision weapon that could rip through buildings and kill on impact.

And a telescopic, heat-sensing sight that could detect any living creatures within the house.

Will lunged at the door, kicking it open. "Get to the back of the house!" He spun around, dropping low in the doorway. A second bullet struck the door frame, right where his head had been a second before. Sentinel was leopard-crawling fast across the floor, his handgun held in one fist. Will reached out, grabbed Sentinel's other outstretched hand, and yanked him toward the doorway with all of his strength. A third bullet crashed into the skirting board.

Will pulled him to his feet, turned, and sprinted into the hallway and along it. "Move!"

He reached another closed door and threw his body sideways at it, causing it to come off its hinges and fall to the floor. Sentinel was right by him. Both men moved deeper into the room. It was the kitchen. They crouched down, breathing fast.

Sentinel gritted his teeth. "Bastard."

Will looked quickly around. The four walls between them and Razin would make him blind to their position, so Razin would now be moving to get another line of sight.

Sentinel also looked around, his eyes now filled with hatred. "He's not going to leave us alone."

Will's heart raced. "I know." He looked at the back door. "We've got to close him down."

They both knew the only way to do that was with speed and erratic movement. Even then, the chances of success were slim.

"Let's go."

They moved to either side of the door. Will opened it, nodded at Sentinel, and dived through the exit. Crashing to the outside ground, he rolled and dived for cover just as another shot rang out. The bullet struck the ground inches from him, but it had given him what he needed. "He's on our two o'clock. One-fifty yards away."

They ran again, heading toward the shooter, keeping low and sidestepping left and right to make them difficult targets. They reached a point thirty feet from the house. The gun fired again, and a bullet grazed Sentinel's upper arm, causing him to stumble, but he regained his footing and ran even faster.

Gripping their handguns, the MI6 officers sprinted toward the place where they had last seen Razin's muzzle flash. They ran along the track leading away from the house, the whole time Will scouring the rough ground to the right of it, where he thought Razin might still be. But all ahead of them was in darkness, and the faint moonlight enabled Will to see only a few feet in front of him.

Then he saw something move rapidly from a hedgerow onto the track. He raised his gun, but whatever he saw had now disappeared. Sentinel dashed to his right, jumped off the track, and disappeared into the darkness. Will knew that the officer had also seen the movement and was trying to flank whatever it was. Will ran faster but was now almost blind in the nighttime.

Sentinel shouted from behind Will, "I've found the rifle, but there's no sign of him here."

Will cursed, desperately looking left and right as he ran.

It all happened in an instant. The man appeared before Will, rushing at him with tremendous speed. Still running, Will raised his gun and shot, but the man twisted, dodging the bullet, and punched a fist into Will's jaw with enough power to not only stop Will dead in his tracks but to also lift his body high in the air, hurtling backward. As Will thumped to the ground, his grip on his handgun involuntarily released and his weapon went flying away from the track into the darkness. His body was in agony from the force of the punch and from the impact on the ground. The man was over him. He looked to be in his late thirties, had a smooth face and jet-black straight hair, was tall, muscular, and clearly immensely powerful.

It was Razin.

Will slammed his foot into Razin's ankle, used his other foot to kick his kneecap, and thrust his boot full force into his gut. Razin gasped and staggered back, giving Will just enough time to get to his feet. Stepping forward, Will jabbed his knee into Razin's rib cage, causing the man to double over in pain. He swung a fist at his head, but Razin grabbed his speeding hand in midair, held it still with a viselike grip, and twisted his arm until he was holding Will in a lock. He moved closer to Will. Will instantly twisted his arm in the other direction, pulling Razin toward him, and head butted him in the face. Razin flew backward, holding his hands against his nose. Charging forward, Will dived at him, but Razin sidestepped and banged his elbow into Will's back as he was still in midair. He hit the ground, rolled sideways to avoid Razin's boot as it descended toward his head, jumped up, and took two steps away from the big Russian.

The men stared at each other, breathing fast, their faces screwed up in pain.

Then they moved forward.

Will lowered his upper body and swung his fist up toward Razin's jaw.

Razin punched fast toward Will's cheekbone.

Their fists impacted simultaneously.

The operatives fell away from each other.

They slowly got to their feet, their breathing now even

more labored, and stared at each other. Neither man moved.

Razin gasped, "Who are you?"

Will answered through gritted teeth, "The man sent to stop you, Razin."

Razin's eyes narrowed. "If you know my code name, then you must be an MI6 officer."

A shot rang out from Sentinel's handgun; the bullet sliced across Razin's cheekbone. The Russian special forces commander did not move, but anger was now on his face. "We'll meet again."

He turned and disappeared into the darkness a split second before another of Sentinel's shots raced through the place where he'd been standing.

Will immediately gave chase, running fast but blindly across the rough ground, desperate to hear a noise from Razin. After three hundred feet he stopped, looked around, heard and saw nothing, and stamped his foot on the ground in frustration.

Razin had escaped.

He jogged back to the track. Sentinel was there, his handgun pointing right at Will.

"It's me! Don't shoot!"

Sentinel lowered his pistol as Will came into view. "What happened?"

What *had* happened was unprecedented. In his operational career, Will had engaged in unarmed combat with hundreds of very dangerous and skilled men. But Razin's assault on him was like no other fight he had ever been in. For the first time in his life, Will had come up against a man who was physically his equal.

Will rubbed his hand over his face; the pain behind his eyes and running down his back was immense. "He got away. I couldn't beat him."

Sentinel looked around. "We've got to get out of Russia. But only for a few days. I need to come back to meet another agent."

"What?"

"I've got to, and I've got to notify Moscow Station."

Will couldn't believe what he was hearing. "Your plan failed!"

"Only because we were outgunned." He shook his head. "Razin has to pay for what he did to Shashka."

"Even if it means that another agent loses his life?"

"No." Sentinel looked toward the house. "We need expert help. Do you think you can get a team?"

"What about your Eastern European or Russian assets?"

"They're gifted amateurs, no match for Razin."

Will was still incredulous. "I'm not going to let you put your life and another agent's life at risk again."

"You've got to, because we've just been given another opportunity to capture Razin. Shashka didn't know this, but one of the men he mentioned—Lieutenant General Ilya Barkov, the head of Central Operational Strategic Command—is one of my other tier-one agents. He's the only other general I have on my books, but he's just become a very important one."

"You're going to ask him to activate the beacons so that we can locate Razin?"

"Yes."

"Will he do it?"

"I don't know; he's a difficult man to handle. I need to lure Razin to the meeting in case Barkov says no."

Will could see that Sentinel was exhausted. "You're pushing yourself too hard."

Sentinel muttered, "What other choice do I have?"

"You could trust me to do my job."

Sentinel folded his arms. "Get me a team. Either we'll take down Razin at the Barkov meeting, or we'll get a grid reference for his location and make an assault on him."

EIGHTEEN

Will awoke as the Lufthansa flight touched down in Slovenia. The aircraft slowed to a taxi, and Will looked out of his window but barely registered the snow-covered surroundings or the activities in the airport. Instead, his thoughts returned to his confrontation with Razin.

He tried to understand what he felt about his inability to defeat the Russian. Anger, frustration, perhaps even shame? Yes, maybe all of those things. But there was something else that was far more overwhelming.

It came to him.

More than anything else, his fight with Razin had brought into question everything he'd been trained to do and tasked on. He'd been prepared to make all of the mental and physical sacrifices to endure the Spartan Program because it had been drilled into him that if he successfully completed the course, he would be able to succeed in any mission.

Until yesterday, that had been true.

But now that he'd come up against someone who was his equal, he wondered if the hell he'd gone through for twelve months and the subsequent eight years of constant deployment had been worth it. For the first time in his life, he doubted not only himself but also those who had put their faith in him.

He thought about one of the Program's tests. He'd had to do a HALO parachute insertion from 70,000 feet into Washington's Olympic Mountains, carrying a communications and survival kit weighing eighty pounds. After landing, he'd trekked across harsh terrain for fifty miles in freezing conditions until he reached the isolated house where he'd been told to rendezvous with an instructor who would be role-playing an agent. Will had covertly watched the house for six hours and had seen no one. He hadn't expected to. But as he carefully made his way toward the house he knew that the real test was about to begin. When he entered, men with guns grabbed him, put him in shackles, and covered his head with a hood. He was placed in a truck and driven two hours away before being dragged into a building, stripped naked, repeatedly punched, and forced into agonizing stress positions for hours at a time, throughout which white noise blared from speakers.

He estimated it was twelve hours before the noise stopped, his hood was removed, and he was kicked to the floor. An instructor crouched down next to him, patted him on the head, and said, "So far, so good. But that was just the warm-up. Now we're going to put drugs into you to make you tell us the name of the man you were coming to meet. After one day, every thought and instinct in your body will be crying out to release the information. If you manage to hold out until day two, you'll think you've lost your mind. By day three, you'll want to kill yourself. But you're going to need to last five days to stay in the Program."

Will wondered why this particular memory had come into his mind. It wasn't the worst test he'd had to endure.

Of course. It was what had come after that five-day ordeal that mattered.

When the drugs were out of his system, he'd been allowed to wash, shave, and change into clean clothes. But sleep was not yet permitted. Instead, he was guided into a classroom where an elderly gentleman was standing by a large blackboard. Will was told to sit at a desk and was left alone with the man.

He'd never seen this instructor before; he looked over retirement age. The man was dressed in a tweed suit and bow tie, was tall and thin, and was holding a piece of chalk. He drew two small circles on the board, one in the top left-hand corner, the other on the bottom right. Turning to face Will, he said in a well-spoken English accent, "I know from my experience in the field in the fifties that all of the physical stuff is nothing compared to what you can do with a brain." He jabbed the chalk on the lower circle. "This is you." Then he did the same on the higher circle. "And this is the man you want to capture." He smiled. "Using intellect alone, we're going to see which one can get to the other first."

For the next four hours, the theoretical exercise was played out, with the instructor throwing obstacle after obstacle, new information, and unexpected events at Will, who was trying to formulate an ongoing plan to get to the other circle. Finally, the instructor put a cross through the highest circle and said, "Impressive. You got him." He nodded. "I hope you've learnt more about yourself in the last few hours than you have in the last week."

The Lufthansa flight came to a halt. People around Will started to stand up and extract their bags from the overhead lockers.

Will was motionless. He knew why the memory had come to him. Razin *had* matched him blow for blow. But he had *not* yet proven that he was Will's intellectual equal.

But if he did, Will's future in the Spartan Section was in doubt.

NINETEEN

Will sat at a table and waited. The restaurant provided stunning views of Ljubljana and the snow-covered Slovenian mountains beyond the city. It was breakfast time, but the restaurant was nearly empty.

Kryštof arrived and sat opposite him. The former Czech intelligence officer looked even worse than when Will had last seen him, and he stank of cigarettes and stale alcohol. He shook Will's hand. "Hello, David."

Will smiled. "You look well."

"No, I don't." Kryštof pulled out a cigarette and lit it. "Let's get a drink."

"I've already ordered us some coffee."

"Coffee? Okay." He glanced out of the windows at the view. "Thanks for meeting me here. It saved me having to reroute my flights." He looked back at Will. "I've got a name."

"Excellent."

Kryštof smiled. "I'm not completely off the rails."

"I never thought you were."

"Liar." Kryštof tapped his cigarette over an ashtray. "Richard Baines. British. Operates out of the Cayman Islands."

"He knows Otto von Schiller?"

"No doubt he'll know *of* him. But they don't do business together. Not directly, anyway."

"But he's acquainted with someone who *does* work with Schiller?"

"Correct."

"Name?"

"A Frenchman named Philippe Dêlage. He lives in Paris but spends a lot of time in Berlin, because that's where Schiller's based."

They were silent as a waiter brought a jug of coffee to the table and poured their drinks. After he left, Will said, "The Cayman Islands are a bit out of my way right now."

Kryštof lifted his cup and saucer; his hand shook as he did so. "You don't need to go there. Baines is meeting Dêlage in Munich tomorrow. He's flying into Germany today and is staying at the Mandarin Oriental."

"Today?"

Kryštof took a sip of his coffee. "I've already checked for you. There are spaces available on the 12:40 P.M. Adria flight. It's direct, and you can be in Munich around the same time he arrives."

Will laughed quietly. "You've thought of everything." He withdrew an envelope containing the remaining £5,000 owed to the Czech. "Very good work."

Kryštof secreted the cash. "Anything else you need me to do?"

"No, that's all."

Kryštof inhaled deeply on his cigarette and again looked out of the window. "I thought you'd say that."

Will snapped out of being David. Something was wrong. "What are you going to do now?"

In a near whisper, Kryštof replied, "Something I've been planning to do since . . . since she's been gone."

Will reached across the table and grabbed Kryštof's forearm. "No. You have a future. You're still useful to people like me. I'll get you more work—anything to keep your mind occupied."

Kryštof smiled with a look of sad resignation. "You won't be able to do that for long. Your star's long since waned in the service. I'm surprised they even asked you to do this job." He broke free from Will's grip and looked at him. "You've always been very kind to me. But you need to understand that my mind's made up. It's what I want."

Will was lost for words.

Kryštof's smile faded. "I've been meaning to ask you a question, and given what I've just told you, perhaps you might agree to answer it."

Will waited.

"Is David Becket your real name?"

Oh, dear God. Will's stomach churned. He was facing

a man who had known Becket for years, who liked the MI6 officer, and who wanted to know the truth before he killed himself due to the grief he felt about his daughter's tragic death. Every ounce of humanity within him screamed out that Kryštof had to know the truth.

Will stood; Kryštof followed suit.

Will moved to him, hugged him, said, "Be at peace, my dear friend." Then he stepped back and nodded. "You've always deserved to know the truth. David Becket's my real name."

TWENTY

The taxi took Will away from Munich International Airport and toward the city. Snow carpeted the roads and surrounding countryside, though for now no more was falling.

Will was on his cell phone, talking to Alistair. "Only three?"

"That's all I could get for you at this short notice. They're due to arrive in Russia in three days' time and will wait for you there."

"Equipment?"

"I've told them that handguns won't be enough. Everything's going through in diplomatic bags. The team leader has your John Lawrence number and will make contact when he's in situ."

"Do I know him?"

"I believe you had a drink with him in Washington before leaving."

Roger Koenig.

"Excellent. And what have you got on my man?"

Will listened for ten minutes as Alistair briefed him on everything MI6 knew about Richard Baines. It wasn't a lot, but there was enough on the British arms dealer to give Will the leverage he needed.

"Room number?"

"Cheltenham's tracked his credit card number, and it doesn't show which room he's in."

Cheltenham—GCHQ.

"But I've managed to speak to a contact at BfV."

The German Security Service.

"No mention made of you. They checked with the hotel and got the room. He's in the Mandarin suite."

"All right, but you should have spoken to me first before alerting the locals."

"I'm so sorry. Sometimes I forget that I'm only your boss."

The sarcastic comment made Will smile.

"How's your associate holding up?"

Will thought about Sentinel. "Events are taking their toll on him. But he's a tough bastard."

"Is his judgment sound?"

Will responded, "Even though I disagree with what he wants to do, I can't fault the logic of his plan."

"You have the authority to overrule him."

"I know, but this is happening to his people. If I were in his position, I'd probably do the same thing he's doing."

Will stood outside the Mandarin suite, straightened his tie, pressed the hotel room's buzzer, and said in a loud German-accented voice, "Hotel Management."

He heard a man call out something. He waited patiently.

Thirty seconds later, a man opened the door. He was dressed in a bathrobe, had wet hair, and smelled of soap.

"Mr. Baines?"

The man replied in a south London accent. "Of course."

Will stepped forward, punched his hand under Baines's jaw, lifted him off the ground, carried him back into the room, and threw him onto the floor.

"What the fuck—?"

Will stamped a foot on Baines's flabby belly, causing the arms dealer to retch. He knelt down beside his writhing body and grabbed his jaw again, holding it firm so that they were looking directly at each other.

"Listen very carefully to me." Will leaned closer. "I work for British Intelligence. We know about your deals in Africa, your shipment that's sailing through the Persian Gulf, and the missiles you're about to purchase from the Chinese. You've got a lot of blood on your hands, and we've got enough evidence to put you in prison for the rest of your life. But I'm not here for that. Tomorrow you're meeting Philippe Dêlage. I'm going to be at that meeting with you, and you're going to say that I'm someone you trust and have done business with for years."

Baines tried to break free from Will's grip. "You've got to be crazy."

Will held him firm. "You *are* going to do this for me. And afterward, you're never going to mention this little chat. Fail at either, and I promise that I'll come back for you."

TWENTY-ONE

The three men were sitting around a large oak table in the Mandarin Oriental's business-suite boardroom. Dressed in a Camps de Luca suit, a silk shirt, and a tie that he'd bound into a schoolboy knot, Philippe Dêlage looked at home in the five-star surroundings. He was probably around fifty years old, but wealth, a charmed life, an attractive wife half his age, a personal trainer, or all of those things had made him look ten years younger. By contrast, Richard Baines looked like a 1980s barrow boy banker—pin-striped suit, suspenders over a striped shirt, slicked-back hair, and overapplied eau de cologne. The third man, Will Cochrane posing as Thomas Eden, was dressed as if he were about to have a glass of port in the Household Cavalry's officers' mess—dark Huntsman bespoke Savile Row sports jacket, pink shirt with cutaway collar, regimental tie, cords, and brogues.

Dêlage studied Eden's business card and said in a barely accented voice, "I've never heard of Thomas Eden before." He looked at Baines. "Why is that?"

Baines shrugged. "Fucked if I know, pal."

Dêlage shook his head. "You say you've done business together for years. Strange, given that you and I have known each other for the same length of time and you've never mentioned him before."

Baines pointed a finger at the Frenchman. "Don't be a shit, Philippe. I bet you've got a dozen contacts tucked away who I don't know about."

Dêlage smiled. "Maybe that's true. But why are you revealing Thomas Eden to me now?"

Baines was about to speak, but Will raised a hand to silence him. "Because I'm paying him an introductory fee that equates to ten percent of anything I get out of the relationship."

"Introductory fee to meet me?"

Will laughed. "No. Someone you know."

Dêlage seemed unflustered. "So what's in it for me?"

"Not my problem. I suggest you arrange terms with the man I want to meet."

"And who is that?"

Will smiled. "Otto von Schiller."

Dêlage did not smile as he began rapidly turning over Eden's business card in his hands. "Who gave you that name?"

"I have *my* contacts."

Dêlage held the card still. "What's your interest in him?"

Will looked serious. "Soon I'm going to have my hands on some very interesting blueprints. I'm looking for a buyer, and I think von Schiller might be that person."

"Blueprints of what?"

"I'm not going to tell you."

The Frenchman looked sharply at Baines. "This has been a waste of my time."

Will interjected. "Give him my business card. That's all you need to do. The blueprints I'm talking about—I reckon they've got a market value of around fifty million dollars. If I were you, I'd start thinking about what percentage you want from the deal for"—he nodded toward the business card—"merely handing over a tiny bit of cardboard."

That evening, Will's Thomas Eden cell phone rang.

Philippe Dêlage.

He listened to the Frenchman's precise instructions. Otto von Schiller would meet him tomorrow.

But it was crucial that he come alone.

TWENTY-TWO

Will drove around Großer Alpsee searching for his destination. The Bavarian Alpine lake was tranquil, surrounded by tree-covered hills and low mountains. Snow and icicles hung from the trees' branches.

He felt tense. He was unarmed and had followed Dêlage's instructions to come alone. He'd considered getting armed backup for the meeting, perhaps some of Kryštof's contacts, but had decided that was too risky. If it looked as though he was coming to entrap Otto von Schiller his plan would fail. He'd also hoped that the meeting would have been held in a public place, but the area around him was deserted; it would be easy for men to shoot him in the head and dump his body in the lake without alerting others.

But Will had to follow this through because this meeting was his final move. He hoped that the Ukrainian SBU had sent the SVR the full transcript, that Schiller had alerted his SVR masters to the approach by Thomas Eden, and that they had tasked him to meet Eden urgently to try to ascertain the identity of the mysterious Russian colonel. But right now he couldn't be certain of anything.

He drove for another mile, following the shore.

He saw the place.

A large house, right by the water's edge.

Nothing else around it save forest.

He breathed slowly to try to calm his racing heart beat. He tried to imagine how Thomas Eden would be thinking right now. He had to match his thoughts and mood. Would he be scared, or would meetings like this be commonplace for a man like him? Perhaps he'd be slightly irritated that he'd had to go so far out of his way to meet Schiller. Yes, that's how he'd feel.

He approached the house and stopped the vehicle in a spot that was easily visible to the building's occupants. After walking casually to the front door, he knocked on it three times. There was movement inside. The door opened. Two thickset German men, dressed in suits. They were obviously bodyguards and no doubt would be armed.

Will's expression was terse. "Thomas Eden. I have an appointment with Mr. Schiller."

The men said nothing and stepped back a few paces, keeping their eyes fixed on him.

Will stepped into the house.

The door shut behind him.

Will was about to move forward when one of the men grabbed him and slammed his face against the corridor wall.

"Stand very still."

Will followed the bodyguard's order. The second man began to expertly search his overcoat, suit, undergarments, shoes, and body surface. He removed Eden's wallet, car keys, and BlackBerry before nodding at the man who was holding Will in a viselike grip. That man kicked Will's ankles while simultaneously thrusting down on his arm and shoulder. Within two seconds, Will was facedown on the floor, his limbs outstretched, a boot fixed firmly against his neck.

Will lay still, knowing there was nothing he could do other than let the men do their job. He heard the front door open and a moment later the sound of his car being unlocked. There was nothing in there that could compromise him, but he wondered how long it would take the guard to search the vehicle.

Approximately twenty minutes.

The front door was shut. The guard walked past him and disappeared into a room. He'd now be searching Eden's wallet and in particular analyzing his BlackBerry—sent and received e-mails, calls, files, individuals in his contact list, and his Internet browsing history. The guard would find nothing unusual. Will had crammed the phone with data that showed only one thing—that he was a businessman who worked in military consultancy and was ultracautious about electronically communicating matters pertaining to Thomas Eden Limited. He was, after all, always conscious that he could be picked up by customs, Interpol, or other law enforcement agencies.

He estimated that it was forty minutes before the boot was lifted off his neck.

Red-faced and angry, Will got to his feet, rearranged his clothes, and looked at the two bodyguards now before him. "Was that absolutely necessary?!"

No reply. One of them handed Eden's belongings back to him and beckoned him to come forward. He was led along the corridor and into a large room. Its windows overlooked the beautiful vista of the lake. But inside the room, nothing was beautiful. It was empty of anything save two straight-backed dining chairs in the center, facing each other. The floor was entirely covered with black plastic sheets that had been taped together.

Will had seen rooms like this before.

Sometimes they were used for interrogations.

More often for executions.

He turned and was about to say something, but the bodyguard pushed him forward and pointed at the chair facing the windows. Will sat in it and crossed his legs. He was afraid.

Because that's what Eden would be feeling right now.

The bodyguard disappeared from view. Will checked his watch and waited. Sweat began to trickle down his back. Ten minutes passed. Everything was silent.

Another ten minutes. Then footsteps on wooden flooring, followed by footsteps over plastic sheets.

He stayed still, expecting to feel a gun barrel against the back of his head just before a tiny moment of absolute pain.

The two bodyguards came into view and stood in the corners of the room, facing him. Both held pistols. Will glanced over his shoulder and saw that two more bodyguards were in the corners behind him, also armed. He looked back toward the windows.

More footsteps.

A man came into view.

Small, midfifties, suit pants and open-neck shirt, clean-shaven, gray hair that had been immaculately cut into a style favored by Germany's officer-class soldiers.

Otto von Schiller.

He sat in the chair, clasped his hands together, leaned forward, and asked, "What do you want from me?"

Will answered quickly, "I came here to discuss a business opportunity with you." He glanced at the bodyguards. "I'm wondering why I bothered."

Schiller smiled, though his look was cold. "Of course you are."

Silence.

Schiller kept his blue eyes fixed on Eden.

The silence was unsettling. Will had to say something. "I've been to other meetings where guns have been present—mostly in Central America, Africa, and the former Soviet Union states—and can assure you they achieve nothing."

"Now you can add Germany to that list."

More sweat, this time down his face.

Von Schiller pointed at him. "I've been to meetings where guns *haven't* been present but should have been. I'll not make that mistake again."

"This meeting isn't a mistake."

"From where you're sitting, do you really believe that?"

Will looked around. Despite his circumstances, he had to achieve some degree of control over the situation.

He looked directly at von Schiller. "I want"—he paused, then spoke in a more confident voice—"I *want* you to listen to me so that you can understand that I've gone out of my way to bring you a highly unusual business proposition."

"You could be here to entrap me."

Will looked exasperated. "I rather think it looks the other way around."

Von Schiller glanced away. "Are there men out there, waiting for the right moment to come for me?"

"If there were, they'd be here too late to stop your men from putting a bullet in my skull." Will shook his head. "I came here in good faith. On. My. Own."

Schiller unclasped his hands and leaned back, drumming his fingers on his leg. Clearly, he was deep in thought.

Will muttered between clenched teeth, "We both hate the same organizations."

Schiller stopped drumming. "Dêlage told me that you have access to blueprints. What are they?"

Will glanced again at the bodyguards. "I'm not going to talk to you while under duress."

"And I'm not going to remove my men!" Schiller was motionless. "*If* you are genuinely here to discuss a business transaction that is of mutual interest, then I give you my word that you'll walk out of here unharmed."

"Your *word*?"

"Yes, my word. I've spent thirty years in this business. I can tell you with certainty that I wouldn't have survived that long unless my word meant something."

Will shook his head. "Other men have said the same thing to me. I was proven right not to trust them."

Schiller looked shocked. "I don't have to earn your trust."

When Will spoke, all traces of fear were now absent from his voice. "Yes, you do. Last year my company made eight million dollars profit. All of it came from business associates whom I trust. In the same year, I lost five million dollars to people who turned out to be completely untrustworthy. Trust equals money. It's as damn simple as that."

Schiller smiled again, but this time the look was less cold.

Will rubbed a hand over his face and flicked sweat from it onto the plastic floor. "All right. Blueprints of prototype suitcase nuclear bombs."

Schiller narrowed his eyes. "I've seen similar in the past."

"No, you haven't. These are different. The bombs'

range far exceed anything developed before. They weigh less, and so far trials with them have been one hundred percent successful. They're perfect for special forces, commandos, or paramilitary units."

"But the bombs can only be manufactured by people who have access to weapons-grade uranium."

Will nodded. "That's my problem, because I lack the contacts in that world. Most of my business is in conventional military matters. I tried the Iranians but got knocked back, and it quickly became clear to me that I needed another route in to potential buyers. I've heard that you have access to such people."

"And where did you hear that?"

"From someone I not only *trust* but to whom I also gave my *word* that I would never reveal his identity."

The German stared at him. When he spoke, his voice was quiet. "If your specialty is in conventional matters, how've you come by these blueprints?"

"By chance."

"Who's the supplier?"

Will shook his head. "I can't give you that information."

"Then I can't give you a buyer."

The room was silent.

Will knew that he couldn't be the first one to speak.

More silence.

Finally Schiller said, "I can't approach a potential buyer unless I can persuade him that the blueprints are authentic. To do that, I must be able to say where they come from."

Will looked frustrated. "I have to protect my supplier, including his identity."

"And I have to protect my clients and my reputation."

"Then it seems we are at an impasse."

"I agree."

Will thought through the problem. "How likely is it that you can get an interested buyer?"

"Providing the blueprints are authentic and accurate, it's certain."

Will was silent.

Schiller said, "If you could satisfy *me* that the supplier is authentic, that will be enough. I can tell my client that the source's identity must remain a secret but that I can vouch for his credentials."

Will looked unsure.

Schiller looked at one of the bodyguards and nodded. The guards left the room. He faced Will. "We're going to have to exchange something. You need my client and money; I need a name and the blueprints."

Will was hesitant. "I have your word?"

"I can give you that if you can give me your trust."

Will lowered his head and stared at the floor. Finally he nodded and said, "Okay."

He fixed his attention on the SVR agent. "He's a Russian colonel named Taras Khmelnytsky."

PART III

TWENTY-THREE

Razin looked at the twenty-four men who were busy making preparations in the disused warehouse. They were his Spetsnaz Alpha troops, all handpicked by him for the training exercise. Tonight, their task was to infiltrate the base of the 104th Parachute Regiment in the ancient northwestern city of Pskov. It would be tough, though he wasn't concerned, as he knew they'd succeed. What did concern him was that time was running out, because the exercise could be terminated at any time. If that happened before everything was in place, his plan would have failed.

He moved away from the men, their vehicles, and the equipment and sat on a wooden crate. Withdrawing his custom-made military knife, he looked at the long blade for several seconds before carefully sharpening it with a stone.

All of the MI6 officer's agents had to die, but it was taking too long. That was why he needed to change tactics. The traitor had given him the names and the time and location of the next meeting, but this time he'd not only kill his target, he'd also capture his former agent handler—the man he'd recently found out carried the code name Sentinel. That would speed things up. Sentinel would be forced to summon all of his remaining agents to one location. Razin would slaughter them.

Everything depended on timing. The agents had to be dead before the three American cruise missile–bearing submarines sailed toward Russia. And the training exercise had to still be live when that happened so that he could plant the bomb.

He smiled as he looked at his faithful colleagues. They had no idea what they were really doing for him. It didn't matter, because if they survived the war, he'd honor them for their role in preventing Russia from being crippled. But he'd never tell them the truth about the bomb. Instead he'd say that he'd removed its beacon and detonated it at sea or in one of Russia's vast wastelands to prevent it from falling into American hands. By then no one would be asking questions. They'd be focused on far more pressing matters.

He thought about the big MI6 man he'd confronted outside the Saint Petersburg safe house. He could be a problem, for he was unlike anyone Razin had confronted before. No doubt he'd be with Sentinel at the meeting with General Barkov.

That's where he'd kill him.

TWENTY-FOUR

Roger Koenig shook Will's hand. "We're a long way away from that drink in D.C."

Will smiled at the CIA SOG officer. "Indeed we are." He looked at the other men. Laith Dia was one of them. He was the only other SOG paramilitary specialist to have survived Will's last brutal mission to capture the Iranian mastermind Megiddo. Will was overjoyed that Patrick had sent the two CIA men. He asked Laith, "How's your stomach?"

The tall, black-haired American shrugged. "I've got a scar right across it. Makes me look like I've had a darn hysterectomy." The ex–Delta Force man laughed, shook Will's hand, then nodded toward the third man. "Ross Tark. SAS Increment."

Ross was slightly shorter than the two CIA men but was

still six feet tall. He was an athletic, handsome man with close-cropped blond hair. When he looked at Will, his brown eyes looked dead, a common appearance among special forces men who had seen sustained action. The SAS soldier shook Will's hand and spoke to him with a Scottish lilt. "Nice to meet you. Now, if you don't mind, we need to check through the kit."

Roger, Laith, and Ross silently removed items from diplomatic bags and laid them out on the large dining room floor. Sentinel was standing in one corner of the room beneath a cut-glass chandelier, talking to one of his assets on his cell phone. Will stood watching them, his arms folded across his chest.

They were in a beautiful fourteen-bedroom seventeenth-century house set in the middle of sixty acres of gardens containing whitebeam trees, manicured lawns, wild heathland, stone paths, red and musk deer, and kennels for big Caucasian Ovcharka guard dogs. The house and its grounds were thirty miles south of the Russian city of Kursk.

An elderly lady with white shoulder-length hair and wearing an expensive-looking skirt and jacket walked slowly into the room holding a tray containing five bone china cups and saucers and an ornate teapot. She placed the tray on a twelve-seat oak dining table, frowned, moved across the room, stepped over a Chinese QBZ-95G assault rifle placed on the floor by Laith, and walked to the opposite wall, where many gold-framed paintings of landscapes and stallions were hanging. After straightening one of the paintings, she turned and walked back across the room, this time stepping over magazine clips, and began pouring tea into the cups. Squeezing lemon into the drinks, she looked at Sentinel and spoke a few words in Russian.

Sentinel snapped his phone shut, walked up to her, gently kissed her on both cheeks, and smiled. The woman hugged him, holding the MI6 officer for a long time, then released him and walked out of the room. Roger, Laith, and Ross finished extracting all of their kit. The floor now contained four QBZ-95Gs, five QSZ-92 handguns, spare magazine clips, military communication systems, binoculars, cell phones, battlefield medical kits, plastic waterproof envelopes containing wads of cash, piles of white arctic warfare clothes, stun grenades, and one Chinese AMR-2 12.7 mm sniper rifle.

A silver-haired man came in, carrying a plate of cakes. He was in his seventies and dressed in a three-piece suit and tie. He nodded at the men and said in a soft Russian accent, "Gentlemen, this food is all we have, but my wife and I are honored to give it to you."

Sentinel immediately grabbed two of the plastic envelopes of cash, took the plate, and gave him the money. The man looked hesitant and said something in Russian. Sentinel replied with something inaudible. A slight smile emerged on the Russian's face, and he clicked his heels together, gave a sharp nod of his head, turned, and walked out of the room. Placing the cakes next to the teapot, Sentinel spoke quietly to Will. "They come from previous generations of tsarist Russian aristocracy. Most of their relatives were wiped out in the 1917 revolution; the few that survived were imprisoned or managed to go into hiding, penniless and homeless." He looked around the room. "The couple you've just seen are the grandchildren of some of those survivors. They spent their lives trying to accrue enough money to purchase this house, which was seized by revolutionaries from the husband's grandfather. It belonged to his family line for three hundred years, but in buying the property, the couple used up their entire savings." He looked at Will. "They live in splendor and poverty, waiting here with the vain hope that one day Russia may once again be ruled by nobility."

Roger called across the room, "We're ready."

Will and Sentinel joined the men. Roger stood on the other side of the military hardware, holding a cup of tea in one fist. Ross was sitting on a chair, munching a cake. Laith was sitting on the floor, leaning against a wall, smoking a cigarette.

Sentinel looked at them all. "Gentlemen, Barkov must be protected at all costs, because if we fail to kill Razin he's our last remaining hope to pin down Taras's location." He looked at Will. "Unless my friend's private operation has any legs."

Will smiled.

Laith asked, "You're sure he won't use his Spetsnaz men in the assault?"

"He'll be alone."

Ross shrugged. "Then we'll easily take him down."

Sentinel looked sharply at the SAS man. "Don't think that way."

Roger set his cup on the table. "When's the meeting?"

"I'm waiting for Barkov to call me." Sentinel looked at the weapons. "How do you want to play this?"

Roger answered, "Laith and I will be in the house." The former DEVGRU SEAL nodded at Ross. "Tark will be our sniper."

"All right. Well, there's nothing we can do now but wait."

Sentinel walked out of the room.

Roger picked up his cup and saucer and moved to the window. Will joined him.

Speaking quietly while looking at the garden, the CIA officer said, "My grandfather fought in Russia as a paratrooper in the Wehrmacht's Fallschirmjäger Division in '41. He nearly died here. When I was a kid, I remember him telling me about the Second World War, his battles in Denmark, Norway, the Netherlands, Greece, Crete, Sicily, and Italy and how he earned the Iron Cross." He shook his head. "He reckoned that none of them was as bad as what he experienced in Russia." He leaned against the window frame and looked at Will. "We might have a bigger and better-equipped army, but this ain't a place for American soldiers."

Will stood in the vast grounds of the seventeenth-century house, several hundred yards away from the property. Sprouting through the snow were many pink Luculia flowers.

He folded his arms, deep in thought. He was glad that the paramilitary men were here, but he still felt deeply uneasy about Sentinel's plan to kill Razin. Not for the first time, he wondered if Sentinel was intending to sacrifice his life to take his revenge on Razin.

Movement in the woods. A large brown shape, now gone. In a flash, he withdrew a QSZ-92 handgun and pointed it at the place where he had last seen the movement. His eyes darted left and right, searching the areas of open land between the trees. Big flakes of snow began to fall slowly through the windless air. He heard bird calls, nothing else. His heart pounded, but his hands and gun were steady. He saw the shape again, in a narrow gap between two trees, and swung his weapon toward it, but just as quickly the shape disappeared. Keeping his gun at eye level and held with both hands, he braced his body, ready to shoot.

He saw it again; his finger instinctively started pulling back the trigger, but after a few millimeters the finger released its grip. His body relaxed.

Fifty feet away from him, standing between trees and easily visible, was a huge stag. The antlers of the red deer towered over its magnificent physique. The stag stared at Will, keeping very still. Will lowered his weapon and stared back at the beast. They stayed like that for thirty seconds before the stag moved a few feet toward him and stopped again. Will expected the deer to turn and bolt into the woods, but it remained in front of him, and then it walked even closer, its breath visible out of its large nostrils. The stag lowered its head and moved a hoof back and forth over the snow. For the briefest moment, Will wondered if it was going to charge at him. But then the animal looked up, again fixing his large eyes on Will, came forward, stopped, and tossed his head.

The deer's ears twitched. It stepped back, turned, and darted off into the woods.

"Remarkable." The elderly Russian man who owned the house was walking toward him. "The stag came to my grounds a year ago, most likely from the nearby forests. He's wild and has a doe and two fawns to protect." The man reached Will. "They're very shy creatures, and we rarely ever see them. And I've *never* seen a wild stag walk that close to a human being." He turned to Will. "He's received the call. You're all to leave."

TWENTY-FIVE

Two days later, the team was a thousand miles east of Moscow, in a lodge nestled high up in the Ural Mountains. A hundred miles farther to the east was the city of Yekaterinburg, the location of the headquarters of Central Operational Strategic Command. The early-morning sun was rising and cast its light over a large lake a half mile below the building and the surrounding mountains overlaid by snow-covered forest. A solitary road snaked alongside the lake until it followed a route up the mountainside, ending at the property.

They had arrived the night before, stowing their vehicle in a garage so that it was out of sight, keeping the lodge's lights off, and maintaining an all-night vigil even though Sentinel had never used the lodge before and was convinced that it was not compromised. The place belonged to one of his assets, who had moved out of the home to stay temporarily with relatives in Yekaterinburg within twelve hours of Sentinel contacting him. The asset had left ample food in the lodge for the team, although none of them had touched it. They were too focused and tense to be hungry.

Will moved through the property, passing through a kitchen, a small open-plan dining room and lounge where Laith was waiting and holding a QBZ-95G assault rifle, up bare wooden stairs, through one bedroom containing a single bed and nothing else, and into a second room containing Roger and Sentinel.

Sentinel glanced at Will, checked his watch, and nodded. "Barkov should be here in approximately two hours." He moved next to Roger. "What do you think?"

Roger spoke while looking out a window through the sight of his assault weapon. "I think it's okay. Good lines of sight, almost continuous coverage of the road, very high ground, and thirty miles from the nearest civilization, so minimal risk of interference from locals." The CIA SOG officer nodded. "It's a darn good defensive position, but my God, there's a lot of land and tree cover around us. Razin could come at us from any direction. And unless Ross spots him with the sniper rifle or Razin's stupid and takes the road, our target could get very close before we see him."

Sentinel looked at Will. "Have you spoken to Ross?"

Will nodded. "He's ready."

Ross was a mile away on another mountain on the other side of the lake. He had been there for an hour in temperatures that were now nearly minus twenty degrees Celsius.

Will rubbed his face. "Even with Ross watching over us, Razin could do what he did last time: take us with a high-powered sniper rifle and thermal imagery. Maybe he doesn't need to come close."

Roger spoke without removing his gaze from the window. "He can't do that from the rear of the house because the incline of the mountain behind us is too severe and the angles are all wrong to give him a meaningful shot. But if he chooses to adopt that tactic from the area in front of the house, he'll be in for a hell of a surprise. In the garage, I found enough gasoline to drive a truck for a year. I've put some of the fuel into canisters, and then I took smokeless powder from bullets, rags, and whatever else I could lay my hands on to turn those canisters into crude incendiary devices. I have them strapped high up in trees one hundred and fifty feet from the house, and I doused the trees with the rest of the fuel. The canisters have been positioned very precisely so that Ross has a clear shot at all of them. If Razin uses thermal imagery, Ross will shoot every canister and create a ring of fire around us. Our enemy will be blind."

Sentinel walked up to Will, speaking quietly. "You need to stay very close to Barkov."

Will responded equally quietly, "I'm the best shot on our team. I should be downstairs."

Sentinel shook his head; his next words were almost inaudible. "*Nothing* must happen to Barkov. I'm trusting you with that task *because* you are the best shot."

• • •

"I've got a silver Mercedes on the road. It's about one mile from the lodge, heading toward you." Ross's voice was calm.

"Understood." Sentinel looked at Will while speaking into his throat mic. "The most vulnerable point will be when I greet him at the door. Razin could try and drop us both then."

Roger replied, "We know." The Americans were downstairs.

Will glanced around the upstairs room. A small circular table was in its center, a chair on either side of it. Aside from the windows, the only way to access the room was via the adjacent bedroom and the one set of stairs leading up to the place. Razin would either have to jump onto the lodge's roof from the mountain behind and enter through one of the top-floor windows or access the room from the ground level at the front of the house. Both routes would make him an easy target for Ross's hidden sniper rifle, but even if Razin did breach the house he would be facing four very dangerous and professional men whose sole objective was to gun him down.

Nevertheless, Will felt edgy and knew the rest of the team felt the same.

Ross spoke. "The Mercedes is point five miles away. One driver, no visible passengers."

They all knew that meant nothing. Razin could be hidden in the vehicle, pointing a gun at the driver.

Ross paused. "The Mercedes is slowing, but he's—" There was a sound of static.

Will frowned. "Ross?"

Ross's voice came back. "Yeah, I can hear you, but these damn mountains are interfering with the signal. I was saying that he's still moving, now three hundred yards from you."

Sentinel gripped his handgun. "I'm going downstairs to meet him." He walked to the door, paused, and turned to face Will. His expression looked earnest. "Thank you for helping me with all of this. I understand why you don't agree with me, but—" He smiled. "A four-bedroom property's just come onto the market. It's on the shore of Lake Windermere. Might suit me, don't you think?"

Before Will could answer, Sentinel walked quickly out of the room just as Ross spoke.

"He's a hundred and fifty feet from you. It's crunch time."

Will picked up his assault rifle, checked that his handgun was secure under his belt, opened his upper jacket pockets so that his spare magazines were easily accessible, and waited. He heard a car door slam, the bolts to the lodge's entrance being wrenched open, and voices speaking in Russian.

"They talk by the car, our man ushers Barkov toward the lodge." Ross's commentary was quiet. "I'm keeping my sights on the vehicle. No one else gets out of it. They reach the lodge."

Ross was silent.

Will held his breath.

"They enter the building."

Will exhaled with relief.

He heard the door shut and bolts being put back into position. Then he heard a voice downstairs, clearly belonging to Barkov, speaking loudly in Russian. The presence of Roger and Laith had obviously perturbed the general. There were footsteps on the stairs and through the bedroom, and the voice drew closer. Sentinel and Lieutenant General Ilya Barkov entered the last room.

Barkov walked quickly up to Will. "I'm told that Russia is a dangerous place right now and requires the presence of armed British and American men to protect my interests. But why would I need to be reminded that Russia is a dangerous place when I've known that my entire life? And why have you and your men chosen today of all days to look after me when there have been a thousand similar moments in my life when I could've benefited from protection? Obviously, today is special. Obviously, men are nearby to kill me."

Barkov was quite small and slim, had black hair that had been oiled and swept back, was clean shaven, wore an immaculate woolen suit, silk shirt, gleaming black brogues, and a silk bow tie. He was younger than Will expected, in his late forties, and it was clear that he was a high flyer to have reached one of Russia's most senior military ranks at such an age.

Barkov held a hand out to Will and spoke in a clipped and rapid tone. "But here I am, and here you are. So let's get on with business and hope that we're not murdered in the process."

Shaking the general's hand, he wondered what to say to the Russian, decided that the man before him was exceptionally smart, and concluded that he had to tell him the truth. "One man may be nearby with the intention of killing you. We don't know for sure. But if something does happen, it's essential you do exactly as I say."

Barkov released Will's hand, glanced at Sentinel with a faint smile on his face, and looked back at Will. "There are only two men in the world who have the authority to give me orders. One of them is the commander in chief of the ground forces, and the other is the president of Russia. However"—his eyes flickered—"I will concede that just for today you may have some authority over me."

Will heard Laith's deep voice. "All's quiet."

And he heard Ross's strong Scottish lilt. "I can't see any unusual movement, but I'm having to cover an entire mountainside plus the lake, road, and lodge."

Barkov gestured toward the table and chairs. "Gentlemen, shall we sit?"

Sentinel grabbed a chair. "My colleague will stay with us but not at this table."

"As you wish." Barkov sat down, glancing at Will. "Do what you need to do."

Will sat on the floor, pointing his assault rifle at the door.

Sentinel was leaning forward across the table, speaking quietly to Barkov. "Sir, we have little time, so I'll come straight to the point. We know that a Russian colonel is planning to misuse the weapons in his possession to spark war between Russia and America."

"Name?"

"Taras Khmelnytsky."

Barkov laughed. "Where did you hear this?"

"We know for certain that this is what he's planning to do."

"He's a Hero of the Russian Federation, and he'd know that we'd lose in a war with America. Are you suggesting he's working for the Americans?"

"No. He's working alone."

Ross's voice spoke in Will's earpiece. "I've just completed a hundred-and-eighty-degree sweep of the area before me and—" Loud static sounded.

"Say again, Ross. You broke up." Will concentrated on his earpiece.

There was more static before Will heard Ross say, "Damn terrain. I said, I've seen nothing."

"All right. Laith, Roger?"

"Nothing."

Sentinel's voice was now very quiet. "I think he wants to bring the countries to war so that he can take over Russia."

Barkov shook his head. "You cannot expect me to believe this."

"I can, and I need you to do something for me."

"If you think I'm going to take this to Platonov, you're mistaken."

"I wouldn't ask you to speak to your commander in chief. You'd be compromised. But I do want you to turn on the beacons attached to the nuclear devices in Khmelnytsky's possession."

"And give you the grid reference of his base of operations?"

"Precisely."

Barkov looked angry. "This smells to me like subterfuge."

"It's not. We're desperate. We've got to stop him."

"I think this is a charade . . . the men here . . . the idea that someone out there wants to kill me. A charade."

A shot rang out in the distance. Will instantly jumped to his feet, gripping his assault rifle tight, and ran to one side of the windows. "What's happening? Was that you, Ross?!"

There was static in his earpiece before Roger's frantic voice came over the air. "Ross's just shot one of my incendiary devices. Ross, what's going on?"

There was more static, then another shot. Will glanced out of the window and just as quickly pulled his head and body back behind the cover of the wall. Ross had shot a second incendiary device. Two trees were on fire; black smoke billowed from them very close to the lodge. Will looked at Barkov. "Get flat on the floor by the back wall!"

Sentinel was on his feet, moving to the corner of the room, where he grabbed a QBZ-95G resting upright on its butt. "His communication system's down. But he must have spotted a sniper."

One with thermal imagery.

A third shot rang out, followed by a fourth, fifth, and sixth.

"Ross!" Will pressed one hand against his throat mic. "Can you hear me? Where's the hostile?"

Another three shots rang out.

Laith screamed, "That's all of them! The whole damned place in front of the lodge is ablaze!"

Will glanced at Barkov. The man had followed his instructions and was lying down behind the table.

But Barkov muttered, "Give me a gun."

"Stay where you are!" Will swung his gun through the window's glass, moved the barrel to form a large hole in it, and stood exposed, searching the outside ground for signs of Razin. But the fire from the trees was now abating, and the dampening effect of the snow on them had produced a two-hundred-foot-tall and five-hundred-foot-wide thick black wall of smoke. He cursed. Razin was blind to them, but they were now blind to him without Ross's communications system working. His heart pounded. He looked at Sentinel; the man's eyes were narrow, and he was gripping his gun while standing by one side of the window.

Sentinel muttered, "Maybe Ross's system's not down. This is starting to feel wrong."

"I know." Will shook his head, his mind racing. He stopped shaking his head as one stark thought pushed all others aside. His heart pumped faster; adrenaline coursed through his body. "Roger, Laith, I think Razin's taken Ross's rifle and fired at the incendiary devices. I don't think he's using thermal imagery. I think he shot the devices to make us blind."

So that he could move in close without being seen.

"You could be wrong, Will." Roger's tone of voice was anything but accusatory, but Will knew the CIA man had to make the point.

"I could be fucking wrong!" He gripped his gun tighter. "Ross's communications could be down. But it doesn't feel right."

"I hear you."

Will closed his eyes, then opened them. "Roger, I've got to stay here."

"I know what you're thinking. Laith and I will get him."

Will nodded. "All right. But move fast."

Will looked at Barkov. "If we don't get him, will you turn on the beacons?"

Barkov looked uncertain.

"Will you turn on the fucking beacons?"

Barkov nodded. "All right."

"In that case, here's your weapon." Will withdrew his handgun and slid it across the floor to the general.

The Russian grabbed the pistol, expertly checked its workings, rose to a crouch, and looked at Sentinel.

Laith's words were nearly breathless; it was clear that he was running fast. "We're out of the lodge, moving along the mountainside."

Will looked out of the window, but the wall of smoke was still thick and prevented him from seeing the CIA men.

Sentinel looked at him sharply. "Dash for the car?"

Will thought rapidly. "Not yet. But we need to be ready. All of us, downstairs."

They moved to the first-floor lounge. Will pointed at the kitchen. "In there." The lounge had two sash windows that opened vertically. Will yanked the first one up three inches, pulled out the pin from a stun grenade, jammed the grenade in the open gap, and ensured that it was held fast with the heavy window pressing firm against the grenade's lever. He did the same with the room's other window and his second stun grenade. Moving to the lodge's front door, he took out a thin piece of cotton, opened the door a few inches, primed and placed his last grenade on the floor within the gap, pulled the door closed onto the grenade, and tied the door firmly by wrapping the cotton around its handle and a lock on the door frame. Providing that the grenades weren't spotted, a man who opened the windows or pulled back the door, while easily snapping the thread, would be in for a big surprise. The grenades were primed to explode the instant the levers were opened.

Will jogged into the kitchen and shut the door behind him.

They waited for ten minutes with Will pointing his gun at the door.

Roger's voice sounded in his earpiece. The CIA officer's words sent a shiver down Will's spine.

"Ross's dead, and we've found his rifle. There's no sign of Razin. Somehow he must have got past us. But my God, Ross has been butchered!"

Will shouted, "Get back to us!"

"On our way!"

The noise of the stun grenade exploding in the adjacent bedroom was deafening. His ears ringing, Will dived to the side of the closed door, screaming, "He's here!"

Sentinel dropped low into a crouch, pointing his assault rifle at the door. Barkov did the same.

Sentinel called, "I've got the door covered. Get in there and take him down while he's still disoriented."

Will instantly rose, his weapon held high, and kicked the door open. The front door was ajar, but the room looked empty. It was not. He was grabbed from the side and hurled across the room with tremendous force. Crashing against the far wall, he winced in severe pain, twisted, and started crawling toward his discarded rifle. But then he saw the back of a man, saw that man drop low by the doorway just as one of Sentinel's bullets whistled over his head, heard the hostile's gun fire twice, and saw the man enter the next room. Gasping for air and still lying on the ground, Will reached his weapon and pointed it at the doorway.

Razin emerged from the room holding Sentinel by the throat and using him as a shield. Sentinel's white combat jacket was soaked in blood, clearly from a bullet wound to his upper body. Razin held a handgun jammed against his temple. Razin's large fist was wrapped around not only the pistol's handgrip but also a grenade. Will knew it was not the type of grenade that would merely stun.

Will took aim. Enough of Razin's head was visible for

him to easily kill the man. He started pulling back the trigger, but hesitated. A bead of sweat ran down his face.

Sentinel's expression was one of absolute pain; his eyes were narrow. "Kill him!"

Will tightened his grip on his trigger.

Razin smiled, moving his captive a few feet into the bedroom. "If you shoot me, I'll involuntarily squeeze the trigger and probably kill your colleague. But if I miss his head, my hand will certainly release the grenade and this room will be blown to pieces."

Sentinel's eyes were now wide, staring straight at Will. It was clear that the MI6 officer had not known about the grenade. Like Will, he would be rapidly trying to decide what should be done.

Razin tightened his grip around Sentinel's throat, causing Sentinel to make a choking sound, and moved farther across the room. Will's heart was beating so fast he thought it might explode.

Razin and Sentinel were now ten feet from Will, moving toward the exit. Will kept his gun trained on Razin's head. If he shot him, they'd all die. That was a sacrifice Will was prepared to make, because Razin's death was all that mattered. But it was an unnecessary sacrifice. Roger and Laith were on their way back. Maybe Razin didn't know they were out there. If so, they'd have the element of surprise and could take him down when he was no longer holding the grenade.

The Spetsnaz commander squeezed his hand again. Sentinel's eyes shut; he was unconscious. Razin reached the doorway. "I told you we'd meet again." He flicked the hand holding the gun, tossing his grenade at Will, and instantly returned the gun to Sentinel's head and dragged him out of the building. The grenade was still in midair as Will thrust his body up, sprinted, and dived headfirst through one of the closed sash windows. He heard glass shatter, Razin's grenade explode, and the stun grenade he had jammed under the window ignite and cause brilliant white light and piercing noise to encapsulate his mind and body as he thumped onto the ground.

His body was in agony as a result of the shards of glass sticking in him, though the pain felt as if it belonged to someone else. Nothing seemed real except the noise and light that were gripping him with unrelenting ferocity.

One second, one minute, or one hour later—he had no way of knowing—a hand gripped his arm and hauled him to his feet. He staggered; white light remained all around him, but within it he saw two hazy dark silhouettes of men. They seemed to be talking, though their voices sounded distant and nonsensical. He spun around and vomited into the white light. The voices became louder, sounded urgent, then distinct.

"Will! Will!"

He shook his head, opened and shut his eyes, and tried to think. He breathed deeply, attempting to muster all of his remaining strength to focus his mind and body and make the white light and noise go away.

"Will!"

He felt another arm grab him, felt his body being

marched over the ground while being held in the viselike grips on either side of him, and he heard one of the voices again. "Keep him moving until his balance returns."

The white light began to fade. The noise began to ebb. He started seeing dots and shapes; they grew larger until he realized they were trees. He sucked in a lungful of air; the act caused him to gag and vomit again. But this time he saw his vomit land on a surface that was not light, but snow. He frowned, staring down at his feet for a while.

"Will?"

He blinked, stayed still for a moment longer, breathed slowly, then lifted his body until he was upright. One of the hands holding him released its grip. Will nodded. The other hand let go of him. He heard boots crunch over snow. He looked around. Roger and Laith were in front of him.

"Can you see and hear us?"

Will nodded again. He took a step forward. One of his knees buckled and he nearly fell to the ground, but he managed to put another foot forward quickly and stay on his feet. Looking at his legs, he saw large pieces of glass sticking out of them. He ignored them and looked at the CIA men. "The Mercedes?"

"Gone. It was half a mile down the road before we even got back to the lodge. I'd say Razin's at least five miles away now, probably more. Even if we knew where he was going, we wouldn't have a chance in hell of catching up with him."

"Barkov?"

"Dead. He's got a bullet between his eyes." Laith shook his head. "No one else is in the lodge."

Will looked up at the sky. Large snowflakes fell over his face. He felt utter frustration and despair. "I had him in my sights. I could easily have killed him." He returned his gaze to his colleagues. "*Why's* he taken Sentinel alive?"

Roger shrugged. "To get the location of the remaining agents?"

"I think he already knows their location." Will kicked at the snow. "But if not, there would have been easier ways to find out where they live, rather than risk his life by trying to capture Sentinel alive."

Laith asked, "Where are the agents?"

"Spread out across Russia." Will became still as a thought came to him. "*That's* his problem. Every murder is taking too long." He nodded. "Perhaps it's not information he wants. Maybe he intends to *use* Sentinel."

Roger agreed. "Use him to summon his agents to one location."

Will pulled out shards of glass from his jacket. "Yes, he'll torture Sentinel until the man's mind is broken."

"He resisted torture for years when he was in prison. Razin will know that."

"That was a long time ago. Methods to extract information have become more advanced." Will thought about the drugs that had been put in him during the Program exercise in the States. "Still, he should be able to hold out for a few days." He shook his head. The prospect of

Sentinel's torture repulsed him. It should never have come to this. He should have refused to let Sentinel go ahead with the Barkov meeting. Fixing his gaze on the CIA officers, he said, "We've got two priorities now: stopping Razin, and rescuing Sentinel. I've already set in motion a strategy to get Razin away from the bombs, but I'll need you to help me track down Sentinel's location."

Laith asked, "How are we going to do that?"

"We have cash, passports, spare clothes to make us look normal, a vehicle, and weapons." Will nodded. "We'll use those things to try to get him back."

"You also need to notify the Agency so that we can get their help. They should give us every available resource they have."

Will smiled, though now he felt nothing but anger and a total focus. "For the time being, we can't talk to the Agency."

Laith looked incredulous. "You've got to tell Patrick and Alistair that Sentinel's been captured!"

Will shook his head. "I'm not going to do that."

"God damn it, Will. You're making the wrong decision."

Will breathed in deeply as he looked across the Ural Mountains. "I can't talk to Alistair or Patrick because they would never authorize what I'm going to do next."

TWENTY-SIX

It was midday. Will and his CIA colleagues were still in the vicinity of the lodge. White clouds lay low in the sky; snow fell fast on the ground. The black smoke from the trees was gone.

Will and Laith were on the other side of the lake. Roger was a mile away by the lodge, observing the mountain road in case any concerned civilians had seen the smoke and were coming to offer their help or armed police were coming to investigate the sounds of gunfire. But everywhere around them was silent, peaceful.

Will looked at the mountains, at the tranquil lake, and at the snow that seemed to be cleansing the beautiful grounds around them. An eagle flew from one of the mountaintops and drifted. Will watched its graceful movements. He looked at Ross's dead body. The poor man had been sliced open from the lower abdomen to the base of his chest plate. His intestines, liver, and other entrails had spilled out.

Laith glanced at the distant lodge, across the lake. "We haven't got time to clear up all this mess."

Will nodded. "I'm going to leave cash in the lodge for the asset. But we can't expect the owner to dispose of the bodies." Will kept his gaze on Ross. The Scot's eyes were wide in an expression of absolute terror and pain.

"Well, we've got a problem. There's no boat to take them out onto the lake, and swimming them out there would be suicidal." Laith stamped a foot on the frozen ground. "Plus, no chance of digging graves."

The eagle emitted a high-pitched scream. It moved so gracefully, yet seemed so distant. But Will knew it could quickly swoop on its prey and rip it apart with a brutal and immediate savagery. "I'll bring Barkov's body out here. Let the animals have them. There's nothing else we can do." He knelt down and patted a hand on Ross's blood-soaked jacket. "Doesn't make it right, though."

"Nope, it never is."

"Did you examine the area around here?"

"Yes. It took me an hour to find, but the snow indentations are clear—Razin was lying about five hundred feet away, farther up the mountain. Bastard was watching Ross and the lodge the whole time."

Will stood and rubbed his facial stubble, knowing that Ross's blood would now be on his face. "He must have been here hours before us, maybe longer." Even though he hated Razin's actions, he couldn't help but admire the man's professionalism. "Tomorrow night we need to be in Moscow. We're going to do something unexpected."

"Fine by me." The big ex-Delta man sighed. "But I still think we need backup."

"You'll change your mind when I tell you what we're going to be doing."

Laith smiled. "Patrick told me and Roger to report back if you started disobeying protocols again."

As Will had done in his last mission with the two CIA officers.

"Go ahead, but you'll be making a mistake."

The American said quietly, "We're saying nothing."

Will frowned. "Why?"

Laith moved closer to Will; he was at eye level. "Because we *hope* you know what you're doing." His smile faded. "But we also worry that you've met your match, that you won't succeed."

Will held his gaze. "I'll succeed. The *bastard's* time is running out. Soon he'll make a mistake."

"You're that confident?"

Will studied his colleague. "No."

"I thought so."

"You knew so."

"Yeah." Laith moved back. "I believe you'll succeed. But the question is whether you'll do it in time to stop a war."

TWENTY-SEVEN

Will stood on the side of Ulitsa Noviy Arbat in the heart of Moscow's government district. The large Moskva River was easily visible at the end of the main road. To his left was a thin strip of parkland with tall office buildings behind it. To his right were large, modern-looking government administrative buildings. It was early evening and dark, though street and building lights and a full moon made everything around him easily visible. Cars drove steadily along the road, their headlights illuminating the snow on the ground and flakes falling through the air. There were no pedestrians to be seen; this busy route was for vehicles only. Roger was five hundred feet to his south, beside the river on Smolenskaya Naberezhnaya. Laith was two hundred feet east, directly behind Will on Ulitsa Noviy Arbat. And though they couldn't see it, a mile farther to the east was the Kremlin.

Will checked his watch. It was 6:14 P.M. In his earpiece, he heard Roger's voice. "Nothing yet. But he left at this time yesterday, so stand by to hear from me."

Will wrapped his arms around his civilian windbreaker jacket and felt Moscow's icy air penetrate the fabric of his jeans. He stamped his boots on the ground. "Understood."

Roger spoke again, his voice quiet and tense. "You still have time to change your mind."

"I know, but we're going through with this."

Roger made a sound like a sigh. "This is fucking crazy."

Will glanced over his shoulder. He couldn't see Laith but knew the man was secreted in the parkland by the road. "Laith, all set?"

"Damn right." The former Delta Force operative sounded totally focused.

"Good." Will looked back toward the river. "Remember. Keep everyone alive."

"We know." Roger went quiet for a few seconds before saying, "Hold. The embassy's gates are opening."

Will narrowed his eyes, waiting for Roger to speak again.

"Two BMW saloon cars and one SUV exiting." Roger's words were barely audible.

Will held his breath.

"It's not our target. It's the ambassador and his bodyguards."

Will cursed and checked his watch again.

"The gates are closing." Roger's slow breathing was heavy; his voice sounded frustrated. "I've been watching this place all day. I saw him go in and haven't seen him leave. He *has* to still be here."

"Be patient. I'm sure he's still in the embassy." But Will examined every car that drove past him in case the target had used another concealed exit from the embassy to get to the road to access his home on Bolotnaya Ploshchad'. One vehicle passed close to him and threw up a wave of icy slush off the road and onto his body. Will brushed the slush from his legs and jacket while watching the car's driver. The man looked old and waved a hand apologetically. Will looked in the approximate direction of Roger, focusing solely on his earpiece.

It was a further ten minutes before Roger spoke. "A silver Audi's just pulled up on Smolenskaya Naberezhnaya, a hundred feet from the embassy gates. Two men are inside."

Will grabbed his throat mic. "FSB?"

"For sure." Roger went quiet for a while. "They're just waiting."

"Assessment?"

"They look routine. The same tail that was on our target yesterday."

"Okay." A gust of wind blew snow along the road from the river. Will momentarily shut his eyes as the stuff struck his face. When he opened them, he saw an army truck passing right by him. He held his breath as he casually watched the half-open rear of the truck and the many soldiers inside disappear down the road. For the briefest of moments he wondered if his intentions were too much, too risky, if he *should* abort this mission. But he knew that his only hope of rescuing Sentinel lay in doing something that few would dare attempt in the epicenter of Moscow.

"Gates are opening again."

Will froze.

"Nothing yet. Hold." Roger went silent for several seconds. "Okay, now I've got engine noises, I've got . . . I've got headlamps." Three seconds passed. "Two vehicles. Both Range Rovers. Car in front has two men—definitely the protection detail. Car behind has one driver and no passengers. Driver is . . . yes, driver is target. Repeat, driver in vehicle two is target!"

Will shouted, "Move, Roger!"

"Like I needed to be told!" Roger's voice was nearly breathless. The man was running at full sprint to the team's parked vehicle on a side road between the river-straddling Smolenskaya Naberezhnaya and the road that Will and Laith were on. It was the same side road that their target and his bodyguards would be turning onto in seconds. "I'm at our vehicle. Fuck. Okay. Don't think they spotted me."

Roger had covered three hundred feet of snow-covered ground between his observation point and the vehicle in twelve seconds.

"I'm mobile, a hundred feet behind the protection detail, our target, and the FSB men who're tailing them.

I can see brake lights. The convoy's turning onto Ulitsa Noviy Arbat. You should see them."

Will did see them. He took quick sidesteps into the park so that he was hidden in undergrowth, but the two Range Rovers were still easily visible in the medium traffic on the road. As was the Audi containing the two FSB men, who would certainly be armed but whose job was to merely follow their target, make themselves visible to him, and thereby silently tell him that if he did anything silly in their country they would punish him.

Will crouched low. "Laith?"

"Yeah, I've got them." The American's words were slow and precise.

Roger's vehicle emerged onto the road, four vehicles behind the convoy. Roger said, "Okay, stand by." He went silent. When he spoke again, his tone of voice was one of absolute command. "Stand by. Stand by. Stand by. Okay"—more silence—"let's go!"

Will sprinted out of cover, pointing his handgun at the Range Rover containing the two bodyguards. At the same time, he heard Laith's AMR-2 sniper rifle fire two rounds into the SUV's engine block, causing the vehicle to skid, then stop suddenly. In his peripheral vision, he saw Roger drive his vehicle around four civilian cars, then ram his vehicle into the rear of the FSB Audi, pushing it into the back of the Range Rover containing the target. All vehicles in the convoy were now stationary and trapped between Roger's car and the immobilized Range Rover.

The two guards wasted no time, jumping out of their vehicle with pistols in their hands. Will sprinted to them even faster, and when he'd nearly reached their vehicle, he twisted, dived, and rolled on the road as one of the men raised his gun and sent a shot toward him. Then he sprang to his feet so that he was directly in front of the man. The bodyguard tried to sweep a leg against Will's ankles to upset Will's balance, which would cause him to stagger back and give the man sufficient distance to lift his gun again and shoot Will. But Will anticipated the movement, took one step back as the man's leg swept through nothing but air, stepped forward again, and punched him in the chest with sufficient force to slam him back against the SUV. He took another step forward, jabbed two fingers into the man's eyes, and brought the butt of his handgun down hard onto his shoulder blade. The man collapsed unconscious to the ground, and as he did so, Will ducked low. He was glad he did. A bullet from the other guard on the far side of the Range Rover raced through the air where he'd just been standing.

Laith shouted, "Drop your weapon and get on the ground!" Will glanced right and saw the SOG officer standing in the center of the road, only thirty feet away, with his rifle held at eye level and pointed at the second bodyguard. "Flat, facedown, hands clasped together and arms pointing at the sky. Fucking do it, or I'll put a bullet in your skull!"

Will glanced left. Roger was on foot by the Audi. One of the FSB men was motionless by his feet. But the second

Russian was moving quickly around the other side of the vehicle, a pistol gripped in both his hands. Will called out, "Laith?"

"Yeah, you're clear. I've got this man covered."

Will sprang to his feet and jumped onto the hood of the second Range Rover, ignoring the target, who was still in the vehicle. He ran over its roof, jumped onto the Audi, and dived right over it toward the FSB man, who was now at the rear of the car and had leveled his gun at Roger. Crashing midair into the man, Will wrapped his arms around the Russian's upper body and limbs, pinning his arms tight against his sides before they hit the ground. He kept squeezing him tight. Roger appeared before them, nodded at Will, then smashed a fist into the Russian's head. His head slumped to one side. But he was alive.

Will rolled away from the man just as he saw the target in the second Range Rover try to drive his vehicle out of the area. His Range Rover drove into the stationary SUV in front of it, moving it a couple of feet. He reversed into the Audi but was unable to move that car, as it was held firm by Roger's vehicle. Driving forward again, he pushed the protection detail's Range Rover a further few feet. He now had enough room to make a tight turn out of the stationary convoy and speed away from the trap. Will pushed himself up and sprinted toward the car as he saw it move back one last time and point its front tires right so that it would be ready to escape. He heard the vehicle's gears change and the accelerator being depressed. He ran as fast as he was able and reached the driver's door just as the car started to move forward. Smashing the window, he grabbed the driver's throat, stayed firmly in position as the car swerved right and away from the other SUV blocking it, lurched toward the ignition, and turned off the engine. The vehicle slowed, then stopped.

Breathing fast, Will looked at the target. "You're coming with me."

Pulling the struggling driver out of the vehicle by his throat, Will looked around. The place looked chaotic. Civilian cars were immobile and at odd angles on the road behind Roger's vehicle. The men and women inside them were watching all that was happening before them with looks of shock and fear. Some of them had cell phones planted against the sides of their faces. He heard sirens coming from multiple directions and knew that they would belong to law enforcement and maybe even specialist FSB units. Will wasted no time and began to drag his captive backward until he was by Roger. He looked at the CIA officer. "Is your vehicle operable?"

Roger nodded. "Reckon so."

Roger moved into the driver's seat of his vehicle and reversed the car, and as he did so Will heard the sound of metal tearing apart. Roger stopped the car, kept the engine running, got out, and opened one of the rear passenger doors. "The vehicle's okay. But we need to get the hell out of here, right now."

Will looked at Laith. The American was still pointing his AMR-2 at the head of the prone but conscious guard. Will spoke into his throat mic: "Laith, we've got to move."

The sirens were drawing closer.

Laith smiled at the man close to his feet. In his earpiece, Will heard Laith's words to the bodyguard. "Sorry about this."

Laith spun his rifle around and swept it through the air, smacking its butt against the side of the guard's head. He crouched down, placed his fingers against the man's throat to check his pulse, muttered "You'll live," and jogged over to Roger's car.

Seconds later they were all in the vehicle and Roger was driving the car at high speed along the road. Laith and Will were in the backseat; their captive was lying on the floor with their boots holding him firmly in place.

As they moved steadily along the route that took them west, away from the city, Will looked down and smiled, wondering what Alistair would think if he could see him now.

With a boot on the MI6 Head of Moscow Station.

TWENTY-EIGHT

I t was either this place or a local school." Roger rubbed his fatigued face.

Will looked around. They were in a small Russian Orthodox church, near woods and a tiny village that was fifty miles west of the outskirts of Moscow. Roger had chosen the venue because, like schools, most churches were empty at night, were easy to break into, and usually did not contain valuables deemed worthy of protection by alarm systems. The church had wooden pews to the left and right of the center aisle Will was standing in. The place was in total darkness, save for the light emitted by the flashlights that Will, Roger, and Laith carried. Their beams produced snapshot images of religious icons, prayer books, free-standing lamps, chandeliers, unlit candles, three-barred metal crosses, alcoves, wall-mounted paintings of various apostles and Jesus Christ, and an altar table that had marble pillars on either side of it. In front of the altar was a large chair. Seated within it was their prisoner. His arms and legs had been expertly tied to the chair with rope by Laith, who was standing close to the man.

Will glanced at Roger and quietly asked, "Are you sure we weren't followed here?"

Roger shrugged. "There were only a few cars on the road leading to this place. They all looked normal."

Will smiled, although his mood was cold. "Good." He swung his flashlight back toward the prisoner. The man's head was slumped down, though he was awake and unharmed. "Let's begin."

Will walked to the front of the pews and sat down on them so that he was directly opposite the prisoner, fifteen feet distant. He positioned his flashlight on the pew so that it shone directly into the man's face, stretched out his legs, and leaned back to rest his head in his interlocked hands. Laith sat down on the far right-hand side of the front pew; Roger perched on the far left-hand side of the front pew. Both men pointed their lights at the prisoner. Everything in the church was now in total darkness, save the altar and the trussed man before it.

When Will spoke, his voice was calm, of medium volume, and very controlled. "Lift up your head, please."

The prisoner did not move.

"Lift up your head."

The man remained motionless.

Will let out a long sigh. "Would you like me to lift up your head for you? I could do so in a way that would make you never want to lower your head again."

Nothing happened at first. Then the prisoner gradually lifted his head, squinting as the flashlights' beams struck his face. The man was clean-shaven, had hair that was now ruffled but would normally have been carefully held in place by creams, was wearing an expensive suit, shirt, and tie and had a slender build. He was fifty-one years old.

Will nodded, even though he knew that the prisoner could not see him and his men. "That's better." He placed one foot over the other. "We need to make our introductions. Your name is Guy Louis Harcourt-DeVerre. You are a British national, come from a family of nobility, and hold the aristocratic title of baron. But, more important than that, you are the MI6 Head of Moscow Station."

The prisoner's eyes seemed to adjust to the light. His eyes widened; his expression was one of anger. "A full introduction requires me to know your names." Guy's accent was polished, very well spoken.

Will glanced in the direction of Roger and Laith before returning his attention to the MI6 officer. "We're very dangerous men. That's all you need to know."

Guy smiled, but the anger was still evident. "Judging by the accents I heard in the car coming here, you are clearly very dangerous English and American men."

"Maybe. Or perhaps we're SVR or FSB officers posing as Westerners."

Guy slowly looked around, then back at Will's flash-light. "Is this an inquisition or an execution?"

"That depends on how you answer my next question."

Guy kept staring at the light; he showed no signs of fear. Will had expected as much from a senior MI6 officer of Guy's stature.

Will unclasped his hands and adjusted his position so that he was leaning forward. "Where is Taras Khmel-nytsky, the man who has the MI6 code name Razin?"

Guy chuckled. "I've never heard of him."

Will kept his voice calm and neutral. "Yes, you have. You know about Razin because you work for him."

Guy smiled. "I've no idea what you're talking about."

Will stared at the officer for a moment before saying, "Your response does not help your situation."

This time Guy laughed loudly, his voice echoing around the empty church. "My situation?" His laugh suddenly stopped. "My situation will in all probability lead to my death. You'll do what you want to me. But whatever you do, I can't give you an answer that I don't have."

Will leaned farther forward. "Listen to me very carefully. I've sat where you are now sitting a hundred times. I know all about the games that can be deployed to resist interrogation. I *know* what is going through your brain right now. Your primary objective will be to draw out our discussion for as long as possible, with the hope that you'll be rescued by British or Russian forces. At the same time, you will be making rapid and evolving assessments of your captors: trying to ascertain what our objectives are, what kind of men we are, and how far we are willing to go to get what we need. When you realize that we are men who will stop at nothing, you will start feeding us half-truths and lies to keep our attention and to make you appear cooperative. Then, when that doesn't work, you'll feign shock, fear, and maybe illness to try to bring the interrogation to a temporary halt. And ultimately, when that tactic fails, you will ask us for things: water, food, for your ropes to be loosened, anything to make us think you've moved to a new level of resignation to your plight and are about to give us what we want. Time is the only weapon you have, and I concede it's a powerful weapon. But I regret to say that time is my enemy and you'll have no chance to play out your games."

Guy stared in the direction of Will; his face still showed no fear. "Then we are in a bit of a bind, wouldn't you say?"

"I'd say we're in a terrible bind. But I think I have a solution to our predicament. Do you know what that is?"

Guy nodded. "Of course. You need to torture me. Though I must forewarn you that pain doesn't scare me and in any case I'll just tell you what you want to hear, but it won't be the truth."

"We'll see." Will looked toward Laith and said, "Get the box."

A few seconds later, Laith appeared next to Guy, carrying a five-sided metal box and some rope. He placed the items on the floor, pulled open Guy's jacket, and ripped apart his shirt so that his naked torso was visible. Lifting up the box, he carefully positioned its open side flush against the MI6 officer's belly and began wrapping the rope over the box and around the man's body so that it was tightly fixed into position. Laith looked toward Will, nodded, and disappeared back to his seat on the pew.

Will smiled. "Do you know what that is?"

Guy remained calm. "I've no idea."

Will placed his hands together as if he was in prayer. "It's my means to accelerate matters." He narrowed his eyes. "I need to know the precise location of Razin. You're going to tell me. The box will make you do so."

The Head of Moscow Station shook his head before angling it to one side, frowning and then smiling. "I see. You've an explosive device inside the container. It'll detonate after a period of time unless I give you what you want. The bomb will be small enough to destroy my organs but not large enough to hurt you." He grinned. "I regret to tell you that I don't have the secret you want. And even if I did, my life has been devoted to protecting secrets. I'd rather lose my life in an instant than give you what you want and live out the rest of my life feeling that I had betrayed not only my employers and my work but also myself." His face turned to one of anger; his voice deepened. "Let your bomb go off. I don't care."

Will stretched his fingers. "I thought you'd say that, and for that reason I'll tell you that there's no bomb inside the metal box. An explosive would give you far too quick a death. Instead, there's something inside the container that ordinarily you wouldn't fear. But today you're going to be terrified of it." Will stilled his hands.

"Inside the box is a rat. It's sedated. But I estimate that in fifteen minutes it will awaken. Upon doing so it will feel disoriented and scared and will draw upon its survival instincts to do everything it can to get out of its prison. It will scratch and use its powerful teeth to try to force a route through the metal sides of the box but will quickly realize that it stands no chance of doing so. Then it will feel that one side of its prison is softer than the others. It will decide to bite and claw its way through that surface."

A bead of sweat ran down one side of Guy's face. "A rat?"

"We didn't have time to come up with a more refined solution to our bind. For that I'm sorry, because when the rat awakens you're going to suffer the most agonizing death. It will burrow through your abdominal muscles, tear through your stomach lining, and gnaw through your intestines and liver and kidneys. You won't die straightaway, because the rat will have a hard task. I think it will take at least thirty minutes for the rat to tunnel its way through your torso until it has emerged out of your back. And at every stage of the rat's journey, you'll feel it inside you, scrabbling and ripping through your body."

Another bead of sweat fell over Guy's face before dropping to the floor. "I'll immediately lose consciousness and will be of no use to you."

Will shook his head, smiling. "We'll pump your body with adrenaline and saline solutions to keep you awake."

Guy was silent for a few moments. When he spoke, his

words were slow and angry. "Then I'm in the company of demons."

Will shrugged. "I've not told you anything to suggest otherwise."

Guy looked quickly at the box on his belly before glancing away, clearly deep in thought.

Will kept his attention firmly on his prisoner, studying the officer, wondering whether the man would fall for his ruse. Because there was no rat in the box.

Guy looked toward Will. "I'll embrace the pain . . . let it shut down"—his voice was hesitant—"shut down my mind and body."

"I wish you luck because I've no idea if you'll be able to do that. I've been tortured before, but I've never experienced what's going to happen to you. This is a new experience for both of us." He moved his arm in front of his flashlight's beam. "I'd say the rat could awaken in ten minutes, maybe less."

Guy shook his head; he was now clearly agitated. "Who are you? Who sent you?"

Will leaned back. "I'm a man who must capture and kill Razin. I sent myself."

"You'd let this happen to me? You'd just sit there and watch me die in agony?"

Will chuckled. "No, not just watch it happen. As the rat goes through you, I'll keep asking you about the whereabouts of Razin. And if you refuse to answer, I'll personally strap a metal plate onto your back so that the rat has no chance of escape there and will have to turn around and find another route out of your body."

"Questions and answers won't matter at that stage." Guy's face was now covered in sweat. "I'll be dead or dying by then."

"You'll most certainly *want* to be dead by then. You'll beg me to end your life with a bullet in your brain. I'll be willing to do that if you tell me the truth." Will leaned forward again, and spoke in a near whisper. "But does it need to come to that? There's still time for me to remove the box."

Guy lowered his head; his breathing was fast. When he looked up, his face seemed terrified, confused, but it still displayed some strength and defiance. "I'm an MI6 officer. Men like me don't betray secrets."

"And yet you've betrayed secrets in the past." Will raised his voice. "In any case, we shall have to see if others agree with you. Perhaps some of your colleagues may also have an idea about Razin's location. And I wonder if they will be as resolute when confronted by unimaginable horror. If we don't get what we want from you, we'll follow every other member of Moscow Station to their homes, torture them in the same way, and slaughter their families until we get our answer." He moved his face into the light, knowing that Guy could now see him. "You can end this here, or you can allow me to escalate matters by murdering your entire station. Either way, I won't stop until I get the secret."

Anger was once again on Guy's face. "How could God let you into a place like this?"

"God?" Will laughed, but his tone held utter menace. "God has no jurisdiction over me."

Guy's head slumped down.

"Head up, I said!"

Guy lifted his head; his eyes were wet.

"The rat will be awake in minutes, maybe seconds."

Guy looked toward the ceiling and muttered, "Save me."

"Look at me. The only thing that matters is me!"

Guy did so. His breathing was very fast now.

"You need to make a decision." Will kept his face in the light. "Give me the location of Razin or die a horrendous death just before we leave to butcher your colleagues, their wives, and their children. The decision is yours and yours alone."

The Head of Moscow Station had tears rolling down his face. He shook his body, but the ropes and the heavy chair remained firm. "Get this thing off of me!"

"Not until you answer my question."

Roger spoke. "I reckon the rat will be waking up now."

"Get it off of me!"

Will narrowed his eyes. "I repeat, not until you answer my question."

Guy let out a scream, his face screwed up in terror. Gulping air, he shouted, "I'll tell you anything. Untie the box. Please. Please."

"No."

Guy was hyperventilating. Will stood, stepped quickly forward until he was right in front of the MI6 officer, placed one hand over the box, and pushed it tighter against his body. "It appears my colleague is right. I can feel movement against the inside of the box."

Guy stared with wide eyes at Will. His face was now a mess of sweat and tears. His body reeked of fear. "I'll tell you!"

"Where is he?"

Before Guy could respond, Roger shouted, "Smoke!"

Will spun around, pointing his flashlight left and right. He heard movement to either side of him and knew that Laith and Roger were taking up defensive positions. "What's happening?"

Roger did not answer but instead ran forward, his flashlight held firm against the side of his assault rifle. The beam from the flashlight moved toward the church's entrance. Then Will saw what Roger had seen or smelled. Black smoke was wafting through the air. It was moving from the entrance toward the altar.

Will positioned his flashlight on Roger, who was now on the other side of the church. "Smoke grenade?"

Roger pressed himself beside the doorway, waited a moment, placed a hand against the wooden door, winced, then stepped away from the exterior wall. "Not a grenade. This building's on fire."

Will's heart beat fast; he pulled out his handgun. "Razin!" He swung his light on Guy. "He's come to silence you."

Guy moaned. "Please take the box off me. I beg you."

Will ignored the man and shouted, "Laith! We need an exit!"

From the darkness, the paramilitary officer replied, "I'm working on it."

The smoke became thicker. Will began coughing. He unbuttoned the top of his jacket, pulled it up, and then closed it so that its collar was resting over the bridge of his nose, acting as a crude mask. Then he saw the first flames curling underneath the door. Soon there were more. Stained-glass windows burst as more smoke and flames moved into the church. Curtains caught fire, their dry fabric allowing the flames to accelerate up the walls. Sparks spat across the pews.

Laith shouted, "Run to my voice! I've found a side entrance!"

Roger dashed across the church. Will was about to move to check the exit but stopped as he felt something dripping on him. He pointed his flashlight at the roof. He saw one hole, then another, then many of them. Liquid was dripping through them, but within seconds it was pouring. His heartbeat increased as he realized what was happening. "Gasoline!"

He pulled out his military knife and ran toward Guy to cut him free of the ropes. But as he did so, liquid drenched the Head of Moscow Station. A spark jumped through air, landed on Guy's lap, and set his clothes on fire. Will recoiled from the intense blaze and heat.

"Will, we have to get out of here!" Laith's voice was desperate.

But Will tried to move closer to Guy. The man was screaming in agony; the smell of roasting flesh was in the air. More liquid fell onto Guy, and he became a human fireball. Gasoline from the other holes in the roof turned into columns of fire that rose up from the church floor to its ceiling. In the middle of them all, Guy rocked his body back and forth but could not free himself from his shackles. He stopped screaming. Will stopped moving.

"Will, come on!"

Will lifted his handgun, cursed everyone and everything, cursed himself, but at the same time decided that he was not going to let his prisoner die in agony. He pointed his gun at Guy's head and pulled the trigger.

He turned and saw flames race across the pews toward him. Sprinting to the right, he reached the wall and was grabbed by Laith and hurled out of the side door. He crashed onto snow-covered ground, was grabbed again, this time by Roger, and was lifted to his feet and pulled fast away from the church. After a hundred feet they stopped. Laith ran to them, his rifle held high, scouring the area around them. The small church was now engulfed in flames.

"Razin's got to be around here somewhere." Will gripped his handgun tight. "We split up and hunt him down."

A vehicle's tires screeched in the distance. The three intelligence officers swung their weapons in the approximate direction of the noise but could see nothing.

"He's getting away!" Roger moved his gun left and right. "Vehicle lights are off. He's at least a quarter mile away . . . I've got no shot." He lowered his rifle quickly and said, "To our car. Now!"

They ran away from the church into woods and continued for five hundred feet until they were close to the vehicle that Roger had carefully hidden between trees and undergrowth. Roger and Laith switched on their flashlights, spotted the car 150 feet away, and ran toward it. Will knew that Razin had driven away from the church along the only track leading to the place and that beyond it he would be joining a minor road that would continue for ten miles before branching into different directions. Roger's driving skills would give them an excellent chance of closing in on Razin so that his car would be visible before he took one of the exits off the minor road. But Will wondered why Razin had driven his car so noisily, betraying his exit route.

He suddenly realized why, causing his stomach to churn and his legs to pump harder as he raced to his CIA colleagues. He shouted, "Get down," leapt through the air, grabbed the Americans, and fell toward the ground while still holding them. Before they struck land, the car exploded, sending splinters of metal and glass in every direction.

The men lay on the snow, breathing fast, as pieces of debris fell over them. But none of them was harmed. Will pushed himself off the men, stood up, and stared at the decimated vehicle as it burned and emitted thick, noxious smoke from its melting tires. He shook his head as Roger and Laith got to their feet.

"Quick thinking." Laith brushed ash from his jacket.

Will rubbed his face. "Razin could have driven away

silently. Instead, he deliberately gunned his vehicle to make us dash to our car and either had a pretimed explosive in the car or used a detonator to explode our vehicle when he thought we were close enough." He stamped a boot on the snow in frustration.

Roger checked his assault rifle and handgun. "I've got thirteen bullets left in my rifle and one magazine left for my handgun."

Laith examined his weapons. "Six bullets for my rifle, eleven for my handgun."

Will did not need to check his pistol. "I'm down to seven bullets." He nodded at the burning wreck. "And my rifle was in there along with most of our other belongings." He looked at his colleagues. "How much cash have you got?"

Roger patted a jacket pocket. "Neither of us has used our cash. Between us we've got one point five million rubles."

The equivalent of approximately fifty thousand dollars.

"Which makes a total of seventy-five thousand dollars among the three of us."

A siren sounded in the distance, followed by another. Will said, "Shit."

Laith muttered, "Why the hell did Razin decide to kill Guy now?"

"Because he found out that others knew about Guy's treachery. And the only person who could have given him that information is Sentinel." Despite the heat emitting from the nearby burning wreck, Will shivered. "Like us, Razin must have been watching the embassy, waiting to follow Guy and kill him. But we stepped in first, and he tailed us to the church."

"So he's already started torturing Sentinel." Roger's words were solemn.

Will looked at the CIA officer, then at the distant burning church. "Yes, but I doubt he's broken him yet. I think Sentinel deliberately told Razin that we'd be going after Guy, hoping that it would give us one last chance to kill Razin." He looked down and muttered again, "Shit."

Roger placed a hand on Will's shoulder. "You thought Sentinel's strategy was too risky, and you were proven right. Your strategy to discredit Razin is where our hope lies. But as for Sentinel, there's nothing more you can do."

Will's mind raced. He thought about the profiles of Sentinel's tier-1 agents, every piece of information he'd read about them in the files in Langley, anything that might be useful. One name stood out. He looked at the CIA operatives. "I've got an idea that I wouldn't have tried at the outset of this mission, but now I think it might be worth a shot." He paused. "If I asked you both to stay in Russia a little longer, would you do so?"

"Fuck, yes."

"Damn right."

Will nodded. "Razin can't just detonate the bomb in a Russian installation and hope it sparks a war. His plan must be more precise than that."

The sirens were drawing closer.

"The key to finding Sentinel now lies in finding out where and when Razin intends to strike. And I think I know someone who might be able to get that information."

TWENTY-NINE

It was eleven A.M., and Will was in a cheap hotel room in the center of Moscow. He, Roger, and Laith had arrived at the hotel early that morning, having traveled nearly sixty miles on foot from the church to the city and having discarded all remaining weapons save their handguns. They had paid cash for their rooms and had told the receptionist that they did not want to be disturbed the rest of the morning.

Will stood in the center of the tiny, barely furnished bedroom wearing a towel wrapped around his waist and nothing else. His clothes hung over radiators, drying after he had hand washed them in the bathroom's sink and shower. There was a knock on the door. Will immediately moved to a side table and placed his fist over his pistol. The door opened. Will removed his hand from his gun as Roger entered and let the door swing shut behind him.

Roger smiled. "You're not going to make a pass at me, are you?"

Will smiled. "Fuck off. Did you get the flight?"

Roger rubbed his fatigued face. "I did."

"Excellent." Will picked up his travel bag and swung it onto the bed. "What time do we depart?"

"We need to be out of here in one hour."

"Okay."

Roger laughed. "If we'd been able to wait another fourteen hours, we could have saved ourselves $45,000 by getting a regular commercial flight."

Will snapped, "I can't afford to waste any time."

Plus they needed to avoid airport security so that they could get their guns through.

Roger nodded. "I know. How are you?"

Will frowned. "What do you mean?"

"It's a straightforward question. How are you feeling?"

Will stared at his colleague for a moment before replying, "I'm absolutely fine."

The tall American held his gaze and said softly, "Your plan to capture Guy was a good one. He was our most direct means to locate Razin. And you had no intention of harming Guy, just scaring him."

Will said quietly, "True. But ultimately it was me who put a bullet in his brain." He looked away. "I killed a British national, a senior member of MI6."

"You put him out of his misery." Roger was motionless.

"Some people in a similar position would have just let the bastard burn to death."

Will muttered, "Nobody's in my bloody position."

"I know." The ex–DEVGRU SEAL's voice was one of total sympathy. "That's why I asked."

Will turned on the shower, watched brown water emerge from the nozzle, and waited a moment before stepping into the cubicle when the water ran clear. Raising his face, he allowed the hot water to pour over his head and torso. He washed his grimy body with a bar of soap and tore open a small sachet of shampoo to use on his dark, cropped, greasy hair. Satisfied that he was clean, he closed his eyes and lowered his muscular physique until he was sitting on the floor with the water falling all over him.

He reflected on Roger's words and frowned. A memory came to him, one that he hadn't even known was in his head until just now.

Will was seated on a grass lawn. It belonged to his parents' house in the States. It was a sunny, warm day. He was a barefoot five-year-old wearing a University of Virginia shirt and jeans. His hair was blond in those days, and he had freckles across his nose and cheeks. His American father was walking toward him, wearing a smart dark suit and crisp white shirt. To the small boy, his daddy looked like a giant, but he had a smile on his kind face. Crouching down in front of Will, he rubbed the boy's arm and looked at the toy held in his hand. A green plastic handgun.

Will grinned and proudly held out the gun. His daddy took it, examined the pretend weapon, nodded, and gave it back to his son.

He said something that Will could not quite remember, something about toy guns being okay but real guns being bad.

The boy looked at his CIA father and giggled. He lowered his eyes and glimpsed something on his daddy's hip, visible between his open jacket. He pointed at the real gun.

His father looked down and quickly buttoned up his jacket to hide his sidearm. He looked perturbed as he placed both hands on Will's shoulders. His serious expression was quickly replaced by another smile. After kissing his son on the forehead, he walked away toward his car to go to work.

Later that year he was deployed by the CIA to Iran, where he was kidnapped and thereafter brutally murdered.

Will opened his eyes and swallowed hard to check the emotion he was feeling. He wished his father had been alive to watch and guide his growth into adulthood. More than anything, he wished he could have had the opportunity to share his first beer with the man and give him a promise not to lead a life filled with weapons and violence.

He pictured that little boy sitting on the grass and wondered how that innocent could have turned into a man who could calmly terrify a man in a Russian church before putting a bullet into his head.

He loathed what he sometimes had to do in his work.

No. The truth was more than that.

He loathed the person he'd become.

Forty-five minutes later, Will stood outside the shabby hotel dressed in a dark blue heavy wool suit, white shirt with French cuffs and silver cuff links, Royal Navy silk tie that he had bound into a Windsor knot, gleaming black brogues, leather gloves, and a smart overcoat. He was clean-shaven and had applied Chanel men's lotions and Platinum Égoïste eau de toilette to his body and face. In one hand he gripped his expensive leather travel bag containing his other hand-washed and dry clothes. Tucked into his belt, hidden against the small of his back, was his handgun.

Beside him were Roger and Laith. Both men were also immaculately dressed and carried their own bags. Roger hailed a taxi, and soon they were en route to Moscow's Vnukovo Airport.

They entered Terminal D, the place used for the airport's domestic flights. Roger led the way, walking quickly past ticket desks, passengers, flight crews, check-in desks, retail outlets, and approximately four hundred soldiers who were clearly about to embark on a military flight, until they were by a desk marked PLATINUM BUSINESS JETS. Will and Laith held back as Roger walked up to the man behind the desk, spoke inaudible words to him, nodded at his colleagues, and looked back at the official. The man beamed, jumped down from his stool, and walked around the desk holding a clipboard. Will and Laith moved up to Roger, carrying their bags.

The man shook their hands, muttered a few Russian words to Roger, then asked in English, "What business takes you to Vladivostok?"

Laith looked at him sternly. "Oil."

The man's smile widened. "My best customers are those in the oil industry." He beckoned toward a door marked VIP LOUNGE. "I'll take you through. We have a fast-track process for our guests which avoids the airport's security and baggage checks. You'll have a very comfortable flight with us. Men like you deserve only the very best in luxury travel."

One hour later, they were onboard a super-midsize Falcon 2000EX jet, traveling at an altitude of 37,000 feet. Will, Roger, and Laith were facing each other in sumptuous leather seats. Coffee and caviar were on the table between them. The seven other luxury seats in the plane were empty. A tall blond female attendant was the only other person in the passenger area; her duty was to ensure that they were given anything they wanted during the eight-hour flight across Russia to the eastern coastal city of Vladivostok.

Roger leaned forward to pick up some toast and caviar and took a mouthful of the food. "This is the most expensive civilian flight I've ever taken."

"I'm not complaining." Laith lit a Cuban Cohiba cigar,

supplied to him by the hostess, examined its burning embers, and blew a thin stream of smoke from his lips. "I can't remember the last time I could smoke on a flight."

Will drummed his fingers on an armrest. "Don't get too comfortable. We'll soon be living in shit again."

Roger smiled, taking another bite of his food. "Do you ever relax?"

Laith studied Will through narrow eyes. "Are you sure this trip is worth it? Is your plan going to work?"

"I think I can outsmart Razin and have him suspended or dismissed." Will rubbed his face. "But that doesn't mean I'll succeed in rescuing Sentinel."

"Then why the hell wouldn't you listen to me when I told you to call it in with the Agency and let them decide what to do now?" Laith shook his head; his expression was hostile.

Will frowned. "You've never struck me as a man who follows rules. On the contrary, aside from Roger, I can't think of any intelligence paramilitary officer who dislikes orders more than you."

Laith crushed his cigar in the ashtray. "Don't patronize me."

Roger quickly placed an arm on Laith's forearm, leaned toward Will, and said in a hushed, urgent voice, "I'm not sure I've ever seen a rule book for what we do. But right now I'm in agreement with my colleague. I don't think we should be doing this alone."

Will looked at both CIA SOG operatives. He said nothing for a while, deep in thought, but when he spoke his voice was measured and calm. "The Agency could send us a hundred operatives, but it wouldn't make a difference. So we need to turn this on its head and work with people who can help."

Laith frowned, then laughed. "You're crazy."

Will thought that Laith had a point. But he was still adamant that working with the Russians was the only way forward.

THIRTY

Will and Roger were stationary in an Audi A8 sedan, lent to them for a week by Platinum Business Jets, on Ulitsa Korabelnaya Naberezhnaya in Vladivostok. It was nine P.M., and the area around them was relatively quiet, with few cars passing by. Streetlamps were sporadic, snowfall was heavy, and visibility was poor. But five hundred feet behind them was the port, and moored within it were four easily visible and brightly illuminated Udaloy I destroyers.

Roger placed his cell phone on the dashboard and set it to speakerphone. "Laith, I'm moving in a few minutes."

Laith's response was instant. "Understood."

Laith was in a BMW 3 Series, also gifted to him for a few days, parked close by on Ulitsa Svetlanskaya.

Roger withdrew a pen, a single sheet of paper, and an envelope from an inner jacket pocket. Placing them next to the phone on the dashboard, he wrote a person's name and the words URGENT AND PRIVATE on the envelope using the Russian Cyrillic alphabet. He looked at Will. "Should I leave the sheet blank?"

Will shook his head. "That would look suspicious." He thought for a moment. "Write, 'My normal communications are compromised. I'll call you from a pay phone at ten A.M. tomorrow morning. You must be available to receive that call. Your friend.'"

Roger nodded as he wrote the words on the piece of paper. He folded the sheet and inserted it into the envelope, sealed it, and placed the letter into a pocket. After donning a fur hat, a scarf that he wrapped around his lower face, and thick-rimmed glasses with false lenses, he glanced at Will. "Okay?"

Will smiled. "You look barely recognizable but normal. In this weather, everyone's going to be covered up."

The CIA operative was quiet for a moment before asking, "You're sure I won't be grabbed by the guards?"

Will shrugged. "I can't be sure about anything."

But he hoped that at this hour there'd be only two or three low-ranking sailors at the reception desk who wouldn't dare to do anything to disrupt what should appear to them to be an emergency crash communication between a covert agent and his Russian handler.

Roger opened the door, allowing icy wind to enter the car. "See you soon." He stepped out of the vehicle, thrust his hands into his overcoat pockets, and walked off with his head bent low and shoulders hunched. Within seconds, he had disappeared into the night.

Will spoke loudly. "He's on his way."

Laith's voice responded, "Okay, I'm moving to get visibility of the building's main entrance." After forty seconds he spoke again. "I'm in position. I can see Roger walking to the building. He's stopped. He's checking his watch. He's looking around. He enters the building."

Will shivered, a mixture of fear and cold. Roger had entered the headquarters of the Russian navy's Pacific Fleet. It was adjacent to the naval docks but not part of a military base. Instead, it looked like any other important administrative building in the city. Roger would be handing the letter to one of the guards at the reception. Will hoped that the guard would instantly recognize the act as highly unusual and therefore would not challenge Roger. But if he did, Will had told his Russian-speaking CIA colleague how to respond.

This is an intelligence matter. If you compromise me, you'll be put in a military prison for the rest of your life.

The letter was addressed to a specific Russian intelligence officer. Will had no idea if that officer operated from the Pacific Fleet HQ, and even if he did, Will hoped that the late hour would mean that he had left for home some time before. Irrespective, he was convinced that the naval personnel receiving the letter would have protocols in place to immediately locate and call the officer and that in turn the officer would have no other choice than to go straight to the HQ to collect the message. The officer would then privately read the letter, be confused by its contents, but believe that an agent had tried to make contact and would conclude that nothing could be done until the anonymous agent made the telephone call the following morning.

That call would never happen. The letter's only significance was to try to draw out the intelligence officer this evening so that Will and his team could identify and follow their target.

Laith spoke. "Roger's leaving the HQ. No one's behind him. He's thirty feet away. He's fifty feet away." The line went silent. Will narrowed his eyes, totally focused on the phone. "He's a hundred feet away. Now he's out of my sight."

Will looked quickly away from the cell phone, toward the direction from which Roger should be approaching the car. He saw nothing at first, only driving snowfall. Then light from one of the streetlamps briefly shone over a man before that person just as quickly disappeared into more shadows. Will knew the man was almost certainly Roger, but he pulled out his handgun just in case he was wrong. He looked around, searching for the man. The figure appeared again under a different streetlamp and disappeared again as Will tightened his grip on his QSZ-92. Will held his breath, then swung his gun rapidly toward the car door as it opened. Roger was there, bending low to enter the vehicle.

As soon as the SOG operative was in his seat, he

removed his crude disguise and looked at Will. "There were *four* sailors at reception. Behind them was a security gate with another two armed guards." He smiled. "But it's clear that the HQ is not deemed a target for hostiles. The average age of the sailors had to be about twenty-two."

"They took the letter?"

Roger nodded. "One of them got straight onto a landline after looking at the name on the envelope. I just turned and walked out."

"Excellent." Will looked at the cell phone on the dashboard. "Laith, are you hearing this?"

Laith responded in his deep drawl, "Sure am. I'll stay put to watch the front. But you'd better move to the rear parking lot right now. The target could be close."

Roger turned on the ignition, put the gears into drive, jammed his cell phone into a car phone holder, and slowly moved the vehicle forward. Within a minute they were at the back of the Pacific Fleet HQ, close to the parking lot. The place was nearly empty of vehicles, and those that were there were covered by thick snow. Roger muttered, "We're in position. If the target's arriving by car, we'll see it."

Laith said, "It's a damn shame none of us knows the layout of this city."

Roger smiled. "We'll improvise." His smile faded as he looked at Will. "Staying on the target's tail is the least of our problems. It's what happens after that I'm worried about."

Will looked out of the windshield, staring through the heavy snowfall. "Since when do you worry about anything?"

Roger huffed. "I'm married with three young kids. There's a lot I worry about, including my wife getting a knock on the door from a government man who's there to tell her that her husband died doing something insane." He shared Will's view of the outside downpour. "Not that you'd know anything about domestic responsibilities. You've no such worries."

Will shook his head. "Thanks a lot."

Roger laughed. "If you ever do meet a woman, put her in touch with me before things get serious. There's a lot of stuff I need to tell her about you. Just so she's forewarned."

Before Will could answer, Laith spoke. "I've got a solitary person on foot, approaching the front entrance to the HQ."

Roger instantly said, "Heard."

There was silence for a moment before Laith said, "The pedestrian's not slowing, is walking right up to the entrance, walks into the entrance . . ." The sound of Laith's car engine was clear. "I've just moved a few feet. I can see the person by the reception. The guards are moving. One of them hands something to the person. Can't see what it is yet. The person turns, removes gloves, lifts up something. Hold." Laith was obviously adjusting position again. "It's the envelope. Repeat, the person has the envelope."

"Description of the pedestrian?" Will's voice was urgent.

"Head to toe in civilian winter attire. But judging by the posture of the sailors, this person has rank and is deemed important. Three of the sailors are standing at attention."

Will looked quickly at Roger. "It has to be the target."

Laith continued his commentary. "The person withdraws the letter, holds it in midair, then replaces it into the envelope. It looks like the pedestrian is talking to the guards." Laith said nothing for a moment. "Stand by." Again silence. "The target is on the move, is leaving the building, is heading east on foot."

Roger said loudly, "Any sign of a vehicle?"

"Not yet."

Will nodded. "Then we have to assume the target lives close to the HQ and traveled there on foot. I'm going onto the streets. Listen to my instructions, and be ready for my order to make the snatch." Will jumped out of the car, withdrew a Bluetooth device, which he fixed into his ear, and dialed in his cell phone so that he was on a conference call with Laith and Roger. Instead of walking directly toward the location of the target, Will moved to the far side of the parking lot and spoke as he did so. "Okay, I've got the central ground covered."

Roger drove his car away. "I'm moving north and will hold still after five hundred feet."

Laith spoke. "I've just passed the target and will set my position three hundred yards to the east. Roger, watch the eastern road adjacent to the HQ. If the target crosses it and heads toward my location, I'll need to move before I give the target a double sighting of me."

"Understood."

Will wrapped his arms around his chest; his breath steamed in the icy air. He was alone; no other pedestrians or mobile cars were in the vicinity. Ignoring the snowfall and wind, he focused solely on his earpiece.

Roger's voice was loud and rapid. "The target moves across the road, heading east."

"Shit!" Laith gunned his BMW. "I'm moving farther east. Will, move your ass and pick up the tail on foot."

Will sprinted across the parking lot, his feet crunching deep into the snow. Turning by the northeast corner of the Pacific HQ, he ran fast along the road leading to the port before slowing to a walk. He was right by the quayside. Tall warships were berthed adjacent to the route he needed to take. Looking around, he squinted through the snowfall before spotting the target walking along the quayside. "I'm by the port, have sight of the target, and am taking over command."

Both CIA operatives replied, "Understood."

The target was walking quickly. Will matched the pace, maintaining a constant distance of three hundred feet. Strong winds blew snow diagonally through the air from the port and through the gaps of the Udaloy I destroyers, a *Slava*-class cruiser, and one *Sovremenny*-class destroyer. The target slowed, turned to face the deserted road, looked left and right, and walked across the route.

"Target breaking left and heading north." Will kept his voice at medium volume, even though he knew his prey had no chance of hearing him given the distance between them and the noise of the weather. "I've almost certainly been spotted, although there're no signs the target is suspicious. Roger, stay north but move five hundred feet east. Laith, move three hundred feet north."

"Will do."

"On my way."

Will followed the target north into a narrow side street. As he walked he could feel his handgun, secreted under his overcoat and suit, rub against the base of his spine. The route was straddled by terraced buildings and had only a few dim streetlamps to illuminate the place. He looked at the buildings. All of them were clearly business-related and had no interior lights turned on. He looked at the target.

"Target moving east!" Will silently cursed the fact that he had taken his eyes off his prey. "Now out of my sight. Laith, move two hundred feet further north. Roger, I estimate you'll need to move about a hundred and fifty feet east."

Will ran quickly up the empty street, the icy air causing pain in his lungs with each inhalation. Reaching the crossroads where the target had moved right, he slowed to a walk, stopped, and glanced down the route where his quarry had gone. He saw the pedestrian a hundred feet away, continuing to walk. "I'm in a residential street. The target's home could be here."

"Your instructions?" Roger's voice sounded strained over the sound of his vehicle's engine.

Will momentarily stopped, looked at the target, looked again at the street, which this time was straddled by continuous homes, some of which had lights on, then made his decision. "You both should be a maximum of three hundred feet away from my location. Roger, head south and look west for the road I'm on. Laith, head directly west. You may even be on the far end of the same street." He stayed still, counting in his head. After a count of five, he shouted, "Takedown, now!"

Sprinting toward the target, now no longer caring if he was spotted, he saw car headlights in the distance, racing down the street toward the pedestrian.

He heard Laith say over the roar of his powerful BMW, "I can see you and you can see me."

The target stopped, turning quickly to face Will. Roger's Audi A8 then appeared on the street from an alley on the left, screeching as it turned hard into the road barely thirty feet in front of Will. The target was now trapped between Laith's and Roger's vehicles. But Will sprinted faster, racing past Roger's car, withdrawing his handgun, until he was fifty feet away from the target. He slowed, held his QSZ-92 high in two hands, and aimed it at the pedestrian's head. The target looked left and right but remained in place.

Will walked right up to the target. "Korina Tsvetaeva."

The woman took three steps back, looking terrified and confused. "Yes?"

Will marched right up to her, keeping his pistol trained on her skull. "We don't want to hurt you."

The GRU major looked toward Laith's car, then over Will's shoulder at Roger's vehicle. "Then what do you want?"

Will smiled. "Your help." His smile vanished. "But I *will* gun you down if you try anything stupid."

Korina was dressed in a long fur coat and hat and was in her early thirties. She removed her hat, allowing her long black hair to fall onto her shoulders. Her eyes were still wide with fear, though when she spoke she seemed to be making an effort to control her emotions. "So the letter was a trick to flush me out." She shook her head slowly. The wind receded, and snow fell gently over her face.

Will nodded, stepping right up to Korina. Lowering his handgun, he said quietly, "I mean you no harm. But we need to go somewhere private so that we can talk."

Korina narrowed her eyes. "Who are you?"

"A friend of someone who's important to you, someone who's in danger." He glanced at Laith. The SOG operative was on foot beside his car with his weapon trained on the GRU major. He looked over his shoulder at Roger and saw that he was in an identical stance. He called out, "Lower your weapons." He looked at Korina. "We need to go."

Korina shook her head. "No."

Will silently cursed, aware that at any moment they might be spotted by a civilian in one of the adjacent houses or maybe by a routine naval dock patrol. He stepped even closer to Korina, placed a hand on her arm, felt her flinch, but retained his grip and pulled her body right up to his. He whispered into her ear, "My name is William Archer. I'm a British Intelligence officer. I know who you really are. You're an MI6 agent. The man who's been running you has been captured by a Russian special forces officer who wants to kill you and others like you. If he succeeds, your death won't be the first. Several weeks ago, he infiltrated a naval base and murdered a submarine captain. That man was your father."

THIRTY-ONE

It was ten P.M. Will, Roger, and Laith were in Korina's tiny terraced house. The residence was barely three hundred yards away from where they had confronted her on the street. They were in her lounge, and the place was crammed with full bookshelves, had a small wooden dining table, one chair, a television that looked at least twenty years old, and little else. Korina had removed her coat to reveal jeans and a turtleneck sweater. She grabbed the wooden chair, spun it around, and sat on it the wrong way, with her arms resting on its back. After lighting a cigarette, she silently observed the three Western intelligence officers, who were perched on whatever they could find.

Will studied Korina for a moment, then nodded toward Laith and Roger while still keeping his attention on the GRU officer. "My colleagues are CIA paramilitary operatives."

Korina looked at them and blew out a thin stream of smoke between her lips. "You look like killers."

Will rubbed his cold hands together, then abruptly stopped doing so. "We're hunting a man called Taras Khmelnytsky. Have you heard of him?"

Korina said nothing.

"You know who he is." He nodded. "Khmelnytsky's a colonel and the head of Spetsnaz Alpha. His profile will be well known to someone in your line of work."

Korina continued to stare at Will, before asking, "He murdered my father?"

Will nodded. "Since then, he's killed six other Russian MI6 agents. He's got another three agents to murder. When that's done, the world's going to hell."

He told her about Razin's plan before asking, "You never knew that your father was an MI6 agent who worked for the same man as you?"

Korina shook her head; a tear ran down her face. "And my father never knew about my secret." She wiped her face and composed herself. "Are you trying to trick me?"

"To what end? If we're FSB, we'd have just arrested you."

"Maybe you are who you say you are. But perhaps you're not telling me the truth about the real reason you want Khmelnytsky."

"You decide! But time is running out."

Korina seemed deep in thought. Finally, she sighed

and said, "For obvious reasons, I can't take this to my superiors."

"I'm not asking you to."

She frowned. "Then what are you asking?"

Will leaned forward. "For Khmelnytsky's plan to work, the explosion *must* look like an American strike. Are you aware of anything that the Americans are about to do that, if combined with a nuclear explosion, could spark war?"

"I—"

"Any briefings you've received? Information coming out of agents? Signals intelligence? Anything?"

Korina extinguished her cigarette, pulled out another, and froze. "Oh, no."

"What?"

Silence.

"What, Korina?!"

More silence.

Then she spoke. "An intelligence report. Naval matter. Given I'm GRU navy, I was cleared to read it."

Will spoke with deliberation. "What was in the report?"

Korina lit her cigarette with a shaking hand. "Three U.S. *Ohio*-class cruise missile submarines are going to be sailing in the Barents Sea."

A sea that was above northwest Russia.

"Not unusual."

"No, but this deployment's different. They're going to covertly enter Russian waters. Not too far, but just enough. We believe it's the first time the Americans have tried this."

"A training exercise?"

"The report came to no conclusion, though it did make one stark observation."

Will waited.

"The cruise missiles have a maximum range of fifteen hundred miles."

Will's stomach knotted. "They're entering Russian waters to bring them within range of Moscow."

Korina nodded.

"This has to be the trigger." Will's mind raced. "But it doesn't prove that Moscow is Razin's target. The *Ohio*'s deployment is a test sortie, I'm certain. It's unlikely that a first strike against Moscow would be made by a cruise missile submarine—more likely a ballistic submarine from somewhere out in the Atlantic."

Roger interrupted. "I agree." The former sailor also seemed to be thinking fast. "But if war had already started, the Americans might use *Ohio* subs in the second or third strikes if they felt confident that Russia's missile interception capability had been diminished. I think it's a training exercise, just to see if they can get close enough if there ever is a need to hit Moscow."

Will felt frustration. "Moscow's not Razin's target, because a detonation there will not convince Russian high command that it was an *Ohio* missile strike. While Russian air defenses are at peak performance, it just wouldn't ring true to them. That means Razin's target could be anywhere much closer to the subs. But that still leaves a vast range of possible targets." He punched a fist on his leg. "Damn it!"

Laith said, "Maybe this isn't the trigger." He looked at Korina. "Could be something else that you've not been cleared to read."

Korina shook her head. "No. This is the trigger. Without a doubt."

Will looked sharply at her. "How can you be certain?"

Korina blew out smoke. "Because the intelligence report was written by Taras Khmelnytsky."

Will went cold. "Who was his source?"

Korina seemed hesitant.

"I have to know!"

She looked incredulous. "You can't expect me to reveal the identity of an agent."

"Under the circumstances, yes, I bloody well can."

She puffed on her cigarette. "He's a low-level American sailor, but he works for an admiral and therefore has a higher security status than others of his rank. Razin's his case officer. Beyond that, I'd have to check my database to get extra details."

"Can you get his identity and naval facility?"

"I can, but not until morning. If I log on now, it might look suspicious to GRU HQ."

"Okay." Will clapped his hands together. "There's still a chance. The Americans can put the squeeze on the sailor—get him to send a message to Khmelnytsky saying that the subs are deploying on a different date, that they have to meet in person so he can give him the details. That'll grab Khmelnytsky's attention. Then"—he smiled—"we grab the bastard."

Roger frowned. "Why don't we just get the submarines to turn around so that the incident is avoided?"

"No. If we do that, Razin will strike another target and we'd have no idea when or where that would be."

"He might, but unless he's lucky it would be unlikely to spark war."

"I can't take that chance."

Roger looked incredulous. "And yet you're willing to take a gamble on something that certainly *will* lead to war if we fail."

Will thought about this. "If we've not got him by the time the subs are drawing close to Russia, I'll call it in."

Korina said, "You'll have to move quickly because the submarines will be entering Russian waters in four days' time."

Will's smile vanished.

Four days.

One explosion.

War.

PART IV

THIRTY-TWO

Colonel General Platonov walked through the grounds of his estate. It was late evening and dark, though the driveway's lamps and discreetly positioned halogen lights gave him glimpses of the large garden's brook, oak trees, ornate stone bridges, and special forces men with AEK-919K "Kashtan" submachine guns slung by their sides.

He hated having the bodyguards in his family home, but he was the highest-ranking military officer in the Russian armed forces and protection came with the job.

The man by his side was silent. That was understandable. The Russian president had a lot on his mind.

They stopped on a large rectangular area of concrete, where snow had recently been brushed away to reveal a symmetrical pattern of squares. At opposite ends of the yard were tall plastic chess pieces. On the edge of each corner of the yard, overlooking the giant chessboard, were man-sized stone statues of knights, their bodies and heads cloaked and hooded, their faces solemn, their hands clasped over the hilts of downward-facing broadswords.

Platonov looked at his house. The curtains were still open, all of the rooms illuminated. He could see the premier's wife and his wife talking, smiling, glasses of wine in their hands. Upstairs, the young pajama-dressed children of Russia's most powerful general were bouncing on beds with the children of Russia's supreme leader. They were having a sleepover tonight. Their excitement was palpable.

The two men lit Montecristo cigars. Platonov could still feel the pleasant burn of his postdinner cognac in his throat. The evening had gone well. His wife was an excellent cook and a very intelligent hostess. As he looked at her now, he knew that he loved her as much as when he'd first met her. Then he'd been a muscular, blond-haired, idealistic lieutenant. Now he was a slim, ramrod-backed, gray-haired general with wisdom and a scar that ran from a blue eye down to the corner of his mouth.

A memento from Afghanistan.

A mujahideen knife.

He looked at his premier and spoke quietly. "What are your orders?"

The president blew out smoke. "You'd accept them?"

"It depends on whether they're right."

The president smiled. "Perhaps you forget your status."

"Perhaps you forget whose fucking house you're in."

The premier laughed, then frowned. "I'm tempted to expel the American ambassador."

"Go ahead. But you'll make a fool of yourself."

"I don't need your blessing."

"No, but you'll need my army if it all goes wrong."

"*My* army."

"Your army, if you like." He kept his eyes on his children before turning to his commander in chief. "We're not seven years old. Your army. I don't care."

The president was silent for a while. "Why are you angry with me?"

"Not you. I'm angry with history. Every Russian president has made his general into a psychopath."

"I think you've had too much Hennessy."

"No, I'm stone-cold sober." Platonov looked sternly at his leader. "Don't bait the Americans. They can slaughter us."

"I've no intention of baiting them. On the contrary, they're the ones who're being provocative."

"Then sort it out. Politically."

The president blew out more smoke; it hung in the icy air. "With you in charge, there'd be no slaughter."

"Rubbish." Platonov looked at his wife moving across the kitchen. It marveled him that she'd not lost her effect on him. He looked at the children and felt a chill run through his body. "If you fuck up, I'll send every Russian soldier to meet an American invasion force. They'll all die, but that's what we do and that's how we fight. And I'll just be another psychopath."

"I don't want a fight."

"But you'll have one at the drop of a hat."

"You read me wrong."

"I read you fine."

The president moved closer to Platonov. "How is the nuclear training exercise progressing?"

The question lightened Platonov's mood. "It's going very well. But Colonel Khmelnytsky still has more work to do. In particular, we need to test the feasibility of deploying the devices from sea. The final phase of the exercise will be focused on targeting naval installations."

"Good." The president was keen to get back into the warmth of the house. "Should we be concerned about the three American submarines?"

Platonov laughed. "They're just playing games. But one of our new stealth destroyers will be waiting for them in the Barents Sea. It will make them turn around."

The premier flicked his cigar onto the chessboard. "Come on, let's get another drink." He stepped forward, then stopped. "I'm not going to fuck up, and I hope the Americans don't either. I'm sure it will be fine, but—" He shivered. "My orders. If anything does happen, make sure our entire military is battle-ready."

THIRTY-THREE

Morning broke to reveal a sky filled with gray clouds pouring snow over the city of Vladivostok.

The lounge in Korina's house was thick with the smoke from cigarettes and steam from mugs of coffee. Korina had been out of the room for thirty minutes, and when she reemerged she was showered and had changed into smart charcoal gray pants, a white blouse, and a box jacket. Her body lotions and perfume brought a welcome fresh scent into the musty room.

She looked directly at Will. "I'll need an hour in my office to go through GRU databases."

"All right. Can we wait for you here?"

"Sure. Just don't go through my things." Korina smiled, donned her outer garments, and walked out of her home.

Will glanced at his watch, waited a few seconds, looked

at Laith, and spoke with a stern voice. "Get on foot and tail her. Roger, I want you in one of our vehicles. I'll parallel Laith's route. All cells dialed into my number. Listen to my commands, because if she does anything stupid we'll have to move *very* quickly."

Thirty minutes later, Will was standing close to the quayside of Vladivostok's naval port. Snow pelted his face, and he pulled up the collar of his overcoat to further shield him from the bitter weather. Placing his hands back into his coat pockets, his fingers caressed his QSZ-92 handgun. He heard Laith's voice in his Bluetooth earpiece.

"She's been in the base for ten minutes. Four soldiers are guarding the main entrance. So far, all looks quiet."

It seemed that the GRU offices were not in the Pacific Fleet HQ building, as Korina had entered one of the nearby militarized and restricted naval zones of the port. Will imagined that the naval GRU probably had only a few offices in the zone, the rest of the buildings being used by hundreds of navy sailors and administrators. Laith was barely a hundred and fifty feet away from the entrance to the base. Roger and Will were farther east, with Roger covering the northern flank of their surveillance box in the Audi A8 and Will covering the south. Only Laith had visibility of the militarized zone.

Will heard a loud horn from behind him. Turning, he saw a huge aircraft carrier, fully laden with MiG-29Ks and Su-33s, cruise slowly close to the port. Sailors were on deck, moving quickly, clearly tasked with numerous jobs. The horn boomed again before the massive vessel turned and began sailing away.

Will shivered, but not from the cold. "Anything unusual at the base?"

Laith responded, "You'll be the first to know if there is."

Roger said, "Nothing where I am except a few crazy pedestrians who think today's a good day to go shopping."

Will wrapped his arms around his chest, shivered again, and saw his breath steam into the icy air. Wind blasted him from the sea, carrying with it even more snow. He looked at the other destroyers and frigates moored in the port. All of them were illuminated and had signs of activity. Some were taking on fresh provisions from four-ton trucks parked on the big piers adjacent to the vessels. They were clearly making ready to sail.

Forty minutes later Laith said, "Unmarked SUV stops at the entrance to the base, two men inside, ID cards are shown to the guards, the barrier is lifted, the SUV drives into the base."

Will immediately pressed his hand against his earpiece. "Were the men uniformed?"

Laith muttered, "Couldn't see from my position."

Roger added, "Uniforms or no uniforms, these militarized zones will contain as many civilian workers as sailors. The vehicle's probably normal."

Will let his hand fall to his side. He knew Roger was most likely right. But he felt unusually tense and, despite his attempts to try to relax, could not help feeling that right now everything was out of his control.

A further twenty minutes passed before Laith spoke again. "The barrier's being lifted; something's obviously coming out, as there's nothing in front of the base." The line went quiet. "Okay, I can see the same SUV."

Will and Roger said nothing as they waited for their ex–Delta Force colleague to speak again.

"Two men in the SUV I saw earlier . . . yes, same two men in the front, but . . . something else in the back, can't see yet."

Static sounded in Will's earpiece.

"Vehicle approaches barrier, front male passenger waves a hand at guard, who is at attention and saluting, vehicle slows, then indicates right, then accelerates." There was nothing for several seconds before Laith shouted, "Korina's in the back. She's called it in and betrayed us!"

Will shouted, "Direction?"

"Quayside, heading right toward you."

Will's heart pounded. "Roger, I want you east by a quarter mile, then south by five hundred feet. That will put you on the quayside road, ahead of the SUV."

"On my way." Roger gunned his Audi.

Laith shouted in near-breathless words, "I'm moving east as well. Running parallel to the SUV. Catching glimpses of it, but they're not looking my way. They're about two hundred feet to my right. Speed approximately twenty miles per hour."

Laith was at full sprint and so far was matching the speed of the SUV.

Will scrutinized the quayside road adjacent to him. Three hundred yards away, one of the four-ton trucks pulled onto the route from a pier and started driving slowly toward him. "I can't see the SUV. Four tonner is blocking my view."

"It's right behind the truck!" Laith was clearly still sprinting. "Get out of sight, Will."

Will dashed across the road and into a side street and took the next right turn. As he did so, Laith nearly crashed into him. Will immediately sprinted alongside his colleague so that they were running parallel to the quayside road. "Roger, where are you?"

Roger shouted above the sound of his vehicle, "Just turning onto the quayside. Hold."

Laith stumbled as his feet struck ice on the side street, but Will grabbed him with one hand and kept him moving at full sprint.

Roger said, "I'm stationary. The four tonner is about a quarter mile away, coming straight toward me. No sight of the SUV. Correction . . . SUV overtaking truck. I've got clear visibility of the target. Instructions, please."

Will's mind raced, desperately trying to decide what to do.

"Instructions, please," Roger repeated. "I've got my rifle pointing right at them. I can easily take them all down."

"Wait!" Will ran even faster; Laith kept right by his side.

"She's called it in, Will." Roger's voice was calm but

menacing. "But she might not have had time to tell them everything. If I take them down, we stand a good chance of getting out of the city."

"Not yet!"

They moved past occasional pedestrians wrapped in full winter attire, with shoulders hunched and heads bowed against the driving snowfall. They seemed to take no notice of the two men dressed in expensive suits, shoes, and overcoats sprinting through the snow and ice.

"They're three hundred yards away from me." Roger sounded as though he was speaking through gritted teeth. "I need a decision."

"Come on, Will!" Laith's words were urgent and angry.

Will said nothing.

"Five hundred feet away. Will?"

Will grabbed Laith, skidded to a halt with the man, and spoke rapidly into his Bluetooth. "Abort. Get out of there, and head straight back to her house."

"What?"

"Do it, Roger. We'll meet you there. But move like fury."

Laith stared at Will with a look of bemusement while he bent over with his hands on his knees, sucking in air.

Will ignored the expression and pointed northeast. "Her house. We've got to be there before she gets back."

Laith pushed himself upright, half turned, and immediately led the way. They ran to the end of the street, turned left onto a main road, sprinted straight across it while dodging slow-moving vehicles, ran into another

side street, and kept moving for three hundred yards
before making the turn onto the street containing Korina's house. Laith and Will did not slow, running at full
speed for a further five hundred feet until they were
at her front door. Roger pulled up next to them, and
Will was relieved to see that his Audi was still covered
with frozen snow. Nevertheless, he and Laith immediately started gathering up some more of the stuff from
the roadside and patting it onto places on the car where
metal was exposed.

Will told Roger, "Get in the house, get coffee on." He
looked at Laith. "You too, and start chain-smoking to get
the room feeling like we never left the place."

Will placed one final lump of snow onto the Audi's
hood, decided it would have to be enough, heard an
engine noise in the distance, and raced into the front
entrance just as he saw the hood of a vehicle emerge at
the end of the road.

Will dashed toward his colleagues, who were furiously
stamping the snow off their feet. Grabbing their outer
garments, he sprinted upstairs to the bathroom. Holding
each coat over the bathtub, he punched them to release
the snow, ran hot water to melt the snow that had fallen
into the bathtub, turned the tap off, and returned quickly
downstairs. Hanging the coats up, he scrutinized the
floor of the lounge and kitchen, grabbed a kitchen towel
to mop up a few spots of melted snow, tossed it back onto
a kitchen surface, and breathed deeply. Laith was sitting
in an armchair in the lounge, and he had managed to get

through two cigarettes and was lighting a third with one hand while holding a fresh mug of instant coffee with the other. Roger emerged from the kitchen holding two more mugs of coffee. He gave one to Will and sat down on a dining room chair. Will remained standing, trying to calm his body to make it appear as if he'd just spent the last hour doing nothing more energetic than replenishing coffee cups within the small terraced house. But his heart pounded within his chest.

Directly outside the house, car doors opened and slammed shut. Will took a gulp of his steaming hot coffee, pulled out his QSZ-92 handgun, and pointed it at the front door. In his peripheral vision, he saw Roger and Laith do the same.

The door opened; Korina entered the house. She paused in the narrow entrance leading to the lounge, staring at the three men who were aiming their weapons at her. She shook her head and said urgently, "William, this is not what it seems."

"We expected you to come back on foot"—Will took another sip of his coffee while keeping his eyes and pistol trained on Korina—"not pull up outside your house in a vehicle containing two men." He gripped his handgun hard. "We kept our side of the bargain, waiting for you here, trusting you."

Korina sighed. "I know. I'm sorry. But I had to make a decision, and that decision was that we needed help. I've not told anyone else you're here. The two men with me are totally loyal and are experts at keeping their mouths shut."

Will narrowed his eyes. "Then you'd better bring them in so that we can introduce ourselves."

Korina turned, beckoned to the men who were waiting outside, then moved fully into the lounge. One man entered the room. He was of medium height, had a powerful build and a shaven head, and was dressed in a dark suit.

"This is Vitali."

The man eyed them coldly, saying nothing.

The front door was shut, and the second man was there but had his back to them as he wrenched the door's bolt closed. His task complete, he turned to face the room. Like his colleague, he was dressed in a dark suit, and he looked powerful and athletic. Unlike his colleague, the man was tall and had cropped blond hair and a face covered in scars.

Korina pointed at him. "And this is Markov. They're Spetsnaz GRU."

Will stepped toward the two special forces men, checked to see that Roger and Laith still had their guns pointed at the Russians, lowered his weapon, and tucked it into his belt. For a moment he wondered what to say. Having decided, he said, "If you're here to do me or my men harm, I'll kill you both before you have a chance to move a muscle. If not, you would do well to understand that your presence here could be deemed treacherous by your Spetsnaz officers. If Korina has not made that clear to you, then I'm giving you the chance now to turn around and walk out of here while you still have a job and your liberty."

Vitali gestured toward Korina while keeping his attention on Will. "Major Tsvetaeva made *two* things clear to us. First, that she needed our urgent help to stop the destruction of our country. Second, that we would be breaking the laws of Russia by doing so." He glanced at Markov, who nodded, before looking back at Will. "We understand our situation."

Will looked sharply at Korina. "If these two men are absent without leave from Spetsnaz, they'll be a liability to our team, as their unit commanders will issue orders for their arrest."

Korina shook her head. "I spoke to their superior and gained formal clearance for their immediate short-term attachment to me. I also spoke to my boss in Moscow and fed him a lie. I said that one of my agents had contacted me and said he had information about U.S. naval movements but suspected that he was compromised and needed to urgently meet me in the western borders of Russia. I said I needed a few days to get there and meet him and had requisitioned two men and equipment from Spetsnaz GRU to help protect me during my meeting." She smiled, pulling out a cigarette. "As far as our superiors are concerned, the three of us are on official business and will be difficult to contact during the next few days."

Will looked at the Spetsnaz men. "Why are you willing to help?"

Vitali answered with a smile, "What man wouldn't like a short-term *attachment* to Major Tsvetaeva?"

Will didn't smile and repeated his question.

Markov pointed at the major. "Because we both trust her judgment. All of the Spetsnaz men based here think that way. She's one of us."

"Have you been told who we're looking for?"

Vitali nodded. "The head of Spetsnaz Alpha."

Markov added, "Major Tsvetaeva told us outright. In case we had a problem hunting one of our own."

"Has either of you ever served with him?"

Markov shook his head.

Vitali answered, "No, but I saw him once. I was on an advanced sniper course. There were ten of us from various different Spetsnaz units. We were testing a prototype rifle, and each of us was given the task of trying to hit a playing card, one mile away. Colonel Khmelnytsky was observing, along with four other commanders, because two of the students were from Alpha. We could hear the other commanders talking, saying the new weapon was rubbish given that none of us could get a bullet to within five feet of our playing cards. But Khmelnytsky stayed silent. Instead, he walked up to the sniper on the left of our range, picked up his rifle, took aim while standing, and fired the weapon. His bullet struck the center of the playing card. Then he walked along the line, doing the same with each of our guns, until he'd fired ten bullets from ten rifles and struck ten playing cards as if they'd been only a few feet away from him." Vitali smiled. "After he dropped the last rifle, he strode off, walked past the other unit commanders, and muttered loud enough for us all to hear, 'The weapon's not rubbish, but every man around me is.'"

Will looked at Korina. "Why did you bring these men here?"

Korina inhaled deeply on her cigarette. "Two days after the intelligence report was issued, Taras instructed the agent to abscond from the U.S. Navy and use an infiltration route to enter Russia. He did so on the pretext that the agent could be in danger, although from what we know I suspect his real motive was to get the agent out of his game. But he needed official clearance to do that, as the infiltration route belonged to the SVR and required their assistance. His request for the agent's exfiltration from America's Kitsap Naval Base was officially recorded in our files and was approved. As a result, the source is now residing in a dacha on the outskirts of Moscow. The records show that the man has low-level security protection from the SVR, is not deemed a threat, and can come and go from the property as he pleases."

Will's anger vanished. "We need to meet the agent and put the fear of God into him to make him panic." His heart beat fast. "After that meeting, I don't think he'll dare discuss his situation with his agent handler on the telephone in case the SVR is monitoring his calls. I think he'll want to meet Taras. Hopefully, he'll lead us straight to him."

Korina's eyes flickered. "I thought you'd say that." She looked at Roger, Laith, then Will. "But that hope rests upon the ability of you and your men moving through my country as if you were GRU officials." She nodded at Markov and Vitali. "That's why I asked for these two men.

Together with me, they will front the team and diminish the threat of scrutiny on the three of you. They'll also help with equipment and transport." She smiled, flicking her cigarette onto the floor and stubbing it out with the heel of her boot. "And they can handle themselves very well in a fight."

"That's all good, ma'am, but"—Laith was still pointing his handgun in the direction of the GRU personnel—"I don't speak fluent Russian."

"Then you'll just have to keep your mouth shut."

Will frowned. "The SVR will never let us meet him without clearance."

"Correct. That's why I called them and told them that I needed to have a formal meeting with the man." She looked serious. "Technically, Taras's intelligence falls within my jurisdiction, as it relates to a naval matter that is happening within seas that come under the scrutiny of GRU Vladivostok. That means I have every right to reevaluate the intelligence, up to and including challenging the source of the report." She nodded once. "The SVR had no choice other than to grant me an audience with the American agent."

Will nodded. "Okay. But we need to meet him tonight."

"Tonight?" Korina looked shocked. "He's an eight-hour flight away in Moscow."

For the first time that day, Will smiled. "I'm sure that right now there are plenty of military flights traveling back and forth across Russia. I'm confident you can get us on one."

·   ·   ·

Will and Korina were alone. The rest of the team were in the next room, quietly talking to one another, the Russians trying to get the measure of the Americans and vice versa.

Will asked, "Can we work together?"

Korina studied him. "We'll have to find out." She lit a cigarette and pointed it toward him. "But I warn you, I'm no fool. If you try and trick me, I'll make you and your men suffer."

"I've no intention of tricking you. I came here because I need your help." He frowned. "Is this a place they'd normally post someone with—"

"A pretty face like mine?"

"That's not what I was going to say."

"Then what?"

"It's just that you look like you'd be better suited to Moscow HQ." Will wasn't sure he knew what he was saying. Perhaps it was that Korina's elegance seemed at odds with the harshness of this part of Russia.

Korina inhaled smoke. "I have no family now. I never knew my mother—she ran off with another man when I was a baby. And when I was old enough to look after myself, my father was often away at sea for long periods. I suppose it toughened me up a lot. I didn't want a cozy desk job in Moscow. So I volunteered to come out here."

Will understood. The tragedies in his early life had driven him to seek out his extreme existence. "I'm sorry about your father."

Korina lowered her head. "They wouldn't tell me at

first how he was killed. No doubt they thought it would be too upsetting. But I pulled some strings and found out everything." She looked up. "That bastard savaged him."

Will hesitated before placing a hand on hers. "I know how you feel."

Her expression steeled. "How?"

"My parents were killed."

"An accident?"

"Murdered."

She squeezed his hand, released her grip, and muttered, "So here we are, filling the void." She nodded once. "Yes, I think you and I can work together." Extinguishing her cigarette, she added, "There's something else you should know. When I was in my office, I checked my telegrams. One of them was from GRU Moscow HQ and was marked URGENT. It was sent to me and every other GRU station chief based in Russia but outside Moscow. The telegram stated that we must store all intelligence files in our possession within burn boxes, ready to be incinerated if our offices are overrun by American forces."

THIRTY-FOUR

By midmorning they were in the SUV, traveling to the outskirts of Vladivostok through driving snowfall. Korina spoke quickly and sternly into her cell phone. "There are six of us, three from GRU plus three from a special division. We—" She went silent as she listened to the person at the other end of the phone. Then, "If you want to refuse us entry, call GRU HQ and explain to them why you wish to hinder a major intelligence operation." She listened again, smiled, and snapped the cell shut. She glanced at Will. "There's space for us on a transport aircraft. It won't be the most comfortable ride, but it's the next flight out of here and leaves in forty-five minutes."

"Excellent. But how are my men and I going to get through perimeter security?"

Korina shrugged. "Everything will be fine, provided my identity is valid."

From the front passenger seat, Markov looked over his shoulder at them all. "We're minutes away. In addition to your own bags, in the back of the SUV are five Bergen rucksacks containing Spetsnaz battle kit, MR-445 Varjag pistols, tactical communications systems, cell phones, and spare ammunition. Strapped to the Bergens are AS Val assault rifles with sound suppressors. Vitali and I grabbed them from our base as soon as Major Tsvetaeva called us. I've no idea if the kit is going to be right for what you need, but we didn't have time to be selective."

Roger nodded. "I'm sure it will do just fine."

Vitali called out, "Time to shut up. We're approaching the base."

He drove the SUV off the main road onto a wide lane. Signs with crosses told motorists that they were entering a military restricted zone. An armed soldier stood on one side of the lane, waving them onward; soon they passed another doing the same. At the end of the lane they were confronted by a large arch, within which were four soldiers and an electronic barrier. To either side of the entrance was a twelve-foot-high razor-wire fence.

Vitali stopped the vehicle, opened his window, and showed one of the soldiers his Spetsnaz GRU identity card. The soldier looked inside the SUV, examining every occupant. Korina leaned forward, showed her ID, and spoke rapidly to the guard. He returned the document to her, then fixed his attention on Will and his colleagues.

He asked them who they were, at which point Markov
opened his front passenger door, walked around the
front of the SUV until he was right in front of the guard,
and grabbed the soldier's jacket in a bunched fist. Pulling the guard close to his scarred face, Markov muttered
something inaudible. The smaller guard looked terrified.
He appeared to speak urgently and called out to his colleagues, who immediately raised the barrier. Markov
released his grip and shouted at the four soldiers, who all
sprang to attention. He nodded slowly at them, his face
still furious, then reentered the vehicle. Vitali gunned
the SUV. They drove onto the air base.

Markov shook his head. "Fucking idiots. They'd received
the order to let us through once they saw Major Tsvetaeva's
ID. But they took it upon themselves to make a more thorough check of our vehicle in order to try to impress their
commanders that they had initiative and were doing an
excellent job." He smiled. "I changed their point of view."

The base was big, dotted with multiple runways and
feeder routes, huge hangars and other buildings, and
strewn with large and medium-sized military transport
aircraft. Although it was daylight, everything was lit up
by halogen lamps casting strong light through the leaden
gray air and persistent snowfall. Some of the planes were
taxiing, some stationary, others landing and taking off.
Ground crews and other military personnel were moving
on foot and in jeeps along tarmac tracks adjacent to the
runways. Snow-clearing vehicles moved up and down
the tracks. Vitali was clearly familiar with the layout of

the airport as he drove his SUV with confidence, changing routes several times until he brought it to a halt adjacent to a building.

Korina glanced at Will. "Stay here." She looked forward. "Markov, come with me."

The two Russians got out and strode into the building. Vitali lit a cigarette, lowered his window a few inches, and looked toward the runways. Will and his CIA colleagues followed his gaze. Approximately a thousand troops were standing in lines, carrying heavy packs and rifles, near to two large troop-carrying aircraft. Other men, presumably their NCOs and officers, were walking up and down the lines. They were probably barking orders at the soldiers, although nothing could be heard beyond the thunderous drone of the aircraft. Across the base, some of the massive hangars opened their doors and more soldiers emerged onto the tarmac until what must have been several thousand troops were visible. All of them were waiting to board planes, patiently standing as thick snow fell over them.

Vitali muttered in English, "They belong to the Fifth Army. Their commander, Lieutenant General Viktor Fursenko, has ordered them to mobilize to Western Operational Strategic Command."

Will asked, "Why?"

"It's all presentational—show the West that we're big boys and need to be taken seriously at the negotiating tables."

"The soldiers out there won't have been told that."

Laith's tone was solemn. "I expect that their commanding officers have told them that this is for real."

Vitali nodded slowly, puffing on his cigarette while keeping his gaze on the troops. "Of course. They have to be ready in case there really is a fight." He sighed, flicked his cigarette outside, and closed his window. "My younger brother will be one of the soldiers standing out there. He joined the 60th Independent Motor Rifle Brigade two years ago. I tried to persuade him not to because he was never cut out for the army way of life and had far better options."

Markov reappeared and leaned into the vehicle. "Time to move. Grab your kit. If spoken to, say nothing."

Vitali immediately jumped out and strode to the back of the vehicle. Will, Roger, and Laith joined him.

Markov had the trunk open and began throwing the heavy Bergens at each man. "It's good that we're all dressed in suits and overcoats. The fact that we look different from everyone else here means we look special. We're less likely to be confronted."

Will slung one strap of his Bergen over a shoulder, grabbed his other bag, and watched the rest of the team do the same. Korina emerged from the building, picked up her own travel bag, and nodded at Markov, who led them all across the air base to a large Il-76M transport aircraft that was positioned away from the mass of troops. An airman was waiting, holding a clipboard. Korina spoke to him, nodded at the team, and then beckoned for them to come forward.

As Will climbed into the airplane, he expected the craft to be nearly empty given that the brigades he had seen a moment before had been assembled on the other side of the base. But the plane was filled with soldiers, sitting on their packs and with their assault rifles cradled over their legs. They all wore distinctive sky blue paratrooper berets. Will followed Korina down the center of the plane, walking between the soldiers, who eyed them with looks of confusion, until he and his team were at the back of the aircraft. There were no seats. Will put his rucksack down and sat on it, leaving a space between him and the rearmost paratrooper. Roger took that space.

The airplane immediately started moving and then accelerated hard for takeoff. The noise within the craft, deafening at first, receded to a low drone as it leveled out. Will looked to his left at Laith. The SOG officer was either asleep or pretending to be so. Opposite him, Korina was trying to make herself as comfortable as possible. Markov and Vitali were next to her, talking to each other. Will glanced at Roger. He was frowning. He followed his gaze and saw that one of the paratroopers opposite Roger was trying to strip down, clean, and reassemble his AKS-74 assault rifle. The soldier looked to be barely eighteen years old; he was sweating, and his hands shook as he clumsily tried to put the weapon back together. Two of the soldiers next to the paratrooper were also watching him, chuckling. Roger leaned quickly forward, grabbed the parts of the rifle, expertly stripped it down again, looked at the inside of the barrel to ensure it was clean, checked the other working parts, rapidly reassembled the weapon until it was fully functional, and held it out to him. The paratrooper took his weapon, smiled with a look of relief, and gripped the rifle tight enough to whiten his knuckles. As Roger leaned back, Will saw that Markov and Vitali had stopped their conversation and were looking at Roger with their mouths slightly open.

Roger cupped a hand around Will's ear and said quietly, "Russian or otherwise, no soldier deserves to have a faulty weapon."

Will looked around at all of the soldiers in the airplane. Some of them were laughing and joking with one another in an exaggerated manner. Others were busying themselves with unnecessary tasks. But most of them were quiet, looking apprehensive and lost in their own thoughts. Will knew all of this behavior very well. He too had sat as a young paratrooper in military airplanes, waiting to go to war. And the smell in the airplanes then had been the same smell that enveloped him now. It was the smell of fear.

THIRTY-FIVE

It was midevening. Will, Korina, and Markov walked quickly down a long, winding driveway illuminated by lamps and surrounded by trees. Ahead of them was the dacha. The villa was quite large, and the lights were on. Two stationary vehicles were by the front entrance. The place was isolated in the forest and looked beautiful and homely, with gentle snow falling through the dim yellow glow of the lamps. They were forty miles outside Moscow and were here to interview the American traitor.

Markov knocked on the front door and stepped back. A voice called out. Markov responded, "Major Tsvetaeva. GRU."

Bolts were unfastened; the door swung open. A tall, dark-haired man wearing a suit and a holster containing a Serdyukov SPS self-loading pistol stood in the entrance. Korina stepped forward and showed her ID, speaking quietly. The SVR officer scrutinized her identity card and, glancing over his shoulder, called out a name. He was joined by someone wearing similar attire. Markov pulled out a packet of cigarettes and said something to the men, then laughed. They smiled and stepped out of the doorway, joining Markov for a cigarette. Korina and Will stepped into the house.

The dacha was thick with tobacco smoke. As they walked along the hallway, they could hear a TV. Passing a kitchen, a cloakroom, and two bedrooms, Will saw that nothing inside was as homely as the villa's exterior suggested. Instead, the interior was minimalist and functional. They turned into a large lounge and saw the bright screen of the television. The light from the set was the only illumination, and it flickered over the surroundings to produce snapshot images of a man sitting on a sofa.

Will said loudly, "Turn the lights on and the television off."

The man seemed startled. He scrambled for a controller, switched off the TV, and simultaneously switched on a table lamp. "I thought you guys were coming tomorrow." The American looked hesitant as he slowly lowered himself back onto the sofa. He was slight, in his midtwenties, hair shaven at the sides and back, barefoot, and wearing tracksuit pants and a sweatshirt that had U.S. NAVY BASE KITSAP, NOT SELF BUT COUNTRY emblazoned on its front. He picked up a bottle of beer and took a swig. "I'm an important person now. I don't need fucking surprises."

Will stepped forward. "There's a lady present. I won't tolerate foul language."

The American seemed to relax. "Well, fuck me." He took another slug of beer.

Will moved closer, but Korina put a hand on his forearm and said to the American sailor, "You're clearly a stupid man. If you don't change your attitude, I'll make sure you stay here forever."

The American grinned broadly. "Good, because things have never been better for me. Twenty-four/seven protection, free food, booze, and cigarettes." He lit a cigarette, sucked on it, and then tapped ash into an overflowing ashtray. "Plus the SVR has given me American cable TV." His smile vanished and was replaced by a look of contempt. Directing his gaze at Korina he muttered, "The only thing the Russkies haven't given me yet is any Eastern pussy. Is that why you're here, lady?"

Korina looked urgently at Will and said, "No, William—"

But Will ignored her, took two steps toward the sailor, and slapped him hard.

"God damn it!" The sailor put a hand to his red face.

Will stepped back. "Next time it'll be worse."

The American spat angrily. "How come a Russian speaks perfect English with no accent?"

"Because that's how it has to be." Will threw himself down into one of the other armchairs.

Korina said, "We're here to ask you about the intelligence you supplied to Taras Khmelnytsky. We want to know if you were aware that the intelligence is no longer true."

The sailor sniggered. "I only answer to Khmelnytsky and"—he looked around—"my new SVR hosts."

Korina snapped, "You'll answer to whoever has authority over naval intelligence matters. And right now that person is me."

Korina was about to speak again, but Will interrupted. "How did Taras recruit you?"

The sailor glugged beer. "He told me, 'You don't need to live like scum anymore. If you give me what I want, I'll make sure you live a life that would be the envy of your arrogant officers.'"

"So that's it?" Korina leaned forward. "You spied on America because Khmelnytsky could deliver to you your vision of domestic bliss and maybe even"—she smiled, though her look was venomous—"Eastern pussy."

The American said nothing, his face defiant.

Korina pointed at him. "We've learned that the three *Ohio* submarines will be entering Russian waters on a different date, but that's all we know. I'm here to find out if you know anything about this."

The sailor shook his head. "The dates of deployment were specific. I never heard anyone say that the subs might sail on another date."

Will asked, "Were there any protocols in place in case the deployment was delayed for whatever reason?"

The American looked puzzled. "No."

Will sighed and looked at Korina. "This has been a waste of time."

•   •   •

As they reached their BMW sedan rental car at the end of the driveway, Korina spoke to Markov. "Join Vitali, Roger, and Laith on surveillance detail. Let me know the moment the target leaves the dacha."

Markov disappeared into the night. Will and Korina jumped into the vehicle. The GRU major looked at Will and said softly, "Thank you."

Will shrugged. "It was nothing. Getting a stupid man to do something rash is hardly worthy of thanks."

Korina shook her head. "That's not why I'm grateful."

"I know."

She touched his hand and let it rest there for a moment. "It felt nice to—to have someone stand up for me." She faced forward, moved her hand to the steering wheel, and started the engine. Her next words were strident. "We need to take up position." Engaging the gears, she drove the vehicle forward. "We'll wait out of sight a mile up the road. The moment the rest of the team spots the foul-mouthed cretin leaving the dacha, we'll follow him until he leads us to his master."

It was pitch-dark both in the car and outside. They were a few feet away from the road, on rough ground surrounded by trees. Will and Korina had waited in the vehicle for hours, barely speaking. Only occasionally had she turned on the ignition to generate some more heat.

Korina's cell phone rang. She listened in silence. "They watched him walk out of the house, argue with his SVR guardians, who wanted him to stay, then get into a car alone and drive off. Our team is tailing him in their two vehicles. He's heading toward Moscow."

Will muttered, "We'll let them pass us, wait a few minutes, and then follow team and target." He briefly opened his door to trigger the interior light and checked his watch. It was a few minutes after four A.M.; they had entered a new day. Everything rested on the sailor making contact with Razin, but so far everything that Will and Sentinel had done to try to trap him had gone wrong. He began to sweat, his mind racing with uncertainty before landing on one thing that was a certainty.

In three days, the U.S. submarines would be entering Russian waters. When that happened, Razin would detonate his bomb to make it look like a U.S. strike. For Russia, that would be an act of war.

THIRTY-SIX

Fifteen minutes later, Korina was driving fast while Will used a small flashlight to study the rental car's road map of Moscow. He noted that the city was surrounded by an outer, a central, and an inner ring road and that nine motorways led into and out of the metropolis. His cell phone rang; he put the map and flashlight down to listen to Roger's voice.

"We're on the M-10, approaching Moscow from the northwest. We've just passed signs for Skhodnya. Target is driving at normal speeds."

"All right."

Keeping her eyes on the road, Korina said, "We're only three or four miles behind them."

Will spoke again into his phone. "We're going to gain

speed and try to overtake your two cars and the target. Instruct all of the team that we need to switch to military comms."

"Understood."

Korina further depressed the BMW's accelerator, switched lanes, and sped up the motorway. Will leaned to the rear passenger seats, rummaged through his Bergen rucksack, and withdrew two waterproof tactical communications systems. Pulling open his upper garments, he placed one of the sets on his body, using strips of black masking tape to fix the flesh-colored wire containing the earpiece and throat microphone to his skin. As he finished buttoning up his shirt and jacket, he said, "I need to put the other one on you." He smiled. "Either I can tape the cord on you, or I can get close and personal and fix it to your body in the manner that most female surveillance operatives prefer."

Korina also smiled. "My skin reacts badly to tape."

Will opened her jacket and blouse and strapped the set onto her waist. Holding the wire, he threaded it underneath her bra, alongside one breast, and out of the top of her underwear until the system was secure. After turning on the set and selecting the correct channel, he gently fastened her clothes and said, "Right, we should all be linked in." He turned on his own set and spoke into the throat mic. "Roger, Markov: can you hear me?"

Markov replied, "We can." He and Roger were in the vehicle closest to the sailor. Roger was the driver.

"Vitali, Laith: what about you?"

Laith answered. He was the passenger in the other vehicle. "Yeah, we're getting everything. We're about a quarter mile behind the target. We should switch over in one mile."

Roger said, "Agreed."

Korina was now driving at ninety miles per hour. The motorway had lights straddling its route, but they were spread out and required her to occasionally flick on her high beams as she raced along the route.

After five seconds, Roger said, "Okay, we're slowing down to fifty. The target's moving away from us. Vitali, get your vehicle into point."

"We're on our way."

Will looked at Korina. "We're about nine miles from the city's outer ring road. We've got to be ahead of the target before he reaches that point." He reached for his MR-445 Varjag pistol and said into his mic, "Any sign of cops where you are?"

Laith said, "None."

Markov replied, "Nothing."

Will glanced at Korina. "Increase speed to one twenty."

Korina gunned the engine, and within moments they were traveling at the required speed; the road lights now sped past them.

Will checked the workings of the handgun. "You should see us any moment now. We'll maintain speed as we pass you. Let me know if the target gets spooked."

They drove past civilian vehicles, occasionally switching lanes to overtake any that were in their way.

Twenty seconds later, they spotted Roger and Markov's car. It had picked up speed again to match that of the point vehicle and the target. Will said, "This is us, coming past you."

Ten seconds later, they were approaching Vitali and Laith's vehicle and three hundred feet ahead of them the target's vehicle was easily visible. Laith said, "You pass us . . . you pass the target . . . hold . . . he's continuing as normal . . . don't think he's spooked. And I tried to get your license plate but couldn't because of your speed, so there's no way the target could ID you."

Will glanced at Korina. "Keep the speed up until we're out of sight." Into his throat mic he said, "Let us know when we can slow down and to what speed."

Vitali answered, "Not yet."

Will waited, silently counting the seconds.

Vitali came on the air again. "You're out of sight of us and the target. Our speed is seventy-three MPH."

"Heard." Will nodded at Korina. She immediately braked until they were traveling at exactly the same speed as the cars behind them, and then she moved the vehicle into the middle lane. Will spoke into his throat mic, "We must be very close to the MKAD outer ring road. Has the target switched to the right lane yet?"

"Negative," Laith answered. "No indication yet that he's going to exit the M-10."

Will silently cursed while examining his surroundings. More flashing lights ahead, but this time they covered two of the lanes. He said to no one in particular, "Large military convoy ahead. Given that you don't think the target clocked our plates, we're going to stay behind the convoy and hope we don't look suspicious to him."

They drew closer to the convoy until they could see a column of twenty trucks containing troops in the central lane and nine trucks holding massive 9A52-2 BM-30 Smerch 300 mm multiple rocket launchers driving in the slow lane. He nodded at Korina. "This will do. Get in behind them."

She did so, now driving at forty miles per hour. "The convoy's heading into Moscow. The army's preparing to defend the city if everything goes wrong."

"Vitali, you should see us and the convoy at any moment." Will spoke sharply.

A few seconds later, Vitali replied, "We've got you." The line went silent for a while. "Target's maintaining speed, slowing down, he's coming right up behind you, he's overtaking you, no chance he's taking the exit."

"Vitali, Laith: take point. Markov, Roger: stay behind them. We'll fall in at the rear."

They drove for fifteen minutes, passing the exits to the central and inner ring roads. The target was heading into the heart of Moscow.

Ten minutes later, Markov said, "He's holding something in his hand, close to his head. But unless we pull up alongside him, it's going to be impossible for us to know what it is." Silence. "He's slowing down, has got the option of an exit, not indicating, slowing further . . . Fuck! He's taking the exit at speed, no indication. He must have spotted us!"

Will's stomach churned. "He's holding a cell phone."

He withdrew his handgun and looked around. "Sailor boy knows fuck all about antisurveillance. He's not spotted us. But someone else has, and that person's telling our target what to do. Taras is mobile and nearby." Will wasted no time. "All of us: follow him in. Don't worry about being spotted."

Moscow was now before them. Only a few other cars were on the road.

Will said, "Taras is guiding him to their meeting location, but he's going to do it in a way to make us lose our target. Markov, is he still on his cell?" Will breathed deeply to try to calm his rapid heartbeat.

"The whole time."

Will looked around, but this stretch of road was deserted. He wondered how Razin was able to stay so well hidden. He decided he knew how. Speaking to everyone, he said, "Taras has gone ahead, probably to the meeting place. He doesn't care about our team and formation now, because the target is going to use a preprepared antisurveillance route."

Laith said, "Maybe we should take the target down—force him to tell us where he's meeting Taras?"

"No, Taras hasn't given him the route yet, and when he does he'll only supply him with bits of it at a time. Right now Taras doesn't want the target to know where he's meeting him, in case we do precisely what you suggest."

Markov picked up the commentary. "He's slowing down again, he turns left into a side street, no other vehicles are here, he drives on, I see his brake lights . . ."

Silence. "I see him stop, reverse lights are on, he backs up, he moves his car into a parking space."

"He's going on foot!" Will's heart thumped faster. "Markov, jump out and get close to him. Roger, park, secure your vehicle, and join Markov. Concealed handguns and spare magazines only. Vitali, Laith: move further into the city. Then park until we have an idea where he's going." He glanced at Korina. "I'm getting out; I want you to stay mobile." He told everyone, "We're getting close now. But watch out for police patrols. If any of you get stopped, try to use GRU ID to get out quickly, but don't get delayed. If it looks like they're suspicious, do what you have to." Will put his pistol and spare ammunition into his overcoat pocket, opened the car door, and jumped out onto the street.

Markov muttered, "Target's on foot, looking right at me. Now he turns, walks away."

Roger and Markov were two hundred feet away from Will. He saw them start to walk, tailing the target.

Will followed but kept his distance in case he needed to suddenly change direction. Speaking quietly, he asked, "Description of sailor boy?"

Roger answered in a near whisper, "Hooded, black down coat, jeans, running shoes. He's walking quickly."

"Cell phone out?"

"Not right now."

The sailor had as yet been given the directions for only the first leg of his journey on foot.

Large snowflakes fell through the black air, illuminated

by streetlamps. The sweat on Will's face immediately turned icy cold; he rubbed it away before it froze. He thrust his hands into his overcoat pockets and gripped his handgun.

They walked past terraced residential and commercial buildings on either side of the street. All of the properties were in darkness. As they neared the end of the street, Roger muttered, "He's stopped. He's turning. He's facing us, standing underneath a lamp. We're a hundred feet from him, easily visible." Roger went quiet for a few seconds. "He's reaching into his pocket, pulls out something . . . could be his cell . . . correction, it's a pack of smokes. He lights a cigarette, still watches us, remains still."

Will stopped and waited fifty feet behind the CIA operative and the Spetsnaz soldier.

"He's got direct eye contact with us . . . bastard's smiling. He checks his watch, smokes some more, flicks his cigarette away, turns his back on us, but he's still waiting."

Will's mind raced. He briefly wondered if this could be the place where the sailor was meeting Razin. He thought it was unlikely, that it was too risky when Will's team was right by the target. But so far Razin had not cared about risks or opponents. Will said quietly, "Watch your perimeter. Taras could come at us from any direction."

Five minutes passed. Nothing happened. Will, Roger, and Markov remained static, watching the target but also keeping their hands firmly fixed on their hidden pistols in case they were attacked.

Ten minutes passed. The target did not move.

Fifteen minutes. Markov advised them that the target had just lit another cigarette.

Will checked his watch. It was 5:16 A.M.

After seventeen minutes, Will was about to tell the rest of the team to drive their vehicles closer to the area.

But Roger spoke first. "He drops the cigarette, stamps on it, and walks away."

Roger and Markov walked. So did Will.

"He's running!" Roger immediately broke into a sprint.

Will sped after them, shouting, "What's ahead?"

"Main road." Markov was breathless. "He could be heading there for a mobile pickup."

"Unlikely." Will increased his speed. "Anything else on that road that could be useful to him?"

There was silence for a moment before Markov said, "Not sure."

A thought suddenly entered Will's mind. "What time does Moscow's subway system open in the morning?"

"Five twenty." Markov went silent for two seconds. "Shit! He was waiting for the system to open. Tverskaya and Chekhovskaya stations are on the road he's headed toward."

Will was now at full sprint, running across snow-covered pavement, between parked cars, and along the center of the street. "Are they interlinked?"

"Yes. Between them, there are three lines through the complex, giving six possible directions."

Will grabbed his throat mic. "Korina, drive one mile north. Wait there. Vitali, Laith: get to any station east of me. Park there and await updates. The rest of us will follow him in on foot."

Will reached the main road and saw his colleagues sprinting right, then crossing the route. The target was ahead of them, running fast.

"He's gone into the Chekhovskaya entrance." Roger was only fifty feet behind the sailor.

Will called, "Markov, do these comms systems work underground?"

"Most of the time."

Will's stomach tightened. "We'll have to hope they do. I'm taking the Tverskaya entrance. Keep talking to me inside."

He ran into the subway station. Aside from one official, it was empty. Grabbing some notes of rubles from his pocket, he approached a ticket machine, bought a one-day pass, cursed the few seconds he had lost, and sprinted to the barriers. "Which line?"

"Don't know. We're following him further into the station, but he's not yet committed to a platform."

Will moved through the barrier and along a corridor; then he paused by a map of Moscow's subway system and memorized the names and locations of the other stations in the vicinity. He saw that only the green line traveled through Tverskaya, although he could access Chekhovskaya and its other two lines from within the complex. He moved forward, desperate not to lose communication with Markov and Roger.

Markov's voice came into his earpiece, speaking in a

slow, deliberate manner. "He's going to take the purple line, heading east."

"Damn!" Will searched for signs to Chekhovskaya.

"No, wait." Markov's voice grew quieter but was clear. "We've got seven minutes before our train arrives. Check what time the next green line train heads south."

Will ran to the platform and saw that a train was due to arrive in less than one minute. He relayed this to Markov.

"Good. If you take that train, change at the next stop at Okhotny Ryad, and then head north on the orange line, you can be at our next stop at Lubyanka before we get there. If the target gets off at that station, you'll be ahead of him, and we can drop out of sight."

As Will stood on the deserted platform, watching his train emerge from a dark tunnel and come toward him, he said, "Provided my connections are swift."

Roger spoke. "It's a risk, but I think my friend's right. Taras could have us running around all day as long as we're stuck like glue to the target. Maybe we should gift him a deliberate mistake."

The train drew nearer. Will desperately tried to decide what to do. By getting onto the train, he could be rendering himself useless to his surveillance team. Or, if the risk paid off, he could take up point in a way that would make the target think he had lost his current two followers. The train slowed and stopped, and its doors opened. Will sighed and stepped forward. "I'm getting on the train."

Three men were in the carriage. They looked to be in their late twenties, had shaven heads, were brawny, and carried bottles of liquor. They eyed him from the end of the carriage. Will lowered his head to avoid eye contact with the drunken group and remained standing by the doors. "I'm moving south. Mobile units, can you hear me?"

The line crackled for a moment before Korina said, "Yes, William. I'm stationary near Belorusskaya subway station, north of you."

Over static, Vitali said, "Laith and I are northeast of your location, outside Chistiye Prudy station. We're not going anywhere until you tell us where."

The train rattled as it continued its journey. Will tried to imagine where Razin was waiting within Moscow. He wondered if Razin might not even be in one of the other carriages on this train or on the train containing Markov, Roger, and the target. Or maybe he was now watching Korina or Vitali and Laith, readying himself to walk up to their vehicles and use a knife to gut the occupants.

The train stopped at Okhotny Ryad. He stepped out of the carriage and began walking. So did the three men. They were laughing.

Roger spoke, but his words were distorted.

"Say again." Will held his throat mic. "You broke up."

This time the words were clear. "Three minutes until we depart."

Will followed signs for the orange line, walking quickly along a brightly illuminated tunnel. He heard the sound of glass smashing behind him. The drunken men laughed again.

"Two minutes until we leave."

Will walked out of the tunnel and onto the orange line platform. Looking at the electronic timetable above him, he saw that his train was due to arrive in one minute. Checking his watch, he said, "It's going to be very tight."

The three men emerged onto the platform. They were looking at him. One of them called out in Russian; his words were slurred. Will shook his head, walking away from them until he was farther down the platform. He heard the noise of his train, and soon it was thundering alongside the platform, its bright interior and exterior lights causing him to wince. When the doors opened, he walked into the carriage.

Markov spoke, although it was impossible to understand what he said. Will was about to respond but stopped as the three men jumped into the same carriage he was in. They looked at him, grinning. Two of them took swigs from their liquor bottles. The third held his by the neck. It had been smashed in half and was nothing but jagged edges at one end.

Will pushed his throat mic flush against his skin, and said in a near whisper, "Not sure if you can hear me. I'm on the orange line."

The train pulled away. Will moved farther down the carriage. The men took several steps nearer to him, until they were only a few feet away. One of them took another big slug of spirit, then spat the liquid at Will. Will shook his head again, moving farther away from them until he was at the end of the carriage.

"Our train's arrived, we're—" The voice was Markov's but was replaced by a crackling noise.

Will said loudly, "Say again."

The Russian men heard his words. The largest of the three big men muttered, "American?"

The men's grins vanished, replaced by looks of hostility.

Will said nothing.

The Russian holding the broken bottle pointed its deadly shards toward Will's head, while nodding. "American."

Will momentarily closed his eyes and silently cursed. He had no idea how long the journey to Lubyanka would be, but he thought it would be only a minute or two before he arrived there. Under no circumstances could he be delayed. He smelled bad breath and alcohol. Something sharp touched his cheek. Opening his eyes, he saw that the men were right by him. The largest held his makeshift weapon against Will's face.

Will smiled. Quickly, he swept his arm to knock the bottle away, stepped forward, and punched the flat of his hand into the man's nose, crumpling it into a bloody mess and sending the man staggering back, clutching his face and screaming. Will dropped low as the two other men tried to punch him in the head. Using the heel of his shoe, he kicked one of them in the base of his knee, thrust sideways and upward, and used the power of the movement to smash his elbow into the other man's jawbone. Both men fell to the floor. The big man with the broken nose shook his head, pulled his hands away from his blood-covered face, bellowed, and rushed toward Will. Will took one step to the side, moved low, and swung his fist upward into the man's gut as the Russian raced forward. The force of the impact lifted the man's entire body weight off the floor and caused him to vomit the liquor and all other contents from his stomach.

Will looked at the three men writhing on the ground by his feet, then walked quickly over them to the train's doors. The train was slowing. Into his mic, he said, "I'm approaching Lubyanka station."

Roger answered in a clear voice, "Keep sharp. We've no idea what the target's doing. He's sitting at the end of our carriage, looking at us with a grin on his face."

"Which carriage are you in?"

"Second from the front."

Will's train stopped. He ran out of the carriage and along the platform's exit, searching for signs of the purple line. As he did so he said, "Vitali, get your car to Kitai-Gorod station in case the target stays on this line. Korina, move further east in case the target switches lines and goes north."

They both replied, "Understood."

Will reached the purple line platform. A few other people were there, and most looked like early-morning commuters on their way to work. Will was glad of their presence, as they would give him some cover. He moved to the far end of the platform so that he would be by the back of the train when it arrived, away from Roger, Markov, and the target.

Markov said, "We're slowing down, approaching Lubyanka."

"I can hear your train." Will looked along the platform. Some more commuters emerged onto it and joined the others, who were now moving closer toward the incoming train. "What's the target doing?"

"Still sitting, but close to the doors."

"Where are you?"

"We're both in seats, far enough away from the exits to lose him if he bolts as the doors shut."

"Good."

The train emerged and slowed as it traveled alongside the platform. Grinding to a halt, the train's doors opened. No one got out. Everyone on the platform started walking in. Will started moving with them, staying close behind the couple in front of him.

Roger's words were quiet and controlled. "He's still sitting, looking at the doors . . . we've just received the signal we're about to depart . . . doors are closing . . . he still sits . . . now he's up and running. He's moving out of the train!"

Will looked rapidly along the platform. At the other end he saw the sailor sprint out of the train just as the doors closed behind him. In the same carriage, Roger and Markov were now standing, their palms pressed against the window nearest to the platform while they shook their heads and stared at the target. Their play-acting seemed to work. As the train began to pull away from the platform, the sailor turned, smiled, and raised a finger at them before spinning back and continuing to run. He had not seen Will.

Will said, "Roger, Markov: your next station is Kitai-Gorod. Get out of the subway there." He moved along a corridor until he was heading toward the station exit. The target was walking fast and had his cell phone planted on his ear; he was clearly receiving new instructions from Razin.

Will followed him through the exit barriers, squinting as his eyes adjusted to the daylight outside the station. The snow was heavy, the air was freezing, people and cars were on the streets. Keeping a distance of 150 feet behind the sailor, Will matched his pace as he walked along a sidewalk. After thirty seconds, the target stopped, kept his phone against his head for a moment, then snapped it shut and put it into a pocket. Will waited. The sailor looked around, but not back at Will. Beside the man was the Lubyanka building. It was the current headquarters of the Border Guard Service, and it also contained one directorate of the FSB. But during the era of the Soviet Union it had been a notorious prison for political dissidents and spies. It was the place where Sentinel had been incarcerated and tortured for six years.

The target was about to walk across the road but stepped back as fourteen military trucks quickly turned onto the route. Pedestrians and cars stopped on the road to give way to the convoy. As it thundered past them and the target, spewing up snow from the road, Will quickly glanced at the military vehicles. They were stuffed with armed paratroopers wearing sky blue berets. As the last truck passed Will, he saw that one of the soldiers at the back of the vehicle looked familiar. In an instant, he recognized him as the young soldier who had been unable to assemble his rifle during the flight to Moscow. The man was looking not at him but at the weapon Roger had expertly assembled for him.

The target crossed the road. So did Will.

Will spoke into his throat mic, "We're heading southeast."

"You're heading toward our position outside Kitai-Gorod." Vitali's voice was clear.

"And us." Roger sounded as though he was walking fast or jogging. "We're just about to exit the same station."

Will nodded. "Roger: you and Markov are compromised so can't be seen on foot. Take over Vitali's vehicle and head a few hundred yards further south. Then wait there."

Markov answered, "We'll go to Nikol'skiy Pereulok."

"Okay. Vitali, Laith: get on foot and stay outside the station. Korina, the target might be heading for the river. Get mobile, and see if you can find somewhere there or near there to wait."

After another minute of pursuing the target, Will saw the subway station. He examined all the pedestrians near it and spotted Laith standing to the left of the entrance and Vitali about thirty feet away from him. "I can see you both. If the target goes into the station, I'll drop back to allow you to take point but will follow you in. If he doesn't go in, take point and I'll go ahead of you all."

Vitali and Laith shifted position. Neither man spoke.

The sailor walked up to the station and stopped suddenly. He was right next to Laith. Reaching into his pocket, he withdrew his cell phone and listened to it. Will watched him, motionless. The target closed his phone and kept walking, passing the entrance and continuing down the street. Laith walked behind him; Vitali moved to the other side of the road to follow him. Will waited where he was for a few moments, then walked quickly across the road. He moved into another street before turning left onto a road that ran parallel to the route containing the target. Now that he was out of sight of the sailor, he broke into a jog, dodging pedestrians on the ice- and snow-covered sidewalk. As he ran, he passed a stationary vehicle. Inside it were Roger and Markov.

Vitali said, "He's still walking, same pace."

Will replied, "I must be ahead of you by now. Let me know if he deviates from the road." He reached the end of the route, broke left, and continued forward until he was back on the same street as the target. He stopped. "I'm at the end of the road."

Laith said, "We're halfway along it."

Will started walking away from the team behind him.

"Target's increasing pace." Vitali's voice was quiet. "William, I can see you, and we're getting closer to your location. Increase speed."

Will did so.

"Target moves through crossroads, keeps going straight." Vitali's voice grew louder. "Korina, we're following the target toward Moskvoretskaya Naberezhnaya, on the river. Where are you?"

Korina answered, "On that road, close to the place your route joins it."

Will said quickly, "Go east before he spots you." He kept walking fast until he reached the main road and the adjacent Moskva River. "Roger, Markov: I'm turning west on the road. Start driving toward my location."

He walked faster for a while and then slowed to his previous pace. Soon the target would reach the road and Will would know if he was continuing to walk behind him or had instead turned left toward Korina's location. A Russian voice, amplified by a loudspeaker, barked close to him. Will froze, then turned to face the noise. Two powerful river police boats and one military gunboat sped along the river, knocking aside large sheets of ice that were floating on the surface. The Russian man speaking through the amplifier kept repeating the same sentence. Will looked at the various civilian vessels on the mighty river and saw that they were slowing. He understood what was happening. They were being told to berth, that only military and police boats were now allowed to use the route.

"Target's turned left, heading east." Laith's voice was tense.

Will silently cursed and increased pace again as he said, "Markov, Roger: get to me fast. I need picking up."

Roger answered, "On our way."

Will mentally pictured the road map of Moscow he had

earlier studied. "Korina, he's heading toward the bridge at Sadovnicheskiy Proyezd. Are you east of that place?"

"Yes. I've parked, although I'm not sure how long I can remain static."

"Do what you can. If he doesn't go south on the river crossing, he'll be coming toward your location. Roger, Markov: I need you here now."

"We can see you." Markov's deep voice was controlled. "Start running, we're going to have to pick you up at speed as there's nowhere to safely stop on this route."

Will did so. Cars passed him, but none of them belonged to his team.

"We're three hundred feet behind you . . . now two hundred . . . now one hundred . . . now fifty . . . passenger door's open . . . we're slowing . . ." Markov paused. "Look left now."

Will glanced to his side, saw the car and its open door, sprinted faster to keep up with it, and dived headfirst into the rear of the vehicle. Markov grabbed his arm and pulled him in. Roger thrust his foot down on the accelerator, causing the car to skid on a patch of ice before getting a grip and pulling away fast.

Will slammed the door. "Take the next bridge, then double back on the other side of the river so that we're heading east and paralleling the target."

Roger drove fast, taking them right up to the eastern tip of Red Square before turning onto the crossing to take them south, over the river. Once they were over the waterway, Roger turned left.

Will looked across the river. "We're heading back toward you from the other side of the river. Where are you?"

Laith answered, "Target's slowing down, on his cell again, about a hundred and fifty feet from Sadovniches-kiy Proyezd." Laith went silent. "Hold, something's happening." More silence. "His phone's stowed away. He's stopped. Now he's looking left and right along the road."

"He's going to cross it and take the bridge." Will placed a hand on Roger's shoulder. "We must be at the other side of the bridge before he gets on it."

Roger accelerated harder, swerving expertly between two cars to overtake them.

Vitali spoke. "Target's spotted a gap in traffic. He's running over the road. If we follow him we'll expose ourselves, as this isn't a place pedestrians would normally cross."

"Stay on your side of the road." Will's mind raced. "Korina, can you turn around?"

"Impossible on this main road. But I can abandon the car and get closer on foot."

"No, stay with the car. It's vital we retain one mobile unit on the north side of the river." Will spoke to everyone. "Okay, we'll take up point as soon as the target reaches the south end of the bridge. Once we know where he's headed, I'll update you so that we can adjust formation."

"He's on the northern end of the bridge." Laith's voice was quiet. "He's slowed to a fast walk. We're stationary now. He's a hundred and fifty feet away from us. Bridge has got medium traffic in both directions. He walks onward."

Will could see the bridge. Urgently, he asked Roger, "Can you stop anywhere here?"

"Difficult, but I'll put my hazard lights on and fake a breakdown. If cops or other officials arrive, I'll deal with it."

Will nodded. "Vitali, Laith: update please."

"He's slowing"—Vitali paused—"he's stopped halfway along the bridge."

"Stopped?"

"Stopped. Now he's looking around."

Will's heart raced. "Is his cell back out?"

"No."

Roger pulled the vehicle onto the road's hard shoulder. Will jumped out of the car, thrust a hand into his pocket, and gripped his handgun. Roger and Markov also exited the vehicle. Will glanced in the direction of the bridge. "Everyone, the bridge is the likely meeting point. Repeat, bridge is meeting point." He darted a look at Markov. "Come with me. Roger, stay with the vehicle."

Roger looked angry. "I should be with you."

Will shook his head impatiently. "The chances of Taras doing a mobile pickup of the target are now very high. If that happens, you're the only man south of the river who can tail him and take him down. *Everything* depends upon you staying with your vehicle."

Roger smiled; his anger evaporated.

Will and Markov moved alongside the road until they were close to the bridge.

Laith said, "He remains stationary. He tries to light a cigarette."

"I've got another pedestrian on the bridge." This came from Vitali.

Will and Markov instantly stopped.

"He's heading from the south side . . . big guy . . ." Vitali went quiet. His next words sounded confused. "He looks out of place . . . not right for this weather. He's not wearing a coat."

Will snapped, "Vehicle?"

"None, aside from civilian motors going back and forth on the bridge."

Will sprinted, pulling out his gun. "It's him! It's him!" He pulled back the workings of his weapon. "Laith, Vitali: get closer to the bridge so that you're ready for takedown, but stay out of sight of the target for now!"

Markov was running fast by his side, his handgun held at waist level.

Will reached the bridge and turned onto it. He saw cars, heavy snowfall, more military boats cruising along the river beneath him, and a man walking at a steady pace with his back to him, no more than two hundred feet away. Will stopped and grabbed Markov's arm to bring him to a halt. "Wait, wait."

The man reached the target and stopped right next to him.

"They look like they're communicating." Will held his fingers against his throat mic. "No other pedestrians are on this bridge. But why the hell is he here without a vehicle and without an overcoat?"

Vitali said, "We're at the other end of the bridge. We see them both. They're definitely talking. Big man pulls out something . . . can't see what it is."

"Nor can I," Laith added.

"Big man places a hand on target's shoulder . . ." Vitali sounded totally focused. ". . . target tries to shrug him off . . . tries to move away . . . big man pulls him closer . . . something in big man's hand . . ."

In an instant Will knew what was happening. "It's an assassination! Takedown now! Now!"

He sprinted along the bridge, ignoring oncoming civilian vehicles sounding their horns. His feet slipped on the snow and ice beneath them, but he kept upright and ran faster. Markov was right by his side, his gun now at eye level.

Will raised his weapon to shoot. He was only 150 feet away. As he did so, the big man spun to face him, using the sailor as a shield.

It was Razin.

In a flash, the Russian raised a handgun, firing three bullets at Will. One of the bullets sliced alongside Will's face just as he and Markov dived behind a passing car that had come skidding to a halt. Getting to his feet, he could see the sailor beyond the car, lying on the ground; blood-saturated snow surrounded him. Beyond the dead body, Razin was sprinting away, dodging between cars.

Will and Markov chased. Markov shouted, "Vitali, Laith: he's coming right toward you!"

They could catch only glimpses of Razin, too brief to get a clear shot. They heard two more shots from the other end of the bridge, followed by Vitali saying "Fuck!"

Reaching the end of the bridge, they saw Vitali on his knees, his face screwed up in pain, a hand clutching his leg. Laith was running along the river; he fired four shots.

"What happened?"

Vitali answered between clenched teeth. "It's just a flesh wound, but it put me on my ass."

"Okay, get to Roger. Markov, with me."

Laith shouted in a near-breathless voice, "I'm moving east along the river's north-side road. Can't see him."

Roger spoke, "I've abandoned my car and am also going east, checking the south bank."

Korina said, "I'm on the north bank, about five hundred feet from your position. Six military trucks have just raced past me, heading toward the bridge."

"Stay with your vehicle, Korina." Will still needed at least one of his team to remain mobile.

"GRU! GRU!"

Will glanced toward Roger's location on the south bank. "What's happening?"

Silence.

"What's happening?"

More silence.

Then gunfire.

"I'm"—Roger was screaming over the sound of rapid shots—"under attack! Cops and soldiers."

Will saw flashes of light on the south bank; the noise of gunfire in his earpiece was now constant.

Korina shouted, "I can get mobile, drive ahead to find a turning place, then try to pick you up."

"No!"

Vitali said, "I'm with Roger, we're being pushed east."

Will urgently looked ahead. He was sprinting as fast as he could, but he'd no idea if he was still on Razin's trail. "Laith. Anything? I have no visual. Repeat, no visual!"

"Nothing."

They'd lost him.

Frustration surged through Will. "Fuck! Fuck!" He continued running. "Laith, Markov: get across the next bridge and extract Roger and Vitali."

"You can't go after him on your own."

"Just do it!"

Markov moved away from Will's side and took the next river crossing. Moments later, Laith appeared on the bridge running at full pace, his gun held in one hand.

Will kept moving along the road.

Ten seconds later, Markov shouted, "We're heading southeast on Sadovnicheskaya Ulitsa!"

Laith spoke. "Vitali, Roger: we're on the south side of the river now. We should be close to you."

Roger spoke over the sound of rifle shots and bursts of submachine-gun fire. "We've got about a hundred soldiers on our tail." His words were strained; clearly he was in pain.

More heavy gunfire.

Laith shouted, "We can see you! You're coming right toward us!"

Will stopped at a crossroad, frantically looking in every direction. This was hopeless. Razin had vanished.

"William." Korina's voice was full of despair. "Should I go to the team?"

Laith said, "We're all together now. There's too many of them. William, we're going to draw them away from you by taking them south on Novokuznetskaya Ulitsa."

Will cursed and continued running, keeping the river by his side.

"Changing magazines." Roger was clearly running. "Last clip in. I'll cover you all. Run behind me for twenty, then cover me while I move back."

A few seconds later, Vitali shouted, "In position and covering you. Move!"

"Two more hostiles down, now three." Laith spoke over the sound of three shots from his handgun.

Markov cursed. "More sirens, reinforcements."

"Low on ammunition . . . last clip." This was from Vitali.

Will stopped, his stomach sick with failure. "I've lost him. I'm coming to you."

Roger responded immediately, "Get to Korina. Get out of the city."

Will repeated, "I'm coming to you."

"No, you're damn well not! We're surrounded on all sides now. You'd make no difference."

Will pulled out his handgun. "Tell me your location. I'm coming for you."

"No."

"Tell me your location!"

Roger made a sound like a sigh; more shots rang out.

"We're on Novokuznetskaya Ulitsa. It's about half a mile south of the bridge where Taras killed the sailor. But for God's sake, don't come"—rapid bursts of fire interrupted him—"stay away."

Will moved onto the next bridge, ran across it, and headed south toward the gunfight. He ran along residential streets, commercial routes, and roads containing administrative buildings. Compacted snow covered the roads and sidewalks, and pedestrians cowered in doorways, hiding from the gun battle that was taking place farther ahead. Some of them stared at Will as he ran past them, making no effort to hide his handgun. The civilians looked terrified.

Will did not need a detailed knowledge of the city to know where he was going. He just followed the noise of the battle. "I'm very close now. When I see the hostiles, I'll open fire and try to draw some of them away from you."

"There's too many of them." Laith sounded exasperated. "We're pinned down on all sides."

The sounds of gunfire were now very close. Will slowed down as he approached the turning into Novokuznetskaya Ulitsa. Reaching the entrance to the street, he stopped and crouched next to a building. The place was swarming with troops and police, most using the cover of doorways and vehicles to fire at his team. Halfway along the street, he saw glimpses of the four-man CIA-GRU unit. They were about 250 feet away and were using whatever cover they could to return fire. Beyond them, more soldiers.

Will pulled away from the street, desperately trying to work out what to do. Even if he fired shots at them, he would draw only a few of the two hundred or so troops toward him. Roger was right. The situation was hopeless. He glanced again into the street containing the soldiers and his team. He spoke to his men. "I'm sorry. Stop fighting. We've failed. Surrender to them."

There was silence for a while.

Then Roger spoke to his comrades. "Switch your comms systems to any other channel and smash the kit so that they can't monitor William and Korina. No matter what the soldiers do to you, keep your mouths shut."

A few more seconds passed before Markov shouted out words in Russian. Then he walked out of a doorway, his hands placed on his head. Laith appeared from another doorway and tossed his handgun onto the street. Roger moved into view from behind a vehicle, his arms outstretched, his palms facing the soldiers, blood dripping from one of the limbs. Vitali came to his side, arms high in the air, and shouted more words at the soldiers. The troops and police moved close to the four men; all of them had their weapons pointed at the team. One of the cops barked instructions at them. Roger got to his knees; then the rest of the team followed suit. The troops rushed forward. As they did so, Roger looked toward Will and smiled.

The police and soldiers grabbed the men, wrenched their arms behind their backs, and placed plastic handcuffs on each of them. A soldier smashed the butt of his rifle into Laith's head, causing the CIA officer to crash back to the ground, his head now a bloody mess. Another jabbed the muzzle of his gun into Markov's gut, forcing the Spetsnaz operative to double over and vomit. A police officer wearing captain tabs stepped forward, shouting at the soldiers, clearly berating them for their brutality. Some of the troops and cops grabbed the team and yanked them to their feet. At the far end of the street, a four-ton military truck pulled up. The captain pointed at it and shouted orders. Will's team was slowly walked toward it, hands gripping them, the rest of the army and police units continuing to point their weapons at the joint Russian-American intelligence unit. As they were placed into the back of the truck, Will looked at his men one last time, knowing that they would be imprisoned, brutally tortured, and executed.

He turned away from the street, feeling sick, and more than anything wishing it was himself rather than his team who had been caught. Secreting his gun, he turned and walked. His face smarted from the bullet wound, but he didn't care.

Snow fell faster. The air grew colder. He passed pedestrians who were now reemerging onto the streets and were calling to one another, ignoring him and pointing in the direction of Novokuznetskaya Ulitsa. Men, women, children, old and young.

He heard Korina's voice in his earpiece, telling him where she was, telling him what to do. With every step he took toward her location, his stomach tightened and cramped.

He had one remaining option to capture Razin. But the thought of taking it repulsed him.

THIRTY-SEVEN

They were driving south, away from Moscow, and had been on the road for two hours. Korina was in the driver's seat; Will was next to her. It was midmorning, though the sky was dark and the snowfall heavy.

Will had no idea where Korina was headed. He had not bothered to ask her as he did not care. He just sat in silence, feeling sick with failure. During the journey, the scenery had changed from urban to suburban, and now they were moving through forested countryside. As Will looked at his surroundings, he knew that ordinarily the snow-covered trees and rolling hills would seem pretty. But right now he could only imagine how the country-side around him would look in a devastating war.

Korina slowed her vehicle and turned off onto a thin

track that took them into the forest. She drove for another ten minutes before stopping in front of a large eighteenth-century house. She glanced at Will. "My father's house. I couldn't think of anywhere else to go."

Will got out of the car and retrieved his bag and Bergen rucksack from the open trunk. Grabbing her bag, Korina approached the front door, tried the handle, realized it was locked, and looked at Will. "Stay here." She disappeared around the side of the building, returning a minute later. "Dad always kept a spare key hidden in the shed." Korina unlocked the door and stepped into the building. Will followed her.

He walked through a wide hallway containing gold-framed paintings, passed the base of a majestic, red-carpeted staircase alongside a study, a large kitchen which had a breakfast table set for six, and into a big open-plan dining and lounge area. At one end of the room was a Bechstein grand piano, lying on its surface were a violin and bow, and fixed in a stand next to it was a cello. Korina moved beyond an ornate oak dining table topped by a candelabra, stopping by a sumptuous leather three-piece suite, dropped her bag on the floor, and slumped into one of the armchairs.

She tousled her hair with both hands and looked around. "I haven't been here for a while, but nothing's changed. I still pay Dad's cleaner to come in once a week, and I even keep the freezer and cupboards stocked with food in case—well, I don't know why." She nodded toward the instruments. "When I was a girl, Dad would accompany my violin recitals." She half smiled, though the look was sad. "I think he tried his best to make me into a true lady, but in the end, he gave up and allowed me to pursue my own path." Her smile faded. "But it must have been hard for him to see his little girl be like that."

Will nodded slowly, looking around. There were photographs on the walls, and, after dropping his Bergen and travel bag, he walked up to them. One of the shots was of a younger Korina; she looked to be in her early twenties. She was wearing an army uniform and had tabs showing she was a junior lieutenant.

Handwritten, in black ink in one corner of the photo, were some words in Cyrillic:

To my dear Korina, I am so proud of you.

Korina called out, "It was taken on the day of my graduation from the GRU training academy." Her voice grew quieter. "Even though Dad was shocked at my career choice, he seemed so proud of me on that day." She said in a louder voice, "I need to look at your injury."

Will was about to speak, but Korina wagged her finger, got to her feet, and walked to him. Grabbing his hand, she said, "The house contains plenty of medical supplies." She walked him out of the room, up the red-carpeted stairs, and into a big bathroom. Turning her back on him, she removed some items from a wall cabinet and placed them by the sink. Then she took off her jacket and blouse to reveal a white tank top and stuck a cigarette in her mouth. After lighting the cigarette, she washed her hands, grabbed some implements, and moved to him. "Sit on the floor, please."

"I can dress the wound myself."

"I'm sure you can," Korina said while clenching her cigarette between her teeth. "Or you can allow me to do it. You choose."

Will looked at her for a while before lowering himself to the ground.

Korina crouched opposite him, carefully rubbed disinfectant-doused cotton wool swabs over the cut on his face, used more of them to wash away the caked blood around the injury, and finally applied butterfly Band-Aids to close the wound. "It will still scar."

Will got to his feet, and so did Korina. She moved back to the sink, extinguished her cigarette, stripped out of her tank top and bra, and filled the sink with hot water. With her back to Will, she began washing. "I'll bathe properly this evening. But first I want to prepare you some food, and I can't do that without a wash." She applied soap to her body before cupping her hands and splashing water to rinse herself. Grabbing a hand towel, she turned to face Will and stood still. Water from her naked upper body dripped down to the waistband of her pants.

Will looked at her face, her long black hair, her slender arms and shoulders, and her full breasts. He stood still as she walked up to him, dropped the towel on the floor, and wrapped her arms around him.

Bringing her lips close to his, Korina whispered,

"Vitali and Markov will not break in interrogation, but it's a matter of GRU record that I requisitioned them from their Spetsnaz unit. That means the FSB has issued a warrant to arrest me." She raised a hand to his face and gently brushed her fingers against his cheek. "Unless I can get out of Russia, my life is over." She pulled him right against her body, kissing him fully on the lips, holding him tight, pressing her breasts against his body.

For the briefest of moments, Will wanted to forget about everything, to hold on to Korina, to lift her body and cradle her in his arms, to take her to a bedroom and gently lower her onto the bed. Instead, he pulled away from her and said, "Get dressed."

Korina frowned; her eyes moistened. "I thought—" She stared at him for a while before grabbing the towel from the floor, positioning it over her chest, and shaking her head. Her expression now held anger. "I was stupid."

Will sighed. "No." Momentarily he looked away from her, silently cursing himself. Then he locked his gaze back onto her. "I need to freshen up and get into clean clothes. Then I'll help you cook."

Having bathed and changed into his clean arctic warfare clothes and combat boots, Will walked into the kitchen. Korina was there, defrosting a whole chicken and pre-packed vegetables in a microwave. She gathered the food together and laid it out on a large bench.

Staring at it, she muttered, "I now realize that I've never cooked for a man before." She kept looking at the food and seemed uncertain what to do.

Will moved to her side, ignited the adjacent gas burner, placed a deep frying pan onto it, and reached for a large kitchen knife and chopping board. Expertly, he peeled and diced shallots and tossed them into the pan with olive oil and butter. Then he deboned and portioned the chicken, pan-fried it with crushed garlic, pepper, and finely chopped herbs, splashed red wine into the pan, and allowed the alcohol to burn off before tasting the liquid and adding some salt and sugar.

He looked at Korina. "It's not five-star cuisine, but it will work with rice or potatoes."

Korina looked surprised. "It looks and smells better than anything I could have prepared. Where did you learn to cook?"

Will shrugged. "For one of my lessons at school I had to choose between metalwork and cookery. I opted for the latter because I knew I'd be the only boy in a classroom of teenage girls." He smiled. "It gave me certain advantages."

Thirty minutes later they were sitting at the dining table and eating their meal in silence. Korina looked distracted and unsettled. When they finished, she looked out of the window and muttered, "I need some air. Will you join me?"

As they walked into the spacious garden, the snowfall was lighter, though large flakes still drifted slowly through the air. They reached a big oak tree. Hanging from one of its branches was a child's swing. Korina sat on it and looked at the snow-covered ground. "My father loved his country but secretly hated the way it was being run. He believed that after the collapse of communism, Russia was supposed to be a better place. Instead he felt it had become a breeding ground for the worst excesses of capitalism, for mad dogs who would do anything to make money. Over the last few years, I've seen that his views are right."

Will watched her for a while, staying silent, before moving in front of her. "So that's how my MI6 colleague got you. He discovered that, like your father, you hated your country's regime."

It was evening. Will was alone in the dining room, emptying the contents of his rucksack onto the large table. He realized that it had been packed for a Spetsnaz man to operate in harsh, rugged terrain. Carefully, he laid out two mountaineering ice axes, vertical-framed steep-ice crampons, a small spade, a pure down sleeping bag, inner and outer gloves, thermal tops, a white fleece jacket, a fleece-lined woolen hat, tactical goggles, waterproof pants, a compass, a first-aid kit, and a military knife. He stripped down and reassembled the workings of his AS Val assault rifle, attached the sound suppressor, checked his MR-445 Varjag pistol, unpacked and repacked magazine clips, and tested the tactical communications systems that he and Korina had used in Moscow earlier in the day.

Korina came in, barefoot and dressed in loose flannel pants and a baggy V-necked sweater with nothing underneath. Her hair was damp; she smelled of shampoo and soap. Moving to the fireplace, she put firelighters, twigs, and logs onto the grate and struck a match to get the fire burning. At the liquor cabinet, she poured large slugs of Château de Beaulon cognac into two big brandy glasses and handed one of the glasses to Will before taking a seat on the floor in front of the fire.

She took a gulp of the spirit and looked at him. "You call him Sentinel; I know him as Gabriel. I've always known it's not his real name, just as William's not yours, but that's never mattered to me." She glanced at the fire, wafted the cognac under her nose, and took another gulp of the liquid. As the fire crackled, its flames cast flickering light over her face. "Of course, I don't know the identity of his other Russian agents, but I bet they all think about him in the same way that I do. He gives us so much hope."

Will sipped his drink slowly, his gaze fixed on Korina. "He'll crack under torture very soon. And when he does, there's something you need to know. He'll call and ask to meet you. He's going to do the same with two other agents. Then Taras will try to kill all of you."

Korina looked shocked. "I—"

Will held up a hand. "I'm not going to let you get anywhere near Razin. As soon as I get the time and location of the meeting, I'll go there alone and watch the place."

"I'm coming with you."

"No."

Korina looked sharply at him. "I'm a professional intelligence officer. I don't need to sit here doing nothing."

Will sighed. "It's too risky."

"So is staying here! GRU or FSB could come looking for me here while you're away. Plus"—she placed her glass on the floor, spilling some of its contents—"Taras killed my father. I want to be there." She stared straight at Will. "I'm *going* to be there."

Will wondered what to say. Nothing came to him, because he understood exactly how Korina felt. He moved to the fireplace, sat next to her, and placed his hand over hers. She moved her fingers around his.

They stayed like that, not speaking, just holding each other's hands, staring away at nothing.

Both intelligence operatives.

Fugitives.

And with no one else in their lives.

Will stripped out of his clothes, turned off the light, and sat on the spare bed.

He tried to relax his aching body and put all thoughts out of his mind. But images kept racing through his brain.

He saw a Russian submariner lying on the floor with his body cut open, an old woman being torn apart by an explosion, a military commander raise a toast to peace, a noble but impoverished couple giving away their last food, a general expertly checking the workings of a handgun, the dead body of a Scotsman left to be eaten by animals, four American and Russian men throwing their guns to the ground as troops surrounded them, and an Englishman sweeping a hand over prone handgun cartridges with a look of utter sadness on his face.

He wondered if these images now meant anything.

Uncertainty and despair swept over him. He felt that the fate of Russia and the United States rested on his shoulders.

Standing, he looked at the bed before walking to the window. It was dark outside; he could see nothing. But he stayed there anyway, just looking.

He thought about Korina. She had taken so many risks for him, yet he had rejected her. That decision now seemed wholly wrong, because he knew that they were attracted to each other.

And they both knew that tomorrow they could be dead.

He turned away from the window, walked across the room, opened the door, and stood still. On the opposite side of the corridor was another bedroom, its door shut. Korina was inside. He stared at the door for nearly two minutes before making a decision.

It was the right decision.

He walked across the corridor and knocked on her door.

She was now before him, dressed in her bathrobe.

The slightest smile on her face.

A tiny nod of her head.

A minute step toward him.

Will moved to her, held her for a moment, lifted her body so that she was cradled in his arms, kissed her passionately on her lips, and carefully carried her back into her bedroom.

THIRTY-EIGHT

It was six A.M. Sentinel's mind was now almost certainly broken. In two days the *Ohio* submarines would reach Russian waters.

Will was dressed, pouring coffee in the kitchen. As he brought the steaming mug to his mouth, he could smell Korina's perfume on his hand.

When she came in, she was wearing a jacket, pants, and hiking boots; her hair was pinned up, and she had applied makeup. Wrapping one arm around his waist, she kissed him on the nape of his neck, grabbed a spare mug of coffee, and moved to the far side of the room. She turned on a small television, flicking through channels until she found a news program. Will looked at the screen and saw the Russian president giving a press conference. His tone was solemn. At the bottom of the screen, his words were shown in English, French, and Chinese subtitles. As Will read the English transcript his stomach wrenched.

> *Diplomatic relations with the United States of America have broken down. We are working hard to reverse this situation, and we pray that America is doing the same. It is certain that Russia has done nothing to create this political catastrophe. Whatever happens, I promise all Russians that I will continue to serve you with unwavering loyalty. God bless and protect the motherland.*

Korina turned the television off. She raised her mug of coffee to her lips. Her hand shook. "Whatever happens, I can't stay in Russia. Do you think MI6 would give me a home in the U.K.?"

Will nodded. "Of course. They won't leave you to suffer imprisonment or—"

"Or execution." Korina frowned. "I've never been to England. I wouldn't know where to live."

Will kept his eyes on her. "London's as good a place as any." He smiled. "I have an apartment overlooking the river Thames. You could stay there."

Korina moved closer to him and held his hands. "That's a generous offer."

"My home's in need of a feminine touch. It would help me out if you stayed there."

Korina smiled but shook her head. "A feminine touch?"

Will laughed as a mental picture of Roger watching him right now entered his mind. He tried to think of something normal to say. "I'm away a lot. The place rarely gets used."

Korina moved closer to him, smoothed a hand against his face, then unclasped her necklace. She held the chain and locket before him, a smile on her face. "You can open the locket when we're in your apartment."

Will took the necklace, nodded, and secreted it in an inner pocket.

She grabbed her coffee and stared at her cell phone on the kitchen table. "I've destroyed my regular phone because I know that GRU will be trying to track its signal. But this phone was given to me by Sentinel. Only he has the number." She looked around. "My dad and I shared years around this table. What would he think of me now?"

Will briefly wondered how to respond. He decided to tell her what he really thought. "He'd be proud of you."

Korina looked at him. "Yes, I'm sure that's what he'd be thinking right now." She smiled, though her expression was haunted. "His little girl . . ."

They were quiet for a while. Outside, snow was falling thick and fast, and garden trees swayed in a strong wind, but the noise of the weather did not penetrate the kitchen. The whole room was silent.

Then it was not.

An electronic beeping noise reverberated around the kitchen. A small flashing light accompanied the sound.

Korina's phone was ringing.

*   *   *

Will held his cell phone and stared at it for a moment. So much rested on the call he was about to make. And so much rested on the man answering. Doubts raced through his mind. Perhaps the man was right now on a flight, in a meeting, sleeping, vacationing, or doing anything else that meant he couldn't answer.

His finger shook as he began pressing numbers.

When the last digit was depressed he raised the cell to his ear.

One ring.

Three rings.

Will's heart pounded.

Six rings.

Seven rings.

Click.

The man answered.

THIRTY-NINE

Will drove the Toyota Prado northeast toward the town of Shatura. Korina was next to him, checking the workings of her handgun. The SUV had belonged to her father, was in immaculate condition, and carried additional gas in the spare fuel tank and canisters. Next to the sat nav on the dashboard was a worn photo of Korina and her father; they were wearing skis and winter sports clothing, standing on a snow-covered slope with smiles on their faces. Jammed between the door and Will's seat was the sound-suppressed AS Val assault rifle.

Their destination was beyond Shatura. Sentinel had given Korina exact directions to the isolated farmstead that was ninety miles away.

The snow was heavy and strong winds were whipping

it up, making visibility atrocious. Though there was daylight, Will had his car's headlights on high. The road was deserted and straddled by forest and rolling countryside. They drove for one hour, barely speaking to each other, not deviating from the route, the features around them remaining the same.

Will's eyes ached from concentrating on the road and from the disorienting effect of the dots of snow continually rushing toward his vehicle. After rubbing his face, he glanced at the sat nav and saw that they were approximately sixty miles away from Shatura.

"Something ahead."

Will immediately looked up on hearing Korina's words. Driving slowly, he reached the end of the forest and saw that snow-covered fields were now to either side of them. He could not see much beyond three hundred feet into the fields, but he could see enough to make his stomach churn. There were at least fifty of them, probably more were hidden by the snowfall, and all were facing the sky. They were RT-2UTTKh intercontinental missiles, fixed onto MZKT-79221 sixteen-wheel transporter-erector-launchers. Soldiers moved back and forth among the weapons; none of them took any notice of Will's vehicle as he continued driving steadily onward. They all seemed too busy preparing the deadly projectiles.

Will knew that the missiles had a precision-guided effective range of more than six thousand miles and that each carried a 550-kiloton nuclear warhead. They could easily reach and destroy armies in Europe, and if needed they could be sent across all of Russia to strike seaborne landings in the east. Once launched, they were nearly indestructible, being immune to any missile defense system and shielded against electromagnetic pulses, lasers, and even nuclear blasts up to a quarter mile away.

As he passed the last of them, he was sure that in a day's time the missile unit would move to another location and would keep changing location over the following days and weeks so that it could not be compromised. But a small number of people in the Russian military high command would have information about the missiles' exact movements. Will wondered if one of those men or women was a tier-1 agent belonging to Sentinel.

After almost two hours, they were three miles away from Shatura. The road was straight and surrounded by flat, featureless countryside. As he looked at his inhospitable surroundings, a memory came to him. He was a small boy, dressed in an ill-fitting black suit, a white shirt, and a black tie that he hated because it felt tight around his throat. He was in a beaten-up SUV that had cold, tatty plastic seats. His older sister was sitting next to him. She was also dressed in black and was quietly sobbing. His mother was in the driver's seat. Her long silver hair was tied up in a bun by a black band. All he could hear was the sound of the car's wipers and strong winds buffeting the vehicle. All he could see was driving snowfall and endless flat countryside to either side of the road. They were driving west, away from their home in the suburbs of Washington, D.C., to their father's hometown of Lancaster, near Columbus, Ohio. They were going there to hold a memorial for his dead father.

The memory faded. He wondered what his father would think of him now, driving through countryside identical to the Midwest.

Multiple lights ahead. He caught occasional glimpses of buildings. They were approaching the outskirts of Shatura. He gunned his engine and drove quickly into the town. The place had only one main road running through it, and a few cars and pedestrians were on the route; otherwise the town seemed quiet. He drove away from the town for a mile until they were on a long strip of flat land that had a large lake on its left and another medium-sized lake on its right. Soon the lakes behind him were gone. Everything around him was barren. He increased his speed to sixty mph.

They drove southeast for another twenty-five miles until they reached eight large and medium-sized lakes that were positioned from north to south. As Will drove, he counted them until he was sure that he was by the large lake in the south. Soon he could see distant glimpses of a forest.

"This is as close as we dare get in the vehicle." He stopped the SUV, grabbed his rifle, and jumped out of the car. Korina joined him, gripping her handgun.

They moved off the track, toward the lake's shoreline, before changing direction and following the shoreline toward the forest.

Will twitched his gun left and right, searching for the

farmstead and the clearing in front of it where Korina had been instructed to park her vehicle and wait. They neared the forest. A glimpse of color between the trees. Will tapped a hand against Korina's arm and nodded toward the colors. Korina lowered her body into a crouch and moved forward; Will did the same. They reached the edge of the forest, the lake still by their side. The colors belonged to two cars, both parked in the large clearing. Will held his rifle tight, one finger gripped against the trigger. They moved a few feet into the forest, stopped, and lowered themselves slowly onto the ground until they were lying flat.

Beyond the two vehicles ahead of them were buildings. They were spaced out. One of them was right beside the lake and looked like a boathouse, two others were farther inland and were huts, and in between them was what looked like a large wooden barn or workshop. But there was no sign of life.

They waited for ten minutes before Will rolled onto his side, cupped his hand against Korina's ear, and whispered, "We need to move to watch the farmstead from another angle."

Korina nodded; then her eyes widened and she gripped Will's arm hard.

Will urgently followed her gaze.

A big man emerged from one of the huts. His face was obscured by a body that was resting over his shoulder. The man walked steadily across the clearing toward the barn, pulled open the building's double doors, and disappeared from view. A moment later he reappeared, his face no longer hidden.

Will watched him through the foresight of his rifle, his finger on his trigger.

Ready to pull back and send a bullet into Razin's head.

Razin moved back across the clearing, went into the hut, and came out with another body over his shoulder. Reaching the barn, he tossed the limp body into the building, grabbed an adjacent gas canister, and began dousing the outside walls. It was clear that he intended to burn the building and the dead bodies. He checked his watch. No doubt he was wondering how much time he had before the last tier-1 agent arrived. Korina Tsvetaeva, a GRU major and traitor to the motherland. If she was on time, he had thirty minutes to wait.

Will was motionless, staring at the man whom he could easily kill, the man he'd been hunting for weeks. He recalled the encounters he'd had with the Spetsnaz colonel: the fight outside the Saint Petersburg safe house where Razin had matched him blow for blow; the moment he'd thrown a grenade at Will just before dragging Sentinel out of the mountain lodge; the pursuit across the Moscow bridge just after Razin had killed the American sailor.

He was desperate to pull the trigger.

Desperate to end this now.

But he had to wait.

Razin moved into one of the other buildings, and was now out of sight. Will relaxed his trigger finger. Glancing at Korina, he saw that her eyes were narrow, that she'd had her handgun trained on the man who'd murdered her father. He whispered, "Don't do anything stupid."

She replied between gritted teeth, "I don't intend to."

"Okay. Stay here to keep this side of the farmstead covered. I'm going to get to the other side."

Korina remained motionless, her gun trained on the open ground before her.

Will rolled away from her, crawled a few meters back, got to his feet, and moved around the perimeter while keeping low and holding his rifle at eye level. Two minutes later, he was on the opposite side of the farmstead. Buildings blocked his view of Korina, but that didn't matter because between them they now had all of the complex's open ground covered. He lay flat on the thick snow and waited, large flakes now falling slowly onto his body.

Ten minutes passed.

All was silent.

Another ten minutes.

No sign of Razin.

Will decided he had to get closer to the building that Razin had entered. Cautiously he moved forward, swinging his gun left and right. He reached the hut, crouched, listened, but heard nothing save the sound of the icy wind. Moving forward ten feet, he was close to the door and saw that it opened inward and if locked could easily be kicked in. In all probability, he could enter the hut and drop Razin before the man could do anything about it, but nevertheless he wished he had a stun grenade to toss in there first. He moved to the edge of the door, stood up fully, and got ready to make the assault.

The impact from above was overwhelming. Will crumbled down, his body in shock, his shoulders in severe pain, his lungs locked. As his head smacked the ground, he saw the rapid movement of a large man close to him and understood what had happened. Razin had leapt on him from the roof of the hut. A boot kicked his face with sufficient force to roll his whole body over. Another banged into his ribs. Then Razin grabbed his hair with one hand and punched his other fist full force into the side of Will's head. Will's vision blurred; he felt nauseous. Razin pulled his fist back in preparation for another devastating punch. But before he could deliver the blow, Will slapped him in the throat, causing the Spetsnaz commander to gasp, bend closer toward Will, and clutch his hands against his gullet. Still on his back, Will head butted Razin in the face and began lashing out at the Russian with his legs and fists and all of the strength he could muster. Razin blocked some of the blows, screwed his face up in pain as others struck his face and torso, and rained his own punches down on Will.

This was hopeless.

They were killing each other.

Will grabbed Razin's wrist and twisted, causing the Russian to fall to the ground by his side. Releasing his grip, Will kicked at the ground to force his body away from Razin. Both men quickly got to their feet and were about to get back into the fight when they stopped.

Engine noises. Drawing closer. Certainly vehicles. And one of them sounded like a truck.

Razin frowned, then peered straight at Will with a look of utter hostility. "Bastard!"

He turned and ran away, darting between buildings until he was out of sight.

Will didn't pursue him. He didn't need to. Instead he looked around, grabbed his discarded assault rifle, winced from the pain caused by the blows to his body, jogged to the perimeter, and moved along it until he was back alongside Korina.

She frowned as she stared at his bruised and bloody face. "You fought him? Where is he?"

Will ignored her questions.

The engine noises stopped.

A few seconds later there was movement.

Twelve men moved toward the farmstead from the vehicle track. All of them were wearing white combat clothes and balaclavas and had semiautomatic rifles held ready. They moved purposefully and silently toward the buildings. One of them was clearly their leader, communicating with the others via hand gestures. He sent three soldiers to the boathouse; they moved quickly across the open ground, their rifles held high. Two of them paused on either side of the door; the third stood back while pointing his weapon directly at the entrance. The door was opened, and one of the men entered, followed by another. Within seconds, they exited. The commander gestured to others in his team. Four of them approached one of the huts. The same drill. But they found nothing. The leader nodded at the other hut. The same four men moved to it and entered quickly.

Noise.

Shouting.

A shot.

Then another.

Three more soldiers rushed into the building. The commander and his remaining four men were motionless, each on one knee. Two of them ignored the hut while pointing their weapons at the barn; the other two had their guns trained on the hut containing the rest of the team.

A soldier jogged out of the hut, then swiveled around and pointed his rifle at the door. Another two emerged and stood to either side of the exit. A man inside the building called out. The commander shouted back to him.

It happened very fast. Soldiers rushed out, Razin was forced backward, one soldier had his fingers in Razin's nostrils, three others were gripping his limbs. They dumped him in the center of the clearing before fanning out to form a circle around him, their rifles trained on his body.

The commander stood, walked toward Razin, and said in a loud voice, "Colonel Khmelnytsky. You are under arrest for suspected misuse of Russian military property."

Will felt relief and joy overwhelm him.

Because his plan had worked.

His call this morning to Otto von Schiller telling the German that he was taking possession of the nuclear blueprints had prompted the SVR agent to immediately report it to his handlers. And Will had given him an exact time and location for the handover. The beacon in Razin's car had been turned on. His location had corroborated Schiller's intelligence. And men had immediately been deployed to arrest Razin before a British arms dealer walked off with vital documents.

Will hadn't been able to physically defeat Razin.

But he had totally outsmarted him.

FORTY

Razin was on his knees, still in the center of the farmstead clearing. "You're making a big mistake!"

The Spetsnaz commander took off his balaclava and ran his fingers through his blond hair.

Korina whispered, "Captain Zaytsey. Spetsnaz Vympel. I've done training courses with him."

Zaytsey said, "Sir, we're under orders to take you away for questioning."

"Do you know who you're talking to?!"

"Of course." Zaytsey glanced at his men. "None of us takes pleasure in doing this to someone of your status."

Razin started getting to his feet. Two of the soldiers stepped forward, shouting at him. But Zaytsey raised a hand. "Give him some dignity." He looked at Razin. "Where are the blueprints?"

"What fucking blueprints?"

"You were here to meet a British arms dealer named Thomas Eden so that you could sell him blueprints of the nuclear devices you've been training with. We want them."

Razin shook his head, anger vivid on his face. "I was never given any blueprints. Your commanders will know that."

"They do, sir. We assume that you must have had an expert examine the bombs so that blueprints could secretly be drawn up."

"This is outrageous!" Razin looked at the Spetsnaz men. "I'll have you and your commanders court-martialed for this."

The men stayed still.

Zaytsey pointed at Razin. "The order for your arrest was countersigned by General Platonov himself. The only man looking at a court-martial is you." He held out his hand. "Sir, I'll have your sidearm."

"And I'll have your head!"

"Your sidearm, sir."

Razin hesitated.

"Sir!"

Slowly Razin removed his pistol from his holster and weighed it in his hand before thrusting it at Zaytsey. The commander took the weapon and tucked it in his jacket.

Razin placed his hands on his hips and looked at the men. All but Zaytsey still had their faces covered with balaclavas. "Which unit are you from?"

Zaytsey answered, "That's classified."

"Nothing's classified from me!"

The commander stared at him, then nodded. "I suppose it makes no difference. We're Vympel."

"It makes *every* difference." Anger was still evident in Razin's voice, but he showed no signs of fear, his posture now one of a high-ranking officer addressing his men. "You should know that I used to be in Vympel before being given command of Alpha. We're the same, and *we* do not sell Russian secrets."

"If that's true, you will be exonerated. But that decision will be made by more powerful men than me. We're here simply to take you away."

"Fools!"

"Sir, your Alpha men have been recalled and are being questioned. The beacons on the nuclear devices have been turned on. All of the bombs have been retrieved except one. We don't know where it is because its beacon has been removed."

Razin barked, "Removed or is faulty? Either way, I can help you retrieve it."

"They think that's the bomb that was dismantled so that the blueprints could be made."

Sweat began to trickle down Will's back. The fact that the beacon had been removed from the bomb meant that Razin must have planted it.

Slowly Razin turned fully, pausing to look at each man around him before returning his stare to Zaytsey. "You've all been tricked, and I think I know by whom."

"Sir, if that's the case, you must tell your superiors."

Razin laughed. "Oh, I'll tell those idiots everything. But right now you and your men need to know that I've captured the man I'm talking about. He's an MI6 officer, one of the most powerful men in Western intelligence and certainly *our* biggest enemy. He's been hunting me, and I've been hunting him. I got to him first. But this"—he swept an arm—"*farce* was no doubt his insurance; a way to make me look bad to the motherland."

Zaytsey moved closer. "Is he dead?"

Will tensed.

"No. I have him prisoner. But if I don't return to him soon, there's every chance he may escape." He smiled. "Perhaps it would be better for you and your men to return to your barracks with the one man that every Russian intelligence agency has been chasing for decades, rather than"—he thumped his chest—"a man who will certainly be proven innocent and will make you and your soldiers look like a laughingstock within all of Spetsnaz."

Captain Zaytsey's eyes narrowed. "Where is he?"

Silence.

Then Razin nodded. Speaking loudly, he gave them a grid reference.

Korina grabbed Will's arm and said urgently, "He's winning them over!"

Will muttered, "I know."

He crawled forward a few feet, tightened his finger around the trigger, and pointed his gun at the center of Razin's skull.

He heard feet crunching over snow, clothes rustling, saw movement in his peripheral vision.

Too far away to be grabbed and pulled to the ground, Korina strode quickly out of the trees and into the clearing.

Will thought, No, Korina!

"Captain Zaytsey." Her voice was loud. "Major Tsvetaeva, GRU."

Four of the Spetsnaz men spun around and pointed their guns at the approaching woman.

"We've trained together. An interrogation course a year ago." She kept walking. "Colonel Khmelnytsky is lying to you about the bomb."

Zaytsey frowned. "Yes, I remember you, Major Tsvetaeva. What the hell's going on?"

She went right up to the captain and Razin and pointed behind her. "There are dead people in the barn. Khmelnytsky murdered them. Check their identities. I suspect you'll find they are high-ranking Russian officials."

Razin spat. "More like traitors!"

"You're the traitor, Khmelnytsky!" Korina looked back at Zaytsey. "This is worse than you think. Please check."

Zaytsey looked doubtful, but he gestured to two of his men, who walked off toward the barn.

More sweat trickled down Will's back. He had to stay hidden, keep his gun trained on Razin. If he could have stopped Korina going out there he would have, though he understood why she'd done so. But everything now depended upon her ability to ensure that the men carried out their orders.

A minute later, the two men returned and spoke quietly to their commander.

Zaytsey looked at Razin. "An air force colonel and a senior government official. Both natives of this country. You killed them?"

Razin stepped closer to the captain and Korina. "They were MI6 agents, run by the man I captured."

Will adjusted his position slightly. Korina had her back to him and was partially obscuring his view of Razin, though he still had an easy head shot available.

Razin smiled while looking at Korina. "And they're not the only MI6 agents I've been looking for. There's one more. And I think"—he looked toward the perimeter—"that person's been getting help from another MI6 officer."

Korina interjected in a loud, urgent voice, "Captain—the bomb. Khmelnytsky plans to use it to—"

She became silent.

Something was wrong.

Zaytsey shouted.

His men moved quickly toward him.

Korina fell back toward the ground.

With a large knife stuck in her chest.

Will's stomach wrenched; he gritted his teeth.

No! No! No!

Soldiers grabbed Razin.

No!

He was thrown down.

No!

Will banged a fist into the ground, disbelief overwhelming him.

Captain Zaytsey knelt down by Korina. She was motionless. He placed a hand against her throat, fingers against her wrist, then placed his ear to her heart. Rising slowly, he shook his head, moved to Razin's facedown body, and said to the men holding him, "Let him go!"

They moved away.

Zaytsey stood over him. "She's dead."

Every emotion gripped Will.

Dead? Oh dear God, no!

"You killed a GRU major." Captain Zaytsey moved an arm; Will couldn't see what he was doing.

"No!" Razin's voice was urgent. He looked wide-eyed toward the perimeter again, clearly trying to locate Will. "I've more information you need—"

"Shut up!" In a loud, authoritative voice, Zaytsey said, "Colonel Taras Khmelnytsky, Hero of the Russian Federation, soldier of the motherland, I relinquish you of your rank, title, and nationality."

He swept his arm forward.

Razin's sidearm was in Zaytsey's hand.

Will shouted, "Stop!"

But his voice was drowned out by the sound of the pistol shot.

Its noise traveled through the forest, and across the adjacent lake.

The captain slowly lowered his arms and dropped the gun on Razin's body. The back of Taras Khmelnytsky's head had been completely ripped apart.

Razin was dead.

FORTY-ONE

Ten minutes later, Will remained motionless. The soldiers were busy examining the farmstead.

One of them approached Captain Zaytsey and reported that every inch of the place had been searched and there was no sign of the bomb or blueprints. The cars, including Razin's SUV, had also yielded nothing.

Another told him that the barn had been doused with gasoline. He wanted to know what to do with the bodies that were inside the building. Zaytsey thought for a moment before saying, "Put the major and Khmelnytsky in there with them. We'll torch it before we leave. Bring our vehicles here."

After a further fifteen minutes, a four-ton army truck and a jeep were driven into the clearing. The captain summoned the drivers and the rest of his team. They stood around him as he said, "This has been a total fuckup. Ordinarily I should call this straight into HQ and also report the location of the MI6 prisoner so that they can send another team to get him. But I say we have a chance to make this right. I say we go and get the MI6 man ourselves."

Zaytsey studied his men.

All of them nodded.

"Good. Let's go."

The men ran to the vehicles; the engines started.

Zaytsey stayed on foot. He walked to the barn, withdrew a lighter, ignited it, tossed it at the barn, turned, and ran to the jeep.

The Spetsnaz vehicles were out of sight as Will ran to the barn. The whole building was ablaze. As he got to within fifteen feet of the building, he stopped dead in his tracks, his arms shielding his face from the intense heat. He tried to take a step forward but immediately recoiled. The pain on his exposed skin was immense. He tried again but again involuntarily retreated.

He had to get in there.

Just had to.

After taking several steps back, he stared at the barn's large double doors. They were covered with flames. He sucked in a lungful of air, held his breath, braced himself for the pain that was about to come, and charged straight toward the blaze.

It was worse than he expected. Much, much worse. But he wasn't going to stop this time.

He dived at the doors, hitting them with his shoulder and forcing them to burst open. Rolling on the barn's interior floor, he got to his feet and looked around. Korina was there. He ran to her, picked her up, and cradled her in his arms.

Just as he'd done before resting her gently on her bed.

Running as fast as he could, he exited the building, his face screwed up in pain as flames curled around him and smoke wafted into his eyes. He staggered, nearly fell, and placed one foot in front of the other. He thought he might lose consciousness, but he kept moving.

The pain ebbed.

Cold air soothed his face.

More steps forward.

The roar of the inferno grew quieter with each step.

Turning, he looked back at the barn. It was ninety feet away; the fire showed no signs of abating. He moved farther away until he was in the center of the clearing. Carefully, he rested Korina on the ground. His legs buckled, and he fell down until he was kneeling by Korina's side.

The chest wound was bloody. Razin's hidden knife had been plunged so deep that there was no doubt it would have killed her instantly. But the rest of her body and face were untainted by what had happened here today. Will placed a trembling hand against her cheek, leaned forward, and kissed each closed eye, then her lips. Gripping her body, he let his head slump until his face was flush against hers. His body began to shake; he began to sob.

Lifting his head and upper body, he looked up and screamed, "Fuck you all!"

FORTY-TWO

Will programmed the grid reference into the Prado's sat nav system and called Patrick. "Three *Ohio* submarines are sailing to the Barents Sea with the intention of covertly entering Russian waters tomorrow. When that happens, there'll be a nuclear explosion that will make the Russians think the subs have attacked them. You've got to get the vessels to turn around."

"What? Where's the nuclear device?"

"I don't know, but I suspect it's somewhere on Russia's northern coastline."

"That's a very large area. But you're sure it's there?"

"No. It could be in Moscow or just about anywhere else in Russia, but everything suggests it's somewhere in the north. Speak to the admiralty or the president. Just make sure those subs turn around right now."

* * *

Fifty minutes later, his cell phone rang. Patrick.

"It's a no-go."

"What do you mean?"

"They're not going to turn the subs around."

"You've got to be joking!"

"I spoke to the admiralty. They said they're not going to withdraw the submarines after months of preparations and millions of dollars spent."

"Then speak to the president!"

"I did. He sought advice from the admiralty and agreed with them."

Will couldn't believe what he was hearing. "You told them about the bomb?!"

"Yep. The admirals said that I must be crazy to think that they'd deviate from their plans because of some field officer's hunch. Actually, their language was a lot stronger than that."

"Idiots!"

"I'm sorry."

"So am I!"

It was night. Will felt exhausted, and his body was wracked with pain. The sat nav directions were taking him south, around towns, through small villages, forests, over flatlands, undulating countryside, across rivers, craggy hills, and into increasingly rugged terrain, but he barely registered his surroundings. As he drove hundreds of miles across Russia toward the Caucasus Mountains, only one thought was in his mind.

Whether Sentinel is alive or dead, my only hope is that Razin has left some clue as to the location of the bomb.

Night became day.

Today the submarines would reach Russia.

Snow and ice were everywhere, but the sky was blue and clear of clouds. More hours passed. The roads became narrower and uneven. Soon he was driving away from any signs of life; the imposing mountain range was visible in the distance. He continued driving for an hour, until he was within a couple of miles of the mountains' foothills.

The mountain range extended across the entire length of Russia's border with Georgia, Azerbaijan, and Armenia, between the Black Sea and the Caspian Sea, and was more than six hundred miles long and a hundred miles wide. Right now the mountains looked majestic and stunning, though Will knew that from ancient history to the recent second Chechen war they had been the location of numerous bloody battles and atrocities.

He drove off the road and followed a winding track that headed toward one high mountain. The incline grew steeper as he moved into a ravine; sheer ice-covered mountain walls rose up on either side of him. He reached a wooden gate with a sign indicating that the route beyond was private. The gate had been smashed open, probably by a vehicle.

Will drove forward; the mountain walls on either side of him were now only a foot away from the sides of his vehicle. They cast a dark shadow over the entire route ahead, their faces looming nine hundred feet over the track; above them was the severe incline of a mountain that was at least twelve thousand feet high. He put the car into low gear as the track further steepened. Its tires managed to maintain traction, despite the thick snow beneath them.

He braked suddenly. Two stationary vehicles were ahead of him. One of them was a four-ton military truck, the other a jeep. The smaller vehicle was on its side and was a mangled wreck. The truck was a burned-out shell. Will got out of his car and walked to the decimated vehicles. He looked at the jeep. The driver's legs were missing; the rest of him had been shredded by bits of metal. Next to him was Captain Zaytsey. The Spetsnaz officer's face was black and swollen, his blond hair completely singed away, and a large chunk of the jeep's metal undercarriage was protruding from his gut. Will went to the rear of the truck and looked inside. What he saw was horrific. Ten men, ripped apart.

Shaking his head, he muttered, "You bastard."

Razin had mined the route ahead, knowing that anyone who came here to get Sentinel either would die trying or would have to just turn around and leave the MI6 officer to his fate.

He was running out of time. The submarines would now be very close to Russia.

Will decided that there was one other way to get to the mountain lodge, a route that was in all probability every bit as perilous as a road containing high explosives. Opening his Bergen, he turned it upside down and emptied its contents onto the track. He donned the white balaclava, tactical goggles, and gloves, fixed the vertical-framed ice crampons to his boots, placed the MR-445 Varjag pistol and spare ammunition clips in his fleece jacket, and strapped the military knife and scabbard to his waist before putting his hands through the straps of the two mountaineering ice axes and gripping their handles. Head to toe, he was now dressed in white arctic warfare kit.

He looked at the sheer ice wall by his side, stepped up to it, and plunged both axes' spikes into the ice above his head. Pulling himself off the ground, he simultaneously jabbed the crampons' toe blades into the ice. The ice held his weight; he was satisfied that he could begin climbing. Straightening his legs, he pulled out one of the axes and dug it higher into the wall, then did the same with the other, pulling himself up and jabbing his crampons back into a new area of ice. He kept repeating the actions until he was three hundred feet above the track.

He looked down. The ravine was in near darkness, though he could see his SUV and the Spetsnaz vehicles. A light wind blew ice particles off the wall's surface and coated his goggles. Wiping them clear, he looked up, dug his axes higher, and continued his ascent. After five minutes, he had covered another three hundred feet of the ice face. He rested for a few seconds, felt sweat underneath his balaclava and inner garments, and continued climbing. With every swing of his axes and thrust of his crampons, the pain in his body increased.

But he kept moving, hauling his big frame up the vertical mountainside a few feet at a time.

He was now 250 yards above the track. His breathing was labored, and his undergarments and balaclava were now soaked with perspiration. Looking beyond the axes to the top of the wall, he could see nothing but sky. He hoped that meant the mountainside was less severe beyond the ice face and the subsequent climb would be easier. That hope spurred him on; his movements became quicker. He neared the top of the ice wall, swung one ax over it and into the hidden ice beyond, did the same with the other, and then pulled his body up over the edge until he was lying flat on the ground. For a moment he felt relief that he had made the near-impossible climb. But as he lifted his head and looked forward, his heart sank.

The land before him was relatively flat for about ninety feet. But beyond it was another ice face. This one was much taller, and halfway it curled inward to produce a massive overhang at the top. As he looked at the terrifying slope, only one thought ran through his mind. This climb *was* impossible.

He got to his feet, walked fast to the base of the wall, looked up, silently cursed, put the tip of one ax against the ice above his head, hesitated for a moment, and swung it deep into the face. He started climbing, but this time he felt that every swing of his axes and stab of his crampons into the ice was taking him nearer to a place where he would fall and die.

Razin would have known about this terrain; he would have known that the only way to access the mountain lodge from Russia was via the track that he had mined. That was why he had chosen the venue for Sentinel's imprisonment. And in giving Will the location, he had sent him to his death.

Will climbed for fifteen minutes, briefly stopping twice to get more oxygen into his body. The air was now colder; each breath caused pain in his lungs. He reached nine hundred feet above the ledge below him. This was the place where the wall began to gradually slope inward. He looked up, saw the huge overhang towering above him a further nine hundred feet beyond, looked down, and briefly wondered if he should climb back to the base. But he knew he could not do so. He had outsmarted Razin but had failed to save Korina's life and the lives of the other tier-1 agents whom he had been sent to defend, and he had failed to prevent the capture, imprisonment, torture, and inevitable execution of Roger, Laith, Vitali, and Markov. While the odds were now impossible, he had to try to get to Sentinel in case the man was still alive, and he had to search his prison for anything that might tell him where the bomb was planted. This was his last chance to do something right, even if he died trying. But this climb was taking too long.

He moved his arms and legs, just focusing on the ice directly in front of him. His body was tilted backward a few inches; the chances of his axes pulling free from the face were now considerable. His progress was slow. After

every insertion of the ax spikes and the blades of his crampons, he carefully tested their grip on the mountain face
before proceeding. It took him thirty minutes to cover
three hundred feet of the ice wall. As the slope had now
pushed the angle of his body back a further few inches, it
took him an hour to climb the next three hundred feet.
The muscles in his arms, back, and legs now felt as if they
were tearing themselves off bone. His heart pounded, its
noise drumming in his ears. He could taste blood in his
mouth and smell it in his nose. He stopped, his breathing
shallow and rapid, not daring to take his eyes off the axes.
The three-hundred-foot incline above him was going to
get worse, and if he made it to the top he would then have
to move underneath a near-horizontal overhang for two
hundred feet. Gritting his teeth, he continued.

Nausea accompanied his agony. He swallowed hard,
desperate not to vomit, choke, and lose his grip on his
axes. The wind grew stronger, blowing more ice at him.
Despite his exertions, his body was now shivering; the
sweat from the earlier climb now made his garments
cling cold against his body. He tried to count each swing
of his ax, imagining that if he made it to a count of three
hundred he would be off this terrible place and alive. But
he kept losing count, not able to focus on anything other
than getting his arms and legs to move at the right time.

It took him another hour to reach the overhang. His
body was now leaning back at an angle of forty-five
degrees. He looked down. Eighteen hundred feet below
him was the ledge, out of sight, and a further nine

hundred feet beyond that was the base of the ravine. He stayed still and looked up. Directly above his head the mountain face curved sharply. He looked at the over-hang, wondering if he would fall to his death in the next few minutes. He moved.

After two swings of his axes, he was on the overhang, his back now directly facing the huge drop below. He kept his body bunched close, using smaller reaches of his axes and crampons and digging them in at an angle within the surface. As he moved, inch by inch, three thoughts were in his mind: Is the ice strong enough? Am I strong enough? Have the subs reached Russian waters yet?

He managed to get across thirty feet of the two-hundred-foot overhang before pausing. He let his heavy body hang there, deadweight between the small toe blades of the crampons and the thin spikes of his axes. Carefully withdrawing the point of one of the axes, he swung it hard into the ice, pulled on it to test its grip, and moved onward. Thirty minutes later, he had moved another thirty feet along the overhang. One hour after that, he had reached the center of the slope. More than anything, he worried about his hands. The ax straps were around them but were not enough to stop his body from falling if his agonized fingers involuntarily released their grip. He tried to wrap his digits tighter around the shafts of his ice picks, tried to flex them to get blood moving through them when his crampons were in place, but nothing stopped the pain. He thought that he was now dying.

He decided that he had always known that he was going to die a violent death but that it was better to do so through inability to conquer a terrifying ancient mountain rather than by being outmatched by another man. That thought spurred him on. He looked down again. The whole world seemed to be beneath him. It looked so beautiful, so perfect. It looked like a place that had once tolerated his existence, but not anymore.

He slammed a foot against the ice, drove an ax into it, jabbed his other foot into the overhang, gasped for air, and moved his outstretched arm to swing the other ax into position. It all seemed futile now. But he still kept doing this for another sixty feet.

His frozen hands started to slow down and fail. Death, he decided, was now close by. He looked at the overhang inches above his face, stretched his head and neck back to look at the sky, and saw the sun, blue air, thin streaks of cloud, and the endless mountains beyond.

He jabbed the point of an ax farther along the surface, spat blood, watched it fall far below him, felt the skin on his face become taut, swung his other ax, and looked at the end of the overhang. It was now only a few feet away.

He heard a noise. It was barely audible at first, but it seemed to be coming from the sky. He winced as he looked in its direction. He saw a small dot. It grew larger. The noise became louder. His hands and feet were vibrating. The mountain shook. The dot got bigger and bigger. It seemed to be moving very fast. His limbs were now badly shaking. He breathed fast, urgently looking between the thing from the sky and the tools he had fixed in the mountain. The thing grew larger, a thunderous scream accompanying it. Will braced himself, ready to drop to his death.

He narrowed his eyes.

The thing came closer.

Then it banked up, only a few hundred yards away from him, moving back toward the sky. A MiG fighter jet.

It would have been impossible for the pilot to have seen him, and no doubt he was just practicing maneuvers over the range, but as the jet pointed at the sky the mountain shook more vigorously. Will tore his eyes away from the sight and looked desperately at the overhang. But it was too late. One of his axes and both of his crampons shook free from the surface. He fell down and swung like a pendulum, hanging from the one remaining ax spike in the ice. Gasping for air, he stared at the spike, knowing it would pull out at any moment. He tried to thrust his boots at the surface as he swung close to it, but he did not get near enough. His body stopped swinging. Pulling up a few inches with his arm, he swung his other ax toward the ice but missed, his grip on it loosening as his arm moved quickly through the air, the ax very nearly falling away from his hand, saved only by the strap around his wrist. He pulled up with his arm again; the effort was monumental, the pain immense, but he kept pulling, knowing that he had to get much closer to the ice this time, even though his arm felt as though it were going to explode. He kept moving until his arm was at a right angle, readied his other ax, focused his eyes on the spot he wanted to strike, swung his ax, and jammed his spike deep into the surface. Wasting no time, he moved his legs back, then swung them together toward the overhang. His crampons dug into the ice. He moved forward, reaching the edge of the overhang. Blindly, he swung one ax over its edge and felt it dig into something. He did the same with the other.

He heard the jet again. Its noise was growing louder.

Removing one crampon and bringing his knee under his chest, he slammed his boot into the ice.

The roar of the jet was getting nearer. The mountain began to shake.

He moved the other crampon and stabbed it into the surface.

His whole body was vibrating.

He pulled with his arms while thrusting forward with his legs, easing his body around the lip of the overhang.

Large chunks of ice near him cracked and fell away.

With all of his strength, he pulled, finally getting his chest onto an area of flatland on the other side of the overhang. He kept pulling as one of his feet fell away, then the other, until his whole body was off the overhang and lying on the ground above it. He had made the impossible climb.

But maybe it was all in vain.

Crawling forward, he looked around. More of the mountain was above him, but he could see that he would not have to climb any farther. He was on a plateau two hundred feet long. To the left of the mountain was a chasm, beyond it another plateau that had a track leading to it and a lodge in its center. He had found Sentinel's prison.

Getting to his feet, he walked across the plateau and looked at the chasm between him and his destination. It was about fifteen feet wide and hundreds of feet deep. He turned away and, holding his axes at head height, sprinted toward the gap. Reaching the edge, he leapt, lifting his axes until his arms were fully outstretched, and swung them forward as he neared the far side of the drop, digging them deep into the ground by the chasm's edge. His upper body was on the plateau around the lodge; his legs were dangling in the chasm. The pain was intense. But the area around him was covered not in ice but in snow. His spikes moved but failed to maintain any grip; his body weight was pulling down into the chasm. Urgently, he slammed his boots against the surface below him, but his crampons only met more snow. His upper body slid back, the axes carving long grooves in the ground. He was sliding to his death, and there was nothing he could do about it.

His head moved to the edge, then into the chasm. His arms moved off the plateau and were now above him. He braced himself, waiting for the axes to come over the edge, release themselves from everything, and drop him to a place that would snap his neck and every other bone in his body and crush his internal organs.

Then he stopped moving.

He looked up.

A hand was gripping his wrist with tremendous strength. It began pulling him up. Then another hand grabbed Will's arm. He was lifted out until he was lying facedown on the plateau. He raised his head.

Sentinel was standing before him.

The MI6 officer was wearing jeans, a windbreaker jacket, and hiking boots. Deep lines of fatigue etched his face. He put a hand underneath Will's armpit and helped him to his feet. "Razin's dead?"

Will's heart was racing; he breathed deeply. Nodding, he pulled off his balaclava and looked around. "It doesn't make any difference. Razin's planted one of the bombs. Right now three U.S. submarines are sailing close to Russian waters. As soon as they enter, the bomb will go off."

"And war will commence." Sentinel rubbed his face. "We need to go."

"How did you get out of your shackles?"

"I was never in them. Razin drugged me." He shook his head. "That's how he got me to talk. He must have expected to be back here long before I regained consciousness."

"Your agents are dead."

Sentinel slowly lowered his hand. "All of them?"

"Yes."

Sentinel said nothing for a while before muttering, "Then all is lost."

He turned and began walking toward the lodge.

Will stood still, watching him. He recalled Sentinel

telling him how he had recruited Razin, how they had sat alone in the Lufthansa business-class lounge in Frankfurt and talked for an hour.

He reached into his pocket and withdrew his handgun, keeping his eyes on the man who was walking with strength and purpose toward the mountain property. Then he raised his gun and pointed it at Sentinel. "I can't let you go in there."

Sentinel froze, standing with his back to Will.

"You never had drugs in your system." Will placed his finger over the trigger. "But I bet there's a gun in that house."

Sentinel raised his arms outward. "What are you talking about?"

Will gripped his gun harder. He felt nauseous. "This wasn't your prison. Instead, you used the place to wait while Razin did your dirty work for you."

Sentinel turned slowly, lowering his arms. Looking directly at Will, he said with anger, "I survived five days of drug-induced hell and rescued a man who was about to fall to his death. Lower your weapon, and help me get out of here."

But Will kept his gun very still. "Why? I'm not going to help you get out of here. And I'll kill you if you take another step toward the lodge."

Sentinel was silent, just staring at him.

Will's mind was racing and confused. But he was certain of one thing: Sentinel had tricked him all along. "Was everything a lie?"

Sentinel kept staring, his anger no longer evident. He gave a bitter smile. When he finally spoke, his voice was quiet. "To me, everything has been the truth." He looked away toward the mountains. "Can you imagine what it feels like to spend six years in a Russian prison, receiving endless bouts of torture, knowing that the West has given you up for dead?" He looked at Will. "How it feels to be finally released, only to find out that the British government has relinquished you of the one thing you treasure the most: the title of Spartan." His anger returned. "When that happened to me, I hated Russia and I hated the West. I decided that when the time was right, I would bring them both to war so that they could tear each other apart."

Will's head spun. "Why America, not Britain?"

Sentinel's eyes narrowed. "Because it was a CIA Soviet agent who betrayed me to the SVR and led them to me. When the Cold War ended, the Americans should never have let him go back to Russia. I wanted them to pay for their mistake. Plus I knew that Britain didn't have the power to bring Russia to the brink of war but America did." He looked around. "But now that it's about to start, it's only a matter of time before Britain gets sucked into this war along with most of Europe." He smiled. "Everyone's going to die."

Incredulity struck Will. "A Russian CIA agent betrayed you?"

Sentinel locked his eyes on Will. "Razin found out who he was. I tracked him down and killed him."

"You made me capture and interrogate an innocent MI6 officer!"

Sentinel nodded. "Borzaya's story was all untrue. I told him that we were trying to flush *you* out as a traitor and to do that we had to make you confident that we suspected someone else. You had to believe that the Head of Moscow Station was the man who had supplied Razin with the identities of my agents. You did a good job, though Razin ensured he died. He climbed onto the roof of the church and poured gasoline into it." He looked at the sky. "When I first met Razin, we spoke for an hour in the transit lounge, but the content of that discussion was different from the version I gave you. I quickly realized how ambitious the man was; told him a half-truth that I hated the West for abandoning me in a Russian prison; said I wanted revenge, that we needed to spark war; that if he killed my tier-one agents Russia would not be crippled, he would be seen as a hero and could take over the country. Razin agreed to my terms."

Sweat poured down Will's face and back. "How could you work with a monster like Razin?"

Sentinel smiled. "It had always been my intention to have Razin killed when his task was complete. The man was extremely capable but psychotic. Whatever the future held for Russia, I couldn't let it be run by a man who'd want to rebuild it into a superpower."

Will exclaimed, "Svelte was trying to warn us about you!"

He has betrayed us and wants to go to war.

"And your mad dog."

Only Sentinel can stop him.

Sentinel nodded. "My original idea was to plant a nuclear device on a Russian submarine. For that I needed Svelte, but the submariner refused and quickly deduced what I was planning." He spat. "That was careless of me. Svelte escaped and used the DLB before I had a chance to clear it myself."

Will paled. "Is this really what you want? Total war?"

Sentinel glanced at the lodge before looking back at Will. "There's nothing else I need now. Not even my life."

He took a step toward Will.

Will moved a finger along the trigger. "Stay where you are."

Sentinel took another step toward him.

"Stop moving!"

Sentinel came closer. "If you let me get right up to you, I will try to disarm you."

More sweat poured down Will's body. His head throbbed. "You'll be held accountable, but I don't want to kill you."

Sentinel smiled. "My work is complete." His smile vanished. "And now it's over." He walked quickly forward.

In that moment, Will felt overwhelming anger. He thought he'd understood the man; he had respected him, believed that he loved his Russian assets and agents, and believed that Sentinel stood for all that was good. But the man coming toward him now was someone else altogether. He was a man who was prepared to see millions of lives lost in order to satiate his desire for revenge against those who had hurt him and let him down many years before. He was a man who had unleashed Razin to dismember, burn, and decapitate brave people.

But as he pulled the trigger, his anger was replaced by sorrow and pity. At some point, a part of Sentinel's mind had been broken. It should never have come to that. The enormous burden he had carried for all of his adult life had become too much for even a man of his strength. Powerful leaders in the West should have pulled him out of his deep-cover role before it destroyed him. But they'd done nothing, only carried on letting him take enormous personal risks until he was finally betrayed.

The gun lifted a little as the bullet left the barrel, traveled across the few feet of air, and struck Sentinel in the abdomen. The man's eyes widened, his knees buckled, and he slowly fell to the ground until he was kneeling on snow.

He placed a hand over the wound, glanced at the blood covering it, and looked at Will. "The bullet's torn through my liver. I'll be dead in a few minutes. But it would have been quicker to just shoot me in the brain."

Will lowered his gun, walked toward him, and asked, "Where is the bomb?"

Sentinel said nothing.

"You're going to die. But before you do, you have the chance to make this right."

Sentinel smiled. "There'll be no dying confession."

Will stared at him. He thought about how Sentinel

had originally intended to use Svelte. A realization struck him. "The Russians know about the submarines. They'll send an interceptor to act as a deterrent, probably one of their new stealth destroyers. That's where the bomb is! It's on the Russian boat."

Sentinel's smile vanished, but still he was silent.

"I think Razin was waiting to find out which vessel was given orders to prepare to sail. Then he planted the device." His heart raced. "I'm right, I know I am."

Sentinel lowered his head; his breathing was fast.

Will took a step toward him. "I need to know why you stopped me from falling into the chasm."

Sentinel raised his head, looked at the mountains, and smiled. Seemingly to himself, he whispered, "This is a good place to die." Staring at Will, he nodded slowly. "In the lodge, there's a detonator. It will explode the mines and clear a path for you on the track beneath us. At the back of the lodge is a car and spare fuel. You can escape here unharmed and try to leave Russia." Blood was pouring over his pants and onto the snow around him. He looked back at the mountains. "I kept you alive to remind myself of the man that I once was. It wasn't always a lie. Once, I truly did believe in the work that I did. I"—he coughed blood—"really did love my agents."

Will crouched down in front of him. Quietly he said, "You can become that man again. I give you my word that nobody, *nobody* need ever know what you did. I can have you buried in England with full honors. And I can have a gold plaque put on your coffin that has the word

SPARTAN engraved on it. I promise you that I can do that. In return, nod once if the bomb's on the interceptor."

Sentinel stared at him. Eventually he said, "You'd do that?"

"I would."

The men were motionless.

The wind vanished.

Everything stopped.

Sentinel nodded once.

Then he closed his eyes, let out one last breath, lowered his head, and died.

FORTY-THREE

Will walked down the Learjet's steps and stood on RAF Brize Norton's runway. The rain was heavy, but Will didn't care and let it wash over his face. Even though he felt more tired than he'd ever been in his life, he'd been unable to sleep during the flight from Moscow to England. He looked around; the normally busy military airport was virtually empty of other aircraft. He wondered if it had been like that when Sentinel had arrived here after his release from the Lubyanka prison.

Three limousines were close to the jet. Plain-clothed special forces men were in the front and rear cars. Two men were standing outside the central vehicle. They were dressed in suits and overcoats. Umbrellas shielded their faces.

Will walked slowly to them.

They lifted their umbrellas a little.

Alistair looked at him. "Roger, Laith, Markov, and Vitali have been released. The Russians have been reinstated into their Spetsnaz unit."

"And our boys are in the hospital in the States." Patrick's expression was somber. "They were beaten up pretty badly, but they'll recover."

Will rubbed rainwater off his face. "Next time I'm in D.C., I'd like to have a chat with the president and some of his admirals about their decision not to turn the submarines around. I'd like to impress upon them the future need to always do what I fucking say."

"It all worked out for the best."

Patrick agreed. "A superb result for both America and Russia."

Alistair moved closer, his look one of concern. "Have you got anyone you can go to?"

Will ignored the question. People were speaking behind him. He glanced over his shoulder. Four men were unloading a coffin.

Sentinel had finally been pulled out of the field. He was home and would be buried with full honors. Will had kept his word and hadn't told a soul about what had really happened, not even Alistair and Patrick.

Will returned his gaze to the coheads. "One day it will be me coming home in a box."

FORTY-FOUR

Will unlocked his front door and entered his apartment. Stepping over piles of junk mail, he walked through the corridor and entered the open-plan lounge–kitchen area. Placing his grocery bag and newspaper onto the table, he moved through the minimalist room, filled the kettle, and flicked it on. He returned to the table, sat down, and looked at the front page of the newspaper.

The headline story was the same story every other British newspaper was carrying today. Moreover, most of the world's media were giving it their top slot. It told of a remarkable humanitarian action. A Russian naval destroyer had become severely damaged in the Barents Sea to the extent that it needed to be evacuated of all personnel. No Russian ships had been close enough to reach the destroyer before it sank, but three U.S. *Ohio* submarines had. In an unprecedented move, the U.S. president had ordered the submarines to surface and rescue the Russian sailors. All of them had been saved before the destroyer sank to the seabed. As a result, relations between the United States and Russia were now the best they had ever been.

What really happened would be kept secret for a long time. The U.S. president had called the Russian premier and told him about the bomb on the Russian destroyer. The conversation hadn't been easy, but eventually he'd persuaded the Russian leader that this wasn't an elaborate ruse with ulterior motives. He'd also told him that the *Ohio* submarines were the only ones that could rescue the sailors before the bomb went off. They did precisely that and sailed quickly away. The bomb had detonated, obliterating the ship, but by then the submarines had been out of the device's range. Nevertheless, a large area of the sea had been irradiated. Russian, U.S., and European nuclear specialists were collaborating to try to clean up the fallout.

Will tossed the paper to one side.

Alistair and Patrick were right. The mission had been successful, but that success had come with a significant loss of lives. Two of them lost at his hands.

Both were MI6 officers.

Four days ago, another had taken his own life.

Kryštof.

The rest had been slaughtered.

He glanced at the bare walls, the wooden floor that desperately needed some rugs to give it some color and warmth, the functional kitchen chairs, and the plain white sofa. Pulling out Korina's necklace, he looked at it.

She'd asked him not to open it until they were together in his apartment. For a moment, he wondered what to do. He weighed it in his hand. Then he sighed and opened the pendant. Inside was a photo. It was of a man.

Svelte.

A man who had risked his life in driving snowfall to send a coded message to the West. A message that could stop a war. An act of heroism that had cost him his life.

Next to him in the photo was his beautiful daughter, Korina.

A woman who had risked everything to do the right thing. A woman Will would have wanted to get to know. A woman he was sure he could have loved.

He banged a fist on the table, causing some of the contents of the grocery bag to spill out. Shallots, chicken, garlic, and herbs. The same ingredients he'd used to prepare a meal for Korina.

He stared at the food; his fist slowly unclenched. Lifting the pendant, he held it against his cheek. A tear ran down his face; he momentarily closed his eyes.

Standing, he looked around. He hated this place. He hated everything about his life. More than anything, he hated losing Korina.

He grabbed the kitchen table and threw it against the wall with sufficient force to break it. He grabbed the chairs and broke them into pieces as well.

He slumped to the ground, still gripping the pendant. His breathing was fast, but as he held the necklace against his chest, his breathing began to slow.

His cell phone rang.

Alistair.

That could mean only one thing.

Work.

He thought about ignoring the call, instead grabbing a drink in a bar, going for a walk through London's streets, perhaps catching an evening show at a theater.

Will Cochrane desperately wanted to do those things.

But not alone.

With someone special.

Spartan answered the call.

GLOSSARY

AEK-919K Kashtan submachine gun—Russian special forces submachine gun; fires 9 mm rounds.

AK-47 assault rifle—Russian assault rifle in Soviet and Russian service since 1949; fires 7.62 mm rounds.

AKS-74 assault rifle—A variant of the Russian AK-74. It is equipped with a folding metal frame stock, fires 5.45 mm rounds, and is used primarily by Russian air assault units.

Akula I submarine—A nuclear-powered Russian attack submarine. It deploys conventional weapons through its torpedo tubes.

Akula II submarine—A nuclear-powered Russian attack submarine, larger than and with an improved sonar system compared to the Akula I class.

AMR-2 12.7 mm sniper rifle—A Chinese antimaterial sniper rifle that fires 12 mm rounds and has an effective range of up to 4,500 feet.

Antisurveillance—An intelligence drill that is designed to establish whether an intelligence officer is being watched by hostile intelligence operatives. It can be conducted by intelligence officers on foot, in cars, and with the use of many other modes of transport.

AS Val assault rifle—A Soviet-designed assault rifle containing an integrated suppressor; fires 9 mm high-performance armor-piercing rounds.

BfV—Bundesamt für Verfassungsschutz. Germany's domestic intelligence agency, equivalent to Britain's MI5 and the United States' FBI.

BIS—Bezpečnostní Informační Služba. The primary domestic intelligence agency of the Czech Republic.

CIA—Central Intelligence Agency. The United States' overseas intelligence agency, tasked primarily with gathering intelligence from foreign human sources as well as conducting special operations.

Companies House—Britain's register of companies; an executive agency of the U.K. government.

DA—Defense attaché. Typically, a high-ranking serving military officer who is attached to one of his or her country's overseas embassies. DAs are tasked with interacting with the embassy's host country on a range of military matters, including military procurement.

Delta III submarine—Russian ballistic missile submarine.

Delta Force—Alongside DEVGRU, the United States' primary antiterrorist special operations unit, though, like DEVGRU it is deployable in all covert and overt theaters of war and operating environments.

DEVGRU—U.S. Naval Special Warfare Development Group, popularly known by its previous name, SEAL Team 6. It is one of the United States' premier multifunctional special operations units and draws its recruits from other SEAL units.

DGSE—Direction Générale de la Sécurité Extérieure. The French overseas intelligence agency, tasked primarily with gathering intelligence from foreign human sources as well as conducting special operations.

DLB—Dead-letter box. A method of espionage tradecraft that allows one spy to pass an item, using a secret location, to another spy without their having to meet.

FSB—Federal Security Service of the Russian Federation. The main domestic security agency of Russia, comparable to the FBI and MI5.

GCHQ—Government Communications Headquarters. The British intelligence agency responsible for providing signals intelligence (SIGINT) to the U.K. government and armed forces. Comparable to the United States' National Security Agency (NSA).

Groupement des Commandos Parachutistes—A highly trained reconnaissance unit of the French Foreign Legion's Parachute Regiment (2ème Régiment Étranger de Parachutistes).

GRU—Glavnoye Razvedyvatel'noye Upravleniye. The

foreign military intelligence directorate of the general staff of the Armed Forces of the Russian Federation.

98th Guards Airborne Division—An airborne division of Russian airborne troops, stationed in Ivanovo.

217th Guards Airborne Regiment—Part of Russia's 98th Guards Airborne Division stationed in Ivanovo.

Heckler & Koch USP Compact Tactical pistol—A semiautomatic pistol developed in Germany by Heckler & Koch; fires 9 mm rounds and is favored by many countries' special forces and special police units.

Household Cavalry—The term used to describe the Commonwealth of Nations' (formerly British Commonwealth's) cavalry of the Household Divisions.

HS 2000 handgun—A semiautomatic handgun manufactured in Croatia. There are several variants of the weapon, each firing different-caliber rounds.

Il-76M transport aircraft—A Russian multipurpose strategic airlifter airplane.

Increment—The term for the unit within MI6 comprising handpicked elite British special forces soldiers.

60th Independent Motor Rifle Brigade—A unit under the command of Russia's Fifth Army within the Far Eastern Military District.

IR/TG-7 thermal goggles—A rugged, lightweight, and powerful infrared optical device that can be handheld or mounted on a helmet or headgear.

KGB—Komitet Gosudarstvennoy Bezopasnosti, or Committee for State Security. It was the national security agency of the Soviet Union from 1954 until 1991 and was the premier internal security, intelligence, and secret police organization during that time.

MI5—The British domestic intelligence agency, equivalent to the United States' FBI.

MI6—Secret Intelligence Service (SIS). Britain's overseas intelligence agency, tasked primarily with gathering intelligence from foreign human sources as well as conducting special operations.

MiG-29K—Russian all-weather, carrier-based, multirole fighter aircraft.

MIT—Milli İstihbarat Teşkilatı, or National Intelligence Organization. Turkey's governmental intelligence organization.

MR-445 Varjag pistol—A Russian semiautomatic pistol; fires 10 mm rounds.

MZKT-79221 transporter-erector-launcher—A sixteen-wheel Russian military mobile missile launcher that carries the Topol-M, an intercontinental ballistic missile.

OCP—Operational cover premise. Typically, a domestic or business property that is used to support the alias identity of an intelligence officer.

***Ohio*-class submarine**—A nuclear-powered submarine used by the U.S. Navy. *Ohio*-class submarines are deployed with either conventional or nuclear cruise missiles.

Oscar II submarine—A Russian cruise missile submarine capable of firing conventional and nuclear weapons.

104th Parachute Regiment—Part of the 76th Air Assault Division; the first Russian ground forces regiment to be fully made up of professional soldiers rather than conscripts.

QBZ-95G assault rifle—A Chinese assault rifle; fires 5.8 mm rounds.

QSZ-92 handgun—A Chinese semiautomatic pistol; fires 9 mm Parabellum rounds or 5.8 mm armor-piercing ammunition.

RT-2UTTKh intercontinental missile—A Russian missile with a single 800-kiloton-yield warhead. Capable of flying up to 7,000 miles.

SAS—Special Air Service. The world's oldest, most experienced, and arguably most effective Special Operations unit, the British SAS is regarded as the benchmark for all tier-1 units and special forces around the world.

SBS—Special Boat Service. A U.K. special forces unit, directly comparable to the United States' DEVGRU (SEAL Team 6), though the SBS is older and more experienced. Recruitment and selection into the SBS are considered even tougher than entry into the renowned SAS.

SBU—Sluzhba Bezpeky Ukrayiny. Ukraine's security agency, comparable in duties to Britain's MI5 and the United States' FBI.

SEALs—Sea, Air, Land teams. U.S. special operations personnel who can operate in any combat environment. Highly trained and very effective.

Sig Sauer P226 handgun—A popular weapon among special forces and law enforcement around the world. Various round calibers.

Sig Sauer P229 handgun—A variant of the P226 handgun, though more compact and therefore favored for operations requiring weapon concealment or close quarter combat.

***Slava*-class cruiser**—A large, conventionally powered Russian warship.

SOG—Special Operations Group. The paramilitary wing of the CIA's Special Activities Division. Many members are drawn from Delta Force and DEVGRU.

***Sovremenny*-class destroyer**—An antisurface Russian warship.

Spartan Program—The twelve-month-long selection program for premier MI6 officers in which they attempt to attain the code name "Spartan." Only one officer at a time is allowed to endure the program, and only one successful trainee is allowed to carry the code name until his death or retirement.

Spartan Section—The highly secretive unit within MI6 that supports the Spartan MI6 officer.

Spetsnaz—The generic term for Russian special forces. The Russian army, navy, GRU, and SVR all have Spetsnaz units attached to them and under their control. They are wholly separate units. For example, Spetsnaz Alpha (SVR) is a completely different unit from Spetsnaz Vympel (GRU), and recruitment, selection, and training follow different paths.

SPS Serdyukov self-loading pistol—A short-recoil, 9-mm-firing Russian handgun.

Su-33s—Sukhoi Su-33; a Russian all-weather carrier-based air-defense fighter.

SVR—Sluzhba Vneshney Razvedki. Russia's primary overseas intelligence agency, comparable to Britain's MI6 and the United States' CIA.

Udaloy I destroyer—Russian antisubmarine destroyer.

WTO—World Trade Organization. An organization whose remit is to supervise and liberalize international trade. Formed in 1995 under the Marrakech Agreement, the WTO currently has 153 member states (at time of print).

ACKNOWLEDGMENTS

To Jon Wood and the team at Orion (U.K.), David Highfill and the team at William Morrow/HarperCollins (U.S.), Luigi Bonomi and Alison and the rest of the team at LBA, Rowland White, Judith, and the Secret Intelligence Service (MI6).

If you enjoyed

SENTINEL

don't miss

SLINGSHOT

the next Spycatcher thriller featuring

Will Cochrane,

from Matthew Dunn

Available in hardcover July 2013

from

William Morrow
An Imprint of HarperCollins*Publishers*

CHAPTER 1

BERLIN 1995

Each step through the abandoned Soviet military barracks took the Russian intelligence officer closer to the room where men were planning genocide.

Nikolai Dmitriev hated being here.

And he loathed what he was about to do.

The barracks were a labyrinth of corridors and rooms. Icy water dripped over the stone walls' paintings of Cold War-era troops and tanks; the air was rank with must; the officer's footsteps echoed as he strode onward, shivering despite his overcoat and fur hat. Previously, the complex would have housed thousands of troops. Now it resembled a decaying prison.

He turned into a corridor and was confronted by four men. Two Russians, two Americans all wearing jeans, boots, and windbreaker jackets, covering their silenced handguns. The Special Forces men checked his ID and thoroughly searched him. It was the seventh time this had happened as he'd moved through the barracks. Two hundred Russian Spetsnaz operatives and an equal number of US Delta, SEALs, and CIA SOG men were strategically positioned in the base to ensure that every route to his destination was defended. Their orders were clear: kill any unauthorized person who attempted to get near to the men in the room.

The men motioned Nikolai forward.

Reaching the end of the corridor, he stopped opposite a door. Extending his hand to open it, he hesitated as he heard a high pitched noise. Glancing back, two rats in a stagnant pool of water and grease were ripping skin and flesh off the dying carcass of another screeching rat, neither predator attempting to fight the other for the meat; instead they seemed to be cooperating. He wondered if he should turn around and leave while there was still time. Everything about his presence here was wrong. But he was under orders.

He entered.

It was a large mess hall. Ten years ago, he would have seen long trestle tables and soldiers eating their meals. Now it was bare of any furnishings save a rectangular table and chairs in the center. Graffiti covered the walls, most of it crude, deriding the Soviet Union. Cigarette smoke hung motionless in the stagnant air. Rainwater poured from cracks in the high ceiling onto the concrete floor.

Sitting on one side of the rectangular table were a US admiral, a general, and a CIA officer. Opposite them were two Russian generals. Between them were two files, and ashtrays. None of the men were in uniform; the presence in Germany of America's and Russia's most powerful military commanders was secret.

As was the presence of the intelligence officers. Nikolai himself was Head of Directorate S—the SVR's division with responsibility for Illegal Intelligence, including planting illegal agents abroad, conducting terror operations and sabotage in foreign countries, and recruitment of Russians on Russian soil.

The CIA officer at the table was the Head of the Special Activities Division—responsible for overseas paramilitary activities and covert manipulation of target countries' political structures.

At the head of the table was a small, middle aged man with jet black hair. Dressed in an expensive black suit, crisp woven white silk shirt, and blue tie that was bound in a Windsor knot, the clean shaven, man removed his rimless circular glasses, polished them with one end of his tie, and smiled. "Always late for the party, Nikolai."

Nikolai did not smile. "A party requires salubrious surroundings. You've chosen unwisely, Kurt."

Kurt Schreiber nodded toward the vacant chair next to one of the Russian generals. "Sit, and shut up."

The senior SVR officer said with contempt, "You've no authority over me, *civilian*."

Kurt chuckled. "When you and I were colonels in the KGB and Stasi, you'd have called me *comrade*."

Nikolai sat and nodded. "Different times, and I'd have been lying to your face."

Kurt's shrill, well spoken words were rapid, "The Russian premier chose me to chair this meeting. Not you." He placed his manicured fingers together. "That is telling."

"I agree. It tells us how low we've stooped." Nikolai looked at the Americans. "Have the protocols been drawn up?"

"They have." Admiral Jack Dugan nodded toward the Russian generals. "It took us two days."

General Alexander Tatlin lit a cigarette. "It was worth the effort." The Russian exhaled smoke. "The results are precise."

"Seems to me," CIA officer Thomas Scott eyed Nikolai with suspicion, "that you're not comfortable with this."

Nikolai laughed, his voice echoing in the bare hall. "How can any sane man be *comfortable* agreeing to this?"

"Kurt Schreiber's idea is brilliant."

"It's psychotic." Nikolai looked at Schreiber and repeated in a quieter voice, "Psychotic."

US General Joe Ballinger pointed across the table. "Schreiber's right. The act has to shock the fuckers into submission. Man comes at you with a knife; you defend yourself with a gun. Trouble is—we haven't got anyone on our side of the fence who's got the balls to do another

Hiroshima or Nagasaki. So we make the decision, and it's a sane one—as uncomfortable as it may make us."

Nikolai frowned. "You haven't reported the true meaning of the protocols to your president?"

The US commander shook his head. "Nope, and we're never going to. Nor are subsequent presidents going to find out." He gestured toward his two American colleagues. "We're the only Americans who'll know the secret. No one else States-side would ever agree to this plan."

"And that's because they lack my . . . *imagination*." Kurt withdrew two ink pens, handed one to General Leon Michurin, and the other to Admiral Dugan. "Signatures, please."

The Americans signed a sheet of paper inside one of the files, the Russian generals did the same in their files, they exchanged documents and countersigned, and moved both files in front of Nikolai.

The SVR officer stared at the two files. All that was needed to make this official was his signature on both documents.

"Nikolai, we're waiting." Kurt's tone was hard, impatient.

Nikolai looked at the men opposite him; ordinarily they were his enemies. He pictured the two large rats, feasting at opposite ends of the third rodent.

"Nikolai!"

The Russian intelligence officer shook his head. "This is wrong."

"And yet the alternative isn't right."

"If I sign this, millions of people could die."

"Not *millions*, you fool." Schreiber smiled. "*Hundreds* of millions."

Nikolai couldn't believe this was happening. He'd always hated Kurt Schreiber. The man was undoubtedly highly intelligent, but was also untrustworthy, manipulative, cruel, and since the collapse of East Germany had made millions through illegal business ventures. Now he had the ear of the Russian president and that made him more dangerous than when he'd been a Stasi officer. "How can you live with yourself?"

Schreiber shrugged. "I view the deaths as necessary statistics. I suggest you do the same."

Nikolai was tempted to respond but knew there was no point.

Schreiber would not listen to reason.

Pure evil never did.

Nikolai gripped the pen, momentarily closed his eyes, muttered, "Forgive me," and signed both documents.

"Excellent." Kurt reached across, grabbed both files, shoved one at the Russian generals, the other at the Americans. The former Stasi colonel smiled. "The protocols for Slingshot are now in place, ready for use should ever the need arise."

"Great." General Alexander Tatlin stubbed his cigarette out. "So now we can get out of this shithole."

"Not yet." Kurt placed his hands flat on the table. "How can we ensure that no one in this room ever reveals the secret of what's missing in the files?"

Thomas Scott huffed. "Slingshot won't work if one of us blabs. We've agreed that."

Kurt stared at nothing. "We have, but we need more than agreement."

"What are you proposing?"

"Insurance." Kurt looked at the men, before resting his cold gaze on Nikolai. "Time can erode a man's resolve. But fear can keep him resolute."

"Speak plainly."

Kurt nodded. "One day, one of you may wake up with a crisis of conscience and decide that he can no longer carry the burden of this secret. That can't happen. So, my solution is simple and effective. The Russian president has authorized me to activate an assassin. He will be deployed as a deep cover sleeper agent and his orders are to kill any of you," he looked at the CIA officer and smiled, "who *blabs*."

General Tatlin lit another cigarette and jabbed its glowing tip in the direction of Schreiber. "You expect us to live our lives with a potential death sentence hanging over us?"

Schreiber interlaced his fingers. "Yes."

Dugan laughed. "Take a look around this base, Schreiber. We're the kind of men who like to have impenetrable security wherever we go."

"Impenetrable?"

"Damn right." The admiral's tone was now angry. "Send out your assassin for all we care. But, you're going to need better insurance than that."

"There is no better insurance."

Nikolai wondered why Schreiber looked so smug. "Who's the assassin?"

The sound of rainwater striking the concrete floor intensified as Schreiber momentarily closed his eyes. "You know of him by the codename Kronos."

"Kronos?!" Nikolai's stomach muscles knotted. "Why was he selected for this task?"

Before Schreiber could answer, the General Ballinger asked, "Who the hell is Kronos?"

Nikolai looked at the American commanders, as he began to sweat. "He was a Stasi officer, tasked on East Germany's most complex and strategic assassinations. Since the collapse of communism, he's been on the pay-roll of Russia. He's . . . he's our most deadly assassin. One hundred and eighty three kills under his belt. Always successful." As he returned his attention to Schreiber, he felt overwhelming unease. "Why was he selected?"

Schreiber opened his eyes. "Because the Slingshot secret is so vital. We needed our very best assassin to ensure that," he swept his arm through air, "no amount of *impenetrable* security can protect a man who might betray us." Schreiber broke their gaze, and looked toward one of the far corners of the mess hall. In a loud, clipped tone, he called out, "Show them."

Nikolai and the others immediately followed Schreiber's gaze. At first nothing happened. Then, movement from within the shadows of the corner of the room.

A big man stepped into the light.

Standing directly underneath one of the streams of water pouring down from the ceiling.

Was motionless as he allowed the icy rain to wash over his head.

His handgun held high and trained on them.

Kronos.

Schreiber smiled and looked at the others. "He got past all of your men and has been pointing his weapon at you from the moment you entered this room."

General Michurin slammed a fist down onto the table. "How dare you make fools of us?!"

Schreiber responded calmly, "It wasn't my intention to make fools of you. Rather, to demonstrate to you that you do indeed have a potential death sentence hanging over you." He looked at Kronos. "Give them what they need."

Nikolai felt fear course through him as he watched the German assassin take measured steps toward the table, his gun still held high. Though Nikolai was one of only a handful of SVR officers who was security cleared to know all about the Kronos operations, he didn't know the assassin's real name. Moreover, this was the first time that he'd been in the presence of the man. Kronos was nearly two meters tall, muscular, had black hair, and was wearing clothes identical to those Nikolai had seen worn by the base's protection detail.

Kronos lowered his weapon, withdrew a piece of paper from his jacket, tore it in half, and slapped one piece of paper on Admiral Dugan's chest, before moving to the other side of the table and doing the same with the other bit of paper on general Michurin.

Schreiber spoke to the Americans. "I suggest you bury your paper deep in the vaults of the CIA." Then the Russians. "Put yours in the SVR vaults." He cupped his hands together. "*Never* combine them, unless there is reason to do so."

"Reason?"

"One of you needs Kronos to put a bullet in your head."

"You . . ."

"Enough, admiral!" Schreiber composed himself. "The relevance of the two pieces of paper will be made known to you if the need arises. Until that time, Kronos will vanish. No one, not even me, will know of his location. He'll wait for years, decades if necessary, until he is . . . needed."

Thomas Scott shook his head. "Our men have been here for three days." The CIA officer felt disbelief. "And when they arrived, they searched the entire base."

General Ballinger shrugged. "There's no way he could've penetrated the base today. He must have entered the complex before our men arrived and hid in a place they failed to search."

"That's the only possible explanation." Admiral Dugan pointed at Schreiber. "Next time we'll be more thorough."

Schreiber grinned, though his expression remained cold. "Kronos—show them where you were two and three days ago."

The German moved around the table, placing a

photograph each in front of the Russians and Americans. Incredulity was on all of the men's faces as they stared at the shots.

Each showed the inside of their homes in America or Russia.

A local newspaper clearly showing the day's date.

And Kronos pointing the tip of a long knife toward family photos.

"Bastard!"

Kronos retrieved each photo, placed them in a pile in the center of the table, and lit them with a match.

Schreiber watched the flames rise high. "Our meeting is concluded. You will take the Slingshot protocols back to your respective headquarters. You will secret the torn papers as instructed. You will keep your mouths shut. Otherwise, my assassin *will* find and kill you."

Kronos stepped away from the men, hesitated, then turned to face them again. In a deep voice, he said, "Gentlemen, I left all of your men alive though I must apologize for the harm I had to cause some of them." He backed away across the room, raised his handgun so that it was pointing at the conspirators, and boomed, "No one in this room is safe from me."

Then he disappeared into the shadows.

CHAPTER 2

POLAND TODAY

Will Cochrane looked toward the end of the cobbled street. It was night and a cold sea mist lay motionless over the northern city of Gdansk, patches of it visible within the golden glow from ornate streetlamps. The city's Old Town seemed deserted, though Will knew that close to his position in a café's doorway there were twenty armed and dangerous men. Some of them were his allies, some not.

The tall MI6 officer, codename Spartan, attached his earpiece and throat mic, glanced in the opposite direction along the street, and walked briskly across the route. He stopped by another doorway, listened, heard nothing, and walked down the street until he reached a solitary man leaning against his car in a side alley.

He whispered, "The Russian defector should be here in less than one hour."

The man stared at Will, his eyes cold, anger in his hushed voice. "You're making a grave mistake going ahead with this operation. If we get this wrong, the repercussions will be catastrophic."

Will looked up and down the street again. On either side of it were jewelry and antique shops, restaurants, residential properties, and wine bars. All of them were built in the gothic style, having been carefully reconstructed from the rubble of the old Gdansk to replicate the city after it was destroyed in the Second World War. Everywhere was shut up for the night. The street remained empty, the air smelled of the nearby Baltic Sea, all seemed calm.

He glanced at the man. "Luke, nothing will go wrong if you follow my orders."

Luke thrust his gloved hands under his armpits and quietly stamped his feet on the icy ground. "Your orders?" Though barely audible, his tone was unmistakably sarcastic. "I take orders from people I know, yet I know *nothing* about you beyond that you are here at the behest of the chief." The MI6 Head of Warsaw Station pulled up the collar of his smart overcoat. "Poland's my patch. I resent your presence here and I resent your intended course of action."

Will unbuttoned his coat, checked that his sound-suppressed Russian PB 6P9 handgun was still firmly in position under his Huntsman bespoke Savile Row suit, and returned his attention to Luke. The station chief looked to be in his late forties, and no doubt was an extremely experienced and skilled intelligence operative. "I'm here to do my job. Nothing gets in the way of that."

Luke frowned. "Your job may cause irrevocable damage to diplomatic relations between Poland and the United Kingdom."

Will shook his head. "It won't come to that. Even if things go wrong, no Poles will be killed tonight."

Luke seemed about to respond, then put his hand into a pocket and withdrew his cell phone. Silently vibrating, its screen was flashing to show he had an incoming call. He depressed a button, placed the cell against his ear, and listened. Ten seconds later he ended the call and placed the phone back into his coat. "Still nothing out of the ordinary at the Embassy."

Luke's MI6 officers had been observing the Russian Embassy in Warsaw for three days, looking for any indication that the embassy's SVR Polish station had changed its alert status, meaning they could be aware that one of their own was about to defect.

Will felt tense. Russia's foreign intelligence service, Sluzhba Vneshney Razvedki, would do everything they could to stop an SVR traitor getting into Polish hands, including killing the defector and any Poles that were here to meet him. He checked his watch and exhaled slowly, his breath steaming in the icy air. It was nearly two A.M. In the distance, a port foghorn droned, its noise echoing off the nearby buildings. As the sound abated, he asked, "Do you know anything about the Polish operatives who are out to play tonight?"

"All I know is that six men are from the state security service . . ."

Agencja Bezpieczeństwa Wewnetrznego,

" . . . and two from its foreign operations service,"

Agencja Wywiadu.

Luke's reaction seemed bitter. "In all probability, I've worked with some of the men you're planning to render unconscious tonight."

"One of the two AW men will be the defector's handler." Will rubbed fingers through his short, dark hair. "You're certain your team's hidden from them?"

Luke shrugged. "I can't be certain of anything. But I got all twelve of them from London. They arrived this morning. They're MI6 Q operatives."

Men who knew how to stay hidden. Q operatives were all former British Special Forces.

Will asked, "What are the Poles wearing?"

"Windbreaker jackets, jeans, and combat boots."

"And our men?"

"Similar, but just before the green light's given they'll don black baseball caps so that they're distinguishable from the Poles."

"What weapons do the Q men have?"

Luke muttered, "Silenced pistols and tranquilizer guns."

"That's all?! I asked for them to be armed with suppressed semiautomatics."

"And I decided to ignore your request." Luke shook his head. "We shouldn't be doing this to the Polish operatives. This is their country, and the defector's coming to them. Bloody hell, I liaise with the Polish intelligence services every day. The moment we got the tip off, I should have been tasked to use my influence with the Poles to see if they could share the defector's intelligence with us."

"Impossible. You know that would have meant that we'd have had to tell them how we got the information."

Luke sighed. "So you decided to turn everything on its head, overrule my authority, and construct a kidnap operation."

"Not kidnap, a sleight of hand."

Luke responded angrily, "When this is over, I'll make an official complaint about your actions."

Will grabbed Luke's jaw. "I've had enough of your crap!"

The shock on Luke's face was vivid.

"We're not here to snatch the defector from the Poles. We're here because you told the Russians about the defector. And because of that, we had no choice other than to come here to protect the Poles and ensure they got their man."

Luke's eyes were wide with fear. He tried to speak.

But Will squeezed harder. "Save your breath. You've been under investigation for weeks, your burst transmissions monitored by GCHQ. But rather than have you lifted, we wanted to let you continue speaking to the Russians, with information that we fed you. False information, of course. But when you told the SVR about the defector's use of the exfiltration route, matters had to be accelerated." He pulled Luke's head close to his. "I couldn't tell the Qs what was really happening in case they accidentally let slip detail that would make you suspicious. It's a *real shame* that you under-equipped them." He smiled though felt nothing but anger. "I'm told that money was the reason behind your treachery. Pity really. I'd have had more respect for you if betrayed us for other reasons. Still, doesn't matter now because you're screwed."

Will thrust Luke's head back.

Luke winced and rubbed his bruised jaw. "I . . ."

"Shut up!" Will pulled out his Russian handgun and placed its nozzle against Luke's head. "Is there anything you want to say to me?"

"My family . . ." His voice trailed.

"I'll make sure they're comfortable, are looked after, and are told that you were killed in the line of duty. No one needs to know."

Luke closed his eyes and quietly said, "That's kind of you." He bowed his head. "Pull the trigger."

Will hesitated.

"Pull the trigger!"

Still, Will did nothing.

"Please! I can't face the disgrace."

"You're already disgraced." Will gripped his gun, but

his trigger finger was motionless. Even though he was under orders to kill the traitor, something was holding him back.

Luke opened his eyes, raised his head, and looked at him with wet eyes. "Do you pity me?"

Will felt confused, no longer angry. "Perhaps."

Luke nodded slowly. "I don't deserve your pity. Men are going to die tonight because of me. Do your duty! Pull the trigger!"

Will sighed, knowing Luke was right and spoke with a genuinely bemused tone. "Why did you do this?"

Luke shrugged. "The world's full of self-seeking charlatans. I'm just one of many."

Will frowned. "And men like me have to clean up your mess?"

"It appears so."

"I wish I didn't have to keep doing that."

He shot Luke in the head.